SOUTH of BURNT ROCKS

WEST of the MOON

G. J. Berger

SOUTH of BURNT ROCKS WEST of the MOON

G. J. Berger

GJ Berger Publishing

San Diego, California

South of Burnt Rocks—West of the Moon

Published by GJ Berger Publishing
Cover artist DLKeur, zentao.com
Cover model image licensed to the author by iStockphoto
Cover image of horse by CoralieM Photographie for use of her photo of the Arabian Stallion, Zarife El Mansour
Interior design by White Cottage Publishing Company, whitecottagepublishing.com

Printed in the United States of America
for Worldwide Distribution

ISBN 978-0-9883982-0-7 (hard cover)
ISBN 978-0-9883982-1-4 (soft cover)

For the three women in my life
in the order they appeared—
Katharina,
Virginia,
and Edna.
Each in her own way was
every bit as strong as Lavena,
and I am blessed for that.

Praise for *South of Burnt Rocks West of the Moon*

"A spare and intense novel of a people half-lost in the mists of history, resisting to death and beyond the conquering power of Rome." Elizabeth Loupas, *The Second Duchess* and *The Flower Reader.*

"G. J. Berger has written the stirring tale of a Celtic girl at a time when bravery was a child's first weapon. *Burnt Rocks* is a heart-stopping read." Elizabeth Cobbs Hoffman, *Broken Promises, A Novel of the Civil War.*

"In Berger's captivating debut historical fiction, a young Iberian-Celtic she-warrior makes a stand against the invading Roman army. Smartly written, the novel moves quickly, building prose with quiet strength unencumbered by the heavy style. Its bare-bones flow seems to fit the time period. The simple yet powerful narrative relies on a commanding cast of characters, many of whom are indeed women, celebrated for their resiliency and constitution. These women are the leaders of the resistance and they rely on no man for guidance. Berger beautifully crafts them as more than one-dimensional warriors bent on revenge. They're strong yet vulnerable, desperate to protect their land and people. Berger also builds an elaborate world full of small details that add depth and historical context. A wonderfully crafted balance of Roman-era drama and the fierceness of battle." Kirkus Reviews, September 2012.

PART I

The She-Warrior

Chapter I
Hard Ground
184 B.C.

Early on a spring morning in the year after she turned eleven, Lavena's father said, "Daughter, come with me today. Time you learn the work of men."

She jumped up from the bench next to her mother at the loom and put on her sandals as fast as she was able. At last, it was her time. All older unmarried girls helped in the trades of their fathers. Her closest friend, Aunia, had already for months pounded hot iron into tools and belt buckles.

They rode bareback on her father's mule, out and away from their Village on The Cliff. She knew this was the biggest, strongest mule in the region, had to be. Her father ruled over everyone within a half day's ride.

She peered forward over his shoulder and smiled inside. She would have shouted for excitement, but girls did not do that in the presence of adults. It was time to ride with grownups, even with her father.

They passed goats and sheep, their herders and dogs, heading to that day's pasture. The men smiled and waved, and her father waved back.

Another good thought tumbled in. Her father might spot his favorite guard dog, Little Bear, and whistle him over. White and shaggy with a black snout, every time Little Bear saw Lavena, he'd run to her, lick her face, and wag his tail furiously. Every time, she laughed out loud and let Little Bear rest his big paws on her shoulders.

Years before she had asked, "May we keep him at our house?"

"No, no. He belongs out here with my animals. He's slain many wolves."

But on this morning they did not spot Little Bear.

They reached a fallow plot marked off by low stone walls. An old farmer waited next to a heavy ard, but no animal to pull it.

From the back of the mule, Lavena saw only the top of the highest tower of her village. The distance made her uneasy. She silently scoffed at her fear. Everyone knew herdsmen or scouts farther out whistled warnings of any approaching wolves or strangers, and guard dogs patrolled the boundaries of her father's territory.

The old farmer welcomed her with a nod, as if he knew she would be coming. He had a kind face, an expression that said he took great joy in preparing the dirt for new seed. He quickly strapped the mule into a leather harness attached to the ard.

"Off you go." Her father lifted her up and set her on the hard ground. "Walk beside us and watch, listen, so you can do what we do."

He urged the mule forward while the old farmer pushed on the ard post to sink the pointed tip into the soil covered by old growth. From time to time, the two men switched places.

The going was slow, two or three paces before the tip stuck, and the mule could pull it no more. They backed up, one of the men tugged at the upturned clumps and dug around them with a well-worn spade. Then they started over.

Some places the soil was loose enough that the men let Lavena lean into the wooden ard post with all her weight and strength. The tip cut into the earth and broke it out and upward. That made her feel useful.

The next day after a line of good progress, Sinorix dismounted and said, "Get up here. You do it."

Lavena grabbed the mane and pulled herself up. She slapped the reins onto the mule's neck and kicked its sides with her sandaled heels. It moved out. Over the day it obeyed all her commands to go, stay in line, turn left or right, stop, or stop and back up a step to release the ard stuck again. Sometimes she walked by the mule or in front letting go of the reins, and it followed.

Satisfied, her father left them.

Lavena wanted to ask him to stay, wanted to say that if there was trouble she was too young and untrained. She glanced at the old farmer, who carried a big stick he used for prodding the mule, and again pushed away her fear.

From then on, Lavena worked the mule all day and rode it back to her village every evening. That made her feel a pride greater than she had ever known, not for riding—she had always been good at that—but that her father trusted her with this mule.

When the first plot was done, they moved to another nearby. After days of working with the farmer and the mule, she asked, "Does this hurt resting spirits of the dead before they come out of the ground again?"

He thought for a while, then, "No, no, Daughter of Sinorix. The spirits live down deep, deeper than the deepest silver mines in the south."

She had heard talk of silver mines. "What's a silver mine?"

"The spirits of the dead have great power, Daughter of Sinorix, greater than when they come to live among us. They cannot spin wool or cotton. But they turn the deep earth into gold and silver and push it up to the top, close to their kindred and friends. We must dig far down to get it, and clean away the rocks and dirt before it shines and lets us see our faces in it. The place where we dig is called a mine."

That satisfied her, and she asked no more questions.

Lavena's hands and fingers blistered, the blisters hardened, and her arms grew stronger from pulling on the reins and helping the farmer loosen the dirt when the ard stuck. Every evening, she wanted to stay out later and later, turn more dirt, until at last they reached the final small untilled corner of the last plot.

She had not seen him before, a solitary rider out of the late afternoon sun. No one whistled, no guard dog barked a warning. This one must have been a herder or scout coming in for the night. Maybe he would go in with them.

When closer, Lavena saw he wore a leather helmet, heavy leather jacket, and a short sword hung from his left side. She had seen men who looked like him, who were dressed the same, but never this close. Her villagers pointed at their backs and whispered—Romans.

"Old man, we're short of mules. Unhitch it." He said it loudly, confidently, in their language, but with a strong accent.

The old man said, "Sir, the mule is not mine to give away."

The Roman looked down from under his leather helmet visor at the old man on the ard post, looked at the mule, slowly as if appraising its health and age, and then straight at Lavena sitting high on that mule. He licked his upper lip, the tongue reaching his nose. "The mule or this one, old man," he said, pointing first at the mule and then at Lavena.

The farmer moved up between the Roman horse and Lavena's mule. "Get off our land, you bastard son of a goat." He clasped his long stick and stood ready to fight.

The soldier leaned forward in his saddle—and waited.

The old farmer jabbed the end of the stick into the horse's snout, and it backed away shaking its head, snorting.

Lavena glanced in the direction of the village and could make out only smoke rising from late afternoon fires. No sheep or horses grazed near them. No herders or village scouts were in sight, not within shouting distance. A new feeling rose in her. This Roman must have watched them from a secluded clump of trees or a hill far away, and come up to them after all their protectors had left.

"Get away," yelled the old man, and the horse backed up farther.

Lavena dared not get off her mule, dared not utter a sound. For a moment, she thought the Roman would not approach closer against the brandished pole, that he would leave.

But the soldier's look hardened. He jumped out of his saddle, pulled his sword, and charged the farmer. The old man swung his big pole hard enough to whip the air. But he missed with first try, and the Roman ducked under the second swing. The hard swings made the old man turn away and exposed his back. The Roman plunged his sword into the old man's side until only the hilt stopped it from going deeper. The soldier grunted, as the farmer gasped for air.

The old man's loose gray top blossomed red. He screamed once, a short burst before all strength and air left him. He crumpled to his knees and fell face down onto the dirt. As he fell, the Roman pulled his sword, the shiny metal mixed with red wetness.

The mule kicked, but not high enough to topple Lavena. The soldier's horse stood calmly. That felt wrong to her, as if his horse had seen this before.

She wrapped the reins tightly around one hand and grasped the mule's hair with her other hand, didn't know what else to do despite a great urge to do much more. She felt more than thought that if she held fast right there, this soldier could not make off with her, the mule and the ard attached to the mule. To take the mule, he had to unhitch it. To take her, he had to get her off.

The Roman stepped on the shoulder of the farmer, then on his head, grinding it into the ground. Lavena did not want to look, but could not help looking. It was all too close, and the horror, poised to turn her way, drew her in.

The old man wheezed through his last breaths, blood from his face and mouth darkening the freshly-turned dirt in his mouth and under his chin. Though face down, his arms reached up and out, hands still opening and closing on his stick up above his head and trying to swing it at the legs of the one who had done this.

The soldier kicked the walking stick away and turned to the mule and Lavena. "*Eia! Quid hoc*?" Then in her language, "Well, what do we have here?" He laughed a laugh of triumph. "From back a ways, I thought you a boy—not a boy, eh? I'll show you why we keep our women inside, and why your Keltoi men here in Hispania know nothing—stupid *barbari*—letting their girls out."

She knew that strangers from far away referred to her people by the Greek *Keltoi* and her land as Hispania, but that other word—*barbari*—she did not know. The rest of what he said flashed white hot, flashed of what strange soldiers did to young girls when their fathers and husbands lay dead. She and Aunia had talked of such things, and her mother had many times told her to run from strange men.

She pushed those flashes away. That could not happen, not here, not now, not to her.

The flashes did not go away. They grew brighter, hotter, into a white whirling panic. But she knew she had to do something, anything, to jump off on the other side and run or yell… something.

He strode to the mule and Lavena, dripping sword hanging from his right hand. He reached his big hand for her thigh.

She tried to lift her leg out of the way. His free hand caught her above the elbow, and pulled down hard, harder than any pull she had ever felt. Her tight hold on the shortened reins and hair of the mule prevented her from getting pulled off—though only for an instant.

The soldier hoisted her arm and shoulders up and away. That push, too sudden and too much reinforced by her own pulling away, spilled her off the mule on the other side. Her hands still held the mane and allowed her to stay upright and land on her feet. The tumble, landing on her feet, a moment to think took away the panic.

The big body of the mule shielded her from him. While wrestling boys and girls many times, she had learned that a wall at the back or a horse around which to duck and dodge gave some protection. If he came around, she could duck under the mule and run away from the other side. If he ducked under the belly of the mule, she'd have a head start.

His eyes across the back of her mule, wide open and unblinking, made her say in the firmest voice she could muster, "Here, this place, is the land of my father. You must leave now." She said it again in her learned Latin, "*Excede statim! Ager patris mei hic est.*"

He frowned when she spoke in his language, had not expected this. He looked around too. They weren't that far from the village, with some daylight left. She sensed this killer had not decided what he was going to do next.

She looked for anything on the ground, anywhere, looked for the best route to run. All the stones had been collected up and set along the edges of the field, the nearest line of rocks and boulders too far off. She slid off her sandals, might be able to outrun him to her village. She ran as fast as most of the boys her age and some of the older ones. And this one had heavy boots and heavy clothes and that sword. If she could get a start on him, if—.

The soldier laughed. He had decided, and his laugh was of the kind that had brought on the white terror. He reached his free hand across the back of the mule and beckoned with his fingers for her to come to his side. At the same time he leaned to his right, then to his left and laughed some more as she took a step the opposite way. He leaned up on the mule's back and said something she did not understand, but the sounds through the words he made—low rasping grunts—how he breathed—short bursts out of his mouth—told her everything.

He brought the sword up with his other hand and jabbed it at her face, snorted, and ran around the front of the mule.

But Lavena had turned away and into a full sprint on the shortest path to her village, yelling, screaming, shouting with all her might.

A new sound, from behind between her own bursts, did not register. Were there more men running her down now? Had he too kicked off his boots? She yelled louder.

A fast shluffing of soft feet on the ground mixed with the clomping of his boots running after her. A deep growl smothered the shluffing, and the clomping of boots ended.

And she got it. The thump of a body hitting the ground, the growling turned to snarling, then big teeth ripping skin, muscle and sinew, a bone cracking and screams of sharp pain.

She dared to slow enough to look back, and then stopped, stared. A giant white dog had him by the elbow and arm, he on his back. The big dog threw him from side to side. With his free hand, the soldier tried to punch the shaggy shoulders and neck, mere slaps on the enraged guard dog.

Lavena turned away and did not stop running until she reached the family house.

Fighters from her village found the mule, the ard, the dead farmer in the same place and reported what they found to the many villagers gathered. Lavena and her mother, Edereta, waited with them.

Little Bear lay by the mule, the soldier's sword flat under his front paws. His muzzle was bloody, but the rest of him unmarred. They said that, by all the tracks and markings, Little Bear had let the soldier run to his horse and flee when Lavena was safe. One of them said for all around him to hear, "Little Bear grinned at what he had done."

Lavena allowed herself to imagine Little Bear grinning. The big dog would do that.

Haltingly, suppressing tears of anger and fear, clasping her hands tightly to hide their shaking, Lavena said to her mother and the men and women around her, "He"—she realized she had never learned the old farmer's name—"yelled at me to run, and I obeyed. He fought that bad man with his mule stick for a long time. That bad man never touched me. Then Little Bear came, and I was safe, and ran in as fast as I could."

She knew that was not true, not all of it, but she wished it, and it felt better to tell it that way. The old farmer would have done that if he could, if they had both been ready for the killing treachery of the stinking Roman.

Chapter II
Father's Gold

When they were alone, Edereta tended to her daughter. Down in the nearest bathing area for women, Edereta searched with her finger tips and eyes for the truth of what had happened. She found only little burrs on Lavena's clothes and scratches on her legs and feet.

Edereta said, "I will tell Sinorix as soon as he is back. He must know, and I must tell him before anyone."

Lavena could not remember her mother calling him Sinorix, and not Father or, your father. But deep down she understood other things too had changed on this day.

Edereta continued, "I must talk to your brothers about this."

Father had not returned from wherever he had gone. And she had not seen the brothers in many days. They did not often come round to the family house, not even on this evening.

Edereta set out the meal of raisins, dates, walnuts, bread and honey. Lavena did not want to eat, but her mother implored her with her eyes and hand gestures. After a time, cool water and the freshly baked bread tasted good.

As the day left them, Edereta started a small fire in the pit built into the north wall of the main room. She was the best at starting fires Lavena had seen—with the first quick strike always making the rough stone throw multiple sparks onto the waiting ball of dry straw. But today it took Edereta's shaking hands many tries before the straw lit.

Lavena wanted to tell her mother that she was all right, that this would not happen again. More than that, she wanted to ask about Romans, where they went, where they came from, why they were here. But she kept quiet. Children did not start conversations about such things with elders.

After they finished eating and sitting in silence, Edereta, her hands in her lap, eyes closed, said more to herself than to Lavena, "First time since the treaty they do such a thing. Where were our sentries this day? Father will know."

Lavena dared to ask, "Mother, when will Father get back?"

"Oh, Lavena, I don't know."

Edereta rose from her bear skin pile and stood next to the fire. It made the old wood crack and throw sparks. "They broke the treaty today."

Lavena yawned and said, "What's a treaty?"

Her mother smiled weakly, and Lavena felt more than saw her sadness and worry. "A promise, Lavena. A promise to us and to all their gods and ours. Go now, it is time for sleep."

Lavena ambled over to the door on the far side of the main room. The child part of her wanted to sleep and wake up covered by her blanket, and the realization that this day had not happened. The adult part of her roiled in the dark contours, in the ugliness of how close and how horrible, the details too frightening to let in fully. She looked back and saw her mother's own dark thoughts as if hovering in the light cast by the fire and the candle, and that made her say, "He, that bad soldier, will never come back, will he?"

"Not as long as Piso governs. Sinorix must confront Piso."

"Who's Piso, Mother?" Lavena yawned again.

Edereta shrugged as if she didn't know how to answer, or wasn't supposed to answer. "You should ask your father."

"I'll stay awake until he comes home."

Her mother remained quiet, head down, for a long time. Then she came to Lavena, put her arms around her, pulled her close and hugged her. Through warm tears that fell on Lavena's shoulders, her mother said, "We must give thanks tonight, give thanks for Little Bear and Father's old farmer."

She laughed softly through her tears. "I don't know that farmer, don't even know his name or his family. They must live in one of the houses far out away from here. And...we must pray the Romans don't want more than we can give them."

Part of Lavena did not understand about giving anything to men such as that one on this day, though the other part, the older part of her understood it all and more. Lavena whispered, "What do they want more than we can give, Mother?"

Edereta answered without hesitation. "In the end, they want our gold, all of it, they want everything, everything we can give them, everything we have, everything we are."

Lavena had glimpsed gold on the necks and wrists of the nobles and sometimes on warriors riding out. Grownups talked of gold slowly, deliberately, with lowered voices and wide eyes, a kind of reverence they showed when they talked of the main gods. She didn't know if she ought to like gold. Surely she must like it too if ever she saw it closely, but until this moment had not cared. "What gold do we have to give them?"

Edereta breathed deeply. "You don't know, do you? All the noble families hide it in secret places until they take it out to show their power. Some say your father's gold is the finest. His gold gives him the power to command—and we all follow his commands."

"Why, Mother, does Father have so much gold?"

"Lavena, you do ask too much."

Lavena felt the little sting. She had asked too much, too much at once, asked of things it was not her place to know, but on this evening it felt right to ask about anything. "Do we have the most gold?"

Edereta looked at the dirt floor again and then up and around where the stone wall met the wooden beams under the thatched roof. "No one must know. No noble in Father's tribe tells another all he has or where he hides it."

"Can I see our gold?"

Her mother stood up. "It's time, but don't, don't ever tell anyone what I show you now, or where it is. Swear it, swear it, now, and for all time."

Lavena looked directly at her mother. "I swear it, now and for all time."

Edereta, standing on her toes, tried to reach an unmarked stone high on the wall to the right of the fire pit. She could not reach it and pulled cut logs against the place in the wall. She stood up on them, placed her hands on a stone in the top row of the wall, leaned in and pushed hard. This stone slid sideways. She reached into the hollow behind and pulled out a yellow rope.

As she brought it down, she twisted the thick rope into a circle as big around as a girl's waist, the rope's ends now nearly touching. She handed the rope to Lavena. "Here, look."

Lavena grabbed this fine slithery-looking thing but, not ready for its weight, nearly dropped it. It wasn't a rope, didn't slither but was solid and heavy. The facing ends were heads of wolves, sharp ears pointed up, dangerous teeth over tongues hanging, and eyes of green stones.

The heavy metal shone in the light from the fire, and the wolf eyes flickered at her, green then black, then green again. She felt her mother waiting for her to react. She could think of nothing until, "Can I have it, Mother?"

Edereta's laughter burst out. "Not yet. Let us keep it. If others know you have this, they'll chase you till they capture you." Edereta stopped laughing. The look on her face told Lavena that her mother understood about others chasing and capturing. Edereta lowered her voice and turned her head as if she did not want Lavena to hear, but said it loudly enough. "We must get ready for that day when they ask for this, and after that ask for more than we can give them. Go, sleep now."

As Lavena passed through the door to the next room, Edereta said, "Tomorrow I'll talk to Father. We must make ready for the day when our tribute's not enough, when they take Piso from us. That day will come too soon, I fear."

Lavena burrowed down into the animal hides—though the air was too warm for heavy covers—and wished the Romans stopped wanting whatever more they wanted, wished they wanted nothing more, and that her father came home while she slept.

The next morning, her mother woke her. "Get up, work to do. Father's back. He knows about his farmer and Little Bear and you. Do not tell him."

The day passed slowly. Lavena didn't pay attention to the teacher in her language and numbers class. She helped her mother prepare the evening meal, and that made her forget for a while.

Village elders gathered at the family house. Unlike other meetings when they kept Lavena awake, this time they didn't yell and get drunk on her father's beer or wine, didn't sleep sprawled around the rooms or on the path outside. They left sober and slept in their own houses and huts. Her father and mother let her stay up.

Father said to them all, "This village can't hold for more than three days if any of their big armies, like in the old days, comes at us now. Don't have enough men. Our neighbors won't unite with us. We don't know how to fight anymore." Her father shook his head and grinned. "Piso won't even let us raid the other tribes for practice like we did before the treaty."

One of the other old men said, "That's why we made our treaties.... Piso helps us all live in peace, respects us, has for a long time...."

Her father said, "His men show us less respect than they show their dogs. Roman Praetors always leave after they've taken what they want from us. Tomorrow we must begin to make ready for when Rome recalls Piso, for the day when other Romans come and want more than we can give them."

After that evening, Lavena did not see her father for many days. Her mother said he had gone to each of the houses of the other village nobles. Together they had arranged a meeting with Praetor Piso at the Roman encampment far to the north. Lavena never heard what had come of that.

They sent the old farmer off to his next life in the same manner as great warriors. His body, dressed in his finest clothes—though they were not very fine—lay on a platform built on a nearby hill, with the stick by his side. Vultures and crows would take him far into the land and clouds, where the spirits of all great warriors lived until they returned to earth. They buried the bones that remained and marked the place with a big round stone.

Chapter III
Making Ready

Every day that summer, the grownups woke Lavena at dawn. The training sessions started before the sun broke over the hills to the east. Many of the boys and the few girls collapsed before the training sessions ended and struggled to go on.

They got no water and bread lathered with the drippings from a roasted pig until after they were done. She didn't mind. Each lesson brought her closer to the day she might ride out with fighting men, to the day she could defend herself.

Besides, she had no choice. Her father had selected six girls to train with the boys.

On this day, the children stood under the east-facing wall of her Village on The Cliff. She squinted into the white sun at the tall woman, naked except for her locks yellowed by limewater, a short sword and ax both tucked into scabbards hanging from a leather belt.

Lavena had wanted to run naked too, but her mother said, "Have to wear shirts and pants till you stop falling." Lavena did not protest. The cloth protected her elbows and knees. She did fall, and the big boys tossed her around too, though not with the easy power of that Roman.

The instructor yelled, "Boys, to the wrestling ground. Girls, come up to me."

Lavena and the five other girls came closer, slowly like pups to the mother dog after the mother had bitten them. This instructor had many times hit the girls hard across the face with a snake-quick open hand. She hit them for talking out of turn, for not standing still, or for no reason. Each time, the instructor said, "Duck under, jump back…catch my arm. The spear and arrow fly faster than any hand."

Now she implored rather than commanded, "Come on, come on, close to me."

The girls approached within striking distance, each ready to duck, to jump back.

The instructor bent down, her head at the same level as the girls and pointed at each one. "Listen to me and never forget." The words came out with the guile of whispered secrets meant only for them. "Look at me and never forget. You see I wear no cloak, no leather, no chain vest. Look at my nakedness."

The instructor stood up to her full height and turned slowly for each girl to look, admire, and remember. "We chosen women, the strongest, biggest, the very finest of all women in the region, fight with no leather and metal pulling us down. Lets us run fast and jump high, makes them miss us."

Lavena thought, *I know, you and many have told us so. Let us fight or play in the river*. She was not prepared for what came next.

"And for us, for us women, there's another purpose. The Greeks, the Romans, the Africans don't let their women fight, don't let their women go alone where strange men can look at them, can stare at their woman parts until their blood rushes them into a mating frenzy."

The instructor held her hands on her breasts, and on the place where her long, muscled legs joined, first on the front then on the back. "Stinking soldiers do without women for many days. Dark ugly men with boils covering them will stop and stare here and here. They'll stare harder when you run at them—and think only of mating you there in the field, in the forest, on the rocks, wherever they find you."

Lavena heard the words and the words not spoken, about the allure of the female, the strong stallion mounting mare after mare, about young men in her tribe trying to lure girls to isolated places, especially the girls who had not yet mated. She heard the words not spoken about the farmer who died for her, and most of all about what lay ahead for her, for all the girls, with the certainty and power of this summer's hot sun.

The instructor seemed to now stare at her and her alone. "They won't expect you to hurt them, and they'll want to keep you alive, your fine young skin not cut and bleeding. They'll want you fresh the first time and later again, and for as long as taking you pleases them."

Lavena tried to block the images, the details, the feelings of that other evening, but could not. And that made her listen all the harder.

"They don't know she-warriors. When it happens, and it will, you'll have the first strike. Make it count." The instructor waited.

The girls stood still as statues.

"Now go, start with sword fighting. Learn well, my beautiful strong warriors. Remember always—you'll have the first strike. Go now to the sword fighting ground. Hurry."

Lavena raced to the assigned place behind the main stables, arriving ahead of the others. Perhaps today they would let her shed the wooden sticks, give her a real sword and teach her how to use it.

Not long ago, her father had let her try his long sword. Her two hands barely closed on the handle formed in the shape of a man. She lifted the sword, scraping the tip on the ground around her in a long arc. Once moving, the sword's weight spun her round until she toppled sideways.

Sinorix laughed. "Children wield weapons too heavy for them and die young. A child with a good knife is far more dangerous than a grown man with a sword he knows not how to use." He said those kinds of things often.

The sword instructor had been waiting. He motioned for them to watch, held a short sword by the blade gently in his palm, flipped it up and caught it by the handle. He did it again, but turned away and caught it behind his back.

"This is your best weapon. Our metalworkers make the hardest edge, sharp after many cuts it slices through bear hide like through a baby's skin." He paused. "Honor the gods of the falcata by learning to use it better than you use your hand."

Lavena and the other girls stared at their hands, turned them over as if they had not before been aware of the power of the sword in their own hands.

"Feel its balance. Knocked away in the night, feel where it flies and find it fast." He handed each a short sword.

Lavena grasped the handle of bone and slid her thumb along the blade edge. The gods of the falcata scolded her haste by cutting the fleshy part of her left thumb. She must not let that show.

The instructor said to the little group, "You try now."

Lavena hoisted the falcata over her right shoulder and swung around and out at the exposed chest of the target in front of her, a leather-draped man of straw. The sword bounced off. She tried again and once more, still nothing. Her thumb stung. Its blood crept over the sword's hilt, and she couldn't grasp tightly with the left hand. The hollowed out eyes in the hollow skull of the target mocked her.

She swung at the straw and at the memory of the Roman as if he stood in front of her, until tears and sweat flew onto the target, and she kept swinging. Arm weary and every attempt weaker, she stopped.

The instructor started clapping softly, joined by the other girls, who had given up on their own targets before Lavena.

The instructor took her hand still holding the sword, and moved it into a slicing motion. The leather hide opened easily, and he jabbed the point through the opening, twisting as he thrust in until he hit wood. "A man's skin's easier, and he'll fall sooner than the bear or wolf with this in him, but he'll smell a lot worse. Don't let his foul smell stop you."

By the end of the second lesson, Lavena made the short sword cut the hide easily, and shoved it in to the hilt or until it hit solid wood.

Chapter IV
What Children See

Everyone in the village always listened for the warning whistles from far outside the village. One whistle meant Romans had been spotted. The children quickly formed into groups at play, and ran any weapons into the nearest house or storage hut. Then they played like children were supposed to play, chased each other or drew pictures in the dirt until a second whistle.

After days of learning how to use the sword, axe, pike and sling shot, the bow and arrow, came running and wrestling without any weapon, then how to kick at the knee, gouge out the eye, and bite the neck and face. She didn't mind any of that, but until the very end of the summer the pike was too heavy for her to thrust with power.

By the time of the fall harvest, she handled the falcata easily, tossed it up and caught it by the handle, threw it so the point buried into the target. But deep down she felt as fake as the straw-man targets. She sensed that nothing she had learned would have made any difference that other time.

She had watched the slaughter of a used-up sheep, cow or horse. She had lugged water and brought food to dark huts where old men wheezed out last breaths or women died in childbirth. Even animals, their legs tied and struck at the perfect place on the neck, did not die easily. They kicked and cried, dropped heavily, tried to stand while spraying blood before they flopped down one last time and lay still. Old men and bled-out women did not go quietly.

The adult part of her knew any real target of the sword would shout next to her ear and bite it off if he could, pull away from her bloody hand clutching a slippery grip. If he had lost his weapon and her blade sat deep in him, he would still writhe for his life, his hands on her throat, his thick thumbs in her eyes and his feet kicking into her more violently than any dying sheep. And any Roman soldier would be many times heavier and stronger than she. All the lessons did not comfort her.

For years before the training days started, she had wrestled other girls and boys, joyfully, laughing, seldom inflicting real pain, more like open-mouthed puppies frolicking. The bigger, older boys seemed to seek her out, smiled as they picked her up and rolled her to the ground and let their hands slide over the non-wrestling parts of her.

All that changed on the day the Roman killed the farmer. From that day on, she wrestled against the village boys with a different purpose. On that day, Lavena found a greater strength and new meanness.

She grabbed the base of their thumbs and twisted until even the stronger boys had no choice but to fall away awkwardly and pull out of her grip. She slid her backside under their midsection and tumbled them over her shoulders so they fell hard, then stepped onto their necks as they hit the ground and before they could jump to their feet.

She felt from them a restraint born of fear and of that other thing too. They held back not because she was the daughter of Sinorix, but because she was someone's daughter. The young men of her own tribe yielded to the mysterious power and fierceness of a fighting woman. Soon, even the older ones circled away from her and found another wrestling partner unless the instructor ordered them to fight her.

Only one, Turibas, son of a noble family, never shied away, never held back. She had learned how to evade or slither out of the grasp of others her age, but not out of his clasp. His laughter even when he fought, sometimes a leering laughter, slowed her and made her want to relax into him, wrap around him, even as she struggled against his holds.

After he tripped and pinned her down, he whispered loud wet whispers. "I'll keep you under me when I get you alone, you know what I'll do then…"

Other times he said, "Drag you into the winter straw hut if you don't come with me…"

Or, "If you weren't his daughter, what I'd do to you."

Often he just laughed softly and held her down.

Lavena did not respond to Turibas' taunts, did not know what to say, her feelings too strong. At a level deeper than conscious thought, she knew that she made Turibas utter those things, that her body pulled those words from him, stirred him to places that in the end stirred her too and stayed with her long after the training sessions.

The months of training did not quiet the insides, did not stop the cold sweats in the night with no fever, the dreams and the memory. The Roman killing the farmer was not the only cause of all that.

From that day, Roman soldiers on horse seemed to spot her often. They rode up closer, looked directly into her eyes, at all parts of her lean body. Always she ran to the nearest hut or down a narrow path between houses nearest the village wall, where a horse could not follow and many of her tribe could protect her.

The intruders yelled after her with a laughing yell. She imagined the killer must have talked about her and how close he had come to taking her.

One morning Lavena said to her mother, "They always find me, look for me. Will they come to our house?"

Edereta thought a while. "It's your hair. Your hair's the color of the sun at morning, easy to see from far off. Their women have dark hair, and smell like goats."

Mother and daughter laughed, and later that day Edereta cut Lavena's hair so that from a distance Lavena looked no different than boys her age.

After a time, Lavena understood the bad men did not single her out. Sometimes she spotted them ride right up to her village walls and around the outlying houses, shops and storage sheds as if they owned the land and all that came with it. They haggled with the sentries at the gates, stopped to talk to farmers out in the fields and chased mothers out of vegetable gardens back into their huts shuttered by heavy wooden doors.

Sometimes she saw Roman soldiers grab a young pig or chicken and ride away teasing the owner by holding the stolen thing up high as the owner, yelling, ran after them.

Each time, Lavena tightened inside. Each time, she yearned for the day she could help her villagers and ride the Romans off.

Here and there Lavena thought she spotted the one who killed the old farmer, but never well enough to be able to say, that's him. These Romans showed only eyes, mouths, hands and knees. She wondered how they could fight and run and dodge carrying all that leather and metal. Everyone knew that grimy unwashed clothes poisoned any serious wound.

Many evenings that summer and fall after the killing, farmers came to her father at the house. They met with him in a closed-off room where no one else could see, but Lavena heard enough. She heard men cry about what had happened to them, heard them beg her father to fight back, to throw the marauders off their land. Some nights, the grown men shouted and cried loudly and deeply. Men in her tribe rarely cried in front of other men.

Lavena saw her father give them one of their family's chickens or take them to the family pens to select a larger animal, saw them hug her father, bow and wipe away tears as they parted.

She saw her father's stooped shoulders and clenched fists, his silence. Once, she saw him hit the stone walls in the main room of their house with his bare hands until his hands bled.

She was sure that when the time came, when her father judged he had enough ready fighters, her tribe would beat the Romans badly. Until then, she knew she had to stay alert and close to others of her tribe and to her village.

The only safe place, where no strange Romans could touch her, was deep in water, far out in the flow of the river that ran below her Village on The Cliff. There everyone started as equals, and there she had become better than all the rest.

Chapter V

God of the Eberus

After the lessons, after they had wrestled and run, after they had eaten and rested in the mid-summer afternoon heat or bundled up against a cold wind from the north, the grownups let them play in the river.

Lavena and her tribe called it Our River. Her instructor, Alexandros, said the river had a proper name, Eberus. He said it was the longest in all the land south of the mountains. He said that on the other side of the mountains where many more Keltoi lived, far wider and longer rivers flowed in every direction. Lavena did not believe him.

No river could be longer or wider than her river. Alexandros said the mountains were named after the Greek god, Pyrene. Lavena did not believe that either. Everyone she knew called them Burnt Rocks and that's how they looked from a distance.

At the summer's end harvest celebration after her twelfth birthday, many in her tribe travelled far downstream where the river widened and flowed without anger. There Lavena beat all men and women in races across and back. Her father's deep voice yelled the loudest. She heard him from the opposite shore and all the way back but was not embarrassed. Other family members yelled and sang out for their own swimmers.

She had no memory of any mortal showing her how to swim. One day she just did, and from that first day swam faster and stronger than all the other children, soon faster than the older ones and now faster than everyone.

At times close by her village, her mother swam with her alone or with all the children.

One day after the two of them finished, Edereta said, "Lavena, come, sit a while with me. You trained well today. The evening meal is ready and we can linger."

They sat at the river's edge and watched egrets dive and pull out wriggling fish. They watched shadows of the catfish and big bass leave ripples on the surface, watched the day drift down soaked up by the river.

Edereta said, "Lavena, you swim like a fish. That will help you after Father and I are gone."

Lavena looked at her mother, at her strong arms and wide shoulders, and was not sure if she meant what Lavena feared. "Where are you and Father going?"

Edereta laughed. "Not like that, not for many, many days. When our eyes have the fog and we can't hear, when our teeth crumble, then we'll go over to the place of all the spirits."

"When you die, Mother?"

"Yes, Lavena." She paused to let the meaning settle. "When Father and I are gone, know that the land and rocks and mountains are of men. Heavy clouds and the rain out of them, streams and rivers are the earth's fertile women. They give life to all things. The flowing waters are yours and mine and will be there whenever we need them."

Lavena's face must have revealed her puzzlement.

Edereta laughed again, a mother's laugh of delight at her child, and of being able to give her child lessons to last a lifetime. "No, no, not that way. The spirit that makes water flow is the same that moves our bodies. The soft rain that cools and the hard rain that makes everything grow, share the same spirit that is in you, in me, in all women, but only in women. Heed that spirit we call Reue, listen to her. Let her shield you from the heat and dryness of men."

Mother's words comforted that first time and every time when thoughts of evil men intruded, and those thoughts intruded often.

At night, Lavena listened for frogs, for water gurgling over rocks at the base of the village wall. She never felt the day complete unless she had let the sometimes warm and muddy, sometimes cold and clear water envelop her so she became part of it, so its spirit merged with hers.

#

On a day later that autumn, the clouds stood high in the west. They promised the god Reue's water would mix with her groans and sparks from her cloud-cleaving sword. Lavena led the youngsters and the two instructors out into the deeper water.

Too late she noticed the swifter flow, the stronger push, her separation from the others. She heard them yell, "Lavena, stop… let us catch up…we must stay together." Then, more faintly, "We're getting out…. You should get out…." She heard fear in their young voices, and warnings mixed with anger in the adult voices.

The rush of water round her took them out of her hearing—and that pleased her. Real war, real fighting did not wait for quiet, for times of no storm.

When she next rolled onto her back and looked to the west, the clouds had darkened, and the village's outer wall on the cliff above the river appeared small and far away. Anxiety crept in.

She pulled hard sideways in the direction of flat rocks sloping low into the river where she might easily climb out. But the swifter flow around these rocks did not give her any place to grab hold. Her hands slid off the slippery wet surfaces. There at the edges the water churned white as if at a shallow place, yet her feet could did not find the bottom.

She next aimed at a stand of trees and roots far enough downstream for her to slide at branches and exposed roots that made good hand holds.

Now far from her village, she knew she had to watch for what might lurk on the shore. She lifted up out of the water as high as she could. She saw no one, but that did not calm her. She would have felt better if she had seen many village farmers coming in for the day. Without them, a solitary Roman could wait in those trees unnoticed.

Her worry about strangers on the shore distracted, caused her to lose focus on the target branch, and in that instant the water swept her past.

Around a rocky bend she spotted the next cluster of trees and grass and still water without eddies. She pulled hard at this place, where she could rest until the others arrived or until she decided to run home. She got close enough this time.

As she reached to grasp the nearest root above the surface, her feet touched a muddy bottom but did not hold. The water pushed at all parts of her. It tore at her arm and shoulders, forced her hand off the root and pushed her down against more roots under the fast-moving surface. The roots grabbed her left foot, then the right. The water shoved harder against her legs, pressed them at the tree and bent her down backwards. It tore her searching hands off the muddy bottom and into a tangle of leaves and branches.

Not two long strides from the safety of the shore, the water pulled all of her under. It pinned her face against the underwater grove. It pressed harder until, unable to move, to breathe, to shout out, except silently to herself, she no longer heard the heavy water gurgling into her nose, over her eyes and ears. Until she heard no sound and saw nothing, except the screaming urge to breathe, knowing she dare not or would surely drown.

Light and air came back, and she felt hands pushing on her chest, heard a noisy, slurping breathing, then the distinctive voice trying to say, "Lavena, foolish, strong and foolish, cough, cough and sit up." It came out, "Habema, foosh, song and foosh, ca, ca and si up."

Lavena obeyed, but had to cough for a third time, lie down and cough again before she could stay upright.

Aunia stood over her in front of other children and the two instructors, a man and a woman, assigned to watch them on this day. Behind them other adults peered down at her, and behind them horses snorted.

Aunia talked fast, talked in her gibberish forced by a mouth whose upper lip had never closed, whose upper teeth came in crooked and open. She talked a talk only her family and Lavena easily understood. Many times the village priest had proclaimed there would be no greater sacrifice to the gods than Aunia, better than the big ram or bull in heat. But they had let Aunia live.

Lavena thought of Aunia as an old grownup in a girl's body, in a face with a twisted open mouth that did not allow her to talk like anyone else. A year older than Lavena, Aunia spoke of boys and men, of wolves and bears that came into the low country in winter when the deer left the mountains. Aunia told Lavena of the Romans, and that their Senate that had sent Piso to watch over them and take tribute back to the greatest city anyone had ever seen. Aunia knew more about more things than teacher Alexandros.

The others did not interrupt. Everyone in the village knew of Aunia's special gifts.

Aunia moved to the river's edge and bent down. "Look at my hand, at the water pressing against it." The swift water crested and cascaded over and around Aunia's hand, a hand pinned against the tree root protruding out of the water. "Reue takes careless men with her roots and branches. When angry, Reue traps the strong cow until the cow drowns, and you, Lavena, don't have the strength of a cow." Aunia laughed at that last, as did some of the others.

Lavena, daughter of Sinorix, had to respond to this scolding from another youngster, had to save face. "I dove in from the same rocks, like the older girls and boys, and the teachers, like always. I swim as good as them, better. How do you know, anyway? You can't even…." She stopped, before her next hurtful word. The gap in Aunia's face, never to be closed, could not keep water out of her mouth. Aunia swam slowly, head held high, and never entered water where she could not stand on the bottom.

Aunia finished the scolding. The adults let her, and the children listened. "Lavena, you do swim best. But Reue lives and laughs and cries in anger like we do. When she swells and flows faster than a horse runs, she knocks down everyone in the way. Listen to her. She'll tell you when and where you can cross, and where she does not allow you to enter her."

Aunia pointed to the darkening sky. "Watch for clouds heavy with rain upstream from every river. Even the little creek swells and crashes with Reue's anger and breaks houses that invade her land. On days like today, Reue tells those who listen to stay out of her way."

Aunia pulled Lavena to her feet, and they all gathered for the walk or ride back to the village. The best friends walked together. Lavena said, "Father has told me too. I didn't listen to him."

Aunia tilted her head away, away from them all. She did that automatically often, to hide her face, even from her best friend. Her black hair hung down to her slender waist. In recent days Lavena thought that soon many men would want to mate with her, would be taken by her wisdom.

Aunia continued. "Hah, children listen to their mother and father last. Better others teach them. Just remember this day—and until you're older never swim alone. Yes?"

"Yes, never swim alone." The other children walking with them repeated the phrase more than once.

"Before winter, you and I will come back here, and I will teach you much more about the Eberus and Reue," said Aunia.

By the time they reached the village, Lavena had taken notice of the throng that had run and ridden along the river after her. A time or two she glimpsed Turibas hanging back, nonchalant, but looking at her too, nodding and shaking his head slightly as if to tell her she had been too bold, that he had worried. That made her feel warm inside.

#

After night replaced the day and the storm had passed leaving a gentle cold rain, Sinorix sat by his daughter under her pelts. Her mother sat by her often before she fell asleep, told her stories of living people and of those who had left to return to the spirits in the ground and sky, but Sinorix not often.

Able to see with enough light from the fire in the other room, Lavena took in her father's wide strong face. She saw his age, old and tired, the skin drooping under the eyes and from below the chin. She wondered for how many more river races he would be with her. She took in his upper arms, relaxed but as muscled as those of any man Lavena had ever known, and his big bare chest, still hard as stone. As always, she felt safe in his presence. No one, nothing could harm her if her father was near, though he was gone too often and for too long.

His deep voice said, "I, your mother and I, your brothers and this village almost lost you today. Mother gave you your name, and you leaving us too soon would dishonor that name."

She knew her name was short for "great joy". Before this moment she had not cared about what others might have thought of her boldness, how others might have felt if she had left them. "Sorry, Father. I was.... My head is most strongly foolish."

"Yes, my daughter. Your head is stronger than your body now, but soon they'll have the same strength. We need you to grow strong, to become wise, to stay with us for a long time."

Lavena looked at him, puzzled. What was he saying that she did not hear?

Sinorix must have sensed her question. "Lavena, many years ago, all the tribes of this region were as one fist, one sword, one scream of freedom, and no one challenged us. We forced even the mighty Romans to kneel and beg for a treaty of peace." He stopped and turned away as if weighing how much to reveal, of his past, of himself.

"Your brothers are fighters, not thinkers. We'll need you to gather the tribes back together, to be free once more. Not today or tomorrow, but soon enough we'll be ready. We'll have to be. When that time comes, and I pray it does not come too soon, your brothers will need your help. Our neighbors, the wives of all the nobles, heed our great she-warriors as they heed no man. You, your life, your future days with us, are too precious to waste. Promise you'll not be so rash as today. Promise me you will always be patient until the one right way reveals itself."

"I'll try, Father, I'll try as hard as I can, Father."

Her father's face relaxed, and he touched her left shoulder. "Sleep quickly now. Tomorrow's training comes early."

He left, and did not ever mention her foolishness again.

Chapter VI

Festival of First Blood

On the seventh night of the twentieth moon after the river god Reue nearly took her, Lavena's body whispered that her childhood had ended. Ten days earlier a new pain had sounded in the lower belly, strong enough that she wanted to lie down and curl up but did not. On this night, a new wetness sloughed out of her. She lay still. What to do, at this moment, what to do in the morning and after that?

She had been waiting, expecting, and it did not surprise her. Small soft breasts had formed over hardening chest muscles, and for many months her insides had told her it was coming.

She prayed silently that the stain would not show on her gray winter night shirt or on the dark brown fur skins under and over her. She would not tell her mother or even Aunia, and no one must notice, not this time. By the end of her next cycle, she would hide the traces, wash them out before anyone suspected.

If her mother or Aunia knew and Lavena could not convince them to keep it secret, her mother and father would summon the nobles and every member of their households for another Festival of First Blood.

Four months back, Aunia's time had come. The next day, her mother and father had announced the festival for their daughter with the mouth that never closed.

All the nobles of the village and some from neighboring towns and every member of all their households came to it. Strangers, poorer men, older and young, joined the invited, in case fortune might be with them. After the early rounds of drinking challenges, no one cared about uninvited villagers.

At sunset on Aunia's festival's first day, the hundreds in the main village plaza and the great hall next to it stomped in unison. Hot and sweating, they shouted and cheered, "Aunia, Aunia, beer, beer, drink beer." They yelled it until she drank beer for the first time.

She didn't seem to mind the taste nor the foam that covered over the ugliness of her mouth. Soon after, someone brought her a flagon of wine.

Lavena, who had remained by her best friend's side all that day, looked for Aunia's mother. Edereta and Aunia's mother stood next to each other not far from their daughters in the great hall. Gesturing through the din, they told Aunia it was all right to try the wine.

Aunia looked at Lavena, as if to ask Lavena if she, Aunia, should drink, as if to ask what would happen, as if to ask Lavena to protect her from whatever the spirit in the wine would do to her, and what other people might try to do to her when the wine's spirit took over. She lifted the clay flagon and said, "Lavena, stay with me?"

"Yes, yes, I'll stay by you." Lavena touched Aunia on the elbow, then held her arms firmly to help her balance the full flagon and not slop the wine over the awkward mouth, down her young chin and neck, and over the gown of golden silk chosen by her parents for this celebration.

Aunia drank and coughed and drank again and smiled at the throng roaring louder now.

As if signaled by Aunia's smile, different than any other's smile, the crowd started yelling the chant of every Festival of First Blood.

Aunia, Aunia, come to the man who you take as your man.
Be one with him,

Mate with him,
Bring glory to those who brought you, by
Bringing them your own new life.
Aunia, Aunia.

They yelled it again and again, laughing, cheering. After each chorus, they took another swig of whatever they had been drinking, and swung their arms high. Some held swords or knives, others clutched bones with cooked meat hanging off the bones.

It was time for young men to start hovering over the guest of honor, to fight each other in front of her, for her. This was the time when the mother or father might bring a chosen young man to their daughter, and, if their daughter agreed, send the two off to a selected pile of pelts away from the guests, there to mate and sleep as one until morning.

But only the stooped older men and ugly boys hovered round Aunia.

Through the cheers Aunia eased down to the pelts against a wall in the great hall, lowered her head as if to hide her face and not encourage the ugly boys. She held tighter onto Lavena's arms.

Aunia settled deeper into to the pile of pelts, curled up into an ever smaller ball, never looking out, never looking at any of the men standing over them close enough to reach up and touch if Aunia had wanted to.

For a moment, Lavena thought the wine spirits had taken over. They had not. Aunia began to cry quietly against Lavena's shoulder, the tears not stopping, her hands not loosening their grip.

The collective attention eased away from the two unresponsive girls huddled inward against the wall, and the nearer men drifted away. Soon all the men went back to their drinking, eating, fighting, and flirting with other women, or faded to drunkenness. After a time, only Aunia's mother and father and Edereta stayed near. With her eyes and hands Lavena asked them permission to take Aunia to her own family house.

Aunia's mother motioned to the girls to get up, helped Aunia prop herself on unsteady legs. Then she turned into the room, shrugged and pointed, as if to announce she was taking these two out to the waste areas or outside away from the heat of the hall, as if they would soon come back.

Aunia's mother and the two girls did not stop until they reached Lavena's house.

The two best friends slept holding each other until morning. No young men or drunk old men found them, or if they found them did not dare bother them sleeping at the house of Sinorix. Lavena knew only that deep sleep came quickly and no one disturbed them.

On the second night, two men wounded each other fighting over the left hind leg of the last roast pig. The next morning they lay bleeding in the yard outside the great hall. Sinorix said, "Leave them be. The gods will decide how long they should sleep and if they should awake here or below ground."

On the third morning, both men managed to stand up and stagger away together, each holding up the other, to treat their wounds with hot water and honey. Lavena thought her father must have known they would recover easily.

Aunia's festival lasted for three nights and days, until all the women had taken away their drunken men, and all the fathers had dragged off their drunken sons, until all the men without fathers or their own women had returned to their houses or lay in and around the great hall or in one of the three rooms under it.

On the second and third night when the attention was not all on them, the maiden of honor and her best friend again eased their way to Lavena's house and there slept together.

As they parted on the last morning, Aunia took Lavena's hands in hers and kissed them, drew her close and hugged her as she never had. "Lavena, thank you. The gods of life will walk with you all your days for helping me through my festival of first blood."

#

In the times of waiting for her own first blood, Lavena vowed no festival would be called for her, though she knew hers would not play out as it had for Aunia. All the best single men of age and many older ones would hover, challenge each other, and, if they felt invincible in their youth or drunkenness, fight for her to the death. At the first hint of having been chosen by her, the chosen one would carry her off and mate with her.

She knew, as was the custom, that if she liked the first mating, she might take the selected man for life, and birth and grow many children, thereby bringing great joy to her mother and father. Lavena didn't know a healthy girl who had stayed unmarried much past the age of fourteen. Her body said loudly it was ready to take a man and bring new life.

Her mother breathed deeply in sleep not an arm's length away. Her father, in the other room, snored but not loudly.

Perhaps she should crawl over to her mother and whisper what had happened, and, if Edereta wanted, let the Festival be announced. She had already chosen—strong, lean Turibas.

Every waking moment, she yearned for the feelings reflected by him, for his response matching hers, increasing in her and in him, each leading the other on. She saw his grin contracting and hardening as he looked at her without seeing her but with an increasing urgency, seeing only, seeking only, his way into her.

In recent days, she had allowed him ever so close. One moment more with no adult shouting out for him or her, one more exchange of his warm breath on her face and her breath on his, and they would have joined. On this night, Lavena understood that only the many people of her village, all the mothers and fathers looking out for their children and each other, the constant training and, when not training, the work demanded of everyone kept her from mating with Turibas.

If she told her mother, soon the mating, when it happened, would make her squeal as loudly as other girls and women in the village squealed, and the next morning her face would be as red as any of the young women after their noisy nights.

Those thoughts brought on the same sensations they had every time, took her to a half sleep of feelings unreleased, sweeter than the sweetest grapes. She could increase or diffuse their intensity by the power of her thoughts. By that control she made the feelings last. She made herself see Turibas' face, his alert blue eyes, the smile that turned to a centering leer drawing her closer.

When she or another broke the spell by shouting out for one of them, Turibas always laughed, a laugh not of regret at another missed chance. His laugh said he knew how she felt because he felt the same, he responded the same as she did, and he knew the inevitability of them together.

As those thoughts lingered, as those feelings peaked and waned, the other thing intruded. It flitted in quietly from the head, cooled the heat in the rest of her, made her pull away while she could. Her head, the place where all Druids said the soul dwelled, spoke other commands.

The images changed, first at the edges and then completely, to the laughter and the face of her first Roman, and all the Roman faces, dark and ugly.

From the days of the dead farmer, and weeping village men seeking her father's protection, her head brought on another urge, in the end more constant and powerful. Other things to do, other yearnings to fulfill.

Her hardening hands, wrists, arms and shoulders, her legs that allowed her to jump and flip so that no part of her touched the ground until she landed balanced on her feet, her every breath, had one purpose—to become a she-warrior, to make the Romans rush at her, unprepared for her first strike. She and only she could make the noble wives listen. Only she could make them take some of their gold from the hiding places and pay farmers to become fighters. All the nobles had done that when her father was young. They even paid the best fighting men from other tribes to join with those from the Village on The Cliff. Together they could chase the bad ugly men off her land and back across the Great Inland Sea.

Taking a husband, carrying a child, birthing and caring for young lives would halt all that forever. Turibas, and she with Turibas, had to wait.

Now to hurry, things to do before the roosters crowed and the village woke up.

She got up and made her way out two doors to the waste area behind and below the house, each sitting place sectioned off by roofless walls for privacy of the body's lower parts. Jars of standing water iced over in the cold night. The limestone place for her hands and seat were as cold as the ice. But she was grateful to all gods of women and new life that no rain fell this night, that mounds of fresh straw lay at her feet, that she was the only one in this waste area and could wash until she felt clean and dry, and was able to creep back without rousing anyone.

Chapter VII
Giving Life

Early the next morning, she heard her oldest brother's voice from the main room. "Someone's been stealing our sheep and running off our horses on the eastern edge. The herders and our scouts can't tell if they're Romans or our neighbors."

Loud noises of swords clanking and shouts of others jarred her fully awake. She didn't want to leave the warmth of her pelts after the interrupted night, not for today's training

"They've come three times, each on the first night of no moon. They find one young sheep they can carry, scatter our horses and ride away in darkness. They come when the ground is hard and leave no tracks, and our best dogs can't follow.

"Tonight's the first night of no moon, and the ground's hard again. We're going out there. If it's Romans, time we teach them." He paused as if for any reaction from those in his room or outside the front door. There was none.

Lavena couldn't tell who else was on the other side of the door, but thought her brother must have told her father of the plan. Her father owned more horses, cows, and sheep than most of the other nobles, perhaps more than any of them. But why did her oldest brother make this speech now, why here on the other side of the door?

The oldest brother—most called him Sinorix The Younger—sounded as if he had moved closer to her doorway. "Lavena, Mother and I say get up and get ready. You ride with us. It's time you learned what we do to thieves."

His tone left her mother no opening to protest and no doubt that he wanted Lavena to hear.

This oldest brother, out of her father's first wife now dead, stood as tall as her father. Most times, he acted as a stranger to Edereta and his half-sister, never laughed with them, never ate with them in this house, never sat with them at any of the festivals, and never touched Lavena or Edereta as might a brother or a son. The two younger brothers followed this one's lead.

Lavena didn't know how to fit them into her structure of who she was, who her family was. They were not strangers but not brothers either. In recent times, she could not miss the resentment of the sons against Sinorix's second wife and his new daughter, a daughter given to an old man who favored her more than he favored them. Lavena feared her oldest half brother.

She jumped up and changed fast into warm day clothes, opened the door to the main room—and, before stepping out, closed it again. In the night, she had used up loose smaller scraps of pelts she found by groping near, and now had nothing to hide or clean any further flow out of her. She couldn't ask her mother and didn't know what her mother used during her own cycles.

She grabbed an extra strip of cloth hanging from a post on the wall, for tying back her hair or sleeves when practice fighting or riding. It would have to do.

The outside was cold, colder than in the night, so that her breath made little clouds and her hands and bare feet quickly became cold, first so cold they hurt, then colder still so that she could barely feel them. If she had to ride and fight, she would not wear boots or even sandals, had never trained in those, and had none that fit anyway.

The ground, dry and hard, was free of snow, but the mountains to the north stood white in the bright morning sun. This winter, deep snow had come farther down into their valley than in years. Ice hung from the bare trees, and the wolves howled nearer to the village than Lavena ever remembered. For months, a cold rain mixed with snow had come down. When the snow and rain stopped, the air and ground became even colder.

Many in her village complained they had not seen such a long and hard winter since before the Romans, said that maybe the gods were angry and would drive the Romans off their land. But on this day and in the night to come, the traveling would be easy—for Romans or for any thief.

Before Lavena grabbed the mane and jumped onto the bare back of her horse, Edereta pulled her close. Her eyes told Lavena nothing, except this was no time for talk. As always, her mother's touch, the warmth of her, brought peace. This time, her mother hugged her in a way that made Lavena think she knew after all but would let her daughter announce the first blood in her own time. Lavena hoped that was true.

Sinorix the Younger said loudly, "We ride now and don't wait for girls." Some of the horses pawed at the ground. He jumped on his to join the other riders already mounted, and led them in a circle out and away. Their brightly-striped cloaks trailed on the cold wind they made riding.

Lavena had never owned anything like those war cloaks, had not painted her face, and carried only her falcata. Once she sat high on her horse, she did not look back.

Six fighting men, armed with long swords, spears and sling shots, their horses carrying shields, tent cloths, ropes and bed rolls, and one girl rode out to stop thievery on moonless nights. More villagers than usual gathered to watch a small fighting party leave. They collected at the outer gate and on the outer wall, shouted, whistled, and said loudly between the shouts, not caring if Lavena heard, some plainly wanting her to hear. "Bring back the thieves alive..."

"Look, the daughter of Sinorix goes with them.... Bring back their heads...."

"Lavena...she's too young...too small.... Where's her war cloak?"

"Hush, she's our leader's daughter…and fights like him…." More laughter and whistles.

Soon they were out of sight and sound of the village and outlying clusters of shops and farm houses. They, Lavena last in line, rode east.

Lavena knew what happened to thieves. Their severed heads would be soaked in a slurry of cedar wood, dried and mounted so they stared out from the outer wall of her village. That way, their spirits could never come back in another body to make more mischief.

Her insides clenched a bit at what she might have to do, what her brothers might demand of her, clenched on top of the sharp ache from her lower belly.

They rode below the ridges of the hills, hugged the edges of stands of oak, hazel nut, elm and cork trees. Good winter grassland was hard to find at this time of year, and the herd was far out, too far to come in every night and go out again in the morning on the short days. They tried to follow a stream bed between rolling hills, and finally waited in a low point for the day's last light to leave. Any thieves watching the herd from a distant hill need not know that armed men had come to help.

They found the herders' camp, all fires out, no torches lit, no food waiting. A few herders greeted them with grunts and single words. The shapes and sounds of the horse and rider in front of her told Lavena where to go, where to stop. She would not have known where to dismount in the snuffling, clomping animals, all their noises louder in darkness.

The outline of a dog flitted out there through the herds, vanished and appeared again in another place. As her eyes separated the shapes, she spotted smaller dogs circling, then coming in close, fading away and coming back. All the farm animals followed the dance, seemed to stay within shouting distance of this dark camp. In time, they settled and the sounds softened.

No one opened bed rolls. No one talked. They all peered out at the stirring animal shapes set against a dark landscape and star-lit sky.

Lavena did not move away from her horse, kept hold of its long reins. She was not sure the herders and scouts still at the camp knew who she was, was not even sure they knew she was there.

As the night grew darker, she lost sight of her brothers. For an instant she wondered why they had not made her stay near them. They must have thought she was too small, too weak and not ready for any real fight against grown men. Not too far back in the past, a big dog and an old man had to save her from a single Roman. They had taken her this far only because she was her father's daughter and he forced them.

A tired helplessness crept in, a not knowing what to do if a stranger moved on her, not even being able to tell if that stranger was a villager or a thief. Her short sword felt too light and flimsy. Any excitement had leeched out.

After a time, she made out several men at the camp tying short ropes to their horse's front legs and letting them go. She dared to do the same to her horse. The men unrolled their pads and lay down. She only sat down, ready to jump up.

Footfalls of boots crunching came close, but too noisily for a thief. A soft strange voice, close to a whisper, said, "Daughter of Sinorix, do you see?"

"Only the stars and shapes of the animals, sir?"

"You must see with your ears when your eyes can't."

She had a notion of what he meant. "Yes, sir."

"Hear their foot beats of our dogs, softer than any of the hoofed animals, their breathing when they run, then standing still and even lying down to rest, no growling, no whining. That all tells us what we need to know better than in the day's light."

"Yes."

"No thief comes this night."

Lavena's body relaxed, as if permitted to flop down, get warm between her pelts and sleep, but that would show weakness. From the place of The Great Hunter in the clear sky, a long time remained for a thief's raid. "How can you tell, sir? There's time yet for them to come."

"Your Father's best dogs are quiet. They'd tell us about trouble as if they could talk. They know every one of their animals, smell each as clearly as we can see them in daylight. They know if even one's missing. They know the thief from far away and we would know their restlessness."

"What would they do if one's missing?"

"Run and bark and whine and pester whoever tried to take one of their animals, and then run in here to get us if we did not hear them first."

Lavena looked again for the dogs, tried to spot each one. But they were too quiet, blended in too well, or were too far out.

After a time, the stranger said, "Roll out your pelts, Daughter of Sinorix. Nothing will happen before light. A tired fighter's a useless fighter." He laughed softly as if he did not mean that last, as if he meant, *Lavena, tired or alert, you'd be of no use.*

She was sure they had taken her only because she was Sinorix's daughter, one more sheep to watch over. She curled down tightly, as small as a hiding rabbit. That fit how she felt on this night, in this open cold space, at this time of her first cycle.

#

Loud bellowing of men woke her. Drops of cold water slicked her top pelt and wet her face. Daylight oozed in through a dark cold mist.

Men shouted, ran for their swords and spears, untied the ropes on their horses' front legs and rode away over a rise until out of sight.

By the time she stood up and grabbed her falcata and wool cloak, she was alone at the camp—of so little value no one needed to stay to watch or protect her.

Her horse, hobbled off to her left, snorted as if waiting for her to release the tethers and ride after the others. It seemed to tell her what to do, and doing something blunted her anger and loneliness.

As she mounted up, she glanced over the clumps of pelts and food pouches, water gourds and fire-making flints next to piles of burned wet wood. She wondered if the cows and horses might tromp over it all or the sheep tear into the food pouches. She wondered if she should leave it all for them.

But the animals too had turned in the direction of the commotion, and one dog circled the camp. She rode off after the others.

Out past a line of leafless trees and brown grass not yet all eaten to stubble, past a meandering stream and beyond another rise, her band of riders and others on foot formed a circle. Whoops of victory mixed with shouted words came to her. "Thief…low caste scum out of swine…lesson…teach you. Take his head…yes, take it now…."

Her oldest brother from atop his horse looked down into the center. The circle opened for her to move her horse up to his right. She was relieved they let her see.

On the ground, two men of her tribe held onto the ears and necks of two shaggy gray-haired herding dogs. The dogs sat still, neither growling nor pressing forward. Lavena thought these dogs must have run ahead of the men after the thief trying to hide, though this was no country for hiding.

In their center on the hard red dirt, a small man lay on his back. He held up his legs to kick out, and pointed a sword upward. The sword, bent and rusted, looked heavy enough to hurt. He held a knife in the other hand. His head moved rapidly forward and back, side to side, as if readying for the dog or man who might first attack him. His eyes never set on Lavena, she no threat

Lavena thought he must have been chased to this spot and used the hard ground to protect his back—as she had been taught—though the rest of him looked silly and no match for any one of the men around him. Bones, not muscles, of the arms bulged under loose skin, the skin covered loosely by thin and tattered garments. The knees seemed too large for the thin legs ending in boots with his toes sticking out.

One of the men on foot lifted his hand for attention. "I ask you once more. Who are you? What are you doing here?"

The man ignored the questions. Lavena sensed a mixture of starvation and contempt, a spirit that once had been bright but now as gray as the sky.

The herdsman or scout who had spoken first looked over to Lavena's brothers for what to do next.

Sinorix The Younger repeated, louder, "Who are you? What are you doing here?"

The man on the ground turned his head and opened his mouth but said nothing. He had heard and likely had understood.

One of the footmen said, "Why that rope and netting?"

Lavena noticed the coiled rope and mesh lying at the man's feet. She thought this little man might be one of the wild ones, as shy as the fox, who hid in the mountains far from any village. She had heard about the little mountain men but had never seen one.

Sinorix The Younger said, "You brought those to throw round a young sheep and run off?"

The man rasped out a hissing response. "Mighty Sinorix can spare one sheep to let us live through the winter."

Lavena, they all, grasped the things not said. This one knew of her father and spoke like they spoke.

And then it hit her, changed everything she had supposed about the thief, about this wretched little man, about what she must do. She kicked her horse to move up.

Sinorix the Younger said, "The gods have decided today is your last." He jumped down and pulled out his sword, as heavy and sharp as her father's, gleaming even in the moist grayness. "But first we'll lift your head."

As he raised the sword's handle to his shoulders and pointed the tip down in the direction of the thief's throat, Lavena dismounted. "Brother," she called out and stepped in front of him on the line between sword and target. "Stop this foolishness."

The others made noises of surprise and amazement.

"Only Father can decide this old man's fate—and our father will let him live."

"Out of my way, weak little girl," shouted her brother. He planted his feet one behind the other, bent at the knees, and reared his upper body while raising the sword high.

"Don't. Not now, not here."

Her brother hesitated long enough for her to finish. "Let our father decide. Listen to me."

The instant her words stopped, he shrieked as loudly as she had ever heard anyone shriek. He pushed her aside with his shoulders and chest, rose up on his left foot to brace on it for the strike over his right shoulder down and through the little man now crouched partially behind her.

A thousand training sessions kicked in. Ten thousand practiced thrusts of her feet took over.

Her left foot caught brother's back foot at the right instant, at the right point on the instep. As he rocked forward, her foot swept his free back leg up and behind him. He pitched forward, all balance lost.

Unable to break his fall with either the planted front foot or back leg trapped by her high kick behind him, his whole body flew off the ground and forward following the wild swing of the heavy sword. He landed sprawled on his hands, elbows, face, and chest. The sword pitched up free when his hands hit the cold hard ground and clanked harmlessly, well past the little man.

Quiet.

The quiet of shock from what they had witnessed, at the rage to come, at the skill of a young girl a good hand shorter and far lighter than the man she flattened, at the good fortune of the thief who might live a while longer—or die right now with the girl who tried to save him.

She knew she had to shift this madness before the shock of what she had done wore off.

"Listen to me. Listen well. One of you—I don't know who—taught me well in the deep darkness."

She had them, at least for a moment, even oldest brother who rolled over but did not try to rise. "One of you taught me what Father's well-trained dogs know. They know before we do, they tell us before we can see or hear the thief. Look at your two dogs sitting quietly. Think about your other dogs back there, none caring about this little stranger, even if he is the thief."

She waited. They did all scan the two dogs, sitting undisturbed. They looked back in the direction of the herds, out of their sight but watched over by all the other dogs and not one human.

"This man," she pointed with an open hand that did not accuse, "knows Father's dogs, and they know him. They don't growl at him, don't even look his way. Perhaps he was Father's man. Only Father or the gods can decide when this man's life is done."

Her oldest brother stood up, but left his sword where it lay, rubbed his right elbow and touched his chest, winced a little when he touched it. No one else moved, though from them a grumble rose up, a grumble of wonder and agreement.

She had more time. "The leader of all the dogs, Little Bear, is out there somewhere. He cared nothing about this little man, not this night, not on the other moonless nights." She looked directly at her oldest brother. "Let's go back. Let's take this one to Father."

Long before they reached the village, a crowd had gathered again, soon swelling to a bigger throng than when they had left. Sinorix waited for them in the village center plaza. He walked up to the thief riding bowed over, helped him down, and half carried him into one of the storage huts by the plaza. Sinorix said to the riders, "Thank you. You've done well—for bringing him in. Leave us now."

Late in the evening, the three half brothers came to her father's house. The left arm of Sinorix The Younger rested in a cloth strip hung round his neck. They came with their wives and children, some babies but others older than Lavena. All twenty-five family members sat or lay on pelts in the main room warmed by the fire or in the doorway areas of the three adjoining rooms. They ate bread baked that day. The men and some of the women drank beer, but slowly. None wanted to get drunk. None talked and would not until Sinorix began.

After a time of looking hard at Lavena, then at his three sons, sometimes shaking his head as if not believing his own thoughts, Sinorix said, "Your sister has learned well, they tell me."

"Too well." Sinorix The Younger looked down, shook his head low so none could see his eyes. After what seemed a long time, he looked up at his father, at Lavena and her mother, shook his head again—and began to laugh in small bursts more like a cough. The laughter built in him until it was strong and sustained, carried over to his brothers, to the children and the women. None could stop laughing. None could stop slapping the other family members while they told, in between bursts of laughter, what she had done.

"Did you hear? She knocked him down…with a feather's touch…made him fly like a field sparrow with a broken wing."

"Like he was made of straw…without one stick of wood inside him."

Sinorix raised his hand, and they stopped to listen. "That starving thief's sleeping now, warm and well fed for the first time this winter. He's the son of the best dog handler I've known. The son, that very man you brought in, trained and bred dogs with the same skill as his father. One day, spirits of the dark side of the earth entered the father, then the mother and oldest sister, made all their skin, then fingers, noses fall off. The gods cursed them with the curling hand."

Everyone in the room quieted. Lavena had heard of this curse. None of the high druids and doctors knew how to banish it once it entered a human. Sinorix The Younger opened his mouth as if he suddenly remembered the story, had known the dog trainer but had forgotten in the haste to punish the thief.

Sinorix looked at his daughter. "Your Alexandros and his people call it aphre lepras. They kill anyone who has it. Kill them with stones and arrows so it does not jump to them, burn their bodies to ash.

"I and most of the fighting men of all the tribes were far from here fighting the Romans. After we beat them and I came back, the dog trainer and every member of his clan had been turned out. Our villagers would have killed him if he stayed, killed them if they ever came back. I tried to find the outcasts, leave them food or pelts, but they didn't let me find them. The whole family must have been too ashamed."

Sinorix slapped his own knee, stood up and said loudly, "From this day, he and whoever is out there with him need not starve. I told him to come in before next winter, and I'll give him food and pelts. When the curse leaves them, whoever is left can come home."

#

The next day, her father gave the little man the cleaned carcass of a freshly killed sheep, a coat made of deer skin, and as many blankets as his horse could carry.

From that day Lavena was allowed to join the adults training to fight.

From that day, the villagers no longer jabbered like crows when Lavena passed, no longer smirked when she rode out with a band of men.

The young men of the village stared at her but looked away when she looked back. All except Turibas. He had already been promoted to train with the older fighters and farmers.

The first time they were alone after she spilled her brother, Turibas took her face in his hands. "Lavena, fair Lavena, I will wait for you, for you to say when we will mate and marry." Then he smiled that smile. "But don't make me wait until I am an old man."

He let go, looked down and away from her and clenched his fists as if he understood his next words were hard and weighed on him. "If I must wait until then and you have not taken another, I will." He brought his gaze back and, by his look, he meant it.

Lavena moved nearer to him and whispered in his ear—that always made him smile and lean into her with his whole body.

She put her arm around his waist. "You won't wait long, not that long. I cannot." And she meant that too.

From that day, her brothers, all three, came to the house more often, crowded in with their wives and children and some nights stayed too long. The house, though the biggest in the village, was not big enough for all of them to sleep in comfort.

Chapter VIII

Broken Treaties

180 B.C.

The faint clanking of swords on shields mixed with high-pitched shouts of scouts far out made her stop pulling the reins. This mule had finished hauling the cabbage and turnip cart for the day but didn't want to enter its paddock.

The distant sounds grew louder and closer, "It's him....Our chief and his men....Make ready for them...for the good news they bring...."

After three months without any sign or rumor, the scouts relayed that her father had returned from that distant place called the City of Rome. He had much news, and it would be good.

Praetor Piso had left Iberia, and Father followed him soon after. Though Lavena had heard of Piso many times, of his arrogance and demands, most times Piso had kept his men under control. Lavena thought it likely the Romans had learned how well the village had prepared, that they had extracted enough tribute. Soon every Roman soldier would be gone from Father's land, she thought.

At last the mule walked through the gate where fresh water and cut grass waited.

Lavena and many others ran to the outer wall and up the stone steps. She shouldered her way to the front on the walkway that ran along the top of the wall above the main gate and stood as tall as she could—and she had grown taller than most women around her.

A dust cloud rose in the east then horses and chariots out of the dust.

Lavena fixed on him, riding high and fast in the lead, until she made out his face and his white locks flowing behind—that he might spot her and wave, but he did neither.

She jumped down and ran to the outer gate, arriving as her father rode through. He did not acknowledge the greetings and shouts or look for anyone. Unlike other times, his horsemen and chariot drivers did not follow him through the outer gate, or to the inner gate and into the central plaza to the cheers and mounting anticipation. The returning men headed straight for the paddocks and storage houses outside the walls and let their leader enter alone.

He dismounted and strode to the tower by the great hall in the village center, the same hall of Aunia's festival. He shouted in a voice of warning. "Gather the elders of all the noble families, the head blacksmith, our merchants, the head horseman, the head foot soldier, now, everyone." He bellowed the last, "On their lives, get them here."

Lavena chased after and caught up to him. He did not hoist her up, did not reach into his cloak for a coin or colored stone, or smother her against his chest as he had so often when returning after a long time away. He climbed the steps to the top platform of the tower and stood motioning for all to hurry closer.

She sensed her mother next to her before she saw her. Though Lavena watched the top of the tower where her father waited, she felt and heard villagers come up from the rooms built against the walls and under the plaza, from the leather and blacksmith shops and weapons store rooms, from the mill works and tailor shops, and from farm houses and fields farther out.

One by one her three brothers, some of their wives and children, came up to the front. No one blocked the family view of Sinorix. Lavena understood this deference to her family, and it made her uneasy. Her father had earned respect, but she had done nothing worthy in this short life.

Sinorix raised his arms for quiet and spoke slowly, not his rousing shouts after a victory over a neighboring tribe. "They will not honor their promises, ripped up the treaty scrolls and threw them at our feet, spat on them."

Murmurs of questioning and disbelief from all sides and behind.

"The Roman Senate—we met with them three days—demands surrender, our gold, this land, everything."

Many of the listeners clanked their swords on other swords and on their own shields, and many talked at once, first to those next to them, then ever louder so their leader might hear, might hear the anger and disbelief, the words cascading to a flood.

"Sons of swine...."

From close by, a deep voice bellowed, "Surrender, I'll surrender the pimples on my old ass."

Laughter, and, "You told the Romans to mount each other from the back like dogs, yes...."

"We'll send them off howling...."

"Like mongrel dogs sick with the red eye sickness."

Sinorix raised his arms for quiet. "We have only four hundred trained fighters, five at most. We're not ready for what they bring—at us."

The swords on shields clanked again, and many voices shouted. "That's enough...."

"Half that's enough...."

"We've trained years for this day...."

"Let them come...."

"We're ready...."

Sinorix shouted back. At first, his shouts went unheard.

Then the crowd next to and behind Lavena quieted, and those behind them until everyone froze to listen.

"They bring not one but two new armies of thousands, one for our region, the other for the silver mines in the south. Their war galleys followed ours, carried parts for siege towers and battering rams bigger than the biggest Hannibal threw at them in days back. They say they'll kill everyone who raises a sword and have their way with all survivors—unless we surrender."

The shouts grew to screams, and Lavena had to look out for helmets flung into the air.

"Not with me, not with mine...."

"Off with their heads, out with their tongues...."

"Our neighbors will help...."

In the growing din from somewhere behind a woman's voice yelled, "Our she-warriors alone will beat the Roman dogs."

That got Lavena, made her understand what was and what might come too soon, made her shut out the noise, forget those around her, and dwell on her own arms, legs, hands, all of her, on her place in the coming carnage.

Not yet, don't come this day, or this season, not this year, I'm not ready, she shouted back silently to herself. No woman rode to war with the fighting men before age seventeen, before she had mated with a soldier in darkness and bested him in hand-to-hand combat the next day. She, barely fifteen, had not done any of that, had not yet sliced real human flesh, drawn the blood of another fighter trying to kill her or make her his.

Sinorix's louder voice intruded. "They come with horses out of Africa, carried them in bigger galleys than I've seen, ever."

Lavena knew her father had seen many galleys, and the approaching Roman galleys must be monstrous.

Ever more women joined the yelling. Edereta shouted up, and those near them quieted to listen to her. "Why did we give them a seventh of our crops and live animals...for this?"

Sinorix held up his hands, pushing his palms out and down as if pleading for quiet. "Their Senate says that Piso had no power to make his treaties, not with us, not with any of the tribes. The great Roman Senate sacked Piso, some wanted to drown him for treachery."

The clanking swords eased off, the shouts and yells lessened.

A man behind her grumbled, "We should have killed Piso for them, weak son of Roman dog whores."

"We treated him like any honorable man that gives his word," said Sinorix.

Someone said, "They're worse than dogs with the water sickness."

"Romans aren't like us. They live in great houses five times higher than this tower," said Sinorix.

A woman's voice shouted, "No, that cannot be. Their houses will fall on them." Those near laughed.

"I tell the truth," said Sinorix.

Alexandros had taught Lavena and other noble sons and daughters about those great houses, drew pictures of them in the dirt with shapes of little people next to the columns and under the roofs. The people were tiny compared to the columns and buildings.

"Then they don't need what little we have," said another followed by murmurs of agreement and dismay mixed with shouts, more clanking and roars that the Romans should come and meet their slaughter.

Sinorix waited for quiet once more. "They're more greedy than in days back. I saw the young men they enslaved, the young girls they turned to whores, more than ever before, many thousands of them in Rome."

That last brought total quiet. Lavena tried to not hear, as if by not hearing about them the bad things would never arrive.

Then her father said, "And they always want fresh ones."

After a long time, one near the front and behind Lavena yelled, "So we fight. Death's not the end."

And another shouted out, "They'll die too, and we'll find them in the next life and take out their eyes before we take their heads."

Sinorix said, "Or we flee this place, this land."

"Never...."

"No...."

"Where can we go?"

Sinorix responded, "Maybe we'll cross the Burnt Rocks, maybe we'll go west of the moon and across the big water to the land we came from, to our brothers and sisters in the cold country."

He let the choices linger, the murmurs rise and die. "The council of elders will decide. Meet now."

Lavena, Edereta, scores of single women and young children stayed in the village. Men watched from the walls and roof tops of dwellings and store houses. All the village scouts not already on patrol mounted up and headed to the far perimeter of their territory.

That night Lavena began to understand fully something that had puzzled her. On his last day, Alexandros had told her class, "I've always said my time with you lasts as long as Piso is with us. I must leave with him tomorrow for Rome, but will return with him or the next Praetor, certainly."

Alexandros, the apprentice teacher with him, the wool and cloth workers from Greece, and the jewelry makers from Sagunto on the shore of the Great Inland Sea had all left within days of Piso's departure.

Now Lavena knew none of them would ever come back to her Village on The Cliff. Whatever she learned from now on about the languages of Greece and Rome, their buildings, their tricks with numbers and counting, and everything else about them she would have to learn on her own.

At dawn, the leaders of the noble families emerged out of the main room at the side of the great hall in the main building and spread the mandate of their unanimous vote. Anyone wanting to flee had permission to leave with their treasures, all livestock they could control. For all those who stayed, the nobles had one short command. "We fight until only our blood in the dirt remains for Roman spoils."

Chapter IX

Promises and Forebodings

Lavena saw no one flee, heard of no one who left. But the village population swelled beyond what she had ever seen. Families that belonged to no tribe or village swarmed in, set up camp crowding below the outer wall with their donkeys and horses, pigs and chickens in crates, and their wagons.

She knew of smaller tribes, no larger than extended families—"out-villagers" they called them. They lived in wooded hollows or in mountain valleys far from any village but close enough to come in at times of no game or danger. They were one level up from crazy little men of exiled clans.

In normal times, the out-villagers came in up to four times a year. Her father and mother welcomed them, though others laughed at their accent, their ragged clothes. The out-villagers brought small carts piled high with pelts of the badger, ferret, bear and deer, intricate leather belts and harnesses, and potions made from wild mountain flowers and ground up bird beaks. They left with spices and salt, metal weapons and tools, woolen clothes, and hair brushes. They never stayed after their bartering was done.

This time, Lavena thought they might not leave for a long time and worried. If they all crowded inside the walls, there would not be enough space to fight—or run.

In the organized chaos, she lugged water buckets to cement mixing tubs and up ladders to soak the thatched roofs. She ripped cotton sheets and woolen blankets into bandages, made splints out of wood scraps. From outlying huts that raised bees, she collected jars of honey mixed with garlic and crushed poppy seeds.

In darkness, she planted sharpened soft wood spikes, points up, in holes around the outer wall beyond the out-villager camps, then covered the holes with thin slats and dirt.

At night the youngest children and pregnant women without families of their own crowded into the three rooms under the village center. Somehow the children knew they must keep quiet and try to sleep. Lavena prayed to the gods of the earth to keep all the children safe from the Romans and allow them to live above the ground a while longer.

Here and there she heard her father's shouts. "Faster, move, come let me help, move, move for your life." She glimpsed him run among work parties that filled in weak areas of the walls with new posts, stones and clay or cement. He chased off older horses, cows, pigs, sheep and their protecting dogs. She knew the farm animals would add to the coming chaos and interfere with the defenders. If the villagers survived, they would find their animals, or the livestock would drift back.

Late each evening before sleeping a few hours, Lavena and Aunia found each other. They tried to talk of things that did not matter, that would not burden either of them all the more, but could not hold that for long, both wanting—needing—to talk of what the next days might bring.

On the third night, Lavena said, "Aunia, do you remember your time below the ground, the time between your last life and this?"

That made Aunia laugh, loudly, and turn serious. "Yes. I think I do."

"Well, tell me. Please."

"I had a mouth like yours, Lavena, and all the young men fought for me. I liked that, and picked the strongest one with the hardest chest."

"Well, then, if Father's right and we can't beat them, I'll see you there and all the young men will fight over you and me too."

They both laughed at that, but with a tinge of uncertainty. After all, Lavena thought, what Aunia said might be true.

In the days and nights of preparation, Lavena did not see Turibas. Most of the village fighters stayed far out, watching on the perimeter, or down with the blacksmiths, preparing their weapons. Her father and mother did not allow her out there with them.

In the evening of the seventh day after Sinorix's return, word flitted through the village. "Our scouts have spotted them on the move…"

"The Roman army didn't stop at dusk, kept moving deep into the night. It's coming…fast…at us."

That evening, Edereta said, "Lavena, get your falcata, tie it to your leg under your shirt where they can't see it until you pull it out. Stay with me in the main room under the plaza. Help me with the children. Help me with the women heavy with child and no husband. Help with the wounded when the fighting starts."

Lavena did not need to ask why. In the few times of great danger for the whole village—from a storm or marauders—the orphaned children and pregnant girls without a family slept in that main room. Her mother stayed with them until the thing had passed.

Then Edereta said, "I pray you don't have to use it, but if you—and I and all our sisters and children—must, use it knowing it's the will of our gods for you to not live as a slave in Rome. That is no life at all."

As Edereta spoke, she held Lavena by the shoulders. Her mother's strong, kind hands told Lavena more than the words, though the message in those hands terrified her. Lavena didn't know if she would, if she could, if she had the courage to do what those hands asked of her.

Lavena and all the women of her village, especially the young women not yet dried up, might have to use those short swords on the Romans, and if the Romans kept coming, then on the young children, and after that on themselves. *Only our blood in the dirt for Roman spoils*, the village nobles had commanded.

This night was calmer than any the last week. The villagers had done everything that could be done in the time they had.

Lavena, exhausted, fell asleep in a room under the plaza surrounded by the orphans, her right hand on the falcata strapped to her right thigh.

Before the roosters crowed, Sinorix bounded down the steps, his hair matted, his tunic soaked—both pale orange in the light cast by the one candle flickering on a ledge in the wall. Lavena had not been this near him since his return from Rome.

He had not slept in the family house since then. His great sword hung from his waist. His left hand held his massive black-headed axe. The golden rope on his neck, the one her mother had secretly shown her that night more than four years back, drew her gaze. She had never seen him wear gold, not even when he had left for Rome.

He looked around, his head and eyes unsteady, tired, crazed, his jaw hard, as if not seeing, as if thinking about things not in front of him now.

Lavena rose from her sleeping place and looked over at her mother, awake too and sitting up against the opposite wall. Some of the little ones rolled over, stirred, or made noises, but none woke up. They had learned to sleep—or pretended to sleep—despite the troubles they had seen in their young lives.

This was her chance, perhaps the only one she would have. She half said, half whispered, "Father, Father, let me go to the outer wall, with my short sword and a shield. Let me fight—the gods will protect me."

He turned in her direction and sounded like the father she knew. "You may. It's time you see."

At the first sound of his voice, gentle and tired, Lavena wanted to lift the burdens from him, wanted to tell him no Romans could beat the village fighters, could scale or break through both inner and outer walls, that soon his worry would end, but kept quiet, anything she uttered too impertinent.

He continued softly, apparently also not wanting to wake the youngsters, "Don't hurry. Their army's still a long way off. You have time to fetch your best sandals, lightest cloak and best waist ties, your falcata, and get out to the far wall."

"Thank you, Father. The gods will help me fight well."

"No, Lavena. I forbid that. You must come back here when the fighting starts, come back here to help Mother. More mothers and their tiny ones, wounded soldiers will come here once the fighting starts—and they will need you. Let your brothers repel the Romans. That will be enough."

Lavena said, "Father let me fight…let me have that. Let the gods decide if I'm ready."

Sinorix shook his head. "Daughter, I command you to come back into this room when the first stones and arrows fly. Your place is here—until I or your brothers summon you. Understand?"

His answer, his real answer, struck her as clearly as if he had said it out loud. If he expected the battle to go well, he would not command her to flee to the safest place in the village, to hide among the orphaned and young children with their mothers, to make ready for the wounded soldiers before the battle had begun. He had seen the City of Rome and the army it brought, and he expected the Village on The Cliff to fall.

And what did he mean by *until I or your brothers* summon you?

No time to think more, no time to ask more. His stare, his weapons and power, his size made her say only, "Yes, Father, I understand. Come back here until I'm called."

He left, and total silence came back into the room, though Lavena did not sleep any more that night.

#

Before the sun rose, Lavena headed for the outer wall. Old men, women, and children covered every open place. The crippled sat on litters. Every adult carried a long knife, sword or axe. Barrels stood packed in against every wall, filled with water, others with heavy pikes and smooth stones for the slings, or rolled up bandages and spears pointed ends sticking up. Here and there, fires glowed under and around metal pots.

As she passed, some in the plaza whispered, "Lavena... Daughter of Sinorix...the gods are with you..."

"Fight like your father and brothers..."

"Fight for all women and our children..."

"Call for us and we'll come."

Lavena thanked them with her eyes and hand gestures but knew she would never ask them to come to the walls. All villagers who could wield a weapon already stood out there on the walls.

She stepped around them and the bundles of their last and most precious belongings, through the narrow open space at the gate of the inner wall, through another yard strewn with more villagers, to the stairs up to the walkway that ran around the inside of the outer wall. Along the base of the wall stood large pots of boiling water and melting sand tended and stirred by more old men and women, and children too. Smoke enveloped her, stung her eyes and made her cough.

On the wide walkway atop the wall, all the defenders looked out, their backs to her, but only one row of fighters deep. And that surprised her. Her father had been right—the village had at most four hundred trained and ready defenders, not enough to stand even two deep at any long section of the walkway.

Smaller fires smoldered under smaller pots hanging from metal supports in among the defenders, and more pots sat next to the fires. The fire lights flickered on the backs of nearly naked bodies as if cast from spirits who had once walked this ground among the living.

Lavena worked her way down to the outermost point in the wall above the outermost gate, where she thought the first strike must come. None of the fighters turned to her. If they glimpsed her, none seemed to care.

She spotted the instructor, who had first trained her group, naked to the waist, her legs covered by trousers and light boots. The instructor stared out into the night and took no note of her former pupil.

Some of the men wore bright cloaks or jackets of chain-mail, others naked to their mid-sections. One or two stood naked except for their weapons and helmets. Each fighter carried a spear or axe in one hand, and a sword or falcata hung from the waist. Bows and arrows lay at their feet along with shields and piles of hard round stones.

And then she saw him—Turibas—right in front of her A long sword hung from a belt on his naked waist, his hand held a spear, and a shield propped against his bare legs. For the first time in this flickering light up his back, she noticed how he had grown into a man, how his shoulders had widened, how he looked like a warrior, a worthy one.

She reached out to him but not touching. As if he felt her nearness, he leaned back, leaned until his strong shoulder touched her outstretched fingertips. He reached his right hand across to hold her hand close against his shoulder for a long moment. Then his fingers closed on hers and gently guided her hand around to his hard chest and over his heart. He pressed her hand flat so that she felt the beats—strong, slow.

The village fighters on either side were close, but their stares remained out into the darkness, and for a moment, perhaps their last, they seemed alone. He leaned back and into her and whispered, "Lavena, if the gods let us live, I will look for you until I find you. If they do not, I will wait for you on the other side."

"And I too, I too." She could not say more, the words did not come without tears behind them and sobs after that.

He moved her hand off his chest, squeezed it as he pushed it away in the direction down the wall. "Go now. You and I have other things to do."

Once more, he focused fully on the dark land out beyond him. The stillness of his body, every part of him, told her to leave.

She eased farther down the walkway to a place with an opening, and on her way never looked back at him. There she stopped and looked out straight ahead with all of them.

After a time, the fighters on both sides glanced at her and let the glances linger, as if they knew who she was and did not mind that she stayed there with them and waited.

Chapter X

The Battle

As morning light swallowed up the night, murmurs rose along the wall—"The army...."

"See it...?"

"Yes...."

"Out there, it's here."

"Let us crush it."

Pieces of the land far beyond the last houses outside the village wall lifted out of the ground—and moved closer. As the pieces neared, they broke apart and each piece took on the same shape, rectangles with edges that kept in a straight line even as the chunks moved forward over uneven ground.

Lavena saw the separate dark masses against the darker ground clearly enough to count. She counted more than fifty groups of whatever they were, ten groups across the front with many more coming up behind. As they came closer, the groups crushed vegetable gardens next to vacated farm houses, knocked down the weaker fence sections of empty livestock paddocks, crawled over or through some of the hillocks of cut grasses the village farmers had carefully piled up for winter hay and roofing straw.

She had never seen, never imagined, any living thing able to move with such unity and power. The carts and bullocks that came back to the village on harvest nights were tiny, insignificant compared to these things crushing in.

Twenty or so paces from the outer wall, the moving rectangles stopped as one, stopped just beyond the dirt and slat-covered holes with the upward pointed spikes, as if they knew, as if they had watched Lavena and the women set the traps.

The out-villager camps, carts and animals outside the wall had melted away, though Lavena did not know where, perhaps back to the mountains or perhaps into every free space inside the walls.

By sight and sound and a new smell carried to her on the morning breeze, each of the marching forms revealed the forms within them—eighty or so Roman foot soldiers carrying bowed shields locked at the edges, with spear tips over their helmeted heads. Almost below her now, their breathing, wheezing, coughing, restless stomping told Lavena they had marched hard for a long time.

From behind and to the sides of the foot soldiers, riders moved up to the front and into the open spaces.

And there they stood, every Roman soldier in each cluster, every Roman horse, and did nothing. They stood until they had caught their breath and finished coughing, finished snorting, until silence snuffed out all sounds.

The silence became so deep that birds again sang their morning songs in the upper tree branches and rooftops. The silence continued until the sun pushed away the mist on the ground. The silence gave Lavena and every villager on the outer wall time to finish counting, to comprehend this Roman army and the terror it could unleash.

The numbers of this force were not hard to add up for any of the villagers who, like Lavena, had been taught how to count numbers and multiply the easy ones. In that long silence she counted and multiplied many times. Well over three thousand men, carrying heavy pikes, short swords and arced shields, made an impenetrable forward-grinding mass, protected from behind and on the sides by horses and riders.

And she understood. Without intervention of the gods or all the fighting men from another ten villages, the life she knew could end before night.

She ached to find her father, to run back to her mother, to find her brothers. She thought of Aunia and where she might be...and how Roman soldiers might treat a maiden with a mouth that could not close. And under those thoughts, she knew she might never see Turibas again in this life. She shuddered and hated that she was still so weak.

Suddenly she saw and heard more, though this army could not have come with more. Behind the foot soldiers, two giant wheeled carts rolled up. Each carried a tree trunk, its front end tapered and encased in metal—battering rams.

Many men and two oxen pulled each cart forward with ropes, grunting in unison until they reached the backs of the foot soldiers. The oxen and carts stopped far enough out to be protected on all sides by many men and horses but close enough that all the villagers could take notice.

From the front line, one of the riders nudged his horse forward and stopped. Lavena knew his path was safe. None of the holes with upward pointing spikes lay directly in the pathways to the village gates—too dangerous for villagers and friends trying to enter or rush out.

This lead rider pulled the reins on his horse, its head bucking then rearing but not high, not wanting to throw the rider, wanting to charge. She saw his plumed metal helmet, leather gloves, a shield and leather leggings, and a mouth with no front teeth, though she could not make out the rest of that face. And she easily heard his every shouted word. This Roman yelled mostly in the language of her tribe.

"I bring you greetings from Tiberius Sempronius Gracchus, your new praetor. He should like to meet you all, and I ask an audience with your leader, to arrange that meeting."

Silence again.

"If none of you will meet with me, I'll tell you his message. He beseeches you to come out now. Women and children first, come on...come on, *melior vivere quam mori est*, life's better than death. Throw your arms over your little wall. Surrender and glorious Rome will treat you well."

More silence.

"What, you have no leader to speak for you, to respond to my generous offer, or does a sickly woman lead you? *Quis respondebit?*"

Sinorix's voice—young and strong—stirred the horses in the front to snort and back up. "Leave our land or we'll nail your heads onto this wall. Vultures and crows will eat your eyes." Lavena had not known where he was until he yelled from the highest point of the outer wall to her left.

The Roman leader rode down to Lavena's left to get closer to Sinorix, to get a look at him. "Old man, we have ten times your men and horses. Your walls are little steps to mighty Rome. Save your people from certain death. If you are the leader of this little hamlet, let us meet now in friendship, and hear my offer."

"I, Sinorix, honor my treaties—and piss on your lies and the lies of your worm-infested Rome."

Grumbles and laughter rose out of the Roman mass, and its horses snorted and stomped. The Roman leader said, "Old man, let your people decide, don't let them die. Rome will treat them well, and they'll all live long lives."

"Leave or die." Sinorix shouted that last the loudest. Every fighter on the walls echoed his scream so loudly that they stirred men and horses to the far end of the army.

After the roar subsided, the Roman leader shouted back, "Last time, old man. All you on the wall and inside, don't listen to that old man. He will die soon anyway. You, who have long lives to live, come to us."

For an instant Lavena wondered. Her father was old, older than most if not all the fighters, and he would rather die fighting than surrender. She thought, *me too, me too. I will too.*

Sinorix responded. "You and yours will follow soon enough, and on the other side, we'll take your heads." He said it in a voice that made the front horses back up hard again, some tossing their heads at his challenge. More grumbles and laughter rose out of the rectangles of foot soldiers.

After all around him had settled once more, the Roman leader yelled, "*Nihil amplius.* Nothing more."

He pulled out his sword, raised it high.

Lavena heard the arrows whistle in their descent, a sound longer and stronger than made by any of the arrows she had shot in her training days, heavier arrows shot out of stronger bows by stronger arms and hands. Screams ran along the top of the wall, repeated in the open village areas behind and below where she stood.

A cluster of village soldiers, shields held out and over her, crushed in on Lavena until the arrows stopped. Peering out between the big men protecting her, she saw something new and strange and unexpected that took her a moment to comprehend—ladders lying flat moving forward across the tops of many men until the ladders reached the outer wall right below her.

Before the ladders were set against the outer wall, the Village on The Cliff responded.

From her right and left came the deep loud sounds of carnyxes, war horns held upright and topped with a face of a wolf or bear. She had not seen them on her way here. At the first blast, the doors to storage huts and shops surrounded by the Romans, and even some of the grass hillocks nearest the outer wall burst open.

She was able to glimpse large men and women, each naked at least to the waist and taller and stronger than the Roman footmen, charge into the invaders. They swung heavy swords and axes, cleaved through shields and light armor, sliced tendons or broke the legs of horses backing and rearing onto each other, tossing off their riders.

The defenders easily evaded awkward and slow thrusts from the tight clusters of Roman infantry. For an instant Lavena dared to think these Romans acted like farmers forced into battle, not fighters trained to fight.

Suddenly, the men on either side of her reached down to stones and arrows lying on the path around the wall and shot down, then dipped some of the arrows into the fire pots. The wilding chaos in the Roman army increased.

Cries of attack and power were matched by shouts of panic and screams of pain. Horses and their riders at the front broke formation, reared in fright, and backed away, some trampling on the tight formations of men behind them.

The Roman foot soldiers retreated, crowding on the ones behind. The men on the inside of each rectangle had no room to run or even swing their weapons except at their own. Many stumbled and fell.

A new feeling surged in Lavena—helplessness. Her falcata was flimsy, her arms and legs weak. All she could do was duck low so only her eyes and the top of her head peeked over the wall between fighting men on both sides of her.

Somehow, out past the noise and chaos below her, the tightly bunched horses and men, she saw other Roman riders in saddles shouting and fighting bare backed horsemen from her village, though not many, not nearly enough.

The sounds quieted and the slithering dust and grime below her fell away. The Roman masses retreated—but not for long. The invaders formed up closer to the oxen and carts and again faced the village.

The Romans jeered and whistled louder, loud enough to hear them above the sounds of her village war horns close to her. The ambushers and village riders raced back into the gates—even the gate right below her. There were not many, far fewer than she expected.

One of the men next to Lavena said, "Only daughter of our leader, get to your mother. If you do not go now, Sinorix ordered I take you there." He had to say it again before she acknowledged she heard him, before she left.

For most of that first day, Lavena stayed in the main room under the plaza inside the innermost wall. She, and all of those with her, followed the battle from words passed through the masses in the yard above and down the steps. "They retreat...."

"They come back, but not the horses..."

"Ladders, many ladders on the outer wall...ropes and grappling hooks...."

"The great battering rams move up."

The yells and shouts from outside the walls and the answers from her tribe began to mix with screams of pain and confrontation, of vengeance, and small victories, at times a seamless chorus of human agony spun through with the sharper sounds of metal hitting hard on metal.

More young women came to the room, as if one child or the other belonged to them. Lavena thought they came because they could do nothing out there, and might live a little longer here.

In the heat of late afternoon, both sides quieted, to almost stop, and Lavena dared go up to the plaza once more.

The inner plaza seemed safe, no arrows or fire or spears raining down. The villagers huddled more quietly than on that morning, nothing left but waiting for the end. Here and there a village soldier lay face down or crumpled up among the civilians never to fight again. The village surgeons and a druid knelt next to one and moved on. More and more fighters of her tribe, those no longer of use on the outer wall, made their way to this area.

One soldier, hunched over, headed for the stairs down to the underground rooms. Lavena was drawn to follow him—and nearly lost consciousness at what she saw. That soldier stumbled and fell on the last step down. As he fell, he turned onto his back, not able to use his hands to cushion the fall. He needed every finger and thumb of his bloodied hands to hold together the opening in his gut.

As he landed, her mother and one of the village surgeons were by him with bandages, needles and thread, and strong wine. Other women motioned the nearest children to not look, to move back, but there was not much room for them to distance themselves.

Lavena now understood her father's command. As long as he lived, he would do everything still in his power to prevent the same mutilation of his daughter's young body. And she had lost all will to get up there, to fight and perhaps soon stagger back down here like this fighter. Right now she understood her own death was near, the only decision she might control was how.

Late in the day, the cries and screams rose again to the intensity of mid-morning. More and more young women and wounded soldiers came to them, and Lavena thought she heard or felt the first shocks of the rams battering the outer wall.

Chapter XI

A Night of Sadness

As darkness fell, the sounds stopped and new kinds of words came down to them.

"They retreat…to camp…raise many tents…."

"Ready for them in the morning, at first light."

The Romans must have paused to eat and drink. Even from the interior plaza, Lavena heard their howling and laughter.

Lavena said, "Mother, I'm going down to the wall, have to see, for me and for you and for everyone in this room."

Edereta braced and stiffened as if she wanted to shout, to forbid her daughter to leave, but let her go.

The way to the outer wall was strewn with the same clusters of non-fighters as before—but many more lay dead or dying, moaning, the less hurt among them screaming, blood oozing from them. Here and there lay more soldiers covered by their shields or cloaks, dead, others alive but soon to die.

Lavena stepped through and around them to the outer wall. The fighting had stopped, but far fewer men and women looked out than the last time she had been here. She did not see Turibas at his place on the wall or anywhere. She wanted to burst into tears but could not, the suffering of all those around her too great.

She found her father on the wall almost at the same place as in the morning, a group of fighters on both sides of him.

"I did not summon you."

"I know Father," and then she lied. "Mother sent me—to find you, to report back."

He looked at her as if he did not believe her. "Then you can stay with me and watch our best she-warriors try to save us, those of us who can still walk and do not bleed."

In the distance, the fires of the Roman camp silhouetted the men, horses, dogs, carts. The battering rams sat closer in, pointing, it seemed, straight at Lavena. She had no idea what her father meant.

A long time later, old men and women brought buckets of water and bread to everyone on the wall. Everyone ate and drank, saying nothing other than thanks. No one on the wall tried to sleep, but some fighters simply slid down to a sitting position, their heads bent forward, and they snored.

When the night was its darkest, Sinorix said softly to Lavena so that none of the others on the wall near them could hear, "When light left us, they fell back." He chuckled. "Our little spike pits you helped build did that. By day, they can find them, but in darkness not without torches that make easy targets. They know they can outlast us by waiting, not risking more losses. In the morning, they'll be back and the next day and the day after that—until only you and I are left on this wall."

Lavena waited for him to say more—or send her back to her mother.

"Come with me to the back side of our village. All our fighters on horse perished this morning in that first battle. I sent them away, to find a safe village far up river." He laughed softly. "But you know our fighters. They do not run from a good fight, not ever. Our she-warriors asked to do what comes next, to swim to the village downstream—while the Romans are drunk and happy—and beg them to send soldiers. If we all don't make a stand here, they in that village will fall."

Lavena said, "Father, let me go with them. I know the river, and you know I swim better than all of them, ride better than any."

"No, Lavena, you stay. If they succeed, we might be safe. If not, you have other, bigger tasks."

Lavena puzzled at his *you have other, bigger tasks*, but did not ask.

He led Lavena back around on the outer wall to where the Village on The Cliff rose high above the river, straight down to rocks and water and no invaders.

Others, women and men not armed waited there too, and more drifted to them. It was too dark for Lavena to tell how many, who they were or how they knew to gather here.

Not long after they arrived, off to their right at an opening in the wall below them and closer to the river, she heard a splash and another and six more, the splashes so quiet that in normal sounds of day she may not have heard them at all. Her father whispered, "Pray the Romans have bad ears. Pray for wind."

But no wind muffled new strange sounds. Too soon after the splashes, men yelled from the darkness outside the wall. They whistled and dogs barked from the direction of the Roman camp. The dogs came running to the river at the base of the wall. Soldiers on foot and horse, carrying lit torches, approached fast round the wall too.

Sounds of crunching and screams rose as the staked pits got them, but not enough to stop them from coming on. Their yells, whistles and the commotion drew more to the place below the wall from where Lavena and her father watched.

Through the darkness and confusion, the light of torches reflected on the river water, roiling from ever more men joining the chase. The first pursuers yelled in surprise and pain as the women in the river sliced and stabbed, dove below the surface to not come up until farther downstream and then fought them off again.

But the Romans were too many, their horses and dogs too strong. The raucous throng came back up the river to just beyond the wall. Two of the swimmers must have died and the soldiers let them float off into the night, the remaining six not so lucky or so brave.

The invaders hauled them out and dragged them back to bare dirt and scrubby grass within plain sight of Lavena and all who stood near her, the lit torches revealing more than anyone dared watch.

One of the she-warriors, naked except for an empty scabbard, her hands and feet held by four men, managed to bite one of their wrists hard enough that he yelled out and let go. Her hands free, somehow she grabbed his short sword and sliced the other hands or arms holding her.

For an instant, she rolled up to her feet in a fighting position. But someone slammed her head and shoulder from behind and smothered her last resistance. As she fell, she pitched forward onto the short sword she held. The soldiers around her left her where she fell.

They all now encircled the survivors, each inside her little circle of jumping cheering men waiting their turn. They cheered so loudly that only faint short yelps, like the last cries of a bird caught by a wild cat, escaped from the centers to reach Lavena.

Lavena could not look but could not help looking, though she saw only wilding men pressing three and four deep into the circles' centers. She pressed her eyes closed as tears came, and prayed her instructor was one of the bodies which had floated away, or the one that lay lifeless below the wall.

Some of the soldiers broke out of the insides of the circles and ran up to the wall to point and laugh at the sobbing mothers and sisters, cursing fathers, until one of the defilers fell under a hail of arrows shot from close to Lavena.

In time, the circles broke up, and big men dragged their prey by the hair or arms or legs away from the village and to the army camp.

Through the humiliation, none of the villagers charged out of the gates into a certain slaughter that would not have saved even one of the village daughters.

When the night was still once more, Sinorix said, "The mothers and fathers each knew what their daughters would try this night. They had the right to be here. But do not tell your mother. Stay with her, stay there, this time until I summon you."

Lavena did not sleep that first night of the battle, too many soldiers to fetch water for, too many bandages to cut and slather with opium ointment, too many crying children to comfort, too besieged by what she had seen from the high wall over her river.

Chapter XII

The Battle—Day Two

Before dawn while most of the children still slept, Edereta said to the women, "Pray to the spirits of our men who left us yesterday, pray they give us their strength—and protect our women the Romans took." She could barely get out the last words.

Some of the others said, "Who…?"

"Have you heard who?"

"No. They didn't tell me their names, their family."

Another said, "I'm glad none of mine is old enough to fight—no, I wish he could fight. This waiting with him here is worse. If he was old enough, I would be up there with him."

Edereta whispered to Lavena, "Your brother—your oldest brother—left us yesterday. He was with our riders. Every rider fought them from behind the army…until they could fight no more."

This time Lavena could not stop her quiet weeping and hated that she wept. A young male fighter would not cry so easily. She wept for Sinorix the Younger, for Turibas, who surely was with her brother, for all the women and children in these rooms and out there, for the she-warriors. She wept that courage and honor were not able to overcome power and greed. She wept for this sometimes sweet life ending too soon.

By mid morning of this second day, the screams and shouts came closer, grew louder, and more fighters found the rooms under the last plaza.

One, about the same age as Turibas, held his right forearm with his left hand, the right hand a bluish white. Lavena knew the blood vessels to that hand had been cut.

As he passed Lavena, they looked at each other in recognition. He had trained in her class, had fought her in those silly mock fights. He looked directly at her as he headed for the wounded and the surgeons and said, "The outer wall is breached…couldn't hold the battering rams…not enough hot sand, not enough fighters left."

Then he put on a cheering face, used a cheerful voice. "Lavena, when they come in here, fight them like a she-warrior, fight them better than you used to fight me."

He was the first of many who came to them on the second day, the first of more she knew. Some of the later arrivals she knew well, the sons of other noble families with whom they had gathered and laughed at the end of the harvest, at the annual festival of winter held on the longest night, at the first blood festivals of other daughters.

When the sun stood high, Lavena came out to the plaza long enough to look around, long enough to pray before she again retreated underground.

The remaining defenders crowded on the ramparts and walkways of the inner wall, on the top of the tower in the central plaza, on every stairway up the walls and to the tower.

Below the inner wall the villagers huddled and crushed in on each other, covering every place a body could stand, lie, or sit. Only the wounded made any sound loud enough for her to notice through the shouts and screams of the fighting men above them.

Most villagers stared silently out of bloodshot, darkly circled eyes, resigned. A few noticed her, leaned her way as if to say something, as if to ask her for help, as if to ask if they could enter the underground rooms but then thought better of it.

She had expected this from the many cuts she and the women with her had tied off, the many broken bones they had splinted, the deep wounds they sewed closed and slathered with opium and honey ointments, from the men they sent back still able to wield a weapon and stagger up the stairs to fight a while longer.

Yet the sights in the plaza stunned her in the ugly finality of what was to come.

A time or two, Lavena imagined she had picked out her father's voice bellowing instructions, a warning, or screaming at a Roman too near. She imagined him at the front of a cluster of defenders, but could not spot him through the backs of her village's last fighters.

Before she retreated to the badly wounded, to Mother and the children, she scanned the tightly packed throng in the plaza, scanned for Aunia, and Aunia's mother and father, but saw nothing to tell her what might have become of them.

In the afternoon of this second day, fewer fighters stumbled down to them. Too few remained alive.

Suddenly, her father stood at the bottom of the steps, looked around as if to adjust to the darkness, as if he did not know where he was. Lavena, tending to another wounded man, would not have noticed if others near her had not stopped what they were doing and turned in his direction.

He stepped over youngsters, women and the wounded, toward her. Lavena felt her breathing stop, her core tighten. Her gaze locked on his for an instant and then drifted to his white tunic turned to a shredded dirty bloody gray. His white curls clumped by sweat and blood pressed against his head.

His usually neat beard was now ragged and flecked with the red of blood not yet dry and darker spots of dried blood, his mouth covered by spittle. In his right hand he carried his great axe, its usually shiny blade and wooden handle both a dirty red.

His voice broke through the din directly over them, "Lavena, before they crash through our last wall, get to the top of the back rampart and jump into Our River."

Struggling to understand but not daring to ask, she managed, "Father, I will not leave you.... Mother, these women—and I—know what we must do here."

"My last child, yours is to do something else, you must... tell others of these mad beasts."

A tinge of relief from his words, a surge of strength from his gaze, his voice, her beloved father wanted her to save herself in her river, and hide, and flee and tell others. But fear still paralyzed. "The rocks will take me, and I will be with you and Mother after all, and I will not have done what needs to be done here."

"Lavena, better the rocks than Romans. Jump out far, past the rocks. There the water's the deepest. Listen to Reue. She'll protect you."

As he talked, Lavena could not miss his last strength flowing out, his words halting, slow, his mind searching for the right ones of the few still in him, and that made her listen all the harder. "Your grandfather and his Greek friends built this village here, because the river's deepest here. It will hide you, and save you. Follow it, stay close to it until you are far from here."

Lavena wanted to make him stay, to touch his death-dealing hands, to have him hold her one last time, to have him hold her through to that next place. She managed, "Father, the river didn't save them last night."

"None of them swims like you. The beasts that got them will not expect you—too intent on plunder here, will not look for you upstream. Stay under, and they'll think you ended your own life."

The last words came out like a beggar with no hands asking for a coin, but they were all true.

"Father, I don't know if I can...."

"You can, you must....You must tell our brother tribes what happened here.... You must make them unite... as I was unable."

"They don't know me.... I'm...not...yet a warrior...."

"Tell them your name, our name, show them this. There is none other like it, and they will believe you." With his free hand shaking, Father reached under his filthy tunic and brought forth the rope of solid gold. "Everyone in Hispania knows Sinorix owns this… finest of all torcs."

Now he had to yell, yell over the noise from above, though he strained to yell. "If the mad beasts close on you before you escape, throw it into Our River. It will sink into the mud for the earth to reclaim it. I've instructed all the noble families to do the same. The Romans must not find our gold. They'll leave when they find no more."

He pulled two more torcs off each wrist, closed the far larger one on Lavena's neck and the two smaller on her ankles, speaking almost directly into her ear. "Our River will let you swim away under water against the flow as you have a hundred times. Hide by day and travel by night. Do it, tell them what happened here, tell them if they don't unite, they'll.… Take this and tie it to your waist."

He handed her a heavy pouch that he must have carried in his other hand when he first came in, though Lavena had not noticed, and pulled something out of the back of his belt. "Take these reeds for breathing as you have many times."

And then he left them.

Edereta, now shouting too, motioned for those who could to come close and shouted loudly enough for the few men not able to move from where they lay to hear. "We're done. No more wounded come to us.… Lavena, do as your father says. Get to the top. Go now. Our men can cover your way up to the back wall, but not much longer."

"Mother, I won't leave, not you, not them."

"Oh, Lavena, honor your father's last wish."

Lavena's looked down, her mind shut, not able to form a single thought, a single word, the end too near, too inevitable. Her body, no longer expecting to go on, had lost all will to respond to her mother, to anything.

Edereta touched her daughter on each cheek, slid her hands down to her shoulders and turned her out to the steps going up. "Don't stay, don't watch what we must do. The crossing over's always the hardest." Then even louder to all of them, "Any of you can go with Lavena, to the river—and beyond if the gods will it."

Edereta's hands gave Lavena enough life and strength to take the steps up to the plaza. No one followed her. The children without a home or family stayed with the young women, even the pregnant ones, who too had no other place to pass their last moments.

Before she made it to the top step, Lavena felt and heard the giant battering rams slam into the last gates, heard the Roman ladders clatter up to every unmanned section of the inner wall. Above the shouts and clamor, she heard the inner gates crack open.

A few village fighters up the stairs to the back wall motioned her to them. She thought her father must have told them to look for her and protect her as their last act. She made it through them to the top, and then looked behind.

From her high place, Lavena spotted his white hair at the front of the last defenders down by the main gate, saw his axe bury deep into Roman armor, pull out fast as the soldier fell, and strike down four more. But two pikes broke through his mighty swings and into his unprotected torso. Sinorix's head and raised right arm and axe disappeared under Roman soldiers, blood and dust.

The massive main gate in the innermost wall collapsed with a crunch, and a stream of Roman soldiers clambered through on both sides of the battering ram into the inner yard of the village plaza.

Chapter XIII

Her River

Lavena hoisted herself onto the stone of the highest section of the inner wall. She gathered up her skirt, and strange soldiers shrieked even louder from too close behind and below. Their cries sounded wet with spittle, sweat or blood. Hands shaking, she tightened the leather laces of the scabbard that held her falcata fast to her left thigh.

A lone voice of a young man broke through. "Lavena, look out, jump, now..." and was snuffed out.

She slid her boots to the edge and stared over the rampart, at her river, brown and black in the late afternoon shadows. In that instant she knew. No matter whether the gods of life stood next to her, she had only two choices—the river or death by her own falcata wielded by her own hand.

A new sound, wood clattering on stone, and the top of a ladder jolted her right shoulder from behind, pushing her forward. The lead Roman chased up the ladder so close she heard his panting and then glimpsed more soldiers climbing over bodies on the stairs up to her.

Sons of worm-infested goats. No time. She clamped a reed sideways in her teeth, cinched Father's pouch tight to her waist cord, crouched, and sprang out as far as her legs could take her.

The instant her feet hit water, the battle noises stopped, replaced by the familiar and sheltering gurgles. She relaxed through the descent to a muddy bottom, rolled over and searched the silty flow for shadows of boats, of men, bellies and legs of horses or big dogs, but saw not one.

As she relaxed expecting to float up, the heavy gold ropes pulled on her ankles and neck and kept her down. For an instant she thought to stay down until her mouth and nose could no longer keep the water out of her chest, until her river took her, this time without any friend to pull her out.

Her legs and arms would not let her stay and, as if by their own mind, stroked her upward. Lungs screaming, neck straining to open up, legs beginning to burn, she set one end of the reed into her mouth and the other above the surface. It worked. She blew out through her nose and took in great sips of air.

The gold ropes now helped her. She didn't have to work hard to stay under the surface, easily kept her head from breaking out of the water. She stroked over to the far side. There the river bed sloped gently to the shore. In the shallower part, still under water, she half-walked, half-swam upstream, one step planted then another, trusting her memory of the river contours away from her village.

The current pushed against the swollen pouch cinched to her waist and against her loose skirt. She squeezed air out of the pouch and slid it to her back, snugged her skirt up tight and pressed on against the flow. If the invaders chased her, she expected—she hoped—they would look for her down river, farther and farther from where she headed. She hoped that by now they might think her dead.

About two thousand paces upstream the river widened and became shallow. There the Greeks or Romans had built a raised crossing on arches. There it would be harder to hide except in a big storm, too well traveled to risk approaching in daylight. Long before that place, she found a tangle of river grass and trees, clambered out part way and crouched down, feet still in water.

Before her breathing slowed, before her heart quieted, she heard yelling and whooping, bursts of laughter and whistles and cheers. She had not travelled as far as she had thought, not nearly far enough.

Unsure about when or how far up the next hiding place might be, she stayed crouched down low, ready to slide back into the river on the slightest nearby human sound, the slightest movement of man, horse, or dog.

After a time, the gentle upriver breeze brought the aroma of meats roasting. The loudest sounds from the village changed to the steadier hum of many men talking, shedding garments noisily, tending to horses, feeding their dogs.

By now, she thought, the invaders must have stopped searching for any last defenders, must have discovered all the children dead in the underground rooms, must have found no more live women. They would surely start searching for gold and precious stones, pelts and blankets not torn or used up in the fighting, and any remaining treasures of all the village families.

Soon they grew even quieter, and Lavena thought they must have started to gorge. They had likely found the wine flagons and beer barrels stored in the houses of the nobles, but then must have smashed every one. Her villagers, even her mother, had emptied them onto the ground.

She felt as empty as those flagons. The old knowing that soon she would join the fighting women of her father's tribe, stand side-by-side with the best men, had spilled onto sand as easily as the wine. In less than two full days, the Roman Monster had ground the years of mock fights and good instruction to blood and pain. Only the lessons of her river had mattered.

As she listened to her village and for any other noises, she knew she could not stay this close. She knew she had to run far in the night and by morning find a distant place to hide and rest and decide where next to head, what next to do.

As darkness took the late summer day, Lavena eased up and out of her watery hiding place. On dry land she still crouched low and listened for voices, footfalls, or bodies pushing through brush. She waited a long time and only then stood up fully to look around.

She found a flat spot of dirt still warm. She cut river grass and the soft higher branches of bushes, arranged them high round her, and then squeezed the water out of her cloak and the shorter garment underneath.

She had forgotten about the gold torc on each ankle and the larger thicker torc on her neck. For the first time, she pulled open the soft metal arcs and placed all three pieces in the cut grass under her.

The calm evening air could not block the loudest bursts from downriver. Every time she heard one, she listened whether they came closer. None did, but she knew she did not have much time. Perhaps, if the soldiers or their dogs became restless, she did not have even half the night to stay here. Before she moved away from her river, she had to dry out, check her pouch and wait for deeper darkness, wait for the army to sleep, wait for their dogs to be pulled in and leashed.

The heavy bag had survived the leap and under-water hike. She gulped down chunks of cooked salted meat and raisins, which had stayed dry in animal skins. She felt netting material along with a few thin and round and flat hard pieces on the bottom of the sack. Her father must have given her his last coins minted by the metal workers of her tribe, and perhaps the metal disk and rough stone to make sparks and light a fire.

Sadness tumbled in. His last thoughts, last acts in his preparation for war and the loss of his village and all who lived in or near it had been for her—and her survival. For a long moment she could not think, only see his face that last time, see it through her cascading tears.

The image of the face brought up questions, almost as if she could ask him, ask her mother. *Which direction must I feel my way out, how long must I wait, should I swim under water at night against the flow or dare I walk in the shallows, or strike out on the flat area away from the river?* Her father's image faded as her tears dried. No moon came up to allow safe trekking, and no answers came, only more questions and wisps from good days all gone.

Almost comfortable on the damp grass, Lavena wished she had remembered more, listened harder to those stories of earlier invasions, other armies besieging other villages. She wished she had remembered how other locals had survived, had hardened and fought back to reach treaties and peace. None of those stories came to her now.

Silently she prayed to her mother's spirit to show her the way to more food when the pouch held no more, to help her find the next safe hiding place and the one after that, where to find pelts when the nights grew colder. She whispered, "Mother guide me to a secluding place at my time of the moon and help me to cover up the traces."

She saw her mother's wrinkled brown face, her deep stare and silent nods when she made Lavena leave for the last time. Memories of that stare and those nods eased the numbness, told her to accept whatever happened, gave her the strength to pat around her patch of grass and a short way beyond. She made sure she felt no little hills where ants might live. She placed all her possessions where she could quickly gather them up and slide back into the river if a stranger or hunting dog came near, and began to think.

She had ridden past this clump of grass and stand of trees many times with her father and, since the morning of the thief, with her brothers. The land away from the river lay flat with few gorges and hidden crevasses, the grasses mostly low and scrubby at this time of year. Once daylight came back, here and there low hills provided an easy lookout for her, but even easier for a man on horse. Should she strike out now, sliding her feet to not fall, guessing by the stars and the river for the right direction?

She could make out only the top lines of solitary trees and low hills far to the north against a starry sky. Perhaps, later in the deeper night, she would. No, it was more urgent than that. Before first light, she would have to leave here so close to her village and the thousands of Roman Monsters.

A long reach from the grass bed, her hands located stones and rocks warmer than the night air. She pulled several loose.

As the air cooled, she began to tremble, trembled so strongly she could not hold onto the warm stones. She trembled from energy spent, from no sleep, from men clambering after her, and from the last nine days.

Edereta had sometimes said, “Lavena, I gave you that name because of the joy you brought Father and me the day you were born.”

On this night, Lavena took on the permanent sadness of young orphans with all family members gone, but orphans old enough to understand that special kind of aloneness. On this night she took on a welling silent rage, a rage she could not let out for fear that someone might hear, a rage she knew would last to the end of her days, however many the gods allowed, and that made her tremble all the harder.

As the trembling subsided, she curled up holding to her stomach and chest the largest, warmest stone she could pull out of the soft earth.

Soon deep sleep smothered all her unformed plans.

Chapter XIV

Spirits Helping

Birds squawked and sang to their own kind. Her river gurgled a bit louder and deeper. Close by, a frog croaked and again, and roosters crowed from down in her village, all greeting the new day.

A horse neighed from a distance, and that made her awaken fully. The horse snorting closer and her near nakedness jarred her.

Horses chased off by her tribe in advance of the Roman army would, even without the urging of their herding dogs, gather and search out their masters and territory. But a lone horse had to be ridden by someone scouting or fleeing. Lavena knew a man on that horse with a keening dog would find her easily.

Her arms were numb from the rock still cradled to her. She set it down noiselessly, picked her damp outer garment off the bushes, dressed fast, stuffed the torcs into her food pouch and tied it onto her waist cord. She groped for and found the hollow reed. She tried to breathe silently and to quiet her pounding body, knowing that all large animals hear and smell prey from far off, sense even more the fear of a young female of another, softer species.

Other horses snorting, clomping came from her side of the river, a herd after all, going home but on the wrong side of the river. Were they Roman horses or did they belong to others loyal to Rome moving in on undefended territory? Had her village animals crossed the river in the panic of battle?

First light rose in the sky, and she made out the nearest one, walking straight to the river down the gentle treeless slope. This lead horse did not hesitate or meander, but it carried no rider. More horses in twos and threes drew closer behind the lead horse. Big bodies shuffled, sloshed and smacked jostling for position, and thirsty mouths slurped no more than fifty paces downriver from her.

Softer footfalls and a deep whining of a smaller animal broke out of the herd and in her direction. Lavena pulled out the falcata, and eased backward until knee-deep in water again.

The smaller animal whined loudly and lunged at her, splashing her in the last bounds—and for that instant she forgot all that had brought her to this place.

She nearly screamed, *Little Bear, Little Bear. What are you doing out here?*

The big dog would have knocked her over had she not braced against the paws landing on her shoulders, the floppy tongue licking her face. "Little Bear, you have to go home. Father will....He needs you to round up...." She let out a laugh but cut it off.

She grabbed both sides of the snout and ran her hands up to the ears and down the neck to both sides of the dog's chest as she had so often, but felt what should not have been there. His fluffy coat was too wet too high up his sides and shoulders, too tacky for river water or wet dirt. When she touched near the middle of the wettest part, the big dog whined, but so short and low only she could have heard. She knew wounded animals kept quiet no matter how great the pain.

"Little Bear...." She did not know what to do but stroke and calm this wonderful visitor. "Little Bear, how hurt are you? Can you make the horses go back." She searched with her fingers in not yet enough light. "Or did the monsters hurt you badly?"

The big dog dropped off Lavena and lay down.

"They are brutes worse than any, but...they'll take care of our horses better than letting them run wild."

She patted the area of the wound, tried to feel its length and depth, how much blood had soaked his coat, whether a weapon or a piece broken off still stuck in him. The dog did not resist, relaxed on the dirt where she had slept and rolled over onto his good side to let Lavena examine him.

She felt a gash two fingers long down Little Bear's left flank, still open and oozing through the thick coat, but at a place the dog could not reach with his tongue, could not clean or keep clear of fever. She worried more.

"Oh, Little Bear, I pray you crushed one of their fat necks before they cut you...get up now and go... go home with the horses. They'll take care of you if you go to them—if you let them, if you don't bite them...."

She nudged the dog to get up. When he got to his feet, she pushed him toward the horses and whispered, "Go, go. Go home. They can help you more than I can."

Little Bear turned his head to her, looked at her as if telling her he wanted to stay.

"Away, go. Go with the horses back to them, and they'll let you live among them—if you don't bite them." She knew a trained guard dog was worth more than many foot soldiers who were no longer needed to sack her village or slaughter her people.

Little Bear slid away from Lavena. The horses backed out of the water and turned to head down river, all but one. This last horse hesitated, bent its head to the dog, as if it wanted to stay with Little Bear and not follow the other horses unless Little Bear came too.

Little Bear whined and yipped round the horse, then turned back to Lavena. The horse looked off at the herd leaving, at Lavena and the dog, and came closer, snorted and shook its head up and down and scraped the dirt with a front hoof, Little Bear next to it.

Lavena reached out to touch the nose, the cheek and patted it. "Are you one of Father's too? Is that why you came with Little Bear? Do I smell of Father?"

She ran her hands down the foreleg and let the horse nuzzle her head, while her mind grabbed to understand the danger and opportunity, the burdens and wonder of her father's lead guard dog and an obedient mare brought to her by spirits unseen.

She thought a dog and a horse at the river to drink or play would not draw attention, but a young woman on that horse would pull close any Roman fighter. From far away, men with good eyes could see her riding alone, and her father's scouts always had the best eyes and took the finest horses. Roman scouts would too.

"Oh, spirits of Mother, Father, help me now....tell me what to do."

She walked up the bank a short distance to look around.

A black drape darkened the widening dawn.

Smoke, more smoke than she had ever seen, rose from her village and beyond it. She knew this dirty smoke came out of burning houses and unwanted stores and perhaps from bodies piled high and soaked with oil, not the thin reeds of white from camp fires.

The size of the wall from which she had jumped startled her. It loomed near enough that through the tree branches of her hiding place she spotted lookouts leaning over, heads down on folded arms asleep on the ramparts. If she could see them, they would notice her soon after they awoke.

She had not swum far, not nearly far enough. Her light-colored skin stood out from any feature of the land, and she knew that there was no hiding place within a half day's ride away from the river on either side, perhaps for a rabbit but never for a horse and rider.

The sun's light would soon shine directly on her from the direction of the invading army, and that forced her next decisions. She could not feed or, when winter came, shelter a tame dog and horse, did not know if they would stay with her or run off at the first challenge. But without them she would not live out the morning.

She made gentle sounds that meant nothing in particular and stood close to the mare, patted it before leaving it for a moment. She cut the longest green grass stalks at the water's edge then returned to pat it again. Enough long stalks collected, she quickly twirled a crude rope, then a second rope, and one more, and wove the ends of two of the ropes to make a longer one.

The mare did not back away but watched and listened to this young female human and let her place the first noose over its face and down its neck. The mare could easily snag and break the makeshift rope but did not, at least not yet, understand it was made of river grass and not stout hemp.

Little Bear lay down and closed his eyes.

Lavena grabbed the mane on the side away from the village wall and swung herself partway up. She hung on the horse's mane, only her right leg across its back, letting the mare's body and neck shield her from easy sight of any lookout.

"Let's go." And the mare responded. "I don't know what to call you, but whatever your name, take us far away.

"Let's go, Little Bear."

Little Bear whined but did not move.

"Oh, no," she whispered, slid off and knelt down by him. Little Bear breathed rapidly, his snout dry and hot. In the fuller light, she saw his wound, wider open, deeper, bloodier than she had felt. His white coat was a dark red from his back down to under his belly and left thigh.

She thought for a moment but had no time to think longer about what to do for Little Bear, how to help him across. Only one way to help him came to her.

She touched the falcata, pulled it out and held it high with two hands over Little Bear. Her eyes focused on the spot at the base of the head behind the line of the wind pipe, and then upward searching for circling vultures but saw none. She listened for crows but heard none. She put away the falcata and placed both hands on his face. If Little Bear was ready to die, the vultures, carriers of the spirits of noble warriors, would know first. Their presence always signaled death's arrival.

"Little Bear, you must be hungry and weak. Here, eat." She opened her pouch and pulled out dried salted meat chunks and held them to his nose. The dog sniffed, exhaled deeply, but made no move at the meat in Lavena's fingers. He panted rapidly again.

Lavena let the chunks of dried pig and cow meat fall in front of Little Bear and again placed both hands on his face. "God of dogs and all animals that help us, protect him on his last journey, or give him the strength to eat and get up and go where you direct him."

She could not find the courage, and knew it was not hers to decide whether to hasten his passing even if this was his last day, even if he could not muster the will to eat or the strength to stand. She covered him with all the grass and then bushes that had made her bed during the night, and wished he would die before vultures set upon him.

And she knew she could not stay with him, not another moment.

She pulled herself up to the side of the horse once more and rode away on what, in the growing light, looked like a thin trail along the river to the west.

Chapter XV

Pelt Traders

The elm and cork trees slept in the noonday sun. The birds and insects must have slept too. Even the river flowed more calmly, as if resting in the heat.

Her mare splashed in shallow eddies, clopped on stones, sometimes snorted and neighed softly. Each time, Lavena tightened inside and stopped breathing afraid that her horse would broadcast their approach to whoever rode or marched near.

More than once she had debated with herself whether to flee on her own quiet feet, but in the end decided the trees, grasses and tall bushes lining the sometimes gurgling river provided enough cover for a solitary rider. The river was always right there, a last escape route. Carried on the back of this willing mare, her flight was far easier and faster than on foot.

From the higher places, she glanced behind for clouds of dust or any sign of followers. Now and then she still caught sight of her village, many tents circling it, dark smoke still hanging over it. The entire Roman army could not move as fast as she, but if Roman scouts spotted her, this mare was no match for a young stallion.

Through the morning, her horse had not tensed once or squealed a warning, had not fought against the direction Lavena wanted to head. She thanked the god of the horse, Epona, the most respected animal god of her people. Perhaps her mare too wanted to flee. Perhaps the god of the horse in her mare did not trust that the Romans might slaughter the mare for meat and leather.

A healthy Little Bear would have trotted ahead and growled at dangers before she could see them, would have led her away from them. She looked for vultures in the sky above where she had left him, but there were none.

On this day, Lavena had not seen a single child play in the river, not one old woman wash clothes, not one farmer soak while his oxen drank after a half day of hauling wood, not one boat float downstream with a load of pelts. Any other calm midday like this, she would have seen all of them.

She avoided paths that ran to neighboring villages, all too open and likely prowled by Romans. She could not know without getting too close to their sentries and guard dogs whether those villages would be attacked next or were already loyal to or overrun by Romans.

Her forming goal was a village far to the north and west in the direction opposite from where the Roman army had come. She had to go far past other hamlets and small villages closer, had to ride more than four days west, then north away from her river. Perhaps that larger town, called Village on the Hill, still thought well of Father. Perhaps it still had enough time to prepare for the Romans bent on slaughter.

Father had taken his family to this village for the harvest festival when she was little, though she did not remember the year. Its people sang the same songs, danced the same dances, wore the same clothes and lived in the same kinds of houses as her tribe.

She hoped they would listen and make ready or flee before it was too late, take her with them and let her live among them. She hoped she could find them and, if she found them, trust them.

Half dozing on her mare's back, something woke her—not a sound but a feeling from up ahead. She pulled back on the fake rope and her mare stopped. She peered forward, and then into the trees across the river—a line of horses. All the riders' heads were down. None looked out or away, not even the horses. They too were all hot and sleepy. She saw no dogs and felt relieved. Dogs were always the first to notice any stranger.

She slid off her mare and lay flat on the ground, holding only the very end of her grass rope. Her mare lowered its head and pulled up the freshest clumps.

They never spotted her, or, if they did, they thought she was a solitary young farmer searching for his family or lost animals, not worth crossing the wide river to chase down.

After they had passed, she looked at their backs and understood why they moved so slowly, why they did not care about her. A line of captives tied together walked at the rear of the column. The Romans must have attacked upstream hamlets, and took the captives back to the main army. She had to avoid that area.

No place seemed safe, no place to go. She breathed deeply, remounted and moved on, still best to get far away from The Village on The Cliff and the main army, still best to stay close to her river a little while longer.

Late in the day, she came to a circular glade, surrounded by tall elms and dense lower bushes and vines except for the side than ran along the river. Completely shaded and cool, this made a good place to rest, to let her horse forage until dark, to quiet her mind, and build a dam of black mud at the river's edge and let out her netting so that Reue might let her trap a perch. She nudged her horse forward but it refused to advance one more step, to enter the cool shade.

Lavena jumped off, strained to spot any movement in the bushes, strained to hear whatever her mare had heard. She saw nothing, heard nothing. Standing there on the soft cool earth, so moist it collected water round her feet, she began to understand. The ground, covered by a bed of leaves from many seasons with patches of green grass poking up, revealed hoof prints and partial outlines of boots of heavy men. With every step farther into the glade, the prints faded and vanished to smooth black mud unmarked by anything.

A death bog lay less than five paces directly ahead.

Lavena knew of these places, had been warned about them though had never come on this one. Her father and her brothers must have known of it and ridden far around it every time she was with them. Any man who took one step too far had to lie down and crawl out or be pulled out by others. Any hoofed animal would die a terrible thrashing death, sometimes over days.

For an instant she wondered whose bones lay under the inviting surface. One more step could be her last with no one and nothing to pull her out. One step too far by her horse would mean its end.

On foot, she led her horse around to her right where the bushes and trees grew out of drier ground and away from the muck.

The odor of civilization came to her, of smoke, beer and unwashed bodies. Someone had stopped here not long before—her mare trembled and scraped at the layer of leaves. Whoever Lavena smelled was still here.

"Stop, stop where you are," came a shouted whisper from a man's voice in the trees and bushes ahead.

Another from behind, "We have you surrounded."

A third, a woman's voice, "Try to run and we'll kill you. Kneel down."

These were not Romans but frightened people fleeing, who needed to whisper their warnings and spoke in the dialect of her tribe. They made their voices sound stronger and bigger than they likely were, but could not mask their fear and caution. Lavena knelt next to her mare's forelegs.

Two men, one older and limping on a walking stick one younger but older than Lavena, and a woman approached from the three directions.

The woman stood over her. "You're just a girl. What are you doing here?"

Lavena tried to speak firmly but did not look up. "I am Lavena from the Village on the Cliff. My family is gone, everyone is gone." She thought to tell them who her father was, but stopped herself. These poor people might not know him, or if they did, might resent him. There must have been a reason for them not wanting to come to her village ahead of the Roman army.

"Oh, Reue, god of the river and water and life and mother of us all, how did you get away from, from that?" said the woman. The voice was that of an older friend, of someone who cared, and she knew of the river god.

"I jumped off the top of the wall, and Reue was kind, hid me inside her and allowed me to breathe." Still kneeling, Lavena looked up into curious faces and the stronger air of sweat and beer. "Have you visited my village?"

The old man, stooped over, talked like old men who have lost their front teeth. "We're from the mountains, headed to The Village on The Cliff with our best pelts and skins. By the grace of the god of our Burnt Rocks we didn't get there. We saw all we needed to see. By the grace of our god of Burnt Rocks, the army did not see or care about us. And we fled on the first night, couldn't move by day, been here all day until we can move again in the night."

Lavena said, "I and my horse wish you no harm."

The woman, about Edereta's age but even more wrinkled and lean, spoke. "Relax, child, we'll help you. Get up. I want to look at you."

Lavena heard the words, spoken with a new tone—a slight cackle, the cackle of a woman talking to the barren old chicken while considering if this might be its day for the cooking pot. Lavena stood up and placed her left hand on her falcata. She had put the torcs in her food bag out of sight, and thanked the gods for that. "Where did you sell your fine pelts, then?"

The younger man whistled softly, and a donkey brayed from beyond a thicket. "We haven't. They're all over there. Maybe we can sell them to the Romans." The younger man laughed, but not loudly, at the absurdity.

"Shut your mouth," said the older man. "If the Romans hear us, see us and what we have, you won't like their price. You won't like what they'll do to your back side."

"Shut that talk in front of a stranger," said the woman. "Lavena, come into the thicket where we camp. We have enough bread, beer too on the cart. You're safe as long as we're safe. When we get back home we'll be safe. They don't want our donkey and old horses. The cursed Romans don't wage war in our mountains."

"Thank you, for your kindness," said Lavena, relieved to have found these three from among the many others who might have found her, glad they traded with her village and spoke the same. She wanted to tell them the Romans who took her village would slaughter this little family and take everything it owned, whether the Romans found them here and now or later in the mountains. She knew she would have to tell them soon enough, if for no other reason than to honor her father and tell them the truth.

At dusk Lavena, the three ragged pelt traders and a teetering donkey-drawn cart moved out. They turned north in the first dry streambed away from the river. From somewhere the old woman found a cotton cloak with a high collar. "Here, wear this to cover your smooth face and nice hair, and pray we don't stumble into the army. We're finished if they notice and care about us." She cackled again. "You'd make a nice prize, better than this old body."

Lavena quickly obeyed. She knew wolves and bears presented no danger. They had easier game than a tough old donkey and humans riding healthy horses. Only other humans might notice and hunt them down.

Nothing menaced the little group through this night. Lavena's horse followed behind the three, and ahead of the donkey cart. No moon came up to guide them, and at times she could barely make out her hand in front of her face. At other times she dozed as she rode, trusting that these strange animals knew the way to the home of the out-villagers, or to wherever they headed.

At dawn's light, she looked back to the rolling grasslands of civilization far in the distance. Smoke from hamlet and farm fires, normal night-time fires not yet out, rose in the distance. In the farther distance to the east low on the horizon, the smoke from her village still darkened the otherwise clear blue sky. She wondered about Little Bear.

Now away from the invaders, the little band did not rest or stop to hide in the day. The farther away they got, the less likely any Roman would stumble on them.

By the end of that day, the dried fruit and meat in Lavena's pouch were nearly gone. The out-villagers offered her bread and beer, but she thanked them and declined. She had her own food still and did not know them well enough to take theirs. They watched her eat, watched her fetch her own water from the streams. Except for commands to the horses and donkey, they did not speak to her or each other, did not tell Lavena their names. It would have been rude for Lavena to ask them.

Odors stronger than from the horses, as if he had not bathed in weeks, traveled with the younger man. Bread crumbs and flecks of animal fat cluttered around his mouth and down his untrimmed beard to his chest. From the first moment in the glade, he leered at her, smiling, head cocked.

The older man, who might have been the young man's father, had a kinder look, a look that said the urge to mate had died out in him. But Lavena thought the older man could not protect her from the younger when that time came. Yet she was not afraid, did not cower when the younger one came too near. And that seemed to provoke him all the more, made him stay near her when he should have been out front.

She slept so her hands could not be tied up and prevented from reaching the short sword before she woke. She knew that if she had to fight this stinky man she would fight well. She was done with running, at least for a time. This out-villager had no idea of what she had done and what she could do, and that knowing calmed her.

Chapter XVI

Mountain Hide-Out

Near evening of the third day's ride away from her river, they meandered up then down a wooded trail with steep cliffs on each side of a gorge. Only one big animal or their small cart could pass through easily. In the last narrow spot, a human whistled from the trees above, and the old man whistled back.

He pointed, "My other son."

Lavena did not spot the whistler in the trees but understood that any strangers on this path would not know the signal or the response. The old man talked on.

"Home's up ahead. No robbers or Romans will risk the loss of a single man or horse for what little we have."

The gorge opened on a green valley of huts, animals behind wooden fences, vegetable plots, tall green grasses not yet ready to be cut.

Dogs barked a welcome, their tails wagging fast. Smoke and smells from cooking fires outside and in one of the huts beckoned. Children and women came from around the huts and out of shadows. Two naked youngsters, girls both, ran at them, the older one shouting above the yipping of three mongrels. "Grandmother, Grandfather, what did you bring us?"

A young woman, tall and fair-haired, followed behind the toddlers, grabbed and lifted them up against the curves of her hips, one in each arm. The instant the donkey-drawn cart came into her view from behind the four riders, the broad smile on this mother's face vanished. "Ugh? Nothing traded, nothing sold?" She looked up at Lavena still on her mare. "And who is this one?"

The older woman answered, chuckling as she spoke. "Lavena's her name, and she is our guest. Don't work her too hard. I have plans for this one."

The young mother set down the children holding them in place with one hand on each head. "What, what brings you here?"

Each waking moment, Lavena thought about what brought her here, on this day, at this time in the journey of this life. She let the words flow before they turned to tears. "Father fell at the inner gate of our Village on The Cliff, but... killed many Romans first. He made me leave, made me tell what happened there, what they—the Romans—want, what they'll do if they don't have their way. Your people found me."

The young woman said, though not with anger but with resignation, "Go back now—to your village. We have nothing here for you."

Lavena said, "I...cannot go back. I'm the only...survivor of the slaughter."

The young woman hesitated, as if not wanting her youngsters to hear, not wanting to know more of it now. "Oh, may the gods of the mountains and forest protect you...us. But we have nothing for you here."

The other three slid off their mounts, which all stood quietly. Lavena then slid off too. Her mind screamed to tell what had happened until they might listen, until they might show her kindness, shelter her, or until her body shut down and she could not say another word.

The older woman said, "We found her and we'll keep her, perhaps for a long time," and she chuckled again. "I have plans for her."

When Lavena's feet hit ground, she felt dizzy, but steadied herself, had to steady herself, had to get it out, had to try to stay with them if they would let her. She wondered what plans the old woman had for her, but did not wonder for long, too many other things to get done before any of that. "Thank you, thank you very much. I won't be trouble, and I can help with many things."

The tall mother said, "I can use you, perhaps."

The older man, who had brought them here said, "We should let her tell us about what happened. Maybe the Romans need our pelts and will pay for them."

"Sir, they will take your pelts if they want them and pay you nothing. They'll take everything. Not even Father could stop them."

The old man said, "Father? Who is your father?"

"Sir, his name is Sinorix."

The old man whistled, the two women made sounds of surprise, the son whistled after the older man. The older man said, "You, the daughter of the great Sinorix...but dead now. Must have surprised even the gods, every one, to have him join them so soon. The Romans write things down so they never forget—and your father gave the Romans much to write so they never forget. "

Lavena got that, the sarcasm, the mockery, the message that Rome attacked The Village on The Cliff because her father was its leader. But she did not care. Only one thing mattered. She looked up at the mountains on both sides, at the houses and paddocks, vegetable gardens, and few people. "They will come here too. They want land, young women, children, everything."

She waited for them to respond, to say something but quickly realized none of her words registered. These people looked at her as if she were mad or exhausted or in deep shock, and she was all of that. But her message was still true, and she had to get it out, had to try to save these people, had to save herself.

The children clung to their mother's skirt, not comprehending but feeling the seriousness in Lavena's tone well enough. The way the children looked at her, open-mouthed and enthralled, perhaps she could frighten them and then the parents would listen.

"They'll take the little ones, forgive me, they'll take you and me in front of your husband and father and brothers, and laugh when they do that to us, to young girls. I saw it, what they did to ours—long before the battle even."

The old man broke in. "Stop now with this silly talk. The Romans won't come up here, and if they do they'll treat us well. We've given them no reason to harm us."

Lavena could not stop. "If they learn about this place they'll come. Please believe what—"

The old man slammed the point of his walking stick onto the ground. "The only way is the way we came, and one well-armed man can hold them off until they tire and leave. We've set logs and rocks to tumble onto the trail, can stop many before any get through and we scatter into the mountain. Enough now, I'm tired…."

Exhaustion and sadness combined to make her talk on. "We set many traps too, struck first, but there were too many—"

The old man interrupted. "Daughter of Sinorix, enough. We've got to get these pelts stored up, tanned if we can't sell them, the animals watered and fed, and a proper rope put on yours."

Lavena realized she still did not know the old man's name. "Sir, it's not my place to disagree with an elder who protects me, and I pray you're right, but fear you are not. Please, leave, leave this night if you can. For they will find you, and take everything."

"Young Lavena, look around at our small huts and little plots, at our few animals. The villages nearest here are no match for that army even if we went to them."

"They can be if they unite...."

"Quiet, girl. The Romans won't do to us what they did to you. We've never rubbed Rome's face in horseshit."

"You knew my father?"

"We all did. Enough now or we'll take your horse and chase you out on foot. Do you understand me?"

Lavena bowed, and thought she might faint, eased down to the ground where she sat, not able to get up. She had done all she could to warn, but all useless. No more words came.

The old man motioned for the children, and they ran to him. He managed to balance on his legs and pick them both up, all three laughing and their mother smiling once more.

The young mother pointed back up the trail and shouted, "I see Bodo's coming in. He's been out there since you left. Come on, let's unload the cart and get these animals to water. Come, daughter of mighty Sinorix, you can help me." She reached a hand out for Lavena, who took it gratefully, and pulled herself up. "I am Caniné." She gestured at the old woman who had brought Lavena here. "And Stena is my husband's mother."

Lavena noticed other women and children standing outside the huts and in doorways looking on, but they seemed far away and hard to see. She thought she might at last collapse.

Chapter XVII

Stena's Plan

On that and every evening, two other families came in from their work in the fields or carrying fish from streams that could not be far off, out from the small orchards, and from their secret look-out places. They ate out of common pots—green beans, cabbage, and barley sweetened with honey, turnips boiled in goat's milk, and chunks of fish or salted meat from a whole pig or other animal slaughtered some days, even months, back. They drank beer made here in this valley, but Lavena dared not. She needed to stay alert and awake past all the others.

After the eating, the old men talked not unlike the old men of her village, and the children cuddled up to their mothers and fathers. Lavena counted eight adult women—two of them with child—two older girls, three older boys, six grown men, and six toddlers and babies.

Every night, Stena's second son, whose name Lavena learned was Sigilo, looked for her, sat near her if there was room. Sometimes he reached for her as the beer toppled him over and before others dragged him to the sleeping hut of the unmarried men and older boys. In the day whenever he saw her, he stared, but he never said a word.

The unmarried women and older girls sat together and, from the first night, asked her about her big village, about life as the daughter of a great warrior, about the Greeks and the Romans. Some had never known any place beyond this valley and its mountain. She slept with them in their own hut thirty paces from the main hut, where they all ate the evening meal and the married couples slept with their youngsters.

The huts were strong, built of stone walls under thick thatched roofs, not unlike those of her village. The stones were not cut as straight and the walls not as smooth. The doorways, uncovered in the warm air, each faced the other huts, so any shout would be heard by them all. Only narrow window slits faced outward. The village dogs slept outside and down by the paddocks guarding the goats, donkey, and horses.

The first night, Lavena did not relax until all the women in her tent slept deeply and the voices of all the men died out, always the falcata in her hand down by her thigh, always the pouch with her father's last gold tied to one of her feet.

By the third evening, she began to trust. The adults sometimes stopped in their tasks to watch her work, as if to admire her tireless strength. This was no spoiled girl, said their looks, but someone as willing as they to milk the goats, to turn the soil around the young vegetable shoots and cut the grass ready for drying and bundling to straw. This one rode any of the horses as well as the men.

Every morning and evening she took empty water gourds to the stream, lugged them back full, and worked until the last man or woman quit for the day. The young children, whispering and smiling, followed her almost always.

Before the main meal and darkness and after the men had collected in or around the three large huts, the women bathed in their own secluded section of a stream down below the mountain where hanging ferns grew, and they were hard to spot.

There, on the evening of the fifth day among them, the mother of Bodo and Sigilo came close. She was the oldest woman in this valley, and all the others listened to her. "Lavena, you know it's time you take a man."

Lavena had heard the sounds Stena made, had seen and felt the constant unwanted attention from her youngest son. "I know." She dared not yet tell this stranger of Father's last command. None of that would make sense, and she was likely the oldest girl in this valley not yet married. "Father and Mother wanted me to wed the son of another tribal leader, but the Romans…."

She got out of the water and started to put on her robe, her pouch with the gold bundled up in it. She did not make eye contact with Stena, did not want to reveal how much she yearned for the hard flat chest of her own young man, to mate and sleep with someone wrapped around her and she around him. Every day she thought about Turibas.

Every night she touched the bare earth to connect with his spirit, but never felt a return touch. Even here and now, the eyes of the tall younger men stirred her, but not this mother's younger son. Her looking down must have given away some of her thoughts.

Stena, still naked, moved closer. "You like mating. I can tell. Sigilo will please you. His first wife died birthing their first one. The little one died too. No extra women come up here."

Stena tried to slap Lavena on the backside, but in the nearing darkness Lavena slid away. Lavena had learned well to be ready for the unexpected, to dodge the slow hand, but she pretended not to have noticed. She had to say something. "What about the other girls here?"

"Hah, the little ones that sleep with you are not worthy, peasant girls of no learning, no stature. Not like my family. All the good ones leave and marry men from the big villages."

Stena's haughtiness, the tilt of her chin, for an instant puzzled Lavena, but perhaps she could divert Stena from her plans for Sigilo. "Your family has not lived long in this valley?"

"Hah, long enough. My man and I lived in your village for many years before you were born. My man knew your father, knew him well. One day I'll tell you about that time."

Lavena wondered, but couldn't ask more for fear she might break down at the talk of her village and times past. But she could talk about the other unwed women in this valley, strong, wide-hipped, and good company. None of them liked Sigilo either. "Your son will please any woman. After this war with Rome, he can choose from many, all better than me."

"He can't wait for this war to end. He needs to mate often." The older woman drew out the *needs*. "He's not right if he can't mate every day. Try him out. You can have him if you like him. If you don't, you don't have to take him, yes?"

"In my village—my old village—women choose their men."

Stena looked at her sideways, "Here too, but I can tell you want him. Mothers can always tell. I'll talk to him. You don't say a word. Let him think he's chasing you, and then you sleep with him tonight and every night. Before the leaves fall from the elms and oaks you and he can marry, yes? Half of everything Sigilo owns will be yours."

Lavena wondered who else knew, whether they would let her decide or force her to mate with the smelly, leering son. She wondered about this family's time in her village and with Father.

As she returned to the huts, the other women did not look at her any differently than on other evenings. Perhaps she had time, perhaps they did not all know of the matriarch's plan, perhaps she had to flee again in darkness.

That night, Lavena stayed awake longer than she had on any other night among the out-villagers. Thoughts of Sigilo's body, his odor, his teeth, of how to avoid him, how to fend off his mother, of his family having known her father and lived in her village kept her awake.

After the other women in her hut fell asleep, the night wind changed. For the first time in months, it came from the north, hummed through the passes and rustled the dry leaves not yet fallen, the noise of each gust arriving ahead of the wind. Moisture and the distant rumble of thunder rode in. Lavena had learned to fear a noisy wind, not for the hard weather that drove it, but for the sounds of warning smothered.

The thunder closed in and moved away, but the wind strengthened and drops began to fall, increasing to rain, then bursts of rain and hail.

Another woman in her hut got up, closed and tied down the open flaps and brought inside a smoldering torch, placing it in its holder in the center of the hut.

Lavena listened but heard nothing other than the sounds of storm. She knew that one of the men watched the pass into this valley. She let herself fall asleep wishing for morning's light to hurry.

As on every night since the battle, she dreamed of screaming, shouting men and women crowding into her, running from unseen soldiers in her plaza that opened up and grew larger, but running in place, not able to leave, to move. Dogs snarling and barking chased her in that plaza, then water engulfed her, and she held her breath.

She woke from not breathing, at first not sure whether she was back in her village or on the ground by her river. The torch in the center was out. She waited. No other women roused. She heard no sounds of men, dogs or horses stirring through the continuing rain and wind.

She dared not get up and go outside alone, even with one of the swords hanging on the hut's wall. She could not take on real trouble without help but feared waking others for nothing. They would laugh at Sinorix's daughter spooked by a little rain and wind. After a time of listening hard but hearing nothing new, she again fell asleep.

Something brought her back, something that in her sleep warned of more than the season's first hard rain. This time, she felt for her pouch by her feet, still holding the torcs, coins, netting, fire-making pieces and straw to mask all that. She tied the pouch to her waist cord, sat up and looked around.

One torch, still lit but blowing wildly outside under the roof overhang, cast enough light through the spaces around the heavy door flap to let her see the shape of a large man. He crouched just inside her hut. His head moved as if he looked at the sleeping women and girls, one by one, trying to find one in particular.

Lavena reached for her falcata down by her thigh, slid it out of its scabbard, and held it by her side away from the man.

After what seemed a long time, he rose and slid his feet along the dirt floor to not stumble on the pelts or bump against other bodies until he stood next to her.

Sigilo.

He eased to a knee. The odor of stale beer and dried sweat hulked down with him. She felt one hand wrap around her neck and the other grab the top of her right thigh through her night skirt. Rain dripped from his beard onto her bare shoulder. He whispered barely audibly through the wind and rain but coherently enough that Lavena thought he had slept off most of his nightly drunkenness. "Lavena, all the gods brought us together…want us to join…make life. Mother told me you said, yes. After this night, we'll sleep in the hut of the married men and women."

He had not found her free hand, had not clasped her throat so tightly so as to stop her from breathing. Her response came easily. She had decided well before Stena begged her to take her younger son. She would rather accept banishment from the valley or death than mate and live with this man.

He lowered down further, and his wet beard touched her cheek. She turned closer to him—and shouted directly into his ear. "Sigilo, wake up. You walk in your sleep again. You're in the wrong hut." As she yelled, she stuck the point of the falcata into the side of his left thigh but not hard enough to cause great harm.

The big man released his grip on her throat and jumped up. "Ayee, ow! What scorpion stung me?"

The other women, also naked to the waist, bolted out of their sleep and surrounded him, crouched and stared at him as if they might jump on him unless he left.

He grumbled, "I dreamed… Mother told me…." and turned to the door, to leave.

Chapter XVIII

Thunder Down from Mountains

A freshly lit torch slid its light into the hut. Sigilo froze and stared, and all the women did as well. Through the flap, pulled to one side at the middle, the head of another man peered in.

On this one's head sat a dripping metal helmet of a kind not worn by locals, in his left hand a long metal pike. He wore a polished metal breastplate not found in this valley. This one grinned the grin of a Roman preparing to take spoils. Three more dripping helmeted heads peered over and around his head and shoulders. Each of those three grinned the same way.

Before Sigilo had time to react, the lead Roman moved on him, sticking the tip of his pike under Sigilo's chin. Sigilo lifted up onto his toes and put his hands out to the side in surrender. All attention on Siglio, on the standing women, and on three more armed Romans piling in allowed Lavena to roll up into a crouch behind Sigilo's legs.

One of the Romans yelled in a mixture of local words and his own language. "Down, man. On your face. Women, to the middle." With drawn sword he motioned for them to get away from the walls and the swords and knives hanging there. "*Statim, se movete ne moriamini*...Get, now, or you die now." He jabbed the shoulder of the nearest young woman, drawing a fleeting cry and a straight line of blood. It quickly spread on her bare skin. The five unmarried women and older girls, all except Lavena, hands crossed over their naked upper bodies, crowded to the middle of the hut and faced the four intruders.

Sigilo, weaponless, did not drop to his knees. The first Roman thrust the pike farther up under his beard. Sigilo let out a yell, grabbed the pike, and yanked it away from under his chin.

The Roman who held the pike shoved the lit torch at Sigilo's face. Sigilo let go of the pike as he leaned away from the flames in his face. In the same instant, the Roman drove his boot into Sigilo's mid-section sending him sprawling sideways to the ground against the hut wall. The Roman ignored Lavena on the ground at his own feet now.

For an instant everyone stopped, an instant long enough for Lavena to sort out what must have happened. These four and others had waited for the storm to cover their sounds, had evaded or killed the clan sentry standing watch in the gorge, and then silenced the four remaining men of this valley.

The married women and their children...also silenced or far worse. Sigilo's drunkenness and urge to mate had made him miss the warnings, made him miss any quickly-muffled shouts while he waited and searched inside the doorway of her hut. Or perhaps, Sigilo thought those were noises of his clansmen dreaming. Now, that stupid man lay helpless in front of her.

And Lavena grasped everything to come, in this hut, on this night, and afterwards. She would not let it happen.

Still crouching next to fallen Sigilo, her eyes fixed on the Roman's exposed skin—up above the leather skirt and under the breast plate on his left side not protected by the arm and hand which extended out and down holding the pike in Sigilo's face. No better chance, not ever.

She sprang out of her crouch and struck up into him.

Through his quick grunt and long scream, his left hand and the torch in his right hand flailed to find her.

She circled away to his side and behind him faster than he could follow. She felt each shift of his body rip open more of his insides, felt him try to lift himself off the upward-angled blade. His legs buckled, and more of him bore down on her hand and arm and the falcata blade locked under his rib cage.

He slumped to his knees and fell onto his side. As he fell, she held firm her hand and arm, bloody past her elbow and over her right upper torso, until his movements stopped. It seemed like a long time, but was not.

A flash of new light and new smells hit her—the torch, now on the ground, lit the dry sleeping hay and the edges of the nearest pelts.

As Lavena struck, the other three Romans had backed away into each other. Their faces, their garbled words, betrayed they were unsure—whether to wait, whether to kill or maim what might have been their prizes, whether to shout for help against one man on the ground and one strange little fighting girl, or whether to run. They hesitated just an instant, but an instant too long.

Sigilo had grabbed the pike dropped by her Roman, and rammed it into the second Roman. That second soldier fell backward into one of his own in the doorway.

The last two Romans recovered. One of them sliced Sigilo's arm and then cut deep into his gut. Sigilo fell on top of the second Roman, with the pike clean through and stuck in that Roman's neck, its shaft straight up. Sigilo twitched, tried to move his legs under him to get up as he clutched his mid-section, fell forward hitting his head on the pike sticking out of the dead Roman.

In the gagging grunts of life leaving three men on the ground, in the smoke, noise and light of the spreading fire, the last two Romans backed into each other and out of the hut. They turned and screamed, loudly, clearly and Lavena understood. "*Iuava! Da auxilium!* Help, help us." But they did not flee from mere women.

Lavena yanked the near end of the pelt on fire and flung it at them. As these last two lifted their gaze and raised their arms to knock down the flaming pelt, she dove at them low to the ground. With two strong slices she severed the tendons that hold the calf muscle to the heel.

These last two cried a cry of pain, grabbed their crippled legs, and staggered away.

The women charged out into the rain with knives and swords taken off the hut wall. They sliced and jabbed at the Roman necks, faces, legs and arms, under the edges of their breast plates, stabbed them again and again.

Lavena searched the lifeless shadows of the two other huts, listened for any sounds from them through the wind and rain. Shouts cascaded up from behind the huts. The growing fire behind her lit the entire area. New Romans—only four—ran at the conflagration, at their own men lying outside the doorway, at the half-naked women.

They stopped. One of them said loudly, "Martis?" with a question in his voice and then again louder. "Martis."

They stared for an instant longer and ran off from where they had come. They wore no armor or helmets. Their bare chests, backs and shoulders glistened wet in the light from the fire. Only one or two carried a weapon.

Lavena knew that if those Romans got away, the entire army would soon find this valley and everyone left in it. As she grabbed the torch from inside the hut, the torch that had started the larger fire, she shouted, "We have to get them before they get to their horses."

Down near the horse paddock, another torch sat stuck in the ground. It cast enough light that Lavena saw the four Romans reach down to pick up a sword or knife or piece of clothing. One of them took that torch, and they faded into the rain and darkness beyond.

When the women got there, more armor and battle skirts, swords, pikes, shields, knives and helmets lay scattered on the ground getting soaked. Lavena and the women with her all saw why—the Romans had made ready to take these women right there in the rain and mud.

The other women of the valley, the married ones and mothers, even old Stena and two heavy with child, stood upright, naked, blindfolded, mouths stuffed with cloth strips, their arms tied behind onto horse posts outside the paddock. The children of the valley, mercifully blindfolded as well, sat huddled on the wet ground near their mothers.

Lavena and her hut mates cut the cloth ties on the married women and handed the free ones a sword or pike left on the ground, motioning them to free and shelter their children.

No one asked, no one whined or moaned or complained. Each did what each thought best.

Before all the women had been freed, Lavena yelled out, "Six of you with long swords or pikes, come with me. Can't let the beasts get to the horses." Their own paddock stood empty. The Romans had run off the valley horses.

Lavena had no plan about what to do if she caught up to the last four soldiers, now armed, did not know if any of the women other than Stena could use a sword or pike. But she knew they had to catch them, or else armed Romans on horseback would gather in the gorge and finish what they had started.

The last four Romans and their solitary torch faded fast in the darkness ahead. The trail out past the paddock to the woods and gorge entrance where they had likely tied their horses, slippery, muddy, and strewn with stones, menaced bare feet. But Lavena and the women bore in on the faint light carried by the fleeing soldiers.

She, in the lead, saw a strange clump just ahead. Whining sounds came from it. She yelled over her shoulder, "The last one, free this dog and point him this way."

Not far up the trail they found two more netted bundles. The village dogs had confronted the intruders, but the intruders were prepared. It had been easier to net these three than try to kill them in the dark.

Nearing the tree line, she heard sounds as terrible as any on this night—the neighing and snorting of horses. In moments, the four Romans would mount up and leave. As surely as the rain, they would come back here with many more men or return right now against the women on foot.

The uphill trail made the women slip and fall to their knees in mud and wet grass. But they, helping each other up, kept on, had to get there before the four untied and mounted their horses. The three freed village dogs raced up the trail and passed Lavena. She thought they would be no match for four armed men and useless against men on horse.

Other sounds. Deep barking, then more, growling and snarling and shouts of men. The torch of the fleeing men no longer moved away.

In moments, the women caught up to them.

Two men rolled from side to side on their backs in the mud, hands protecting their faces from two village dogs on them. The last village dog and another bigger dog circled and snarled at the last two Romans standing back to back, swords pointing out and jabbing. Their torch stood upright stuck in the mud on the far side, still sputtering out a dying light. On the far side of the torch, horses tied to trees pulled at their reins, kicked out in the direction of men and snarling dogs close to their hind quarters.

Lavena ran at the last two standing and felt the other women close behind. She jabbed at arms and necks unguarded when the two men flailed at the dogs. It seemed easy, far easier than killing the first one in the hut. Lack of any protecting armor and the dogs helping did that. She loosed all the rage that built in her, shouted over the wind, over screams and yells of the men, and it felt good.

When sure the four Romans here breathed no more, Lavena counted the tied-up horses out loud—ten, two more than the soldiers they had killed. The women still did not know if they would be safe for this night. They stared hard into the trees, back at the village, at each other. They made sure the horses were tied tightly and would not pull free to run back to where they had come.

After a time, Lavena said, “All of you, go to the other women, to the children. Go find your men.”

"No, come with us. What if the last two find you?"

"They won't. Take this torch." Pointing, "I'll keep this one. It will be out soon. The last two foul beasts are dead, but if not they won't find me in this night. I need to stay here a while longer."

"How? How do you know? Come with us out of the cold rain."

"Father taught that Romans will never leave their brothers in a fight. The last two would be here if they are still alive. Our dogs would be up the trail at them if there were Romans still alive up there. They lie dead with your men. If I get cold, I'll come in before morning."

The other women left her alone. The three village dogs trailed them back. The horses quieted.

The last dog, the biggest one, stood like a large white sculpture against the dark trees, as if still making sure that no Roman mounted up.

This time he did not run to her and jump up, did not lick her face, or rest his paws on her shoulders. As she approached, he wagged his tail, whined, turned his head to the side to look at her with one eye, lay down where he stood, and rested his head on his forelegs. Even lying down on the cold wet ground, he panted.

Lavena knelt down next to him, listened to him, put her face against his, and once more gently searched his thick fur. After a long time she said, "Little Bear…Little Bear. I let you live. You have repaid me many times."

She covered Little Bear and herself with one of the horse blankets and lay down next to her father's best guard dog on the wet dirt and stones and grass.

She wrapped her arm around his neck and up to his face, stroked his ears and cheek, scratched his head until he stopped his low whining, until he stopped panting, until his breathing slowed and then ended, until he died from two deep fresh sword thrusts into his neck and side. She stayed with him until the light of a foggy dawn together with misting rain brought in the new day.

Soon Stena and other women came to get her, to collect up the Roman horses and station two women at the trail head. They reported that their men lay dead in the main hut with the babies, but the babies were alive. They had not found the two missing Romans or Bodo, Stena's older son, though they were now all sure what had happened to them.

Stena and the village dogs ran up the trail.

Bodo's father had been wrong. His older son could not, on his own, hold off ten trained soldiers. Lavena had been right. Bodo had fallen with the two missing Romans. The rain had not fully washed away the blood still seeping out of the three not far off the trail. From their positions, it appeared that Bodo had jumped at the lead riders, had wounded two badly before the rest disabled him. No one could know for how long Bodo, unable to shout or whistle loudly enough through the wind and rain, kept them from entering his valley.

The out-villager women and Lavena stripped the bodies of fathers, husbands, and brothers, soaked them in animal fat and burned them one by one in the kiln. They buried the ashes and bones, each in a separate grave in deep soft soil along with each dead man's favorite coat, belt buckle, comb or tooth pick. The women kept every weapon.

The new graves sat below the little hamlet close to the stream that ran year-round, down by the older simple graves and large stones placed over each grave in straight parallel rows. They gave Little Bear his own grave at the far end.

They all knew their men would have mounted the invaders' heads over the doorways and on posts, but they hauled the Roman bodies downstream from the hamlet, tossed them into a gully and covered them with rocks and dirt. Neither vultures nor Romans must find them.

They lit no fires outside their main hut and doused that one before each morning, to not reveal their location from far away in daylight.

For three days, the children old enough to walk never left their mothers. The mothers never left each other. They cried as they worked, cried together, cried their children to sleep, and cried until sleep stopped their crying.

For three days no one else entered their valley, and the women stopped watching and worrying long enough to mourn, to begin to talk of what to do, and what to do after that.

They, even Stena, turned toward Lavena when she passed by, listened to her and waited for her to finish when she spoke, asked her who should stand in the gorge at night, asked her about all decisions, large and small.

Lavena had become their leader.

PART II

Paths to Glory

Chapter XIX

The Scout

Marcus watched the men in his group play dice games by the waning light of another idle day. He, their leader, sat away from them on a flat rock. Roman armies did not allow games of dice—or at least wagering on them. But none of his men had much to wager. Other things, big and small, troubled him more.

He had hoped, they all had hoped, to find wine stores in that last village, enough wine so the leaders could ration some to all the fighting men. The only wine they found had soaked into the dirt outside the huts and storage sheds.

Some of the desperate had scooped up the moist soil into head cloths and twisted the cloths until they squeezed a few drops into their open mouths. But they spat it out, said this wine tasted too much of the dead *barbari*. None of his men had tasted wine or found anything else of value since they left Italoi, and that put them all on edge.

A greater worry sparked his dreams and brought misery every moment awake. Where was his tormentor and constant hero, his older brother, Martis?

Martis and his men had left six days before. This army's best scout and all seven of the scouts he led, plus their two pack riders and each of their horses had not been seen or heard from since. They had left the morning after that battle for that village which held no wine. Martis and the scouts with him had orders to follow any fleeing group to their hiding place, to mark that place, but not be seen and, most of all, to follow them to their hidden gold.

For days now, younger brother Marcus had rolled around all the possibilities. Martis never broke the first rule of every scout, the only rule that mattered—outrun or out-fight every hostile man or beast but, above all, get back to the army and report. An army that has lost its scouts lumbers around in a strange land no better than a blind gladiator stumbles around the arena.

Martis' scout group had not been ambushed and all of them killed or captured, of that Marcus was certain. This was no easy country to ambush the cautious, and good scouts were always cautious. They rode with open space to the next rider but within sight or sound of the next one over.

They did this so all the scouts out on patrol could shout word of trouble to the others far back, and the others could ride fast to the main army. And they carried rams horns. Three blasts meant trouble, to come fast or flee. At night, scouts found places to camp not possible to surprise in darkness, unless....

Footsteps running interrupted his thoughts. The runner yelled, "Marcus Flavius, leader of the second contubernium of scouts of the army of Tiberius Gracchus, our Praetor summons you to his tent."

"Now?" Marcus was too surprised to say more.

The light made Marcus slow down, the brightness greater and the number of lit torches many more than he expected. He wondered how many animals had been slaughtered and drained of fat to light this many bright torches every night. But then, he had never come to this rear part of the army camp at night, to the main tent or the other big tents on the right side of the main tent. He knew these tents belonged to old men. Each old man had his own tent. And each old man's tent was far bigger than the one tent for his group of eight scouts and two pack riders.

Both sentries standing guard at the main tent flap signaled him to enter.

He mumbled under his breath, "*Enim patientia, praeda, et imperium hominem patientem sequentur*. Patience, plunder and power come to the patient." Martis had taught him this and their father had said it too. They had both taught him The Great Empire of Rome would be nothing without plunder—young bodies and gold—from its neighbors and the neighbors of its neighbors. Rome took their land too. Power, all of Rome's power came from plunder.

He stepped through the two sets of tent flaps and stopped. Old men in clean white robes lounged on animal pelts and rugs of many colors. A few dozed on deep cushions. Young girls or boys lay or sat next to some of the old men. The scent of flowers from many bowls and vases of freshly cut blooms mixed with the odor of roasted meats.

In the center, a cluster of men sat or lay on cushions facing each other. One by one they turned to stare at him. Four posts, each as tall as two men, held up the tent over them.

A voice, strong and clear with a hint of mockery said, "Marcus Flavius, you of the golden hair and eyes of an eagle, let me see you. Ah, you do look like your father and your brother." The speaker stood up, beckoning him with a delicate hand, not a soldier's or horseman's hand, to come closer.

"*Salve*, I am Tiberius Gracchus." The great man, far younger than Marcus had expected, used the formal greeting for adults deserving respect. He spoke with mirth and no meanness. "Legate Apollonius and my war council want to know how old you are, Marcus, where you've served."

Marcus had to think before he answered. One insult thrown at these men, one stupid response could destroy him. One of these old men would be the Legate Apollonius. He had heard of that one too, a very old man in charge of all the armed men but not a fighter. The Legati always commanded far back from the front and kept their escape routes open. Above the Legate only this man, Gracchus Tiberius, ruled.

"Well, can you speak, or has someone taken your tongue?" More snickers turned to laughter.

Marcus bowed. "I have my tongue still, Honorable Praetor. I'm eighteen. Since age fifteen, I scouted the elusive Ligurians high in our northern mountains. How may I serve you?"

"Good answer, young Marcus." Murmurs from the old men. "Go sit over there until we finish. My servants will bring you what you like."

"Yes, yes, *Optime*, your Excellency, thank you."

He sat down off to the side between two men, heads back, mouths open, snoozing. Dark-skinned servants brought round the roasted leg of a pig. Still hot, it dripped its juices onto cloths hanging under it. They carried it on a pole and cut off chunks from the places pointed out by the guests. The plates, spoons and forks of polished silver, mesmerized Marcus. Next, the servants brought round silver flagons of juice and wine and filled cups held up to them.

One of the servants offered him a silver plate, fork and spoon, but he did not take them. He had to stay alert.

Gracchus broke off from the others and came over to Marcus. On his way, Gracchus motioned with his hands for Marcus to remain seated. He eased down next to him. The men on either side of Marcus woke up and hustled away.

"How did you like the evening meal?"

Marcus felt the blood in his face rise. He did not know that he was expected to eat of this feast. "Forgive me, *Optime*. I ate with my men."

"Good. A leader of men does not live better than they." Gracchus reached into his cloak and brought out tarnished metal rings, four in all, and two rusty coins and held them in his open hand. "Do you know what these are?"

"No, *Optime*."

"*Numi barbarorum*. They use them like we use talents of gold and silver. This iron junk is worthless." The great man paused and leaned closer. "Tell me, Marcus, where is all the gold in Iberia?"

Marcus, not sure if the Praetor accused him or other scouts of having found and hidden the gold, did not look at him when he answered. "I don't know." Instantly he wished he had not looked away—only the guilty looked away when they deny.

Gracchus helped him. "What do you think? Where could it have gone?"

For eight days now, all his men had talked about little else. If this army of Gracchus found the gold Piso had talked about, there'd be so much even Marcus and his men might merit one good piece. One good piece of gold would buy a small plot of land and a stone cutter for a year to build a worthy house.

"*Optime*, I think they hid it well, well enough that we've not yet found it, but we will…."

"You know, young Marcus, my foot soldiers searched every burned out hut, ripped out every fence post, crawled under every bush, but this is all they found of the sweet metal." Gracchus opened his other hand. In its palm sat one small buttery-yellow coin. "Where in the name of Mars is the rest of it?"

The eyes of the great man bore in. A simple plea of ignorance would not do. "Maybe the rich *barbari* in this village gave it to others far from here for weapons and soldiers and horses." Marcus shrugged as if he did not know any more, but he felt he had to say something more. "Maybe, your first scout contubernium found them and the gold with them…and those other *barbari* overwhelmed them before they could return to us."

"*Vero, Marcus, bene putas*. Yes, Marcus, you think well. We thought so too." The Praetor grinned. His white teeth matched his clean white and lightly scented tunic. His thick black hair neatly clipped into short curls lay on his white neck and shoulders. "The Romans before us swore the old leader of the *barbari* owned the finest gold torcs in all Iberia. That gold gave him his power. He would not part with that for a few weapons and soldiers, not this one. You know we had to destroy him and his village first?"

"I don't know why you had to take this one first, *Optime*, but it seems a good choice, the strongest of these villages, perhaps?"

"Hmm," said Gracchus. "You would not know, would you young Marcus, about this one? Children of our Senators learn about this dead one, named Sinorix, in history lessons, about his battles against us when he was young and fought with Hannibal." Gracchus raised his chin. "I, myself, rolled his big bloody carcass over but found nothing on his dead hide." He yawned.

"We sifted the ashes after we burned the bodies. Sometimes they swallow little treasures to take them to their afterlife—stupid people these *barbari* in Iberia."

"And the prisoners have not told you?"

Gracchus looked at Marcus sideways and out of the corner of his eye. "Good question, young Marcus. Legate Apollonius and his interrogators asked the prisoners, asked them directly and not so directly." He chuckled and looked squarely at Marcus, his look saying the words behind the words. Roman leaders took the tongues of those who lied—or didn't give the right answer.

Gracchus talked on. "One is a *venefica*, a witch, you know. She scratches the ground and casts evil spells. And our men are afraid to go near her, lest she cast a spell on them, lest she touch them and they die of her poison. Have you gone near her, seen her in the cage?"

"No, *Optime*." Marcus looked down at his crossed legs. He had heard about the *venefica*, a young one, who scratched the dirt to communicate with the spirits from past lives, and babbled.

Gracchus said, "Well, I am not afraid of that one. Did you know she speaks our language?"

"No. My scouts say no one can understand her."

Marcus wondered why the great Gracchus would talk to him about a witch who scratched the ground and spoke gibberish. Surely, that had nothing to do with his missing brother and all those who went with him.

"But I can. She babbles in our language if you listen well. I have asked her about the gold from her village, asked her without threatening her. You know what she said? She said her people hid it in places that we'll never find or even think to look—

and laughed a strange laugh when she said it. She said it in a way that tells me the gold is out there. We must only look with greater zeal."

Gracchus pointed at Marcus and then at the tent flaps through which he had come. "Tomorrow before the sun is fully up, you will go with my best dog handlers and best tracking dogs. You must make the two dogs understand that your brother is their prey. *Potes facere*? Can you do that?"

"Yes, with the dog handlers' help."

Gracchus stared at Marcus, stared at him until Marcus dropped his gaze. "Don't fail and blame the dogs or their handlers. I have put you in command over these handlers and the dogs. Understand?"

"Certainly, *Optime*."

"Take them to the place you last saw your brother and his horse, let the dogs find the scent, and once on the scent let them run. Can you do that?"

"Yes, I will try my best."

"Come now, Marcus. I thought better of you, of your father and how he trained you. I picked you for this army myself, you know."

"I didn't know, but am greatly honored."

"Young Marcus, if your brother Martis Flavius and his horse are out there, our best dogs will find them. Go find them, and then you will be honored."

"Yes, *Optime*." This charge from the great Gracchus infused in him a confidence he had not expected, had not felt before this moment. He, son of Martis Flavius the Elder, the father who had scouted for the great army of Scipio Africanus, would find his brother unless *Iuppiter* had turned him into clouds, would bring him back if he lived, would bring back his remains if only remains were left to bring back. He sat up straight and loaded his voice with confidence, "They cannot have gone far. I will find them."

"Yes, exactly, you of the eagle eyes."

Gracchus moved closer to him and leaned over so that his face was a finger's width from the side of Marcus' ear. He spoke very quietly, each word clearly enunciated. "I sit next to you because none of them must know what I tell you now."

He paused. "I do not have enough good riders or good horses. The first thrust at us by the fighters from that village brought down too many of my good horses. Their riders from the village fought like mad men trying to save their women and children. They fought until they could fight no more, and we killed them all."

Gracchus was right about that, though Marcus had not seen the great man near the battle. The few *barbari* riders out away from the village attacked the marching army with a death-defying fury until their horses fell, and then they charged on foot until the army of Gracchus swallowed them up.

The Praetor continued, "Do not engage them. If you find your brother but can't take him with you, mark the place and make haste back to us. We'll save him and crush those who hold him. Understand?"

"Yes, *Optime*."

"You do not know, you do not want to know, young Marcus, how much I had to pay, how much the old men over there paid, for the horses, for everything in this army. Do you understand me?"

Marcus' voice could not hide his surprise at the great man sharing these secrets. "Yes, yes, *Optime*." But it all made sense. No army he had been with, no army his father talked about, ever had enough fine horses, blankets, saddles and bridles, medicines or good horsemen.

Gracchus stood up—Marcus did too—and spoke loudly as if he wanted the others in the tent to bear witness. "Marcus, don't come back until you've found your brother, his men and horses—or the gold that Martis stumbled on. Don't come back with nothing. You're useless to me, to Rome, if you can't find your own brother—or gold—in the valley of the Eberus." The eyes of the man, unblinking, bore into him.

"Yes, *Optime*."

"Gold paves the path to greater glory, to the glory of all of us, and all of Rome. Bring it back and you will share in that glory. Find the gold, and you'll be my head scout. Rome will honor and reward you. You have my solemn promise."

Gracchus pulled him in, hugged him, and turned him out. "Go now, keen-eyed Marcus."

As he left through the double flaps, Marcus glanced back. All the old men seemed to be looking at him, some as if they judged him not as a scout but as someone they might like as a toy.

He breathed the cooler air of the night, no more odors of flowers mixed with cooked meats, of old men and perfume.

Gracchus was right about one thing. The one man alive who cared most to find Martis and the lost scouts was his younger brother, gold or no gold. And Marcus was grateful for the task.

Chapter XX

To Live Until Winter

This stallion had stood apart on that first night, from the moment Lavena had first noticed him. In that last fight by their Roman masters, all the Roman horses except this one had bucked and pulled at their reins, stomped and kicked up their hind legs. This horse had kept quiet, head held high, ears rotating. It must have known that struggling against the good leather straps tied three ways on its head and looped many times round the tree trunks was futile.

The women of the valley told Lavena to make this one her own. The other horses left behind by the dead Romans were all better than any in the valley. All the women who wanted a better horse would have one.

For days, the stallion did not let her on its back, circled away to show her its kicking hind quarters or faced her with stomping forelegs. Each time she tried to touch its head or neck, it bucked and bit at her hand. It shook away its head when she offered the freshest beet tops or oats mixed with dried fruit.

After many tries over five days, the big stallion quieted to Lavena's voice, stopped shuddering when her hand stroked his dark hide. He let her grab his mane and swing up onto his back, let her ride him through the valley. That night, he let her brush him and pry out caked mud and stones stuck in his hooves. When she finished and patted the last leg, the big stallion exhaled loudly and turned his head to her as if to thank her.

Lavena called him Roman Horse. Smarter than any horse she had known, Roman Horse soon responded to the new name.

All ten horses had come into the valley with heavy saddles. These confined the rider by four leather-covered metal posts, one post on each corner. Lavena had not before used a Roman saddle. All ten horses came to them with bridles and hard metal bits that cut into the soft lips. As soon as she mounted up into the bulky saddle, she understood why the Roman bit was so rough. In that high and stiff saddle, she lost connection to the horse through her legs and body and could direct it only by the reins and harsh bit in the soft mouth.

After one ride in that saddle, Lavena rode him bare back, and Roman Horse responded to the lighter load and closer feel of his new rider's body and legs.

Lavena thought the mare that brought her to this valley would understand. A slow old horse would not do for what she needed. Only the swiftest young stallion might give her a chance to run when it was time to run, and she was sure such a time would come.

Deep in the nights when all the others slept, Lavena crept out of the main hut, but not out of fear. The village dogs and whoever stood watch out in the gorge would provide good warning on quiet nights.

She traced the top line of the mountain against the night sky and followed the path of the stars beyond. She listened for the spirits in the earth, and scraped bare patches of the ground with a pointed stone. Sometimes she thought she heard her mother's or father's voice in a night breeze stirring the forest or in the hoot of an owl.

Most nights she said, "Turibas…Aunia, can you hear me? Are you there? Tell me anything, and I will listen. Give me a sign of what to do and I will follow it."

She never heard any response.

At the end of the meal on the fifth evening after the battle in this hidden hamlet, a sudden impulse made her say, "Tomorrow or the next day, I must leave."

"No, you can't." The other women responded alike. The children huddling against their mothers shook their heads or implored with their eyes for their mothers to make Lavena stay.

Lavena said, "We must find a village to take us in, must warn the next one and the one on the far side of the next one."

Caniné said, "Other leaders won't listen to you, not after what happened to your village."

Lavena ignored that last. Other village leaders had better listen and unite. She didn't tell them of her father's last request, of her promise to him. "No Roman army will let ten of its best scouts vanish. We need to find a safer place."

Caniné said, "Lavena, those weren't scouts. They were rogues, cast outs. Trained army men don't do what they did, not like that."

Lavena, still feeling her youth compared to theirs, had to let them talk, had to let them find their own way to safety without trying to force them. "Our instructors, our horsemen said scouts are always chosen from the best of the riders and ride the finest horses."

"What Lavena says is true, but these weren't dutiful scouts, just crazed animals," said Stena, all cackle in her voice gone, replaced by sadness.

Lavena responded, "The horses they left here are as good as my father's, not the horses of outcasts, of low class fighters. Their bridles are made of the strongest leather and their bits of the best metal. Their hides have been brushed every day. They're bigger than the infantry horses, not short-legged ponies. Only rich men or scouts ride horses brought up from Africa, like these."

Lavena did not tell them that her father and her brothers rode horses like these. She didn't tell them that he had proudly announced that once he had ridden a horse out of Africa, he would never ride any other.

Caniné said, "If they were scouts, not anymore, all dead and buried deep in the ground far from here. From what you said, the army's so big they won't know they're gone, won't care."

"They'll care. Taking out an army's scouts is like taking out its eyes. The Romans have tracking dogs too. Father said that long before the great war against Hannibal, the Romans used tracking dogs to find their lost men...."

Lavena could not finish. A new thought crowded in, smothered all other thoughts at once: *the hunting dogs will search out lost horses faster and more easily than lost men. Hoof prints sink deeper than boots, and the horse droppings mark their path loudly for any good tracking dog—and all ten Roman horses came right to here—and I've picked the best of their horses as mine.*

Panic wanted to crowd into her fatigue and sadness. Panic made her say, "The tracking dogs will find this place. And I must find a new place before then."

Another one said, "What if you're gone and they find us?"

Stena said, "If that monster army cares more about slaughter and loot than lost scouts, we might be safe here until winter. But I think not, too many soldiers like the ones who found us are down there. Too many locals loyal to Piso and Rome, and now to this new leader, know where we live—and they'll give this place away to save their tongues."

Lavena had no good thought of how she might find a village to take them, a village bigger and more prepared to fight than her own. She had no sense for whether she would ever return once she left. But they all looked at her to say something, to lead them.

After a time she said, "We can't sit in this valley. That army could have moved on. We could be safe until winter and not know. Or the army could have already sent the best trackers to find the men who came here. We'll never know if I don't look for them as they might look for us."

Stena said, "In the old wars, the Romans did always try to stay together—a great strength, but sometimes made them easy targets. In the old days, they gave each group its own name, and every member of the group belonged to his group for life, and was loyal to all others members for life. If they are still anything like that, they will not leave our land without finding this place."

Lavena came back to where she had started. "I must go out there. I must find them and a new village to take us, before the army finds us. Tomorrow."

"Let us come with you," said Stena.

"I'll have to move faster than the fastest Roman on horse… "

"We won't hold you back," said Caniné.

Shifting her upper body in the direction of Caniné's two girls nestled against their mother, Lavena said, "It's too hard for them, too hard to protect them in the open land." The others fell silent. "And I don't want them to see what I might have to do."

"What's that?"

Lavena answered despite some of the children not all yet asleep. Hearing this could do them no deeper harm. "Kill more Romans… before they kill me, before they find this valley."

Stena stood up and came close to the fire in the main hut—the hut seemed bigger now without any of the men. Lavena saw her face in the firelight, her sadness. "My men are all gone. My body won't carry any more babies. My breasts are dried up."

Then to Lavena, "If I cross over, it won't matter, but until then I can help you, watch your camp, watch over you when you sleep. I ride as well as any man and fight as well as most. You'll need a pack horse that I can keep safe. The good trails, the false trails on both sides of this mountain and far away from here, I know them as well as the lines of my hands. And my old horse knows them better than I do." She paused. "And that old horse knows when to keep quieter than the mice around here. It won't give us away."

Lavena began to nod at Stena. Stena had gone with the men on their trading trips because she was their equal as a rider, as a fighter, as someone who knew the land better than they. Lavena said, "Mother of Bodo and Sigilo, thank you."

The older one said, "And I must tell you all of one more thing that sits on me like a great stone. Last time I asked Lavena to do something, I felt for my son's unrelieved heat as if it were mine. It made him crazy, kept him from seeing anything except her, kept him from hearing anything except her breathing. If he was not so crazy to mate, he would have heard them and our men might have lived."

She wiped away tears, and then, "Let me try to wash away the blood on his spirit and on my hands. Let me go with you, Daughter of Sinorix."

Lavena knew, had known from the first sight of the Roman peering into her sleeping hut that Stena was right about this. She said, "Your sleeping men had no chance in the storm, in the noise of the rain and wind."

Stena bowed part way down in Lavena's direction, as if to thank Lavena for what she had just said. "One more thing. We've traded with every village within seven days ride and beyond. Some of the village leaders wear the belts made by us right here. I'll get us entry to other villages where they might devour you, fair Lavena, daughter of Sinorix."

The next morning, no mist provided cover, and every rise presented a view as far as a man could ride in two days, when Lavena on Roman Horse broke out of the far end of the gorge.

She pulled back on the reins gently and on the tight-fitting and spiked Roman bit in her stallion's mouth. It seemed cruel, but he responded to her soft handling and backed into the shade. Lavena jumped off, hid him in the tightest stand of trees and, crouching low, found the best place to look out.

Two clouds of dark smoke hung over the valley of the Eberus, not as large as the cloud that had sat over her village, but bigger and blacker than campfires. From the location of the smudges against the blue sky, she—anyone—could read what the army had done in the nine days since her village fell and in the days after the night of the storm. The Romans had set to the torch more hamlets not far upriver.

Daylight was no friend down there. The Romans likely buzzed over the land like mad hornets. Lavena thought that perhaps the other women were right, and they had to leave—with all the children and everything they could take.

At least now they had extra horses to carry more belongings. But every one of the extra horses was a horse from the Roman army, a horse that any of the Roman dogs would spot. Or—the possibilities started to pile in. Perhaps Roman dogs would smell Roman horses and not sound the alarm. Perhaps, if she wore some of the Roman garb and carried Roman weapons.... She did not need to decide that now, but soon.

As the sun rose higher in its arc and morning light fell on her more brightly, she slunk back to Roman Horse, pulled up onto him and, staying in the shadows of trees, headed back into the gorge.

At the far end, Stena and most of the others waited.

Lavena spun out what she had seen, the choices and the dangers of each choice.

Stena said, "Some winters, snow from the mountains slides down and fills our gorge. Deep snow keeps us safe in this valley—and deep snow is too far off. We must leave, must all leave tonight."

Lavena saw and heard the desperation in the older woman, the panic where courage had dwelt the evening before. Lavena heard the need to flee with all the women, all the children, flee now. Her own feelings that first night with these villagers had been no different, her tumbling words the same.

Lavena understood that losing every close living thing left behind a hollowed out soul. The loss of family and friends to brutality left behind only a child-like urge to get away, to run, to flee until the legs could not run anymore and the body fell, and then a waiting for death at the hands of those who had done that.

She said with all the quiet confidence she could pull out, "Stena, mother of this tribe, fleeing without a direction is impossible. One of the Roman hornets will find us, and that will end us, each one."

She waited for any of them to say something, but they let her decide what they all should do next. She said, "Stena and I won't leave today or on any morning. We must wait for cover of night. Tomorrow, as the day ends, we'll take a pack horse and won't come back until we find a place for us. The gods will help us to that place and will keep us clear of Romans. Many spirits will help us."

Several of the women said, "Yes, the spirits of our men and yours...the gods."

Stena smiled for the first time in days. "Have to hurry and catch fish, fish for the Romans who might find us."

Stena left Lavena and the others standing, while she scurried off to one of the storage huts, soon to emerge holding up rolled up netting. "Fish for the Romans."

Lavena knew these families ate fish, used the stronger bones to pick their teeth, and that the streams near them held far more fish than they could eat. But she wondered if the hard days and sudden loss had brought on spirits of madness. Some of the other women also laughed for the first time in days, repeated, "Fish for the Romans." And that told Lavena Stena had not been struck by madness.

In a short time, Stena and one of the older children caught as many perch and catfish sunning in quiet pools as they wanted.

The women spread out the fish on the roof of one of the huts to dry else the village dogs would get them, but they did not clean or gut them. They left them there to rot until sunset, always one of the children up on the roof with them to keep crows and fish-eating hawks away.

Chapter XXI

To Save Their Own

Late the next day when the entire gorge lay in deep shadows, Lavena and Stena left the valley. Stena took her long sword, each carried a falcata, a pike slung by a rope across their backs, and a pouch holding a sling and good stones.

Lavena rode Roman Horse. Stena took the same horse she had ridden when Lavena found them, and a pack horse trailed behind her. On the pack horse lay rolls of pelts and extra clothes, pouches of salted meat and dried turnips. Behind those, lay a bundle of pine branches, all tied by loops of long ropes. The pine branches covered the fish wrapped in broad leaves and fastened tightly to the pine branches with netting.

Lavena still carried the pouch holding Father's neck and wrist torcs. She had not worn these since jumping into her river and would not. Roman soldiers might have little interest in two stray riders and an old pack horse carrying tree branches. But any soldier would chase down the glint of yellow.

Every woman and child watched them leave.

As they turned to ride out, Lavena said to them all, "Pray we find our next home. Pray the army does not find us before we find it. If we don't come back by the night of the sixth day, cover the trail with fallen trees, roll down as many boulders as you can, then pray for hard snows. Pray that by the time the snows melt, the Roman army will be gone."

The two women rode as long as the day allowed and stopped not far down the mountain.

Before they settled under their pelts to sleep, the light of a new moon rising pushed through the trees, striping the forest black and gold. They did not make a fire.

Stena had not mentioned any particular village she might seek out. Lavena had not asked, not yet. They were not yet close to any village, not even to a hamlet, the terrain still too steep and wooded, not suited for raising farm animals or crops.

As she had on other recent nights before trying to sleep, Lavena scraped the thick layer of pine needles and dead leaves down to bare dirt, and with her pike dug into the rich soil as deeply as she could. She leaned over the gashes she had made and said softly, "Father, Mother, tell us where to go." She smiled. "Turibas, if you are with them, speak to me."

No spirit, no night breeze, no night bird responded.

After she and Stena lay down, a sudden thought, more a command as if shouted by someone unseen, surged through her, made her say, "Stena, in the morning, take me down to my village."

Stena snapped, "What? On all our gods, on the spirits of Bodo and Sigilo, I will not take you back there. They have left watchmen as surely as I'm the mother of dead sons."

"The main army camp must be near my village—or we can find it easily if we start there...."

"Oh, Lavena, we can run or hide up here on my mountain. But down there, once the army's riders see us, we're done. Your Roman Horse can't outrun them all, can't hide from all their dogs. And I can't help you."

Lavena barely heard, the certainty of what she had to do too strong. "We must go there, must get close to see when it breaks out again, in what direction it marches."

"You talk like a child, Lavena. You think like a child. We can see that army from afar, can see where it marches."

Lavena could not give in, the urge too great. "Stena, I need to go to the place where our dead Romans started following us.

That's the place where Roman dogs will start hunting for their masters.... I...will go alone... if I must."

"Lavena, I'm a sad old fool, but not so foolish to run straight to the Roman army. You go where you like, and I'll head back to my women and children."

This time Lavena heard that Stena meant it. Stena would leave her alone, but that did not chill the heat she felt for what she had to do. After a moment of silence, she said, "The army will send dogs to hunt for its missing men. We must see them before they see us."

She stopped, the truth too hard on Stena, but now too plain to keep quiet. She had to say it. "Stena, had we seen those brutal scouts trailing us to your valley before they saw us, before they got there, we could have done something...and your men might still live. Whoever they send to search for their men, we must see them before they see us."

Lavena heard Stena's breathing, the shuffling of her feet on the forest floor after Stena stood up. Against the moonlight, Lavena saw Stena's outline and main features of her face as Stena wrestled to say something, to do the right thing.

After a time, the moonlight behind her, Stena stood close over Lavena. "You never wanted us to find a friendly village, did you? You only wanted to go back to your burned-out slaughter ground?"

Stena's voice turned to loud scolding. "You cannot find search parties by going down to your village. You think you can ask the first Romans, 'Kind sir, where go your search parties? Do they look for us?'"

Lavena stood up close to Stena, closer than she ever had when talking to an elder not of her family. "Stena, we must start near there, and pray we find the searchers before they find us."

"And you think you and this old woman will find the search party sent to find us, and can evade the whole army if we get too close?"

"We'll have the first strike...and we have our fish."

Stena suppressed a laugh. After a long time, the two facing each other closely in the striped moonlight through the trees, Stena said, "We go while the night covers us."

They packed up again and headed down the mountain on the trails chosen by Stena, trails that Lavena hoped would take them close to her village.

At day break, they reached the lower hills covered by alder and pine trees. The horses moved faster on the gentler trails and easy switchbacks. But here they could no longer see ahead as they had from higher places. In the denser stands of trees, they could no longer see more than a few paces ahead. Lavena whispered to herself, "Spirit of Little Bear, warn us, help keep us clear of trouble. Help us find them before they find us."

#

These two dog handlers were as good as any Marcus had ever been close to. Nicator was the older, and Jove much younger, though they acted and spoke almost as one.

They pointed and pushed the big heads of the mastiffs where they wanted them to smell and remember. When the dogs sniffed fast at the right places, the handlers slipped them strips of dried deer meat, patted and scratched behind their heads and on their chests where the dogs could not scratch. Soon the dogs sniffed only at the place in the tent where Martis had slept, where he had sat and eaten his cold food on rainy nights.

Jove picked up the spare bed roll blanket Martis had left behind, and they took the dogs to the corral where Martis and his scouts kept their horses. Marcus pulled out his brother's spare horse blankets and gear from the adjacent shed.

The dogs soon looked up at their handlers, pulled on the leashes, and yelped as if telling they had the scents of that man and that horse, and they were ready to run.

A day's ride from the main camp to the west and north along the River Eberus, Marcus, the handlers and dogs, reached The Village on The Cliff. It was the afternoon of the twelfth day after the battle ended.

Stray horses and pigs scrounged for food down beyond broken paddocks and storage sheds. Marcus thought the army must have taken any chickens for their eggs or a quick meal. A cow stood bleating to be milked. For an instant, he wanted to help that cow. Until he left as a young scout to the high mountains, he had grown up with and every morning milked his family's cows.

Except for lookouts on the top of the highest wall sections and the tower, the village stood empty.

The many houses jarred him. Fires had burned off all the thatched roofs. He had seen burned-out villages before, but none this big, none protected by an outer and inner wall as thick and high as these. He had never seen so many house walls of stone now broken open and reaching skyward. The broken charred walls made him think of upward-pointing feet of dead crows.

Piles of ash lay in open areas around the outer wall and down by the empty storehouses, their roofs burned off too and some of their wooden walls gone. Marcus knew most of those piles held human bones, and one of them the bones of the big leader of these *barbari*.

In the battle, Marcus had remained far away to look for and warn of any attack from neighboring tribes or fighters from this village who might have hidden until the army passed and come at it from behind. After the battle and still now, he was surprised it had taken so many fires to burn the bodies of all the *barbari* from this village.

They had to burn them so vultures and rats would stay away. They had to burn them down to ash and bones to prevent disease from festering in the decaying flesh. The soldiers had to remove from their nostrils, from their clothes and memories, the sweetly souring rotting stench of death.

From the higher ground close to the main gate in the outer wall, Marcus again saw the now broken stone barriers that had protected vegetable plots, their plants now trampled into the ground, and beyond them the orchards and rows of grape vines running up to rolling hills. For an instant that saddened him.

This was good country, good for farming, and good for building a village to defend if the *barbari* had known how to defend against a real army. Stupid *barbari*. The Senate or Gracchus would decide what to do with all this, make it better and more productive for the glory of Rome.

Nicator brought him back to the here and now. "Marcus, show us from where your brother left."

About a hundred paces outside the main gate opening in the outer wall, the mastiffs picked up the scent, picked it up in the jumble of tracks left by horses, men and battering ram carts. This did not surprise Marcus. After the battle, both his and his brother's groups of scouts had mustered on this very spot before heading out for their searches. The scent of Martis' horse, of its droppings, would still sit on top of and be the freshest of all the other scents left on this ground.

For two days, the dogs followed traces no human could know, strained against long leashes tied to the front posts of saddles or wrapped round the wrists of their handlers. They never ran up a false trail or in circles. They ignored pheasants, rabbits and deer flushed out. They tracked silently, heads low with noses sniffing the ground from side to side. Here and there Marcus spotted hoof prints, sometimes horse droppings and a trail trodden not long before.

But after the first day, the big dogs stopped too often. They slumped to the ground, panting, not willing to go on. Marcus, Jove, and Nicator snapped their fingers in the dogs' faces, pulled on their leashes and rode up ahead. But the dogs refused to keep running until they had rested. Marcus thought every half day lost might be too late, might run into another strong rain that would wipe out all tracks, but he could do nothing more.

In the days and nights heading up the mountain after his brother, Marcus had time to understand the lessons, all of them, from his meeting with Gracchus. Gracchus could have his gold, pay all his debts and all his soldiers, return to a triumph in the Colosseum. Gracchus could have a great marble stone house high on a hill overlooking an estate where the soil was rich, the summers warm and the rain plentiful.

He, Marcus, wanted only to ride with Martis for the rest of their days, one small plot of land on which to build his own house, stone by stone, and a wife and children, who would run to greet him when he came back to them at the end of each campaign.

Chapter XXII

Chasing Ghosts

The dogs noticed first. They lifted their heads up off the ground, cocked their ears forward and pulled harder through stands of trees. An instant after the dogs, the three horses broke into a canter, not caring if branches stung their faces or whipped their riders, no longer staying in single file.

The dogs wheezed against the leashes. The wheezing turned to howls snapped off by yips and then louder until the dogs barked deeply with each big breath. The barks rumbled up into the forest and echoed back from granite cliffs high above them.

#

Roman Horse slowed to a stop without any signal from Lavena. He lifted up his head and pointed his ears forward.

Lavena whispered for Stena to stop, and dismounted Roman Horse at the same time, saying fast and quietly, "I'm getting everything off Roman Horse. Stay on yours and close to me."

All three horses, ears up and forward, breathing quietly, focused on something or someone ahead in the trees or farther down the mountain.

Lavena loosened the pike from her back and dropped it near her. She tied Roman Horse's reins to a branch, uncinched her small packs from his back. She tied these packs to the top of their larger bundle on the pack horse as fast as her fingers would let her. She thanked the god Epona she did not have to wrestle with a heavy saddle.

The changeover of all her gear done, Lavena untied Roman Horse, jumped on him again, this time pike in one hand, and waited. They had brought with them hooded capes, but neither woman wore one. No time now, and those capes might get in the way. Lavena knew she—they—might have to run or fight, separately or together. She whispered, "If…I must leave you, do what you said you would."

Dogs yelped. The yelps turned into deep barks that rolled up to them from down the mountain. These were no herding dogs chasing lost sheep, no mongrels that belonged to a family running from slaughter. These sounds—deep, confident, aggressive—came from trackers or dogs of war, the kind her father said the Romans used in the great battles of times past.

She caught that the sounds came from only two dogs, but came at them fast. These dogs ran unleashed or leashed to men on horse.

What to do came to her instantly, clearly, the only actions that gave her and Stena a chance to stay alive for one more day. Roman Horse had shown her. He did not shudder, buck, or turn away. The barking of these dogs did not alarm him.

Lavena jumped to the ground and at the same time pulled off the bridle. She slapped Roman Horse hard and pushed him down the trail at the closing sounds. He hesitated, she slapped him again, and he trotted forward and away.

Roman Horse disappeared into the trees, neighed once and again. After a time, his neighing drew the same response from farther away.

Lavena picked up the reins and bridle, whirled them around at her side like a sling and flung them into a high arc. At the top of the arc, the horse gear caught the branch she had aimed for and stayed there.

At the same time, Stena quickly untied from the back of the pack horse the branches wrapped around the rotten fish, tied the long rope that had held them around her left wrist, and then pulled herself back up onto her own horse.

Lavena climbed onto a small clear space on the pack horse where the branches and wrapped fish had been.

They turned around and headed back up from where they had come. Lavena led on the pack horse. Stena stayed on her old mare, and trailed behind them the branches still carrying the rotten fish held on the underside of the branches by the netting and scraping the ground behind both horses.

#

Marcus glimpsed flashes of a black head and eyes through gaps in the leaves and pine branches, and then heard the nearer thumping of hoofs on the forest floor. Soon his brother's horse came down at them—riderless, without saddle or bridle, but unharmed and as majestic as when he had last seen him. The black hide glistened in the white light of a clear late summer morning.

Jove and Nicator pulled hard on the dog leashes and on their own reins to stop before the big horse reached them.

As it drew close, the dogs started a singing, happy whine. They had found what they had been instructed to find.

The stallion walked down calmly between the two handlers, between their horses and the dogs, right at the horse that carried Marcus.

The dogs, still whining, tails wagging, turned their heads down onto their forepaws and looked up submissively as he passed, picking his way to not step on them. After the big horse got by them, both dogs flopped panting to the moist ground as if done, as if at last this was their time for a long rest.

The stallion and Marcus' horse touched heads and snouts, made sounds in their necks with mouths closed, blew out gently and quieted.

The great Celer, horse of Martis, had been found.

Marcus's intensity collapsed, not from relief at success after a hard search, not from having earned the right to sleep a long sleep, but from fatigue, from too many questions about how this had happened and what to do next, from having finished some great thing but in the end having accomplished nothing—and from knowing too much.

No scout loses his horse in strange country without some foe taking it. No scout lasts long in hostile country without his horse.

He and the trackers had brought extra bridles, and he eased one over a compliant Celer.

First Nicator and then Jove looked at Marcus. Though he was much younger than both of the dog handlers, Gracchus had put him in command. They waited for his next orders.

Marcus peered up into the forest, at the granite heights above the trees, into gaps in the trees for the trail that switched above them. These three would easily be overwhelmed right here or up there by any more than a handful of fighters. The dogs, panting, began to stir again as if they too knew they were not done.

Marcus rode up ahead alone for a short way but not far enough to lose contact, not far enough to draw an attack if a larger force waited. A deep yawn interrupted. Something ahead and above snapped him awake.

He had become a scout not because his father and Martis were scouts before him, but because he had the best eyes of any group he had ever been among. He, and only he, pointed at the hostile raider coming at them out of a setting sun when all others saw only white light turning to yellow and red.

He spotted specks in the sky—vultures circling—long before anyone with him. He saw the eyes of the young deer in the thicket, when all those with him were ready to stop hunting. His eyes never played the tricks that made other men see things not there but real enough to chase, sometimes to their deaths.

With wet fingers, he wiped the crusted sweat and salt from around his eyes. For an instant, and then another, he thought he glimpsed the back or side of a young woman, dark hair and smooth skin of face and neck, up there in the trees or perhaps on a horse hidden by the trees.

There might be one more—man or woman he could not tell. The younger one might have looked back at him. She might have been very fair. Both of them might have had pikes slung across their backs, the points up above them.

He scrunched his eyelids, wiped them with the back of his hand, looked out again, and saw only trees, dark rocks, dusted with fresh snow at the highest points against a light blue sky. He listened for hoofs clomping, for the heavy breathing of a horse climbing, but heard nothing.

He turned his horse around, jumped off and as he walked back studied the trail down from where Celer had come. He saw only one set of hoof prints other than those his own horse had made, and was relieved. No group of ambushers had come through here since the rain some days back.

A rain like that would have run in small torrents down this trail and washed out any prints. Only fresh ones sat here now. But the dogs told him that Martis and Celer had come up this very trail to this very stand of trees. In all the uncertainties, of that he was certain. His brother had been here.

He sat on his haunches and motioned for Nicator and Jove to come up to him and hunch down, no sense providing an easy target.

Fatigue slowed the mind, every move. He slapped his cheek and then stared at his open hand, pretending he had slapped at one of the tiny black flies in higher elevations, but there were no black flies of that kind here. The only flies buzzed around the horses.

At the slap, his scout training clicked in. This was no place to stop for long. They could not see far up the trail or down behind them. Nothing here provided any natural barrier against whoever might come at them.

They could climb higher and let the dogs chase whatever made them restless again. Or they could turn back and explain to Gracchus why they didn't find more or chase farther, and why they came back with only one lone horse.

He said, "Whoever had Celer fed him and kept him well… and is not far from here."

"Why's that?" said Nicator.

Marcus waved up at the stallion. "See his hide, not one bur. He's been brushed and not been out here on his own for long. See how quiet he stands, not hungry."

Marcus wondered how they treated Martis, if they let him live.

"So, we'll take him back now?" said Nicator.

"Can't. If Celer's all we bring him, Gracchus will cut up and boil our kidneys in olive oil and tomatoes for his next banquet."

The handlers laughed but not loudly, and Jove whispered, "Your kidneys, Marcus Flavius, our leader. And Gracchus won't care as much as that old Legate Apollonius. He's the cruel one. He'll take, cook and eat more than our kidneys."

They stood up and mounted, unsure, cautious, watching for any sudden signals from dogs and horses, the forest birds, even the flies.

The little band continued upward. This time the handlers and even their dogs let Marcus lead on the trail that any human with good eyes could follow.

Not far up, Marcus guessed a thousand paces, he rubbed his eyes and rubbed them again at the second strange thing—the flash of metal high in the branches of a tree. At the same time, the dogs again started their tracking gait and sniffed the ground.

Marcus stopped under the horse bridle. He looked up with the other men. "Unless my eyes play tricks, that's Celer's."

He jumped off his horse, and clambered up through the branches. With every step higher, he paused and looked out, thinking there is nothing more vulnerable than a man in a tree.

Again, except for the horse tails swishing flies, he saw and heard only a quiet forest—or did he spot another glimpse of the fair young woman? Mother of *Iuppiter*, he needed to sleep, he needed to take a woman like the one he imagined right now, the same one who appeared a short way back. Must not tell the dog handlers. Sons of Rome, he'd wander over to one of the pock-marked hags in the supply train right now.

No, he'd settle for a good sleep, but this was no place to rest. Maybe he'd search out the barbarian *venefica*, ask her what ghosts hovered over this mountain and led Martis astray.

It took a long time for the horse gear to loosen, the branch it wrapped around too thin to climb out on. He had to shake that branch many times before the gear fell lower into the tree, and then once more before it fell to the ground.

He said as he landed, "Whoever tossed that up there is not far—but was a lot closer a little while back." He shook his head. "*Barbari, astuti.* Clever, these *barbari.*"

He knelt down and studied the ground around the tree, felt it, picked up clumps of leaves, pine needles and dirt, looked up the trail, looked at Celer's hoofs. "Maybe two riders and horses brought my brother's horse to this place, heard the dogs, tossed his gear up there, and ran."

He motioned for one of the handlers to come to him and pointed at depressions away from the base of the tree but close enough to toss the bridle and reins. "A man tossed the gear up there, and wanted us to see it and climb after it—and I did and let him get ahead of us."

Nicator said, "By *Iuppiter*, you're right. Well let's go get him...take him back with us. Then Gracchus will eat his kidneys and not yours."

Marcus laughed softly. "Not so fast. Remember my brother and his men. They came right through here—all eight of them and their two pack riders and their ten horses." He didn't tell them that Gracchus had ordered him to not engage.

Nicator and Jove waited for him again, Nicator with arms folded and a look of disapproval.

Martis, where are you? Talk to me. What was that ghost, that girl, did I see her, did I wish her? Oh, mother of Venus, what is this?

After a long time, he noticed the stares of the dog handlers on him. He said, "Could have been a trap right here. From now on, the three of us have to stretch our line, separate, and watch each other like a mother watches her babies, may need to run fast or fight."

And then Marcus said, as he knew he must, "From now I'll ride lead, up with the lead dog. The other of you, take Celer and stay behind us. If this is a trap, run back, show them my brother's horse and bring the whole army up here with all haste."

The instant the three men and four horses moved out, the dogs started their low-to-the-ground tracking, regained their intensity. More of their targets were somewhere ahead.

Chapter XXIII

Tracking Alone

The barking and neighing quieted soon after Roman Horse was out of sight and had not started up again.

Lavena spotted them behind and below, first a lone rider, later two or three men on horse, moving slowly, carefully, and then with Roman Horse. These men plainly searched for the ten dead Romans and would not make the same mistakes, whatever mistakes they thought the dead men had made—and that caution prevented them from gaining on her and Stena.

The two women moved as fast as their horses and the trailing branches allowed. They made the horses trot on every flat area, made them work hard on climbs. They tried to keep the branches running on the ground behind them without the fish packets falling off. And that slowed them on the rougher ground.

They arrived at a fork in the trail. Stena's horse veered to the higher trail back home, but Stena pulled hard at the reins and made her take the other trail to the left into dense pines and the sound of cascading water.

This forest trail ended in a flat area above a wild stream falling over rocks, at a place where a nimble climber could scramble down and up the other side. But no horse could do this. This trail ended here for any rider on horse.

Lavena jumped off and beckoned for Stena to let her take the ropes holding the branches tied to the rotten fish. Lavena dragged the branches over her every step, then loosened the nets and hurled all but one small branch tied to one small fish out over the crashing stream. She dragged the last branch behind her as she ran back to Stena, climbed up on the pack horse again, and then tossed that last branch and fish over the edge as well. "Pray to Reue that your old trick of fish for the Romans works. Let's go."

#

The dogs' big muzzles snorted and slurped, but did not waver.

Suddenly they stopped at a place where another trail branched left toward noises of falling water. For the first time since they had been on the scent, the dogs ran back and forth, in circles, looked up at their handlers, ran in one direction as far as the leashes let them and came back.

Nicator and Jove, both holding fast to the leashes, jumped off their horses and searched the ground. Soon the dogs stopped their meandering and pulled to the right and uphill. The handlers kept them from running there.

Marcus dismounted too. "The dogs want to chase up there, but whoever brought Celer went this other way."

Nicator was already down the new path, the one the dogs did not want to take. "It's an old trick. They want us to follow where they scraped the ground. My dogs tell us that Martis is up the other way."

Jove said, "The dogs follow the trail Celer came down, but whoever brought him doesn't want us to go there."

Marcus could not tell them what his keen eyes had seen, seen twice. The fair one had scrubbed the ground of her—if it was a her—traces. These traces were real, seen by the dog handlers easily. He had to follow them to the noise of the tumbling water, or wherever they led. "We'll go this way. We must."

"Why must we, Marcus Flavius?" said Nicator, pulling hard on his dog's leashes. "When it's plain your brother went the other way?"

Marcus hardened his tired voice. "*Manete*. Stay here then. Await my return. We are certain that men came here and down this trail to the water, came just now. If we head up there and let them get behind us...we can die on this mountain...on this day. Yes, my brother likely went up higher and Celer came from up higher on the mountain."

He pointed at the trail heading down to water. "But until we check there, that way, we will not head higher."

Nicator and Jove said nothing, stared at him, looked away and yanked the leashes, and spat to the side. The dogs jumped up, wheezing, and lunged up the higher trail, but their masters did not give in. The dogs obeyed and trotted along next to their handlers.

Soon the little search party could go no farther. A chasm in the forest over misting, crashing water stopped them. They tied up dogs and horses, walked close to the edge and looked for places to clamber down and across.

Marcus had to shout over the noise of the water. "Whoever left Celer with us might have gone down there and crossed over, on foot."

Nicator shouted back, "You are wrong, young Marcus. They rode toward us on Celer then ran up to here pulling branches behind and doubled back." He shook his head. "I don't see any footprints down there. They took the other path." Nicator shouted louder, "Marcus Flavius, your father would not fall for this old trick. Let us hasten up the other trail. We are losing them, while you chase ghosts."

Marcus said, "Nicator and Jove, you know dogs far better than I do, but I know the tales that tracks tell. We check down there."

Nicator yanked at the leash of his dog, not because the dog had pulled away but to show his anger. He glared at Marcus, and Marcus heard the old dog handler mumble, "Too young...too young to lead...not right."

Marcus ignored him and worked his way down the semblance of a trail to the cascading water. Like all streams first spotted from a distance, this one was wider and ran more wildly than it appeared from above. The path down, what was left of it, entered the water at a place where the rocks, above or just below the water, invited a nimble man to jump across on them.

Marcus made it easily without his boots slipping. On the far bank, a trail headed up into the trees. No prints showed in the dirt or in the leaves and pine needles higher up here either.

When the two handlers caught up to him, he said, "Only ghosts have come this way today, and we will not chase ghosts."

One overriding message seared through the jumble and told him what to do. The dogs and their handlers had become a nuisance, a loud nuisance, slowed by having to walk the great Celer with them wherever they went. The dogs had brought him to the mountain that swallowed up Martis and the others.

Whoever had brought Celer to them knew he and the others were now on this mountain. To get closer, close enough to see if Martis lived, he'd have to tread on quiet feet. He had to push on without the dogs.

"You two, take the dogs and Celer. Take my saddle. No local rides in one of these. Tell Gracchus I'll find my brother. Leave me your extra cloaks and food."

Nicator said, "Marcus, is that a command? It is not right for you to go higher on this mountain alone." And then Nicator scowled. "You are too young to do this alone."

Marcus caught the threat. But they had not seen what he had seen. And the loud dogs had warned whoever he had seen, had given them time to send Celer down, to hoist the gear into the trees, to get far ahead of them. He needed a larger force not worried about an ambush or had to go on alone. Returning with only Celer was no option. "I command you. *Ite. Ite iam*. Go. Go now."

The handlers with their dogs and the great Celer left Marcus at the rift in the forest cut by the racing stream.

Marcus followed the trail not taken the first time. It headed into the higher reaches, had been used at least as much as the one to the cascading water, and might be wide enough for a cart or two horses side-by-side.

Straight tracks. Here and there he spotted tracks made by wheels. Barbari, perhaps whole clans, lived beyond here, used this trail often over the last summer, and many summers before.

Whoever had dragged branches behind their horses—clever, the one who had done that. The dogs and their handlers were not fooled, but it had worked on him.

Other things made Marcus shudder and slowed him more. How did whoever sent Celer to him know? How did he—or she—know that the dogs would come up this very trail right now? How did she—or he—know braying dogs tracking Martis would stop as soon as they had Celer? This barbarian was most clever.

More fresh horse tracks, two, then three, separate sets, one set made by Celer was larger than the other two. He need not have feared an ambush from these one or two riders, could have chased after them. These were no ghosts, just two riders, maybe three, and three horses, now down to two.

But his eyes had seen women. Had two women brought Celer down the mountain? He laughed out loud, even as he knew he laughed too loudly. No women would do this, but....

That's what happened. Martis and his riders had stumbled on fair women sent out to bait them, and their men ambushed them. Then the women brought Celer back. Marcus laughed again. Why in the name of Venus would women do that, their men let them? To bait him and the trackers now?

Perhaps it was wise he had not chased after the women, perhaps what he had seen was the front end of another ambush. But how did they know he and the trackers came up here? He shook his head and pressed on.

Farther up, no more fresh tracks headed up the mountain. Whoever had brought Celer down was clever enough to not leave on the same trail. If not up this way, if not across the cascading stream on the other trail, where had they gone?

So, this was how it was with all the soldiers who chased ghosts of women running in the forest or followed visions of lakes in the desert, and died chasing them. His brother and all the others were likely dead somewhere up ahead. Marcus wanted to laugh again at the absurdity, at his own conviction spun from nothing.

He whispered, "Martis, I don't know where you are but if you are up here I'm coming. If you live, wait for me. If you are dead, tell me, and warn me of danger."

Chapter XXIV

Confusion of War and Youth

Not far after they started the climb on the main trail to their mountain hamlet, Stena motioned off to a smaller trail that ended in no trail at all. They followed it for a while before doubling back in a stream bed. They crossed and re-crossed the main trail, Stena riding her old mare and Lavena the pack horse still carrying all their supplies and pelt rolls.

The slow progress made Lavena as skittish as on the night she hid after the battle for her village. But Stena's lead made sense. If they rode straight back to the gorge on the main trail, whoever came up this way after them would have a plain path to the women and children. If whoever came after them was not fooled by the fish, they had to try to divert them now.

In the middle of the afternoon, Stena said, "We must stop, let them drink, let them forage and walk unburdened. These horses are not strong like your Roman Horse."

Lavena started to protest, to say something, but she knew better, had been around horses all her young life. These old horses gave what they could but a long half-day's climb took them to their limit of stamina, of sure footing. One broken leg, and they were doomed.

Stena found a stand of trees on a knoll above the surrounding land and off the main trail. It provided a good view back while sheltering them from all but the keenest eyes. A clear brook ran around the back of the little hill for the horses to water.

#

Marcus emerged from the trees to a wide meadow. The craggy mountain mass stretched across the sky as far as he could see in both directions. Not as peaked as the Alps, it was still massive enough for any careless stranger to lose his way.

The goats and deer on this mountain could support many hovels of mountain *barbari*. The canyons and pockets in this mountain could keep them secluded, uncivil and every bit as dangerous as the little mountain men of the Alps.

Behind the mountain, high clouds on a darkening base reared up their white heads. They promised rain soon.

Before he entered the open meadow, Marcus shed his scout coat and helmet and slipped into the plain top left by the dog trainers. Bad enough to be a stranger without broadcasting that he was a Roman. He'd have to stalk like an untamed cat. Get close enough to see and smell and listen but remain out of reach and out of sight.

He walked his horse up the meadow, trying to stay in its shadow, trying to look like a herder or trader coming in on a horse he could no longer ride.

The farther he went, the more the trail became defined, made him sure that he had it right. Other trails crossed it, and he followed some for short distances. Always those other trails faded, and he came back to this one. The wheel tracks became clearer, deeper, had been run over many times. No one would haul a cart up and down this mountain unless a worthy destination lay ahead.

He had never suffered from the kind of fear that made strong men unable to move, turned their legs to water and their arms to straw. But the knowing that Martis and the others had come here and were gone unsettled him, slowed his thoughts about what to do and how to do it, except to stay alert, ready to stop and to run back, or fight if he had no choice.

The meadow ended in a line of pine trees. Reaching them, he decided he best not mount up again. His horse, the same breed as Celer, showed no signs of tiring, but the day was closing down. Soon he would have to decide whether to camp or go higher.

#

Not long after they dismounted on the knoll to let their horses rest and drink, Lavena saw him. She pointed back from where they had come, but Stena shook her head.

Stena said, "My old eyes need you to tell them what's out there."

"A solitary horseman, walking, looking about from the shadow of his horse. No dogs, no Roman Horse."

Stena said, "No lone man walks his horse up to our mountain—not ever in all my years."

"He walks slowly, searching. I saw him before." Lavena knew she could not let him go much farther. If he did, she could not let him find his way back to the army. "Stena watch me as best you can. I'm going down there. Give me your long sword, and come fast if I shout for you. But if you hear noises and I don't shout for you don't come. Go down the back side of this hill and stop him up ahead."

Stena nodded as she handed Lavena her long sword. "Use it well."

Climbing over the rocks, around the brambles, and through the clustered branches noiselessly was not easy and was slow. Lavena slid from tree to tree so as to not show any of her skin or garment, even to one looking her way.

Reaching the edge of the trees, she peeked through pine branches in the direction of his clomping horse. He walked on her side of the horse. That let her see he carried only a dagger at his side, did not have a hardened fighter's look, not like the one who killed the farmer, or the ones in the night at Stena's hamlet. He was young, his skin not hardened and leathery. His hair was full and close to hers in color.

He might have been a herder coming in. But his pace, the careful way he placed his feet, how he studied the trail and then looked up and around but ducked his head to keep it even with the head of his horse gave him away. This one stalked up the trail even as she stalked him.

But she knew he was Roman. The shape of his head, and, when closer, his face, the way he moved were all like the first one into Stena's hut that night not far back.

#

Now back in the protecting cover of trees, Marcus grabbed the mane to pull up and ride again. He froze.

A small piece of color did not belong, then another—gray, and brown—the colors of clothes and skin. Then he spotted eyes, the color of water under a deep blue sky, not twenty paces away. This one was on foot and stared at him too, and it was a she.

He tried to look off, as if he had not seen her at all. But it did not work. She stepped out from the clump of trees that had hidden her.

She was young, he guessed younger than he but almost as tall, and as fair of face as any girl he had ever seen. Her loose cloak caught on and folded into her body at the right places, and instantly he knew that at any other time she would have aroused him.

Was she real? She stood so still that he was not sure. Then he saw the sword—and it made him sure. That sword was as long as any carried by his army, and the blade shone in the shadow of the forest. She tried to hide it behind her, but he caught enough of it to know.

There had to be others, perhaps many others not far behind her. No one armed like that would come this far down the mountain on foot, come down to challenge him.

#

Lavena felt his eyes on her well before she stepped clear of the trees hiding her. As she thought whether to run out and kill him now, he turned from her and started to mount up—yes, she would have to kill him before he got back onto his horse. She pulled up Stena's long sword and held it ready to run and strike—and he glanced into the trees a different way—as if directly at her. He stared at her as if he had seen the spirit of someone dead, his mouth partly open, and then raised his hand to his eyes and head.

He decided before she did, before she got close enough for the final run and thrust, or before she might tease him into staying. He jumped onto the bare back of his horse that reminded her of Roman Horse. He jumped onto that horse as fast as she had ever seen anyone mount a horse, and wheeled back down the trail and into the meadow until out of sight, out of hearing.

#

Martis. This mountain, these clever women and the men hidden behind them must have ambushed Martis and his men just like this.

Marcus did not look back until he reached the far end of the meadow. No one followed him, no noises of men or horses came down the mountain. As fear receded, curiosity made him stop and study the higher ground, made him look for her, for her horse, for others with her. But he did not spot anyone again, and heard only the usual sounds of mountain trees and meadows.

As afternoon shadows crowded into day's light, Marcus made out the beginning of a gorge into a low saddle of the mountain. This trail headed straight for it. Martis must have thought the same at about this point.

Night came fast, helped by the heavy clouds. Diving and swooping swallows promised a good rain. Weather changed quickly in high mountains, and he knew he could not safely travel another five hundred paces either up or down this mountain. He needed to tie up his horse, roll out his heavy woolen blanket and one-man tent to keep dry. He had to go far enough back and far enough off the trail to be safe in case all the men with this woman chased him.

#

Lavena did not feel safe until darkness prevented her from seeing ahead or behind, and only their old horses knew the way home. She told Stena everything she had seen but not how she felt, the feelings too many and too new. She did not know whether in the moment, if the moment had come, she could have killed this almost unarmed young man.

Or perhaps, she felt more than thought, Stena would laugh at her thoughts about this young man. He seemed afraid to stand and fight, he seemed to see in her the power and danger of a fighting woman who had killed harder men.

By the time they reached the opening of their gorge, the air had become heavy. As they whistled their way past the look out and barking dogs announcing their return, rain had started to fall. Lavena could barely see the children who ran out to them ahead of their mothers, could barely see the light from edges of the closed doors and wooden coverings of the wall openings in the main hut.

After they put up their horses, after they hugged all the women and children, after they all circled around the warm fire in the main hut, everyone waited for Lavena to speak. By then, the rain had grown heavy. Its steady patter on the straw roof and splashing on the dirt outside told them it would last the night and perhaps longer.

"Trackers and dogs are on their way up to us, right now."

"May the spirit of my man, Bodo, help us," said Caniné.

Lavena said, "The fish and letting Roman Horse go stopped them for a time. But they know Roman Horse, all the horses and men, came this way. Will not take them long to find us. They won't come in this night of rain. There are not many—but soon there'll be more."

After a time, Caniné said, "We can't stay here, should leave as soon as Reue lets us."

Stena said, "We should leave at first light." She waited, looked at each one in turn, and then announced, "We must leave in this rain, before it ends so it washes out our tracks. Then the Romans will not know how many we are or which way we leave."

Lavena said, "Reue will protect us—must protect us. Pray she watches over us this night."

"Where shall we go?" said Bedule, a younger woman who had two little children and a third in her belly.

Stena said, "Pray that all the villages we traded with think kindly of us. Put the little ones to sleep now. The older ones have work to do. The nights are still short even through rain. The days ahead will test us."

#

It rained the night and into morning, a cold rain through cold clouds that had come to ground by the time Marcus crawled out of his tent and looked around. This was the kind of rain that often turned to snow, the kind of snow that might not stop for a long time. He looked up ahead to try to see how far the snow line came down the high peaks but could not see more than two hundred paces through the rain and low clouds.

A new warning tinge settled in.

He knew from his time in the Alps that he'd best get to lower ground before snow covered this unknown terrain. One hard stumble by his horse, one wrong turn, one snow that lasted a day and a night, and he might have to kill and eat his horse to survive. No, he thought, that's madness. It was far too early in the year for snow, though not for his horse to stumble on wet ground.

He could not stay here and he dared not go higher in this rain that gave no sign of ending soon. Time to mark this spot and bring many men as fast as he could.

The *barbari* up ahead—. One lone rider who ran when spotted would not alarm these boastful locals. Besides, they were too stupid to prepare for what Marcus knew would come at them next.

He looked around concentrating as hard as he could, looked at every large tree, at every rocky patch through the mist and rain, tried hard to remember the sight lines from the afternoon before to tops of the mountain. He would break tree branches on the way back to mark the trail to this place. He wanted to come back here soon for Martis and for himself.

Chapter XXV

Running West of the Moon

The steady rain made packing up more difficult but easier too. The horses and donkey stayed in their sheltering huts and did not resist when the women loaded them up. Some of the horses had to stand out in the rain. With the ten new ones, there had been no time to build a shelter for all of them.

Despite the wet ground, then puddles and mud, the women and older children managed to load most of what they might need for wherever they were going, for however long it might take to get there.

During this last night in their valley, they kept the kiln burning white hot with dried out wood and old logs turned to charcoal. Lavena instructed the others to gather up all the Roman clothes and weapons they could not take. They tossed these extras into the kiln. When the Roman army found this hamlet, it would be best that the vanished scouts remained vanished.

Their dogs, sheep and goats—what to do with them? Stena laughed and said, "If we don't take our dogs, they'll follow us anyway. We'll pack the pups in the cart, and then they'll stay with us, protect us again. But…we might not take all our horses. The Romans left us too many good ones."

That brought a sound of agreement from Lavena and others. "We'll not take the goats and sheep. They'll slow us, and their tracks give us away. Pray someone comes up here and finds them before the wolves of winter. Good meat and pelts."

None of the adult women and the older children slept on this last night in their valley, too much to do in too little time, too much to think about.

At first light, they were loaded, mounted and ready. As they headed into the gorge, Lavena said to all of them, "Reue is with us, will wash away all our traces out of here, but go slowly. Can't have a horse stumble." She had to talk loudly above the noisy rain and wind.

Stena fell to the rear of the column. She said, "Wait for me at the far side. I'll come last and release the rocks and logs that I can, close the trail behind us. They'll tumble easily on the wet hill. Maybe when the Romans leave our land we'll come back to our valley, and we'll find it empty, waiting for us—"

No one protested that the way back would be blocked, that it might take days to clear the path through the gorge. Not one of them looked back at the huts, even the one with the burned-out roof—at the only home some had ever known. The events of the last days had ripped away all affection for their valley, all good memories.

For most of that day, Stena and her horse found trails not washed out. In treacherous sections, she or her horse located passable ground. The vegetation—wild grasses in the open areas, and decayed leaves under pine needles in the trees—lay thick. But the ground beneath drained well, not yet too water-soaked for the horses to find good footing. The trails had not yet turned into flowing streams that might have been too dangerous for heavily-laden horses.

The village donkey, pulling the cart, followed behind Stena's horse as if this were just another trading haul to a friendly village. This time the cart carried crates of chickens, a crate of young dogs, and one more crate with a pig. Extra clothes and pelts covered the crates. The adult dogs walked along beside the horses.

The three oldest boys spared in the night of the slaughter each rode one of the familiar horses from the valley. Now the Roman horses and saddles served a purpose. Three pack horses, their long reins tied to back corner saddle posts, followed the boys. The two oldest girls also rode their own horses. The other six adult women, all good riders, held a young child between their forearms or a baby in a sling pressed against their chests.

The women not yet mothers shared the burden of babies and toddlers on this trek, as they had in the village. From the look of them, Lavena thought the two with child were not close to giving birth. She hoped that days on horse would not bring the new lives too soon.

Only Stena and Lavena did not ride with a baby or child. Without saying it, all the women let them ride ready to challenge and fight.

Each rider carried a sword or knife, whatever they could strap to a leg or across their backs and still get on and off a horse. Some wore helmets the Romans had left behind. Lavena would not have one of those—not yet—the smell of them and spirit in them too foul. But the metal and leather helmets did keep all but the worst rain off the head and out of the eyes better than the helmets of their own men.

The three pack horses carried as many extra weapons and tools as the women had been able to bundle up inside the extra blankets and pelts.

Except for the cackling and fly-bys of curious crows, Lavena had not seen or heard any sign of wild animals. As the first night out of their valley loomed, Caniné spoke Lavena's thoughts. "Pray that the babies and horses do not give up the safety of darkness."

Stena found a level place to camp, its ground firm and not water soaked.

Everyone knew what to do and did it fast. They cut pine branches and interwove them into platforms, then spread pelts on the platforms. They set the platforms at an angle, one edge on the ground. They tilled up the ground against the platform edge to channel rain and run off away from the grounded edge.

Once all the platforms were tilted against the direction of the wind and rain and braced up with sticks at their opening, they tied up one adult dog at the opposite corners of their little camp. The women had made raised covers of branches and pelts for the dogs as well.

Women and children huddled under the lean-tos for the night. They ate salted meat strips and dried beets, not enough time before total darkness and everything too wet to try to start a fire.

Too soon no one could see any other, only hear and touch in the black rainy night.

Lavena asked her mother's spirit to not let the youngsters cry out. Edereta always caressed the little ones to calm their fears. Though they had not seen or heard any sign of the wolf or bear, Lavena knew that rain does not deter the hungry hunter, and a baby's cry draws them from far away.

Stena and Lavena bundled up under the same lean-to. Lavena said, "Stena, to where do you lead us?"

"To the first village that will have us. We've traded with them all below our mountain, fought with some of them in the big wars long ago before you were born." Stena said the plain truth. "Any village will have us with all our horses and young women. Have no fear of that."

"That Roman army moved so fast on our village. We'll have to go far to get clear of it."

"If each village fights like yours, Lavena, that army will tire, will slow."

"Stena, the power and speed of that army are mighty beyond what I can tell you, the Roman soldiers fiercer than I can say. Take us as far as we can go before we have to stop, before one of our babies pushes out."

"Lavena, I know about Roman armies, know how fast they can travel. I saw that army move on your village. You don't know, you can't know the armies my man and I saw in the old days when your father was young. We old ones all learned more than we want to remember about fighting big armies on our land. We've known the brutality of Rome from the old days."

Stena paused as if remembering. "Piso let us live nearly as we had in the past. He made us forget....You and I will take my women and babies as far from here as we can before we can go no farther."

Lavena wanted to ask Stena how this clan had known her father, why their first mentions of him when they learned she was his daughter carried no kindness or respect. She wanted to ask if any of Stena's men had fought with him far back. But none of that mattered now, and she was too tired to start a long talk.

Her wool clothes and the pelt wrapped around her kept her dry and warm, warm enough to sleep. But she wanted to stay awake too, even in the rain and blackness. The last rain and darkness had done that.

She said, "Stena, take your women and children far from here, from this mountain. Take them where no Romans follow." She remembered her father asking all the gathered villagers if they wanted to flee, remembered his words and added, "Take us west of the moon."

Deep in the night, through the rain Lavena thought she heard quiet weeping from the clan leader lying back-to-back next to her, then from another lean-to, then more. But not one of the young children or babies cried out.

In time, she fell asleep until their roosters close by in the cart crowed up another day.

Early on the third day, this second storm of the season waned, and the land jumped with the freshness brought by the rain. Birds made more noise than Lavena had ever noticed. Porcupines, squirrels and lizards found patches of sun and warming rocks. Their dogs trotted ahead, dove into thickets and did not emerge until the clan had ridden far past.

Here and there, they caught a view south and west under a sky not smudged by any smoke from another crushed village.

At a place where they stopped to rest and let their horses drink, Stena said to Lavena, "Time to take us down off the mountain to the next village. Our waiting women need to get off their horses."

Lavena was sure they had not travelled far enough west, far enough away from the cliffs of her village or the army down there, but she said nothing. She might be their leader in a fight, but this was Stena's clan, some of the children and babies her granddaughters and grandsons.

Farmers and herding dogs drove a mixed flock of sheep and goats in a meadow at the base of the mountain. This was the first sign of a nearby village.

Stena said, "Stay in the shadows here where they and whoever might be near can't see us all, can't see we have no men."

The herders, six or seven, and their dogs circled around Stena and her horse. Their movements did not threaten or alarm. Soon they patted Stena's horse on the neck and rump, and looked up at Stena and smiled broadly. Stena pointed at her group waiting in the trees. The herders motioned for them to come.

The women and older children all looked at Lavena. She saw no signal from Stena that they should leave the sheltering trees and motioned to remain here in the shadows.

After a long moment, Stena headed back to her group, leisurely, her horse's tail swishing.

"They remember us. Their village will take us this night, longer perhaps. Summer was good to them, and they have many stores and healthy animals. Their chief went over to the spirits not far back. His oldest daughter, named Daleninar, leads this village. They call it Village on the Hill."

Lavena remembered. This village had been her early goal, but for an instant uncertainty crept in. She had not told Stena of the Romans and their string of captives travelling downriver the day after her village fell. These herders could be loyal to the Romans, could have been won over by Piso. She hoped no Roman fighters had come this far west.

She said, "Do they know what happened down there?"

Stena said, "I did not want to have to tell them, must talk to their leader first." She looked at Lavena as if she could read Lavena's thoughts. "Any herders this far from their village without horses or scouts are not prepared for war. Look at them."

Lavena and the others turned to the herders, some waving again for the whole group to come to them, men at peace tending their flock in a quiet meadow. Lavena hoped the image was right, hoped that it was not because they had allied with Rome.

Chapter XXVI

Sagunto

This village sat on a rise, as if on an island above grass land. Vegetable plots, storage sheds, paddocks, and sturdy farm houses fell away from outside the wall.

Men and women watched over their goats and sheep or worked on the outlying buildings. They stopped whatever they had been doing and looked at the strangers riding in. Many gathered on the wall and at the gate opening through that wall. Lavena thought this village did have scouts out on the perimeter after all, that her group had been spotted far back and the villagers alerted. She wished for them that this was true.

Lavena thought the main village could easily defend against predators and rogue bands. Those who lived outside the wall would have enough warning to get inside. From the top of the wall, anyone with good eyes could see far in all directions, perhaps, she thought, all the way down to the valley of the Eberus.

The alder, elm and pine forests that covered much of the base of the looming mountains started far back and away from these walls. But the gentle slopes up to the main gate would not stop the Romans. None of this was any match for an army with siege ladders and battering rams.

Village dogs came up round the horses' legs. They barked at the strange new dogs but soon settled and exchanged greeting sniffs. Lavena thought they must have been used to visitors or trained to attack only on their masters' commands. She wondered if Little Bear's spirit might be here now, if he told these dogs that Stena's clan and her dogs meant no harm.

Mostly women and children awaited them—quietly, curiously. At times like this after days of rain, the men and women without young children would be out working or hunting. Wherever most of the men were, this village had fewer dwellers than the Village on The Cliff and would have fewer fighters, not enough to last one full day against the army that prowled not far to the east. These people would have to flee. As soon as she found their leaders, she would make them listen to her. They had to.

As Stena's clan pulled to a halt outside the gate, a young woman, not much older than Lavena, stepped out from those gathered. She, and only she, wore the garb of nobility—a long white coat, cinched at the waist with a purple cord, and a gold torc on her neck. Her torc was thinner than the one Lavena carried, with only round stubs at the facing ends, not big wolf heads with eyes of green.

Lavena knew the deep blue in her cord was colored from the dye of the tiny snail that lived in the far end of the Great Inland Sea. Only nobles and the wealthy could afford the tiny vials of dye extracted one drop at a time from those snails.

This noble said something to Stena that Lavena could not hear. But the noble's body language said, *welcome, old friend.*

The noble walked around each horse, looked closely at the youngest riders and the babies in the arms of the women riders. Lavena read the look. It said at once, please come, you are welcome to my village, we honor women and children—but where are your men, what brought you here without them, with these babies and children, with pack horses loaded and a cart too full?

She walked back to Stena's horse, and said so they all could hear, "Come, follow me. We have an empty hut. The babies and heavy women must rest."

They followed her through the main gate up a rising path into the village. At the top of the path stood more animal paddocks and storage sheds, behind them one-level houses of stone walls and straw roofs, the same as Lavena's village.

Daleninar pointed to an empty paddock. "Put up your horses and dogs in here." She yelled to no one in particular, "Fresh oats and water, and meat for the dogs." Then more quietly to them, "We'll find a place for the chickens and pig. Must unload that cart and unburden the donkey."

Daleninar watched them dismount and unbridle the horses, unhitch the donkey and unload the cart. Older boys came up to help carry the pups and crates to a safe place. "Over there, go with the boys. I'll send food and drink, and you rest."

Lavena and Stena, carrying their bundles, followed last.

Though short and young and of soft voice, Daleninar commanded attention and respect from everyone around her. Lavena wondered how she had earned it so soon after her father's death—and hoped Daleninar would listen.

Daleninar, walking along with them, said to Stena, "Tonight you must tell me why you came here, what misfortune befell your sons and husband—and all the men of your clan. Tell the nobles of my village. They must know too."

Stena answered. "Yes, we must tell you, Lavena here and I must both tell you."

Daleninar, for the first time looked directly at Lavena then tilted her head to the side and back. Those gestures asked Lavena's age and what Lavena might know that Stena could not tell her, how someone so young had become Stena's equal, how someone so fair rode far from home without a man. "Good. Later. We must know."

Daleninar held out her right hand palm down at about her own waist. "This high, I remember you. You came with your father and brothers." She said it in a tone that invited no further remembrance of that visit when they both must have been children.

For the first time since Stena and Lavena had taken Roman Horse down the mountain, all the women and children rested together in a dry hut warmed by logs burning in a proper fireplace built into the north wall, as it had been at Lavena's house.

Daleninar sent them bowls of hot porridge stirred with honey and milk, salted slabs of the rib sections of a pig, jugs of water, all the bread they could eat and all the beer they cared to drink. One of the herders who first greeted them said he would wait outside their hut until they were ready, and then take Stena and her helper to the hut where the village nobles gathered.

Daleninar did not command as many nobles as had Sinorix. But by their expressions and the way they all rose—six women and five men—when Stena and Lavena entered, they all wanted to know about these strange out-villager women and children fleeing with not one man.

This house was not as large as the main hall in the middle of the plaza of the Village on The Cliff, though its pelts lying in layers on the stone floor were as fine. On its walls hung swords, heavy pikes, and bows, but Lavena saw no sign that they had been used in recent days. The metal did not shine, and the edges did not look sharp. This village was not ready for battle.

They sat around the fire, but Daleninar did not exchange names or greetings, or again offer beer and fresh bread. She said as if all one thought, "Where did you leave your men? Why did they send you off? How will they find you?"

Stena turned to Lavena on her left, as if talking to her. "Our men will never come back. They went to the place of the spirits—each one." Murmurs and gasps rose from the nobles. "Lavena here, daughter of Sinorix, last child of Sinorix, must tell you how that came to pass."

More murmurs and whispers from the nobles. Lavena watched and waited for their attention, for her chance to honor Father's last command.

Their looks told her that they guessed she was only fifteen and thought she was too young to know anything worthy, too young to speak for Stena. These faces would not listen to her.

As the murmurs died down, several of the nobles said, "Ah, Sinorix..."

"The great warrior of old."

"The besieger of Sagunto."

They looked at each other as they spoke, looks of agreement, and repeated the short bursts of unhappy recognition.

Whoever among them said great said it with a mocking tone. Whoever among them said besieger said it with regret. And then they looked straight at Lavena, not in friendship, not in sorrow. Their expressions, the mouths pulled down at the corners, the heads thrust forward and down, the eyes looking up from under wrinkled brows all said, *Tell us, daughter of Sinorix. What have you, what has he, done now?*

Lavena could not return the gazes for more than an instant. She looked at her hands clenched in her lap. She did not know how to begin, felt the hostility and puzzled at what she might have done or said to cause it. Frustration gave way to fear, each reinforcing the other. She felt afraid of being laughed at, more afraid of being interrupted and not allowed to get out what she had to tell them, most afraid of them ignoring her.

Then she remembered her father's face on that last morning—and found words to begin.

"We humbly come to you, to this village, without any men because the Roman overseer, Piso, left this land, and Rome sent a monster army in his place."

The nobles quieted and leaned in further. Some made sounds at the mention of Piso in a manner that suggested they knew him and thought well of the former overseer.

"That new army has more fighters and weapons and its killing madness is greater than I know how to tell you—and it comes this way." She had them now. "They come for all the gold in this land, for the young ones to take back as slaves—and the young women and girls to ruin in a manner none should ever know."

She told them of her father's return from Rome. She told them what she could of the battle for her village, but not about how her mother and those with her died, not about the real end of the she-warriors. She told them of how she fled.

She had to stop, look away and wipe her eyes, but she made it to her jumping into the Eberus without any of them interrupting.

She wanted Stena to tell the rest. It would come with greater strength from someone near their age and someone they knew. But Stena remained quiet, as if she had never at one time heard anyone tell what had happened inside the Village on The Cliff, as if she wanted Lavena to finish it all. Lavena had never told Stena the whole of it.

Lavena felt, rather than thought, what she must do next to get through, to make them believe in a way that would compel them to summon the will to fight as they might never have fought before. She had to get them to go out to other villages, to gather all the fighters from all villages in the region, and to hide all the gold so that no Roman would ever find it. They had to start the next day or the one after that at the latest. She felt that in the clear weather, the army was surely on the move again and in this direction.

She opened the string that cinched the outer robe around her neck, and let the top of the robe fall. Sinorix's torc, the facing wolf heads hanging below her neck, the stones of the wolf eyes casting their sparkles of green then silvery black, then green again, looked out at them all. "Father gave me this before he left us—and the Romans want this above all else."

Some of the nobles stood up quickly as if prodded by something sharp. Some moved in to look and admire. Some started to reach for it but stopped under Lavena's glare. Even Stena leaned over. Lavena had kept this torc out of sight at all times in Stena's valley.

All the nobles started to speak half thoughts and over each other. "You are his daughter...."

"That's his. That's the one...."

"If the Romans had found this...."

"The old stories of Sagunto..."

"They are not stories..."

"They are true."

"This proves it..., the wolf heads with green eyes."

"There is only one like it."

Daleninar raised her right hand, and her nobles stopped talking. "Lavena, daughter of Sinorix, we too weep with you. But please, finish. You or Stena, tell us how Stena's clan is here now with not one of her men."

Stena finished the telling, of finding Lavena, of the Roman scouts slaughtering her men while they slept. She told them of Lavena leading the counterattack in her valley. At the end, Stena said, "We thank you for your kindness. My clan, what's left of it, will not burden you but will help with anything you ask. When the Romans draw near, we—you and everyone here—must flee again, must find a way to join with your neighbors, and must not let them have what they want."

By her look Lavena thanked Stena for that last, for joining Lavena in the warning.

This time, none of the others uttered a sound. Daleninar stood up and her nobles followed her lead. "Stena and daughter of Sinorix, stay. I need to counsel with my nobles."

They left the two women alone sitting by the warmth and light of the fire.

From outside the door, Lavena heard the voices of the old men and women, the inflections, but not the words, serious tones, many long silences, no arguments, no shouts.

Daleninar led them back into the room. This time, none of them sat. Daleninar looked at Lavena and said, "Daughter of Sinorix, you must leave."

Stena raised her hand and started to say something.

"Allow me to finish," said Daleninar. "Stena, you, your women and children are welcome to stay. But you, Lavena, and your torc are filled with evil spirits." Lavena's open mouth, wide eyes, the surprise they must have shown, made Daleninar explain. "It is your Father and that thing he gave you that you wear so proudly."

Lavena touched the torc round her neck and the two on each wrist still covered by the sleeves of her outer cloak.

"You see, long before you were born, before I was born, your father was the mightiest warrior, leader of many thousands from all our tribes."

She raised a hand in the direction of one of her nobles. "Some of the old ones in my village, even my father, fought with your father. But for a time, he lost his way. He joined the brutes from Carthage, Hannibal and his Barca family, took many of our people with him into that army. Together, all their forces numbered fifty thousand men and ten thousand horses. Then they crushed the good city of Sagunto on the heights down by the Great Inland Sea—eight months of foulest siege anyone here has ever known."

Lavena did not want to hear, wanted to run out and far away. But she had to listen, had to stay for her father, had to learn what she could, to figure out what to do next.

Daleninar continued, "The people of Sagunto, traders on The Great Inland Sea and down to Africa, friends of everyone, did not merit that. The last of them died by their own hands on their own swords or threw themselves on fires they had set rather than surrender. The fires burned for seven days and seven nights up on the heights inside the fortress walls."

She pointed at the wolf heads and spat out the next words, gagging on the last, "That torc, your father ripped that torc from the neck of my father's friend, the kind and gentle leader of Sagunto, as that good man lay dying."

Daleninar stopped, though she was not finished.

Lavena could not help letting out not a word, not a cry, but a wail of pain and denial.

"Sagunto was allied with Rome but friendly to everyone, had been for hundreds of years—and that's why Rome swept over our land back then, made many of our mothers whores and our fathers slaves. In time, we fought back and achieved a truce, but now Rome, as your father said, spits on that treaty. Now Rome attacks your village first. With you here, we are no safer than Sagunto was against your father and that Hannibal Barca. Without you here, Rome may not harm us."

Daleninar was done, stood there, glowered at Lavena. They all did.

Lavena's mind had fought every utterance, and now questions piled in. The man she knew could not have done that, could never have treated honorable people like that. She said softly, "Not Father, no, it's not true...."

Her voice started to rise in anger, and she started to blurt out more. But the cold stares, tight lips, then heads turned up and away refusing to listen, each noble standing over her, snuffed out what more she might have said.

Lavena stood up on shaking knees, breathing fast and shallow, not daring to make strong eye contact with any of them, too humiliated, too young. She searched for signs of hesitation or softness, for a better way, but saw only faces of stone.

She glanced at Stena but felt no support from her. Stena and her clan needed the safety of this village far more than Stena's clan needed Lavena any longer.

After a time, Lavena bowed to show she honored this village chief and to hide her own face and what it might reveal. As she bowed, she softly said, "I will...leave in the morning...if I may stay the night."

Chapter XXVII

Vanished Barbari

On this early morning, the great tent could not hold the warmth of mere men. Though he wore two layers of wool over a silk undergarment, Gracchus shivered. He was hungry. There had been no feast last night. His servants had not prepared for the sudden soaking rain, now in its third day.

Without dry wood and kindling, fires were hard to start and, once started, hard to keep going. On days and nights like this, his army, the old men and their many servants, devoured dry wood for cooking fires and warmth faster than they devoured food.

The infantry leaders reported grumbling from their men. Streams had swollen to rivers, and rivers had become impassable. Hoofs sank into the muck, the wheels of carts refused to roll. His army had not moved, much less sacked and plundered so much as a solitary farm house in more than ten days, had not scouted out the next village for its young bodies and gold.

The few old men left in his tent from the night before munched on dates and strips of salted deer meat. In the darker corners, one or two still snored under pelts. Once his army found bounty and he paid them back, he never again would have to kiss their hands, lavish feasts on them, could kick them out of his tent whenever he wanted.

Gracchus paced as he thought. He knew he looked silly, not able to advance more than a few steps before having to stop and turn at a sleeping body or at the damp tent wall. The first set of scouts had not returned, and now neither had young Marcus. But Nicator's dogs had found Celer.

At first, Gracchus had thought this was something. In the end it meant only that his lead scout had lost his horse and whoever found it had taken good care of Celer. That told him nothing about the ten men and nine other horses. He said to no one in particular, "Where is he?"

The Legate Apollonius, sitting near him, said, "We'll hear soon enough. Don't trouble so much. Our silver will be enough. Don't trouble so much."

Gracchus knew all that. He would be the first to hear when Marcus or Martis came back, but not hearing anything added to his misery, his agitation, his not wanting to eat or sleep, and not even to get drunk.

The Legate, some called him General, repeated himself often. Gracchus was not sure if he repeated from a mind growing feeble, or to hear his own voice.

Apollonius slapped his cushion and blurted out, the way old men slap at the nearest thing and blurt out thoughts suddenly entering their old heads, "It is time for our priest to study his pigeon bones, for *Iuppiter* to tell us what happened to Martis and now to his brother, and what we must do next. Ask the priest to ask the bones. I will do it."

Gracchus despised the priest he had been forced to take, despised all priests. Leaders who consulted priests and believed the fortunes read by priests in the bones of dead birds did not last long as leaders. Leaders who gave their best animals to the great God *Iuppiter* always wasted their best animals for nothing. And after that, *Iuppiter* made them blunder, sometimes into losing whole armies.

But the Senate believed in priests, and priests read bird bones. If he relented, that might provide him cover. The Senate and his sponsors had insisted Legate Apollonius come with him and command his army in all things of war. He'd kick out this old fool Legate as soon as he paid all his sponsors back.

"Yes, General. If Marcus stays away one more day, the priest and his bird bones will tell us what to do."

Curses on this beguiling land. If he had a bigger army, a numbered legion with fighters who had fought before, a little rain would not deter them. But all he could pay for—even with the money from old men who too often crowded into his tent—was this ragged collection of low class mongrels.

Nicator had reported how easily Marcus had been tricked by horse reins hanging in trees and then by a false trail. If Marcus had been older, old enough to shave and think like a grown man, Martis and all his scouts might have already been found and brought back safely. And if he, Gracchus, had more treasure or influence, he could have paid for real scouts, like their father. The sons were untrained, too young and impulsive to figure out the choices, much less select the best one.

Interrupting his thoughts again, Apollonius sneezed hard three times and shouted in a raspy, nasally voice, "Our army is idle. Great armies move, strike, take what's theirs and move on fast to take more. I've told you many times to keep them moving, keep fresh targets in their sights—best of all, fresh women. Keep us moving, and it will be easier for Martis and his men to find us. Fresh women, that's what they want. That's why they fight. That's the prize, the only prize that matters to them."

That was Apollonius, another stupid tactic from his mouth—if Martis was out there trying to find or fight his way back, it was best the army stayed in its camp, at the place where Martis left it.

And women. Gracchus almost said, *All history teaches that the vanquished quickly honor the victors if the victors honor their women. But the vanquished will fight like caged cats—or kill themselves—before they give up their women to men like you.*

He managed, "When the rain ends, they'll all be ready, and we'll move out."

When the fight went well, Apollonius' sunken chest swelled, and he made the scribe record every detail of his brilliant strategy. When the fight did not turn out as planned, when scouts did not return, the scribes would record that subordinates failed to carry out the General's orders.

But Gracchus thought Apollonius was right about one thing. Every leader of paid fighting men knows idleness is the first step on the path to disaster. Doing nothing brings on a special restlessness. After his five thousand men and uncounted wives and followers in the supply train, all their horses, mules, oxen and other beasts had stripped the land around camp, had stolen all the local farm animals, they would have to hunt in unknown terrain.

After all the game had been eaten or had fled, the army would begin to eat itself. Once the army began to eat its horses and bullocks, no soldier trusted another. Without plump targets to seize and plunder, diseases of the mind and flesh crept into every army. Disgrace in front of the Senate and an early death would follow for him as surely as winter follows summer if this army did not soon move out.

Gracchus had to placate the old man a while longer. "We'll sacrifice our best horse to *Iuppiter* this night, and he'll clear the skies for us. It is too early for winter. Then we'll rid this land of *barbari* and reclaim what's ours, what we've been entitled to ever since these traitors killed all our friends down at Sagunto."

The Legate raised a finger high. "Reports from the south are better, yes? The *barbari* down there are all subdued. Do we need more slaves for the mines?"

Gracchus relaxed at that acknowledgement of some success. He sat down on his pile of pelts. "Yes, we have reports that the *barbari* south of here toil for us as they did for Piso. But we can always use more."

The old Legate slapped his knee surprisingly loudly. "Need to step up the whipping. Nothing teaches a man like the sting of leather."

Gracchus, thinking out loud, said, "As long as they dig and haul and tend the mine fires, we give them food and water. When they give out...."

Gracchus was not sure what he felt about this next. "When they expire, we throw them into an old pit. If they crawl out, we put them back on the ore line. If not, we bury them. Old mining pits make suitable graves. The *barbari* believe their dead live in the ground. It's a good test of their stamina, don't you think, General?"

The old man bobbed his head up and down. "Yes, yes, good test of their strength. There's enough silver in that ground, we won't go back to Rome empty-handed. But," he looked up and raised his voice higher than his raspy whisper, and raised his right hand too, crooked index finger pointing up, "Piso and his men all told us, the gold of Iberia sits in this valley."

Through the rain tapping on the tent and splashing in the puddles outside the flaps, Gracchus heard men talking loudly, some shouting, not in anger, but to make themselves heard above the others yelling. The tent flaps opened.

Marcus stood in the entry way, wool cap and cloak dripping. "*Optime*, I know where they are, what happened to Martis and the others. If time and *Iuppiter* favor us, they will still be there when your men arrive to save them. If we make haste, we'll have the *barbari* who took my brother and his men."

Marcus had to beg, but in the end the priest allowed Celer to live in anticipation of Martis' return. That night, the priest and two of his helpers bound up and slaughtered the finest horse after Celer. They drained its blood on a large flat stone east of the camp, the side closer to Rome—the camp's altar to *Iuppiter*.

By early morning, the rain stopped.

At midday, Marcus led eighty fighting men, thirteen riders, and ten pack mules back up to where he and the trackers had found Celer.

The Legate Apollonius himself came out of his tent and out to the gathering area on the far side of the western wall. He staggered when he walked, but brushed aside offers of help from servants on either side.

He found Marcus waiting to mount and said loudly, jabbing with his hands for emphasis. "You have my best marchers. Each of them covers rough terrain as fast as any horse. Use them, make them run—they must run hard and long—and bring Martis back, bring our horses back. Find our gold. No one will stand in your way. The *barbari* are too afraid after what we did up there. Go, find our gold, go find it."

Apollonius coughed, and as the cough subsided raised a thumb at Marcus, "Go, go find it. Bring it back, go now."

Marcus mounted fast, had to get away from this Legate who had lost his mind, though he was right about the locals not standing to fight. Whoever lived in the mountain had already run from a fight against just three men and two dogs.

Once out of the flat easy land and into the treed hills, the footmen did keep up with the men on horse. No dogs ran with them this time, more trouble than help after so much water washing all old scents off the land. Big dogs needed more stops to rest than horses or these hand-picked men. Speed meant everything now.

At the end of the second day, the little army reached the place where Marcus had turned back. Again darkness fell quickly, and they camped in the same meadow where he had spent the night.

The next morning, the short distance to the opening into the mountain surprised him. He had been so near but had not dared to go on.

Marcus ordered four riders, two pack horses, and twenty men to stay at the mouth of the gorge. He had seen ambushes in the Alps and heard tell of many more. Gorges often contained narrows that let through no more than two or three men abreast. On a narrow trail wedged between cliffs or on a ledge over a deep crevasse, two well-armed men could stop the entire army. From the heights above the gorge, other *barbari* could rain down rocks and boulders.

His infantry started to run, and the riders crowded after them. Marcus wanted to slow them, but understood. Few of them had seen what could happen in terrain like this. All of them hoped to find Martis and his men and, if the gods felt generous, gold, much gold, at the end of this run through the mountain gorge.

Not far in they had to stop. Trees cut down, not felled by age or weather, and big boulders lay across the path. Was this the first stage of an ambush?

Marcus and all of them listened and watched for stones dislodged, for twigs breaking, for breathing, for dead silence. But the forest birds chirped and woodpeckers tapped as on any other morning. He ordered the infantry and riders to string out back to the opening, spaced far apart so that one shout, one horn blast, could be relayed to everyone in both directions.

They took half the day to clear the trail so the pack horses could get through, the foot soldiers could lock shields three side-by-side and charge forward, and the riders had a clear path.

At the far end of the gorge, Marcus, in the lead, stopped and raised his hand for those behind to slow.

Ahead of him down the trail lay a hamlet—three big huts, storage sheds, and paddock fences. One of the huts had no roof, its thick stone walls stained dark at the top—burned out. A kiln stood near the center of the huts. No smoke rose from its chimney.

Past the structures, straight rows of beets, carrots or cabbages ran inside stone fences and beyond them apple or pear trees. On the far side, a meadow of tall grass blanketed the ground to the forest beyond. Summer came late to this mountain valley, and the grasses had not been cut, the ears not yet ripened to grain.

Not one dog barked a warning. No horse snorted to announce the visitors.

This trail ended on the far side of the settlement. Deep forests and above them walls of granite rose up behind the hamlet. The only way out for the *barbari* or Martis and his men was the way in.

After a long moment to think, to confirm, Marcus pounded the two posts on the front corners of his saddle. He turned back and yelled. "They are gone—left in the days of rain." He shouted louder, "We are too late." Louder still so those far back in the gorge could hear, "Pass the word, Martis and his men gone, vanished."

He did not send anyone to collect the others waiting at the far end in case of an ambush. There was no need. His little army would head back very soon.

The footmen spread out and searched every possible hiding place, up into the forest and beyond as far as they could.

Marcus spotted rows of round rocks, each rock set on a mound of dirt—a burial ground for whoever had lived and died here. Some of the mounds were fresh. He pointed to the nearest fresh mound and yelled in the direction of the waiting pack horse riders. "He who has a shovel, unearth this one."

They found ashes and bones of a man, one crude comb, and a metal pick. It, Marcus thought, might be a pick for teeth. These *barbari* had some sense of cleanliness after all.

They found buckles for a belt but none like he had ever seen—crude metal with no symbols, no lettering, no head of a god or a leader. He said softly as if thinking out loud, "Someone recently dead is buried here but not one of ours. The *barbari* wouldn't bury one of us with their trinkets."

They dug up more fresh graves. None contained what might have been left of Martis or his men. Their clothes and everything they had brought with them had vanished too.

The fresh grave last in the line held no trinkets, only ashes and the bones of a dog, a large dog unfamiliar to Marcus or the others around him. Maybe they worshiped that dog. He said, "Stupid barbari. They bury their dogs with the same honors as their fighters."

Two horses appeared from the shade of the trees on the far side of the tall grass. These horses stood off, sniffing at the many strangers and their horses. Then they turned and trotted away, stopped and stared back, then disappeared again into the trees. These horses, though not wild, did not take to the many strangers who swarmed over their valley.

Marcus snapped his fingers at two of the other riders and motioned them to follow these horses. He didn't believe it, but yelled, "Maybe they'll show us where the others have gone."

In a short time, the two riders came back. "Those tired nags stopped up there. We can take them with us if you think the army wants more meat for our dogs. They're not ours, have no markings of any owner, and too old and sway-backed to ride. Up there at the edge of the meadow, some goats and sheep graze with the horses. Plump enough if we want to take them back."

Marcus looked up into the heights. He grimaced and then said, "What will Gracchus and his Legate think of us when we bring back sheep and goats after they sent us to find gold?" The others chuckled in return. "We have plenty enough meat, but not enough good scout horses."

He thought then said, "We'll take the horses and the goats and sheep. Gracchus' army is always hungry. But where are the scouts and their horses? Where's the gold? Where's my brother?"

None of them answered him.

Those old horses and the fresh graves provided all the answers as clearly as if they had been written out on proper tablets or parchment. Martis and his men had fought here or close to here and killed six men and one dog now buried in the seven fresh graves, likely wounded twice as many. Marcus wondered how many had lived here crowded into three huts to put up such a fight, lose six, and still have enough healthy bodies left to burn and bury their dead.

Martis and his men had lost this fight—badly. His older brother and the scouts with him would not have buried the *barbari*, not placed trinkets into each grave. If Martis and his men survived the fight, they would have left the dead *barbari* where they fell. If Martis and any of his men survived, Marcus and all his men in this little army should have seen some sign of them.

Then the final truth set in. The *barbari* who survived and fled left behind two of their precious horses and perhaps more hiding up in the trees. They had not needed to take all the horses out of their valley—because with the horses from Martis and his men, they had more than enough. They even had enough horses to drag or carry their wounded until they healed or died.

Thoughts of his father came to him, when he might tell him about his oldest son. He hoped his father would not blame him.

As a last confirmation, he checked the kiln and every place of fire in the huts and on the ground. They were all cold and damp. The deep layer of ash in the kiln had not been cleaned out in a while but held no more heat. He wondered if anyone burned to death in the hut set on fire, but that hut held no other clues.

Marcus now knew the *barbari* of this hamlet had left days and nights before, maybe even on the night after he had seen the fair one back down the trail, the first night of that last rain while he slept not far from here. He again saw her face, the cloak and how it clung, the long sword and how easily she wielded it. She was out there now, and he let himself wonder if he might see her again.

Leaving the valley, Marcus and the others studied the ground. It did not tell them how many riders or horses or carts had fled or where they headed when they broke out of the gorge. The ground lay too wet and now too jumbled by the tracks of his infantry and pack horses marching in. On the far side of the gorge, old tracks of horses and carts spread out in every direction.

And there a new thought came to him. If the *barbari* had taken their sheep or goats, with their different and fresh hoof prints, he might now know which way they headed, which way to chase them. But they had been too clever to do that. This campaign, finding gold for Gracchus, had all the signs of great trouble.

Chapter XXVIII

Bird Bones

Marcus described everything he had seen and everything the little army under his command had done. He told the truth—but did not tell them of ghosts in the high country, of fair women luring men. He did not tell them what he thought it all meant.

Gracchus stood. Legate Apollonius sat in a tall chair to the right of Gracchus, and Nicator stood to the left.

The presence of Nicator annoyed him. All three looked at him not with expressions of interest in his report, but as they might look at a boy confessing what he had done before taking his deserved punishment.

When Marcus finished, Gracchus asked the infantry leader, who had come with Marcus, "Did you see anything that eagle eyes here missed, that he did not tell us?"

"No, *Optime*. There is nothing more."

"Marcus, can we go up there, hide near and wait for them to come back?"

"*Optime*, they will never come back to that valley."

"What makes you so sure?"

"They would not leave the rocks and boulders on the trail if they thought to return… And if they go back, they'll know we've been there."

Gracchus said, "Yes, yes. You did clear the trail in. Well then, Marcus, to the only points that matter. Do the vanished *barbari* have our other horses? Do they have your brother, our scouts? Do they have Rome's gold, the gold Piso swore they had?"

Marcus did not like the answer, the only right answer. "They have our horses as they had Celer. They may have Rome's gold." He had to stop, then, "My brother and your other scouts with him are dead."

Gracchus shrugged and looked at the old legate as if to tell him that he had expected this answer from Marcus. "What makes you say that, say it so surely, young Marcus?"

Marcus responded slowly. Talking about his older brother like this, with such plain finality did that. But on his brother's spirit, he had to tell them and trust the great Gracchus and his legate to understand no one could have done better than he, and that what he said was all true. "The buried *barbari* died all together days ago, the graves fresh."

Gracchus motioned with his hands for Marcus to say more. His face showed he had listened and was interested. The old legate sat motionless.

Marcus continued, "But after the fighting, the *barbari* stayed in that valley for a time. Enough of them lived to burn and bury their own. Whoever killed the *barbari* now in the ground, did not kill or capture them all, did not flee back to us, and did not stop them from vanishing, and did not stop them from—."

Gracchus interrupted. "But how can you know Martis and my scouts killed the *barbari*, that the *barbari* didn't die of dog fever?"

"Celer, *Optime*, Celer."

"Ah, yes. Someone up on the mountain must have fought Martis to get his horse." Gracchus pulled himself to his full height, as tall as Marcus. Palms out, he turned to the old man. "My wise general has consulted our priest and our priest has consulted *Iuppiter*. *Iuppiter* has told our priest the full truth about what happened to Martis." Gracchus waited, looking at Apollonius on his right.

As Marcus too waited for the legate to speak, he fixed on the face. It was the face of one of the tracking dogs, the skin around the eyes down to the nose, mouth and chin all sagging, only the dog's drool missing. But his eyes were alert.

"Young Marcus, Rome thanks you for your report and for finding this empty hamlet. Some day we may build an outpost in that valley." He tilted his head back against the chair, which gave the appearance of looking down his nose at Marcus. He spoke loudly, not with the same rasp as the last time. "Tell us, Marcus, why you took the false trail to the river, why you wasted time chasing up a tree after horse gear—tell us why you lie to us."

So, that was it. Nicator had been festering, had gotten to them, had found a way to please those in power and destroy him. He looked at all three, sure of what he had done, and that made what he had to say easy. "I made the trackers come back because by then I knew, the dogs knew, and Nicator knew my brother had come that way, had lost his horse, and was captured or dead with all his men, all their horses. Three of us were no match for whoever had done that. Three of us could not allow them to get behind us and block our way back. Three of us had to tread carefully and quietly every step up that mountain. And if they attacked us, it was right that I, brother of Martis, fight them alone and allow Nicator and Jove to come back to you and report."

The dog-faced legate said, "But they did not attack you, and if they had, we would not know about what became of you. And that was foolish. Your brother is out there while we talk. We are sure of that."

Nicator must have told lies and stupid things. Marcus set his jaw, clenched his teeth together hard, and then talked with all the power he could muster. He had to turn these men, had to do it now. "If Martis is out there, he is in chains. Whoever fought Martis kept his horse, even brought that horse back to us."

The old man scowled, the folds on his brow deeper. "Yes, very astute, young Marcus." He thought for a moment, "But we know more about these weak and cowardly *barbari*. We know our men better than you do. You need to learn so much, young Marcus. A few *barbari* out of three huts could not have overwhelmed ten of our best armed men. Ten of our best would have easily killed them, everyone."

He leaned forward. "While you were gone, our priest read the bones of a dove. Those bones never lie, always augur the truth. Those bones told us your brother is alive, and safe, but that you and he are not as loyal as you say."

Marcus looked around wondering whether that priest was one of the other old men in the great tent. His insides told him that anyone who searched for truth in bird bones was a fool. But this old Legate Apollonius believed his priest and believed Nicator—and Gracchus dared not override a priest and a legate, both sent with this army by the all powerful Senate.

Gracchus closed the distance between him and Marcus. "As General Apollonius has said, these few weaklings in a three-hut hamlet could not have done all that to us, to my best scout, to all his men. And you, Marcus, are not telling us everything you did and saw when you rode on alone. Our priest said you met your brother and made a plan with him to take Rome's gold. That's why you sent my dog handlers back and went on alone. That is the truth. Yes?"

Marcus' mind froze for an instant and then ran like a cornered rabbit, the charge too severe, too mad. The urge to scream in protest, to strike out at these easily misled and stupid men drowned logic and cleverness. He did not know what to say or do to save himself. Three sets of eyes, three knowingly smug smiles bore into him. He had to respond. He stepped closer to the three, into their space causing the two standing to move back and Apollonius to lean back as far as his chair allowed.

That helped center him. "I have not seen my brother since he left after the first village fell. I know nothing about any gold. I have told you the truth, all of it." As he said that last, he could not help thinking about the women, about her, and that last did not come out right. He stopped and waited.

The old Legate waved his right hand and arm forward toward him. On that signal, five armed men, large men, entered through the rear tent flap. Their leader held a sword out in front, point down. The other four came straight at Marcus. Each one grabbed one of his legs and arms, pinning the arms behind him in strong grips and lifted him off the floor of the tent. He could feel more than see the others in the tent turn his way. He stiffened, but their tighter clasps and the swordsman within an arm's length from him forced him to not struggle.

When hoisted off the ground so that his head was still above his feet but his body suspended helplessly, the Legate said, "One more chance, young Marcus. Have you told us the truth?"

Marcus swallowed and blurted, "Yes, yes, *Optime*. I have not seen my brother, know nothing of any gold."

"Then open your mouth and roll out your tongue."

Marcus had heard of this hot metal test for truth, but never seen it used. He obeyed and closed his eyes, held his breath—and wished he might lose consciousness.

He felt the heat of the sword approach his face then settle flat end on his tongue, heard and smelled his saliva sizzle, and willed his mouth produce more and more, and more. He stretched open his mouth to keep his lips and teeth off the thing. His jaw ached from the strain. He was not sure about other pain, whether his skin and mouth and tongue wanted to cry out in pain, whether he was already burned too badly to feel the damage.

Then it ended, and the four set him on the ground but held him just as firmly.

He caught Gracchus, an expression of relief on his face and in his shoulders, as if Marcus' tongue had not branded him a liar. "General Apollonius, you have heard and seen. Up or down for this one?"

The old dog-faced Legate raised a gnarled right hand, the two small fingers missing, but the thumb fully intact. He turned the thumb down.

Marcus felt as if lightning had hit through him twice now—the only question, how gruesome the manner of his death? He looked at the great Gracchus who returned the gaze, a glint of regret perhaps, or Marcus wished it. He glanced at Nicator, a sparkle in his eyes.

Gracchus leaned down and whispered something to the Legate that Marcus could not hear. The old one tilted his head from side to side as if to say, I can accept that.

Gracchus rose up to his full height. “General Apollonius is wise and merciful, young Marcus. You do not merit a traitor’s reward. If you had lied, your mouth would have been dry and the sword would have burned much more of a liar’s tongue. Your father is an honored scout. But you are too young for your command, your men. You need to learn to be a leader of men. You need to be able to grow a beard.” Gracchus laughed, then the others.

For the first time in his memory Marcus’ knees trembled, from relief, and he had to force himself to not slump like a sack of rye flour, though the others held him up. And he did grow a beard, but the hair not bristly, not dark, like most of the other men.

Gracchus finished. “The bones—and some of your men—said you are good with animals, that you have tended animals, even cows, all your life. My infantry leader will escort you to your new assignment, young Marcus. You won’t need your horse or long sword. Leave those with him. Nicator will take your place as head scout of your group.” He paused. “Go, get away, before mercy leaves the good General.”

Gracchus flicked the back of his hand at Marcus and the infantry leader, as one would brush a fly off the edge of a silver plate. Legate Apollonius got up and headed for the rear of the tent where a servant held a flap open, followed by the five big soldiers. Marcus looked at Nicator for more than a moment, the smug satisfaction on the face of the now former dog handler, before Nicator turned and followed the others.

Chapter XXIX

Oxen and Venefica

"Here, boy," said the big man to whom Marcus reported the next day. He handed Marcus a shovel and two buckets of wood bound by metal strips. "Yours. Don't break them. You break them, you fix them. The carpenters work all day and night on bigger things."

Marcus, carrying all his gear—sleeping bundle, winter cloak, boots, clothes, satchel with a comb, pick, and small knife, one extra belt—had only one free hand. But the bullock driver did not tell him where to put his belongings, made him try to grab the two big buckets.

He stood a head taller than Marcus, his chest and gut as wide as two men.

When Marcus had packed up, some of the other scouts said Bovis liked to talk, talked too much to anyone who listened. Marcus thought now it was his turn to listen to the oxen leader. He had to listen.

His given name was Brutus, but behind his back everyone called him Bovis.

But none was better with the big beasts. The rumors said Bovis trained each of his charges from when they were calves in the hills above Cannae, said he lifted and carried every calf on his back until each grew into a young bull. From then on, all bullocks did whatever Bovis asked of them, he the dominant male.

Brutus said, "After I get them away from their pens down to water or out to graze, clean out their shit, all of it. Take the dry shit first, and dump it downhill as far as you can carry it. Get so far down hill that you can't see and hear us. No flies, no stink, none in our camp's water. Can't have soldiers puking when they have to march and fight. Understand?"

Marcus nodded. He would take their shit far away and bury it and clean out the bucket.

"If there's no downhill from where we camp, go far away. Stay downstream from any stream or lake. Dig holes and cover them with dirt and cover them again. Keep the buckets clean. Scrub them out with dirt where you have no water. Any place we stay more than one night, you do this. But wait until they are out of their pens and away from you. Strangers too close make them nervous, and when they're nervous they shit more and don't do what they're told. I and my sons and soldiers can go near them. But you keep clear of my beauties. Understand?"

Marcus nodded again. Oxen were sullen beasts as was their lead driver, but that seemed right, reflected how Marcus felt. He would keep clear of them. These oxen, lying in pens behind Brutus, were as big as any he had ever seen. Their horns were not the thick short curled-in kind of a milk cow. Theirs extended far out from the massive heads, the tips sharper than the tip of any spear.

"The last mucker didn't understand." Brutus grinned and wagged the index finger on his right hand. "Tossed rocks at one of them. That one jumped up on the fence, broke it down and chased him. My beauty gored his insides all over, stomped on his insides when he was down." Brutus laughed a snorting laugh out of big nostrils that made Marcus think of oxen. "That's why I've got you now. You had fever?"

Marcus nodded once more.

"Good, then you won't get it for a while. Can you talk?"

"Yes, sir. I can talk. Didn't want to interrupt you, sir." Marcus sounded different in his own head than what he remembered. The fear of what had happened the day before and the whole tongue, lips and upper mouth sore and blistered made him not want to talk and sound strange when he did talk.

Brutus laughed briefly and said, "Good boy. I like a boy who listens. They're teamed up, two on each team even in their pens. The leader of each pair gets nasty around any new animal or man. That's the one to keep an eye on. As for you, they don't know you and they don't like you. Let them see you, smell you, but be nice and quiet. When they get used to you and you bring them their grass and clean out their shit, after a while they'll leave you alone. And keep quiet around them. They hate loud noise unless it's fighting noise."

"Yes, sir. I'll keep quiet."

"They're happiest when pulling a load for a fight. Battle clothes and weapons tell them they are marching out. They like it when the battering rams they pulled all the way smash into the heavy gates, into the wall, like to show off their strength."

Marcus looked over the four temporary pens. Four oxen had gotten up and stood near the gate of each pen, chewing on their second chewing, as if waiting to be taken to water. He thought the pens barely had space for two of them, but the metal posts and rails were heavy enough. He said, "They look like they know it's time for me to get in there and clean out?"

Brutus blew hard out his big nose as he talked. "You catch on good. My sons and I will take them down to water, two at a time. When we're gone, you work."

"Yes, sir." Marcus thought he could do this, had to do this, make the most of it. Their father, Martis Flavius the Elder, had said, *War is never predictable. Men fall, and little men rise to take their places and sometimes to glory—but never the careless ones.* On this day, Marcus felt like all the little men of any army, a careless little man for having let Nicator get the best of him, but with the gladness of a man who had entered the valley of death and come out the other side still among the living.

#

Early on the second night after Marcus joined the oxen crew, Brutus said to everyone in his little group, eight men in all, "Our army has a string of new villages to plunder, new *barbari* to chase down—before they run off or all knife themselves." He laughed, and those around him laughed too, but not Marcus. Dead bodies made no useful bounty.

"Tomorrow before first light, it moves out. The main camp stays here. My beauties come with me tomorrow, gates to smash, they tell me—or at least scare the shit out of the *barbari*. Gets them every time. They see my beauties pulling those rams into place, and then they just drop their rusty little weapons and let us do with them whatever we want."

He and the others laughed again, the laughter turned to cheers. Some of the eight men stood up as they cheered and thrust their hips forward as if into a body.

But Marcus remained sitting, quiet. The *barbari* in this area were too clever to let much of any of that happen to them after that first time.

#

Marcus sat on the ground among the women and men of the supply train across a clear area from the cage. This cage held the worthy ones, the *barbari* women not yet with child, not yet broken, or diseased. They wore plain white robes covering them from neck to ankle. Their hands were tied loosely behind their backs so they might not easily kill or disfigure themselves by smashing their heads into the bars or strangling each other. Some had done that in the first days of their capture.

The area around the cage was quiet, quieter than it had been since they had all landed in Iberia. Most of the laborers and women had left with the army two days before. Marcus, and one of Brutus' sons and one other from their little group had stayed behind to tend the four oxen which remained here. When the whole army was in the camp, many soldiers always crowded near that cage—to look at them and perhaps wish for what might be out there for them some day.

Marcus sat for a long time, thinking, trying to decide whether to approach her and how. There was no rule about talking to prisoners. Just yesterday, Marcus had seen two servants of one of the wealthy old men enter the women's cage, grope one of them and make her strip naked, previewing her for their masters. The other women formed a loose circle protecting against stares from incited strangers, and Marcus could not see much, did not care to. It struck him as sad.

A legate or others of wealth could buy any of them at a good price before the slave merchants came and took them away. Marcus understood that some of these women might repay part of the debt Gracchus owed the old men. But he had no such standing, and was already in enough trouble. His tongue and mouth still hurt, and he had to eat slowly.

Only the Quaestor, the paymaster for the army, had the keys, and guards stood at each corner of the slave women's cage. But Marcus had to talk to her.

He had never before looked for or seen her up close, though he had heard of her upper lip that could not close. In Rome, newborns with this thing disappeared the day of their birth.

There she sat, on the floor in one corner, her legs dangling over the edge. The other women in the cage sat behind her in circles so they all faced inward, and Marcus could see only their backs and hair. They must have let her sit where she wanted—the best place to watch the army camp, to warn the other women if anyone came close.

Marcus thought these women might get a good price at auction in that great city on seven hills, the city which devoured slaves—if the army could keep those now in the cage eating, keep their skin unmarked and their hair shiny.

Crazy young women and men brought the best prices. They could talk more directly to the gods than even the priests. Some in the camp said this one—she said her name was Aunia—was possessed of that kind of madness. Even Gracchus had talked about this one the first time he summoned Marcus. Others said to stay away from her, not ever get close enough to be touched by her breath lest the poisons in her enter the body and lead to a slow and painful death. But everyone said she knew far more than any of the other prisoners about this land, its plants, its animals, its very air. And she talked proudly about the things she knew in a lyrical gibberish.

She shifted so he saw her more clearly. She glanced over at him, pausing as if asking herself who this man staring at her might be. There they were, crooked front teeth eternally exposed in an open hole under long black hair under alert dark eyes, in an otherwise fair face.

He stood up and headed for the nearest guard of the women's cage. "Sir, I was a scout in this army and am now a bullock man."

The guard raised his chin at Marcus, as if to say, *So, why do you tell me this?*

"We need to know something about this land. May I talk to the one sitting in the corner of the cage?"

The guard looked at Marcus hard, then relaxed his face. "I know you. Many know you, and knew *frater* Martis. Ask as you like, but if I whistle, be gone fast." As he talked, the guard pointed at Aunia and at Marcus and back to her, telling her with his hands that she should talk to this Roman. Aunia did not react but did not leave her place at the edge of the cage.

Marcus said, "Thank you, kick me away if anyone notices." He eased over to the cage, and dropped to his haunches. Aunia looked straight at him as he approached. He picked up a stone and made patterns in the dirt to not draw attention.

Not sure how to start, what to call her, whether to use the formal or familiar form of address and speaking, he said, "Ah, I am Marcus Flavius. The guard there said I may ask you about this land, the mountains north from here."

She said in his Roman language, "Ask, ask what you like." It came out, *ash, ash what you like*. But he understood her well enough.

"Not long ago I rode out of your old village into the mountains. I looked for my brother and his men and horses. All, I think, dead."

She listened, followed. Her eyes said she understood.

"I found only his great horse....It...someone brought us his horse. At first I thought ghosts brought his horse to us. Are there ghosts north and west of here?"

Aunia shrugged. "*Animi inferorum.* Spirits of all our dead people, perhaps. But I have never heard tell of ghosts—only in stories to frighten children."

That made Marcus laugh too loudly. Ghost stories were for children. "Yes, yes. Not ghosts. I saw them."

"Did you see them well?"

He whispered, "Yes, saw the younger one well, will not forget her, not ever."

"What did they—she—look like that you would not forget her?"

"The one was fair of skin and face, rode a horse like she was born to it, looked at me without fear, with a knowing of what she must do. Would have taken my head if I had stayed one more heartbeat."

"How old was she, this fair one?"

"Younger than me, I think. Your age perhaps, and very clever. Tricked us and our tracking dogs, so she and the other with her got far away."

Aunia lowered her head, shook her hair from side to side. Then she said to the side, as if to herself, "I knew someone like that once...but she died in the battle for our village. If your army had captured her, she would be the greatest prize in this cage, worth more than a thousand men and women all together." Aunia pulled her legs in, rolled onto her back, stood up and turned away.

Marcus said with all the urgency he could muster, "Wait, please. There is more."

Her back to him, she said, "*Dice quit vis.* What would you like from me?"

"Tell me where they have gone, so I can find her." As Marcus said that last, he knew he wanted to find her for reasons of his own, reasons having nothing to do with Martis, with Gracchus, or the Empire. He said softly, more to himself, "I must find her."

"Marcus Flavius, I can tell you only what I know. Get away now. It is foolish for you to talk to me. No good can come of it. I can't help you find her. The one I knew is surely...dead."

He could not leave, not before he asked one more question. "What is the name of this fair one?"

"Get, get, away...Why should I help you?"

The answer came easily. "Because if she is surely dead, I can call out to her in my dreams. And if she lives and the gods will it," he looked around, "I can protect her from these beasts."

Aunia turned part way to him, so her long hair shielded her mouth from his view. "The one I knew was Lavena. That means joy in our language. Some called her Daughter of Sinorix. Now, go. Or I shall never talk to you again."

Marcus did not understand all of what Aunia had said, the words out of her mouth too strange, but he got her name, that her name meant joy, and that she was the daughter of someone called Sinorix.

He stood up and backed away as if from an order. He said softly so the guard could not hear. "*Habeo gratiam.* Thank you, Aunia." Then, "May I come back if I think of more?"

Her back to him, Aunia stopped and without turning said, "If you must and the guards let you and I am still here. You have kind eyes, young Marcus Flavius."

"Thank you, Aunia. You have helped this oxen herder more than you know."

Marcus left Aunia suddenly more awake and alert than he could remember. He sounded out the name which brought on these feelings.

Chapter XXX

Courage

Lavena left the meeting with Daleninar's nobles alone. Many villagers stood outside that hut. Word traveled fast in this compact village. She felt them study her, this daughter of once-great Sinorix, as if not sure whether to revile or admire her, curious about him, about her.

Through eyes wet from anger and sadness, she looked for what she thought was the path back to the hut where Stena's clan waited.

Before she got there, she heard and felt Stena behind and then next to her. Between gulps of air and half sobs, Lavena said, "You knew…about Father…about this place called Sagunto? Your whole clan knows?"

Stena touched Lavena above the elbow. "Yes, I did, we did. My clan lived in your Village on The Cliff. My man rode and fought with your father, side by side, in Hannibal's army. All the tribes in this region joined with them against the Romans. But the Sagunti were our friends too. My man came home, back to me before the siege of their city and fortress high on the hill behind it."

They walked a little farther. Stena said, "The next spring after Sagunto, Hannibal started his march on Rome over the big mountains named for the she wolf. Your father said the trek over the high mountains would kill them all, and left Hannibal, took home with him all the fighters from this region. When your father came back, he wore those torcs—proudly, and banished us for having left him before he came back. We had to leave, wanted to."

Lavena managed, "Father is—was—not like that. He is kind—was kind—to everyone."

"So we have heard, that age changed him, but not all for the good. Lavena, the young Sinorix would not have made those last treaties with Rome." Stena paused, then, "You are not like your father, not like he was then. We owe you our lives. We will not abandon you, not as long as I lead what's left of my clan."

Lavena did not want to show her weakness and youth from trying to talk through sobs. Only children cried while they talked. She pushed the sobs down and was able to say, "Father could not have taken these torcs from a good man when he lay dying. Did he do that?"

"Lavena, about that, no one but your father knows. Many times I heard tell that we offered the Sagunti an honorable treaty, but they refused. They wanted an alliance with Rome, waited for Rome to save them. We all thought the Romans wanted Sagunto as a foothold to enslave Iberia. We had to take Sagunto before the Romans put their fleets in its harbor and their armies in its fortress. After eight months of war when the town and fortress fell, our men still down there charged in at the lead of Hannibal's army—mad with lust, mad for loot."

Instantly, Lavena wished she had not asked and tried to not hear. But she heard Stena's next words well.

"Your father led them into the fortress on the hill through the breach in that great wall. He went in with nothing round his neck and came out with that torc—the one around your neck now."

Lavena shook her head and squeezed her eyes shut to stop more tears. No part of her had been ready for what Stena and the nobles had said, not ready for failing to carry out her father's last wish before she had even begun.

She touched the torcs on her neck and wrist. No matter what she did with them, no matter what more happened this night and the next day, these torcs, the image of her father racing into the burning homes of the good Sagunti and ripping them off their dying leader, true or not, would stay with her for the rest of her days. The last battle of Sagunto would play out for her every time she thought of him, every time a stranger said his name.

She could say only, "Tomorrow, I will leave, will find the Roman army—and I pray the spirit of Father will guide me."

As she said it, she knew she meant it and would do it. Alone. One young life with the power that comes from nothing, not even good memories, left to lose.

Stena faced Lavena, took her by the shoulders and pulled her close, "Lavena, you have the courage of a mother lion protecting her cubs."

Still holding her, Stena looked around at the huts crowded in on each other, at the silent villagers watching them both. "*This place may not be good for us either* in the coming days."

Stena's words lifted her numbness like a fresh wind clears the heavy mist. That last, this place may not be good for us either, restored her purpose. If the Romans had wanted only ancient revenge on her father, they would be done now, would have stopped there. That army was heading this way or would soon, and this Village on The Hill was no place to wait for it.

Lavena said loudly enough for all those nearby to hear, "Thank you, Stena. If you stay, keep a good eye to the east and make ready to flee again. At first light, I'll ride to a high place where I might see far. I must tell you, tell these villagers," she pointed at them, "what's out there—and then I will go and not come back."

Outside their hut, Stena said, "I will ask Caniné to lead the others away from here. You and I together and one good pack horse will make more trouble for that army than a thousand men." Stena's expression, glowing some in the orange light from the summer sun sinking below the edge of the earth, told Lavena that Stena believed what Stena had said.

That night Lavena did not make her bed with Stena's clan. She spread her pelt roll under the roof overhang on the north side of their hut, the side that had no door or window opening. Stena needed to talk to her clan alone and Lavena needed to sleep alone. But she could not, except in short restless stretches.

Before first hint of light, she found a long thin stone and scraped the ground. Not far down the soil was wet, and it loosened easily. Soon she had cut a deep gash into the ground. She whispered, "Father, are they true, the stories of Sagunto?"

Nearby birds under a thatched roof squabbled over the warmest night perch. Otherwise, the night remained still.

After a long time, she touched the torc around her neck. "Father, true or not, guide me now. Tell me what to do."

She crawled back into her pelts. Still awake or dozing—she did not know which—her father's words, said often when other old men came to their house, welled up. She saw his face and heard his voice as if he sat next to her.

Always, the supply train, the back of the army on the move was the most vulnerable. No one protected the last cart, the last rider behind the last cart. No one guarded the scout farthest out. At night, many mighty strangers were no mightier than one of our riders who knew the terrain. Our horses and riders were better than theirs. Roman soldiers march well, but have never learned to ride in those saddles. Our horsemen struck at the rear, in the night, and the big armies of Rome could not stop us, ever.

#

Early the next day, Daleninar sent one of her fighters to show Lavena the best trail. Daleninar must have received word of what Lavena had planned with Stena on their walk back to the hut, and this village leader was no fool. She wanted to know as soon Lavena knew, sooner, what was out there.

They gained elevation quickly, and before the sun had fully crested, the two saw enough. A dark cloud hung in the cool clear air, hung above billows of smoke pouring up from large fires down below. No camp or hut fires burned like this. No sky god had struck in this area for many days.

The scout said, "Sons and daughters of families from our village started that village down there. I pray they got out and come to us. I pray for our village." He turned his horse and raced back ahead of Lavena.

Stena's women and children were all up waiting to hear what Lavena had seen, what it meant, and what Lavena would do.

Lavena's telling did not take long.

Stena and the others seemed ready for bad tidings, ready to run again. Calmly, Stena said, "Lavena, wherever you go, I will come with you. Caniné is proud to lead my clan to the west—or, if they must, to stand and fight."

Lavena looked over at tall, beautiful Caniné, whose expression said she would do it, and do it well.

Stena continued, "She can lead them to a safer place—or until they have crossed over." Stena must have caught Lavena's expression. "Don't be troubled, we'll all cross over, we'll all meet again, I'll see my whole clan again over there, and see you too, in time."

Lavena said, "Thank you, but…you don't have to. I can go alone from here—." Then she smiled a smile of gratitude and the boldness of youth. By that smile she meant to tell Stena that the two of them together had to be reckoned with.

This time Lavena and Stena packed Roman helmets and leather coats stripped from the dead Roman scouts. Several sets fit each of them well enough, and they took the ones that had the fewest tears, the fewest blood stains. They selected the best of the Roman horses, and the best of the Roman bits and bridles and saddles. Their pack horse was one of the two Roman pack horses brought into their valley. They each carried a Roman sword and scabbard but rode bareback—easier to run or fight not crowded into a four-posted saddle. The pack horse carried two Roman saddles.

While Stena and Lavena loaded up, Daleninar stayed close, as if checking to make sure Lavena did leave, but to help if Lavena should need something the village could give her. Lavena asked her for a shovel. A young boy brought one quickly.

Lavena said, "We'll ride out on the same trail as your man showed me. If the army keeps coming this way, we will not return. Then I pray that your nobles were right and Rome, or whoever leads this thing, this Gracchus they spoke of at our village gate, means you no harm." She said it as if she did not believe her prayer would be answered.

Daleninar caught her meaning. "Yesterday after you left, my nobles told me again and more about the great wars of back then, of fifty thousand on each side, ten thousand horses and riders in the armies of Hannibal, told me of the Romans who came to our land and chased Hannibal's brothers off. But in the end, the Romans were far worse to us than Hannibal and his army out of Carthage."

She looked back at her village, at its wall. "My village will not withstand an assault from one of those monster Roman armies. My walls will crack open at one strike from rams you said hit into the main gates of your village. We'll set as many traps as time allows but be gone before they get here."

Stena said, "Where will you go?"

"To the west and north. My father's brother and his family settled there. They'll take us in. Together, we are stronger. And we'll take your women and children with us," said Daleninar.

Stena said, "I thank you, but I must go with this young one." And the three of them smiled.

Lavena said, "Don't let them see your torc, any of the gold of your nobles. This army comes for our gold above all else. It will stay and chase you for all time if it thinks you have gold."

Lavena again touched the torc around her neck under her outer cloak and the torcs on each of her wrists. This time, more than any time since she had first held them, she felt their weight, far greater than the eye expected. Now as never before, she wondered about what she would do with these pieces in the next fight against Romans. She took them off and put them in her pouch then tied the pouch onto the cord around her bed roll.

Daleninar said, "Romans have not changed in a hundred years, more. Rome fights for bounty. There is none better than gold."

Everyone in Stena's clan—and some of the village nobles and their families—sent them off. The clan children hugged them before they mounted up, but none of the children looked them in the face. They kept their heads turned away or down, their eyes too wet to look at Stena and Lavena. But not one child or adult cried out loud.

Caniné said, "Our gods go with you and with us. May we meet again soon in this life—or in the next if the gods will it. After the Romans leave our land, let us gather in our valley in the mountain. It was a good home, and perhaps will be again."

Stena said, "Yes, our valley. We'll meet there. First, we have to kick the Romans off our land."

Stena raised her right hand and looked in Daleninar's direction, several of her nobles with her. Stena turned to Lavena, who stood by her horse ready to mount up. Stena, hand still raised, signaled for all around them to listen.

Then she said loudly, "Lavena, this time I must ask you where you are taking me. What will you do when we get there? That army is not one of the great Roman armies, but still strong, with many riders and thousands of fighters."

Lavena felt the power Stena had bestowed on her, the leadership Stena had given her. Daleninar and the nobles leaned in to hear her, no longer looked at her like the child of a killing thief. The answer came easily. What her father had said about the old wars with big armies had started her plan. Something Stena and Daleninar had said about the big armies of back then locked it in.

She pulled herself up onto her horse's wide back. Then, looking down at all those assembled, she said, "We'll find them. Then we'll watch them from far away. When the time is right and the terrain allows, we'll come up close to them at day's end. From there, the gods and the spirits of those who fought for this land before us will tell us what to do."

Lavena turned her horse out. Stena and one pack horse followed—to find and challenge the army of Gracchus.

Chapter XXXI

First Strikes

They started on the same trail Daleninar's fighter had shown Lavena at dawn, from where they could see far to the east and south of the village. The smoke of early morning still hung over the land to the east.

By late morning, the trail had reached lower ground. Here it wound through or around outcroppings of rocks and big stands of giant oaks and fir trees. These hid them—but might hide from them advance riders of the Roman army.

In these forests, Lavena and Stena slowed to watch and listen. Whenever they emerged from deep shade, they stopped at the edge and then crept out to let their eyes try to catch anyone coming at them out of a bright sun.

Near the end of a large stand of oaks, Lavena's horse lifted its head and picked up its gait. She pulled on the reins and headed it to a massive oak trunk. That trunk might shield them from whatever had excited her mount. The horse obeyed and picked its way over the roots spread like giant fingers out from the base under uncounted years of fallen leaves. Stena, pulling the pack horse, followed.

As Lavena came around the trunk still in that tree's deep shade, less than a hundred paces directly in front of them, a lone rider appeared as if floating on top of the tall grass. He sat in a Roman four-post saddle on a fine mount of the same kind as Roman Horse—facing the trees.

They stopped. Lavena hoped they might blend into the deep shade, that he had not seen or heard them, but all too late. He lifted up as high as he could and peered at them, turned his upper body away and whistled, then yelled what sounded to Lavena like, "Over here. *Veni! Celeriter!* Come fast!"

Lavena instantly understood. This rider carried no long sword or heavy pike, no shield or bow, only a short sword. A horn was slung over his shoulder. A leather helmet sat on his head, but no breastplate or chain mail on his chest. He had not dressed to fight, but to ride fast and alone.

His was to scout the land ahead of the advancing army. This stand of oaks made a good place for fighters to hide, strike the passing army and retreat deep into the forest. Her father's lessons had been learned by the Romans too.

Stena moved up next to Lavena, and they waited, too close to run from him on that big horse, too soon to know what to do.

In what seemed like a short moment, the rider's whistle and shout brought another rider. The two men talked and stared. Both their horses pressed toward Lavena and Stena, but the riders would not let them move up. Lavena thought these two had no idea of how many armed men lurked in this forest.

The riders kept enough distance to turn and gallop away. The first one swung his horse to the right and rode along the edge of the forest plainly looking for others or any sign of a trap.

Stena whispered, "Lavena, we must do something and do it now."

"Not yet. Let them find that it's just you and me and our pack horse. Then watch me."

The second rider swung back, passed where they waited, rode down along the left edge of the forest, and returned to the first rider. The two talked in low tones, still uneasy, still not sure. The second rider pulled his horn around from behind him, rested both hands on it, thinking, talking in low tones to the other.

Lavena said, "Now, I go." She knew what she could not let happen. One or two horn blasts, and half the army would chase up here, surround them and run them down to a quick and brutal end.

She jumped off her horse and handed the reins to Stena. "Tie this one and the pack horse up—stay close, and with the long sword make ready for two stinking Romans."

She shifted her falcata further behind her left side—out of their sight but where she could reach it easily—and walked straight at the riders. She loosened her top and let it fall down her shoulders and off her arms. She untied the cord that held up her cotton trousers, heavy and loose enough that they slid down her legs as she walked. She stepped out of them.

In bright sunlight, she walked first in the stubble of grass at the edge of the forest, then swish, swishing through higher grass. Except for her boots and the leather belt on her hips, she was naked.

As she moved closer to the big horses and the peering silent riders, she measured the distances to them and back. She had to get close enough that they could not help but stare and soon yield to the urge welling up in them. But she had to stay far enough away that she had time to get into the trees. Where she did stop, the grass came no higher than the tops of her knees.

The Roman holding the signal horn never raised it. The other no longer looked into the forest. Both locked on her.

Lavena heard the words at that first falcata lesson many days back, heard the naked she-warrior telling secrets to the chosen girls, as if an echo from distant mountains, but every word clear. *They don't know she-warriors. When it happens, and it will, you'll have the first strike. Make it count.*

Close, as if once again in front of and above making her squint into the rising sun behind the she-warrior, Lavena saw the instructor pointing to the parts of her own body, the parts that these two stared at now.

The words, the memory brought a calm and a knowing of what to do and when. Lavena shook her head from side to side and around. Her hair had not been cut in many months, and for an instant the dark reddish waves blurred her vision. When she stopped, the stares of the two Romans had hardened, and their heads, their hands, even their horses did not move. She knew she had them.

She stuck both thumbs into the falcata belt, slowly shifted her weight from side to side to make her hips call out their invitation. She looked at the face of the first rider, then the second, then back to the first, the whole time her head slightly bowed as if both excited for and frightened by what was to come.

The riders licked their lips, and rose higher in their saddles pushing up on the front saddle posts, making ready to charge or jump off and run at her.

She felt their gazes, where they paused and where they remained fixed. She kept swaying, waiting for the men to cross over to the place where the urge to mate overpowers all thought, floods all caution, where their bodies leave them blind to every thing but one.

The first rider yelled, "*Heus! Eia!...*" and more that she could not understand. He jumped down and handed the reins to the other. That second rider slapped the reins away, and he too jumped off his horse.

Lavena turned away from them and crouched down. When the grass hid her lower body, she pulled out her falcata. Holding it low in front of her where they might not easily see it, she bounded up and raced at the largest oak.

She heard the foot beats and glanced back to see the men fling away their leather caps, toss aside their signal horns and tear off their gloves. Their yells, their feet hitting the grass gained on her.

Before they reached her, she passed the left side of that massive oak's trunk—and Stena standing behind it, long sword raised over her right shoulder.

Three steps past Stena, Lavena stopped and turned to face the chasing men again, stood there beckoning, this time no grass covering any of her.

The Roman in front had enough warning to jerk up his arm in a reflex to protect his face as he lurched forward and then tried to stop on the slippery leaves. He could not.

Stena's blade whistled, sliced off his upraised hand and caught his head above the nose and across the eyes. His legs leaped out ahead, the rest of him jolted to a stop by the blow that cleaved deep into his head. As he fell, Stena yanked out her sword readying for the next one.

The first scout slammed flat onto his back. He uttered no sound. Only his body fluffing onto the carpet of fallen oak leaves reported his sudden end. The impact threw up dry leaves around him that settled to partly cover the jerking, blood-pulsing carcass of a man dying.

Lavena watched it all, and it did not unsettle her. Before the last tossed-up leaf settled, she slipped to her left around the trunk just as the second Roman passed on the other side. That one, two steps behind the first, managed to stop before Stena's second strike. That one had time to pull his short sword.

That second scout, fixed on Stena, never turned to look for Lavena. Or he had forgotten, or thought a naked girl ducking behind Stena and the big tree for protection could be no threat.

This time was easier. Lavena did not have to study where to strike, or wait for the right moment. From around the tree she came up behind him, grabbed his thick black hair and jerked back his head, as her falcata blade found his throat.

She and Stena did not pause, not even to make sure the two were truly dead. If they were not, they would be soon.

Lavena quickly rubbed her hands and arms in oak leaves, rubbed clean leaves on her chest and belly covered in blood, until most traces were gone. Then she ran to gather her garments and put them on as fast as she could.

Stena wiped her sword with leaves. "I thank the metal worker who made this beauty. In the old days our sword makers were better than those of Rome. We must hurry now." She said more softly, "But...I have not done that since before you came out of your mother." And she smiled as if deeply pleased.

Lavena thought Stena looked at her for the first time with eyes that had the color of the sharpened sword she had just used—and the unblinking steadiness of the eyes of the wolf. And Lavena was comforted. She would need that from Stena in the days to come and for however many days they survived.

Stena brought up their two horses, leaving the pack horse tied in the trees.

Lavena mounted and looked out over the land. She saw only rolling grass, here and there mounds of rocks, small stands of trees, and in the far distance the tree line along a stream.

As they approached the scout horses waiting for their men, Lavena said, "We must tie them and take what we want from the pouches...."

She stopped twenty paces from the closer horse. "Stena, Stena, this one is my Roman Horse. I would have known at first sight, but only saw his rider."

As she approached, the big stallion snorted softly and did not back up. He let Lavena pat his head and cheek, let her take his reins. "He knows me, my voice, see?"

Stena said, "Lavena, we have work to do, must cover the bodies away from the horses. You cannot take him. Too many will know him, and you don't look like his last rider."

For an instant Lavena wanted to find a way to keep the great stallion, but then said, "We'll tie them so when they pull hard, they'll be free." She did not need to say that tied up horses make easy prey for the bear and wolf in the night.

They dragged the two bodies by their feet into the forest, stopping at the edge of a gully. They stripped and tossed the bodies down there, and pushed leaves onto them as best they could from above, but they could not do that well. Lavena said, "We can't cover them from up here and have no more time." She wished vultures and other animals would find these bodies before other Romans found them.

They kept the outer garments. They were made of heavy wool, and the boots, gloves and caps of good leather, though bloodied badly.

Ready to mount up again and leave this oak forest for good, Lavena said, “When those two don’t answer the signal horns from the other stinking Romans near here, there’ll be more. It’s time we look like them.”

Both women quickly put on other Roman shirts and leather coats and leather hats they had taken from Stena’s valley, and placed the Roman saddles brought by their pack horse onto their own mounts. Lavena tucked her hair under her shirt.

Stena touched her helmet and cloak, her saddle, and her horse’s head. “I’ll pass for an old Roman horse fighter. I might remember enough how to talk to them…”

Lavena said, “I have had many lessons in their language. You can talk to me in Roman, if you like.”

Stena looked up and down Lavena now also in Roman garb, sitting in a Roman saddle on a Roman horse. “Ah, Lavena, you will make a good young Roman apprentice horseman. Now, let us get closer to our army.”

Chapter XXXII

Getting Closer

In the far distance, single Roman riders, other scouts perhaps, seemed to glide over the grass and were soon followed by ten or so clusters of armed riders. They all headed to the Village on The Hill. Lavena could count each horse and rider, but they were too far off for her to see faces or weapons.

That eased the buzzing tension in every part of her. If she could not make out details about them, they likely could not about her and Stena and their pack horse.

The single riders rode big horses that looked strong and fast, as if out of the same stock as her Roman Horse. The clusters of riders, each of eight men on small short-legged ponies, rode single file sometimes only their heads and long pikes showing over the tall grass.

She thought some of them looked her way and she tried to keep facing straight ahead as if she did not care. But not one veered at them, not one waved at or shouted out to them. She thought, she prayed, that two old soldiers taking a pack horse back to the main army would cause none of them to be curious, not curious enough to divert from the larger prize—the Village on The Hill and other villages beyond.

Stena and she kept their distance, far enough that they could ride off and likely not be caught before they again reached higher ground and sheltering trees. Yet, she still felt the same stark terror of that early morning on the walkway of her village wall before the battle started. If she and Stena did have to flee, they could not keep the pack horse with them.

A new sound welled up behind the distant riders, a deep constant roar as if the land out there readied to shake. Instantly, she felt the same clenching of her insides as on that same morning, when swaths of the ground seemed to lift and move at her village.

She knew this sound, made by many men tromping, breathing hard and talking loudly, many heavy wheels turning behind animals pulling heavy carts. A moment later, the first dark line of the infantry broke out of green grass against the bright blue sky.

She and Stena could not help but stop and watch.

In daylight and from far away, this mass did not seem as menacing as it had out of the misty darkness on that other morning. It ground forward flattening the grasses, slithering around lonely clumps of trees and scattered clusters of rocks. The men on foot seemed to trot on the flat or downhill. On uphill stretches they slowed to a fast march.

Behind the foot soldiers, more riders sat high in saddles, or in many carts pulled by mules and old plodding horses. Next came the most massive beasts—two pair of oxen pulling the two giant carts carrying battering rams. More horsemen rode next to and behind these beasts and their burdens.

Behind the oxen, trudged unarmed men and women, sometimes resting then trotting to keep up. Many pulled hand carts or poles carrying bundles, their ends dragging on the ground behind. A few staggered under big loads on their shoulders.

Straggling horsemen, some pulling bigger carts, followed the men and women on foot. A slow line of armed riders swept up last. The last rider was not alone. This army would not be so easy to attack from the rear.

When the army had passed, Stena said, "From that far away we look like good Romans. I think when the light is right, we can get closer. "

"I'm not sure if that was courage or foolishness."

"What, Lavena?"

"Us, down here, so close. We might wear Roman clothes, but our spirits surely give us away to anyone who watches us. Stena, take us to where we can see them from far off, where they cannot see us."

"Did your Father ever tell you that he had seven thousand fighting men all under his command back then?"

"No, why? Did he?"

"Yes, and more from regions near here."

Lavena got it. "Stena, I think it might have been easier for him to menace an army in strange terrain than for the two of us."

Stena smiled the same smile as after slaying the scout. "But you forget, we are Romans now, and Romans can get close to other Romans."

"Stop that talk." Lavena returned the smile. "It will only take one of them to see that we don't sit in these hard saddles like Romans, that our pelt rolls are not like theirs. From now on, we stay away until the sun falls under the land."

Lavena forced strength into her voice, much more strength than she felt. "In darkness, we'll get close to the baggage train or whatever we decide to strike."

They veered off to the north, ever looking over their shoulders, but saw no one heading their way.

When they were well out of sight of any in the army, Lavena said, "That stinking mass does not look out for any of our people bent on revenge. It thinks any of us still alive have run."

"Lavena, you are older than your years in this life. But how can you know what that stinking mass is thinking about our people?"

"If I had been a scout ahead of that army, I would have ridden at us."

Stena said. "You forget our one great advantage. We, you and I, look like two of their riders and a pack horse."

Lavena said, "Soon they'll find the bodies in the oak forest back there. Then they'll chase every strange rider. May our gods help us then."

After the sun had begun its downward path and the whole army had long passed, the sound of pounding hoofs from the direction of the Village on the Hill came closer and closer.

Three men on big horses cantered at them. Each carried a bow across his back, wore a metal helmet, and a flowing cloak striped in reds and yellows, not much different that the warriors of Lavena's village. A pelt roll was tied to each of the horses. These three meant to be gone from their village for a while.

They shouted happily and waved as they rode up. The lead rider said, "Daleninar sent us, told us you might be wearing Roman garb. No Roman should be up here riding away from the army. Had to be you two."

Stena said, "You leave your women and children to find us when that monster closes on your homes? Why is that?"

The lead rider said, "Daleninar ordered us to find you before the Romans do."

These three were too brash, too loud, and their cloaks stood out against green trees, green grass and blue sky more brightly than fire. These three could not help them. Lavena said, "Romans have already found us, talked to us in their way. Its army has already seen us and left us alone. Go back now. Daleninar will need you more than we do."

The lead rider peered at her then up at the sky, as if he wanted to say, *keep quiet, young girl, if you know what's good for you.* "You tell lies again. You will need us far more than the three of us need you."

Stena rode up to him, put her face close to his. "Lavena does not tell lies. Now leave before we chase you off."

The lead rider's horse backed up, but he was not ready to go back. "Romans already found you, talked to you? How can that be—that they let you ride away?"

Lavena said, "We were the last thing those two stinking Romans will ever find. Bring us a thousand like you or let us do what we must alone. Get away from us and give your leader our thanks."

This time, the lead rider looked around, as if he had a wide audience, as if to say that Lavena could not be talking to him with such lack of respect. "Five are better than two, better than one old woman and a young girl who does not honor her elders."

Lavena stared at him as if she might want to kill him too.

He went on, "You will need us now and in days to come. We know places for shelter and food when cold winds and snow of winter arrive—if you live until winter."

Lavena had not until this moment thought of what to do or where to go when the summer left and cold rain fell, when their dried food was all eaten, when icy streams gave up none of their fish.

Stena scoffed. "I know every wild berry bush from here to the endless sea, every place where the deer gather to mate before winter, and every river where the fish run in all seasons. Go back. Help where you are needed."

The lead rider and the two with him circled Lavena and Stena. Then he said, "What of the stinking Romans you say already found you? We saw horses tied up in the oak forest. We passed far around them…That was them, yes?"

Stena said, "This one, this girl, lured them to us—I took the head of the first one. She took the throat of the other."

Stena jumped off her horse and reached into the top-most bundle on the pack horse. She pulled out a blood soaked woolen top and then another. She tossed both at the one who had been talking. "Their blood is wet and stinks of those two Romans."

The one who had been talking pushed back against the garments letting them drop next to his horse. His horse snorted and backed up. He got off and handed them to Stena, then turned to Lavena still on her horse. "Ahh…Forgive me for doubting you, daughter of Sinorix. Everyone in our village talks about how you saved this old woman's clan—but not everyone believes you did that." He rubbed his moist hands into the dirt. "But the blood on my hands is true."

Stena said, "It's all true. Lavena is right. We have no use for you."

The lead rider bowed. "Forgive us, our rudeness. I am Tultas The Younger. These are Caciro and Habo. We would have found you sooner but had to let the whole army pass."

Lavena said, "Yes, in those cloaks Romans can see you from a half day's ride. Your mothers and fathers and children want you to come back to them. Stay with us and none of us will last this day."

Tultas must have caught the many insults. Head bowed still, he said, "Our whole village is making ready to leave. If we stand and fight we'll fare worse than your father's village. Daleninar sent us to fight with you because…we three do not have wives or sons and daughters."

Stena said, "Then go back and help them flee. Ride at the rear behind the old men and women who cannot keep up."

Tultas, all arrogance gone, said, "Let us ride with you." He looked down at the ground then at the two women. "You two are the only fighters with any courage in the whole region."

Stena pointed at Lavena, saying with her face and hands that if Lavena wanted them, it was all right that Tultas and the other two rode with them for a while.

These three, their brashness, their lean arms and legs reminded Lavena of Sinorix the Younger and her two younger half brothers. Thoughts of how they might help tumbled in, but only if they did as she asked, if they did not behave like untrained friendly dogs.

She said, "We have extra plain clothes. You are no good to us looking like giant squawking red and yellow birds. Put up your bows and arrows on our pack horse. Romans don't carry theirs like that, and if they spot you before we are ready, you best not look like fighters."

Tultas said, "Yes. You say the truth."

They shed their cloaks for plain leather coats and hats Stena retrieved from the pack horse. The smallest of them put on the clothes Lavena had worn earlier that day, though the women did not tell him who had worn them last and when.

Lavena watched them closely, how they moved. These three did not wear the gold of powerful warriors, but they jumped off and on their horses with ease, handled their bows and arrows as if they knew how to use them. The smooth bows and straight arrows with shiny metal tips looked to have been forged by the best arms makers. She nodded at Stena. These three might help after all.

The five rode in a wide circle to keep behind and follow the Roman army from the rear, far enough back to feel safe.

At a place where the two women were separated some from the other three, Lavena said quietly so only Stena could hear, "Father's last wish…it might start with these three young pups sent by Daleninar."

Stena said, "Sometimes courage spreads faster than fear—and it is always stronger."

Darkness allowed Lavena's group to move up closer, stopping on a low ridge behind the army. The ridge could not be climbed easily by anyone coming at them from the west, and they had a good view to the east, from where the army had come.

It settled for the night on an open plain, easy to see but hard—impossible—to approach without a thousand eyes spotting them before they could get close.

The supply train camped closest to Lavena's group. This hive of men and women pitched different colored and sized tents in a disorganized jumble. Laughter burst out often and loudly, mixed with yelled commands and shouts of surprise or anger. Here and there, women raised their voices in protest and sometimes screamed. No scream lasted long.

Dogs barked and horses neighed. Beyond the tents, many mules gathered inside a circle of carts.

Beyond the supply train and the circle of carts, soldiers and riders pitched their tent villages in straight rows. The riders all headed to a place somewhere beyond the soldiers' tents, where the army's many horses must have collected.

The two battering rams floated above the men and women in the camp, floated like big gods resting. From their location lying on their giant carts protected deep inside the camp,

Lavena thought the Romans prized their battering rams more than they valued people.

Once or twice she heard the lowing of big bovines but could not see them.

Dark unarmed men, watched over by armed footmen and dogs, dug holes around the perimeter. Lavena could not tell if they were traps or waste holes, or both. Soon many approached the fresh holes where armed men stood guard. The trap holes needed no guards, and Lavena understood the only safe way to enter the camp was on the paths taken by many.

Fires started up, and a haze of smoke, and dust soon blurred every part of the army and the stars rising above the sleeping sun. Dogs and sentries on foot and horse peered into the growing darkness from the edge of the baggage train.

Clusters of riders continued coming into the camp, the last riders and horses appearing more like faint shadows against the smoky black sky. All the riders headed to the far side of the army camp. With them came a new thought. She said to her group, "Stena, ride there with me. You others, stay here, watch us. If we get surrounded, make noise as you never have and run. After we escape we'll find you. If we don't find you tonight, look for us west of your village or following this monster."

Tultas uttered a sound, the start of a protest, but Stena cut him off and pointed at the eastern sky. "We'll do as she says. You'll do as she says, or get away from us. We were good Romans today and will be better ones under that rising moon."

The two rode down to below the camp on grass the army had trampled flat. They rode at a walking gait, holding the reins loosely. Their horses, heads low from fatigue of a long day, moved as if anxious to come into camp.

They closed to within about a hundred and fifty walking paces of the camp, heading to the far side, letting the horses pick their way and not stumble. Soon their horses wanted to turn into the camp and all the other gathered horses.

Lavena silently gave thanks that they had used the hard Roman bits. Without that barbed and ugly metal in their soft mouths, heel taps and hand slaps might not have been enough to keep these Roman horses from riding straight into this camp with her on her horse's back.

At the far end, hundreds of horses were tied in rows, and from the light of many fires Lavena saw why the army had camped here. The terrain dropped off into a darker line of trees and bushes marking a stream. Men relayed buckets of water from that stream up to the camp.

Here sentries and dogs on leashes pointed in their direction, many more sentries and dogs than Lavena had expected. She, in the lead, did not slow, but made her horse veer off as if also headed down to the stream. The sentries turned away. The dogs kept looking, heads high, but did not growl or pull toward them.

She rode down a short way and then to her right along the line of trees and bushes. Out of sight of the camp and the glow of its many fires, she let her horse pick its way to water. The moon was not yet high up, and Lavena saw only layers of darkness, the bushes and trees darker than the flat land. She and Stena let their horses drink their fill.

They rode back up toward the many fire lights of the camp, but before getting too close, headed away in a big circle to where she and Stena had left the three young fighters.

As they ate their evening meal of dried meat and turnips, Lavena said to her group, "We know enough for this night. Soon we will know where and how to wound that army."

She did not tell them that she had not one thought about how or where they might menace this mighty army, guarded well by trap holes, sentries, dogs and, most of all, by the many eyes in that army. The first strike against those alert and ready men and animals might be her last.

Chapter XXXIII

Hollow Bounty

On the evening of their second day following it, the army camped in the flat land below the Village on The Hill. Its men, horses, carts and tents formed a ring around all the houses outside the walled village.

Tultas said, "My village looks small now. In the morning, when those beasts attack, I must get where I can see. I pray for… them." Tultas stood watch that night.

The army broke camp before first light. Lavena's group crept closer from behind the hindmost Roman rider behind the hindmost straggler in the supply train. Tultas rode last, searching for any Romans who might sweep up behind them.

Lavena, all of them, looked to the rear often. The sun, rising behind Lavena's group, would soon make seeing anyone from behind all the harder. They turned north to higher ground in tall grass for a safer place from which to watch, and set their horses pointing in every direction.

Lavena said to the three new men, "I too pray that Daleninar has taken everyone far away." She did not need to say that this was no time to attack—five lightly armed riders against hundreds of ready riders and thousands of men. She did not dare say more. The crushing might of the army lying before her again left only the urge to watch as one might watch a giant snake—or the urge to flee far and fast.

The infantry formed up in its tight rectangles protected on all sides by curved shields.

As the front of the army neared the village, scattered screams broke out loudly enough to carry to Lavena's group. Soldiers had fallen into the new traps to impale themselves on sharp pikes. The screams were snuffed out almost as soon as uttered.

From then on, the army crept up more slowly, whole sections stopping, waiting, before moving up through the houses outside the wall and then closer to the base of the wall itself.

Again the oxen-drawn carts carrying the battering rams rolled in last behind the footmen, and lined up so they pointed directly at the main gate. This village had only one large gate in its walls, and both rams pointed their metal encased points at it side-by-side.

Lavena held a special hatred for those rams. Once in place with the oxen and many strong men pushing from behind under a canopy of wet boards, no hot sand, no fire dumped on them had bothered those metal-tipped tree trunks. She knew that their great weight, though rolling no faster than a walking man or ox, easily splintered the gates of her village on the first impact. Without them, those gates might have stayed shut days longer.

As before, Lavena saw a lead horseman ride up to the main gate.

This time, no one responded to whatever he shouted out. No fighters stood and stared out from the top of the wall. No fires for the defenders to heat water and sand or set alight arrow tips smoked up the morning. Not one villager waited.

The oxen had lugged the battering rams for days to no purpose. The main gate swung open as if unlatched, and the army poured through like predator ants into termite hill openings.

The men and horses could not squeeze through all at once, could not all fit into the village. The hundreds or thousands not able to enter started a kind of yelling Lavena had not heard—pent up energy released, anger unsatisfied, mixed with bewilderment.

The tight rectangles of men dissolved into shapeless throngs—roiling, racing around and through the outlying huts. Sounds of battle—metal on metal mixed with cries of pain or anger, Romans against Romans—from the area of the main gate reached Lavena's group, as those outside the village tried to get in and those inside tried to get out.

Tultas had stared silently since the first whispers of dawn. Now he said, "Daleninar always does what she says. Her father was like that. Everyone of my village has left—and I can breathe again. My brothers and sisters, their mates and children, my father and mother will live one more day."

Lavena pushed against thoughts of her own family. "And we must find a safer place. Now the beasts will scatter searching for locals, for animals to eat. And they'll ride and run with a new anger that your village and houses outside the walls held nothing for them."

Tultas said, "I pray they don't set our home to the torch."

The group rode farther away out of easy sight or reach of any searching Romans. But they did not go far enough. By midmorning, new smoke billowed out of houses around the outside of the wall and then from the center of The Village on The Hill. Whatever the plans of this army, it left no structure for any locals—for anyone—to soon live in again.

Late in the day, Lavena's group found a place behind rocks and thorn bushes to watch the army collect up for the night. It took longer to settle than on other nights, reminding Lavena of the first night after her village fell. Laborers and riders straggled into the camp until all light had left the sky.

Hard shouts of angry men, screams of frustration, energy pent up, mixed with cheering reached Lavena's group. The cheers sounded as from men watching other men fight over insults or for sport.

Her group shared a small meal of dried meat, hard bread and water. They dared not build any fire. Lavena said, "This is no night to go down there. The wasps are still out with nothing to do, no cause to obey any command, or even spend the night in this camp. They've been out searching for anything and anyone left behind, and some will search the night through."

Tultas said, "If I'm not here when the sun comes up, don't look for me."

The other two men said, almost as if with one voice, "If Tultas leaves, I'm going with him. I'd rather cross over than listen to those monsters... after what they've done to my village."

Lavena said, "Tultas, I pray your people have fled far from here and Daleninar's uncle commands many fighting men. Better you live to help them than end this life running at that army."

"And you, daughter of Sinorix, what are you going to do against that army now?"

She said, meaning it, "I do not know, but I know we must have patience."

After eating, they moved away into a forest of pine trees, far from the noisy men and to a place less likely that any Roman stragglers might stumble on them. They unburdened the six horses, let them drink out of a small stream, hobbled the horses' front feet and unrolled their pelts. Lavena said, "Stena and I will stand up this night. You men can sleep."

Tultas said in his deepest voice, "We sleep best when not sleeping alone."

He still did not accept her leading him and the others, looked at her like Sigilo and the Roman scouts in the oak stand three days back. She did not want this, not here, not now, not with him. She said, "In my time in my Father's village and in times before him, women chose their mates, and men honored the choices made. I think Daleninar's men honor their women too."

Stena said, "Tultas, it has always been so between our men and women. Surely, you know this. We are not like Romans, who treat all women as whores—powerless, with no right to choose."

Tultas kept quiet. After a time, Caciro responded, "Tultas means you no dishonor. What we have seen in the last days has made us all mad."

That ended the talk, but Lavena knew Stena could not constantly protect her, that the same urge to mate rose up in Caciro and Habo. Most nights Stena slept so soundly that a few muffled noises, even screams might not wake her.

Once again, Lavena held her falcata so that anyone who came at her while she slept could not easily find and pin that hand.

Late in the night, she thought of her half brothers, then of Turibas, and started to weep for them all. She thought of the scouts who searched out and destroyed Stena's clan, and prayed that the little farms and hamlets west of The Village on The Hill all lay empty.

In time, the many stars between gaps in the trees calmed her and eased her sorrow.

#

In the morning they found a place farther away than the day before, from where they could still see most of the village and the mass movements around it. The army did not break camp, did not take down the tents or hitch the mules and oxen. Instead, groups of riders, mule-drawn carts and men on foot headed west and south past the scarred and burning village. At least one group came north into the higher ground—closer to them.

Stena spoke first, "We leave now. They will look here and beyond. Must not let them get close to us."

Lavena said, "Tultas, take your men ahead of us. Stena and I are good Romans and will follow behind you. If you hear anyone come up on us, place your hands behind you as if you were our prisoners."

#

At first light on each of the next seven days, riders, carts and infantry headed out of the army camp next to the burned out Village on The Hill, and returned before full darkness.

Lavena's group matched their movements, riding into the wooded hills far from the village camp every morning when the sun might reveal them and easing back closer when the shadows grew long. They never made a fire, never rested for the night where they had stopped to eat.

Tultas usually led on the rides in closer to the army and to his village. He said he had to know first if the soldiers brought back any of his people. Sometimes Lavena's group could see what they brought back—a cow or pig here and there, horses with no rider, but never any prisoners.

Each morning, fresh fires sent up smoke that blotted the otherwise clear sky to the west and south. Every structure within two day's ride must have been set to the torch.

Killing the scouts in the valley of Stena's clan and taking out the two advance riders in the forest had been so easy. A naked she-warrior might have the first strike against one or two unprepared beasts invading her land, but a naked she-warrior against a ready army of thousands would not survive one long moment.

The men and dogs, their many eyes, ears and snouts, their clusters of riders and infantry extending out from the camp protected each of them better than any massive wall. She remembered Romans from their main camp near her village stealing what they had no right to take, killing the old farmer trying to loosen the soil and others she had not seen but heard about.

She had suffered that her father had done nothing to reclaim, to avenge, and silently raged against his own shame. But she understood it all now.

She said to her group, "They use your village hill as a base to take everything from all the land around, take from it whatever they can, and burn what they cannot take away."

She paused, and they waited for her to finish. "I never heard Father say what to do about a Roman army camped like this, down there protected by more than walls, protected by each other."

She pointed at their six horses unburdened for the night and foraging on grass and low bushes at the edge of the trees. "Our horses are getting restless from the idleness. Stena's and my horse and our pack horse want to be down there to rejoin their own."

Tultas nodded, then Caciro and Habo. Habo said, "I hate most how well they eat down there in their camp, over cooking fires in my village, eating pigs and sheep that might be my father's. I'm hungry."

They laughed at that. Their dry bread, meat and turnips had not changed, but the sacks of them were smaller, lighter, and shrank every day.

Stena said, "I'll set rabbit snares this night. But we'll eat what I catch without any fire."

All intensity of that first day out of Daleninar's village had bled away. Stena's eyes had clouded. Her face had become a mask. Some days she said nothing from when she woke up until she bedded down again. From every rise in the land she looked to the west, the yearning the wondering what had become of her women and children written on her old wrinkled face.

On this night, Lavena unrolled her pelt away from the others, but sat on it through the night. She scraped the ground with a rock, but here the ground was hard, and the rock barely made a shallow line.

She whispered, "Attacking that monster, its many eyes, and ears and noses, is madness. I might do that once but will not live to do it again. What can I do?" She repeated it over and over until it became a chant.

Only the owls and crickets answered her.

In the morning, they found two snared rabbits, skinned and ate them cold, uncooked, right away.

#

By the next evening, at the end of the eighth day following, watching the army but never close enough, Lavena had started to feel, to sense, more than think, there might be a way to pester it. She said, "Let us not try to get close tonight. We have work to do that can't be done where they might see us."

She turned to Tultas, "How are you with that bow?"

For the first time since he had ridden up to them, he nearly laughed, for a moment forgetting the last days. "I am—I was—the best in my village."

Caciro said, "He is better with a bow and arrow than was Daleninar's father. Many years ago, Daleninar's father learned this weapon from the Greeks down by the Great Inland Sea. They taught my village carpenters and blacksmiths how to make a strong bow and sharp arrows, and taught many of our villagers how to use them. Today, all the fighters in our village use this weapon well."

Habo said, "I'm the only one Tultas can't beat."

As they talked, Stena untied the three bows and quivers of arrows from the pack on the ground. She said, "Lavena is right. These might be our best weapons."

Quickly, Stena cut pine branches and set them in a pile. She draped over the nearest side of the pile the bloodiest coats of the scouts slaughtered in the oaks.

When done, she said, "Tultas, Caciro, Habo, let us see how you are with your bows and arrows. Then, please allow Lavena and me to try. Our target is those two dark red blotches."

They took care to hit only the rags set on the pile of loose branches and to pull each arrow out before sending the next one. Any arrow broken on impact, any tip blunted, any feathers torn off, became an arrow they could not replace.

In the years of training at her village, Lavena had used bows and arrows many times. The feel for the line to aim, the place on her chin to set her fingers before the release came back to her in three shots.

Tultas, Caciro, and Habo watched her, first with expressions of amusement then admiration. She put her arrows into the centers of the darkest spots as well as any of them. At the last, one by one they mounted their horses and shot the arrows from a walking or trotting horse—most shots still hitting the target.

Tultas said, "If the light were good enough and I had a flat run, I would show you that I can do this from a galloping horse."

Lavena cocked her head.

Habo said, "He can. I have seen it."

When done, she said, "We have forty-four good arrows. We must not waste a single one." She pointed up into the sky, no stars or moon on this evening. Heavy clouds flowed over the mountains. "Reue is stirring. She may help us."

That night rain started before they settled and had not stopped by morning.

The rain made their horses' footing more difficult, clouded their view from most high places, but made them much harder to see as well. They rode back to one of the fingers of trees and rocks that allowed them to see Daleninar's village and the Roman camp.

The army was quieter than Lavena had ever seen it. No clusters of Roman riders headed out. The men and horses, mules and carts, bullocks and even the battering rams formed into a broad swath far longer than Lavena's group could see from end to end, all facing from where they had come.

The army must have finished gathering up or chasing off anything useful within several day's ride, must have burned everything else. This rain would make finding what little was left—animals, fleeing people—harder, and setting on fire any structures harder still.

Tultas said, "I have not seen them bring in one prisoner, one woman or child. I pray that's not because they are all dead, or because we could not see that far."

Lavena said, "The stinking Romans might now believe they are safe from our people, from your villagers, now that they have killed them, and chased all they have not killed far away. I pray the stinking Romans down there think nothing can harm them. Then our patience will find its reward."

Chapter XXXIV

Second Strikes

On its way back to its main base, the army set its first night camp well before dark. The pace of the marching infantry, their horses and mules with heads low to the ground, fit the dreary wetness.

Lavena and her group watched from a higher area at the edge of evergreen forests. The rainy grayness gave them cover. Stena said, "That army has grown tired of chasing hollow bounty."

At dusk, the army groupings circled up where they stopped. This time, the oxen, their big carts carrying the rams, the mules pulling their smaller carts with supplies, all clustered at the western side of the camp, at the end of the long line behind even the men and women of the supply train. This time, no tents and fighting men surrounded and protected them.

As on the nights before, the men and women of the supply train settled down noisily. But as soon as the tents were up, they quieted under cover and out of the rain.

Again the whole army camped in a place that gave it a good view of the surrounding area, and dark men dug holes along both sides of the entire camp. But unlike other nights, no guards stood watch near the holes to protect those who used them. Lavena understood none of those holes were meant to impale intruders. No dogs barked for nervousness or at sounds only they could hear. They too had no taste to sit or stand out in the rain. Late arrivers rode into the camp but not one with prisoners or farm animals.

After a time, a few campfires started up under coverings that kept them dry. Horsemen began to ride the length of the army on both sides and around the front and rear of the long line of the settled camp, and then again.

Stena said, "They still ride about on the outside of the camp." She laughed. "But don't guard the waste holes. Perhaps they patrol more to keep the angry soldiers in and together than for protection against us."

Lavena thought that they had not yet found the two bodies. "We must get close to them, must pester them soon. If they find the dead ones on the way back, they'll chase down every stranger, even strangers dressed like Romans."

Tultas said, "When you go close, this time let me come with you. That was my village, my home, the home of my father and mother, sister and brothers."

Lavena heard the respect for her in his voice. She said, "Stena, let's find a Roman coat and boots for Tultas. We'll need another Roman rider this night."

#

As darkness took over the day, the rain eased and the clouds broke up to scud across a rising moon.

Lavena looked at that moon for a long time. Then she whispered, but only loudly enough for her to hear, "Must find a way. It is time. Must find a place to attack in this night."

And they continued to stare at the quieting camp, to wait.

Suddenly, Tultas said, "See that. What is that?"

Lavena saw it too and wondered, but not for long. At the far end of the rolling grass that covered the ground between Lavena's group and the army, riders came toward them, and then animals without any riders. The four big oxen, free of any yolk, any cart, moved out awkwardly into the thigh-high grass. Tethers on their front feet made for their ungainly walking. Then mules, many mules, followed. The riders yipped and yelled to keep the animals from going far.

She counted the riders, four then six, then eight. More mules moved into the meadow.

Stena said, "In the old days they did this—when they camped, they let their animals forage through our fields, our beds of planted food, our groves. In one night, those big armies stripped a year's crop for a whole village. They…did that in places where we were all dead or had fled far from them." Stena looked at the three men. "Like now."

Lavena said, "Tultas, ride down between us. Tie your bow and arrows across your horse's back where they can't easily see them."

She barely finished speaking before Tultas found his bow, strung it, and collected his long bag of arrows.

Then she said, "Your arrows are for any rider who menaces Stena and me. But don't use them unless you must. Stena, our long swords are for the bullocks first and any mules this night allows." She paused to let the commands settle and for any question or protest. There were none.

"Caciro, ride into the trees. Take Stena's pack horse to a good hiding place. Habo, go with Caciro and break branches to mark the way, then come back here and wait for us. We will need to strike fast and hide fast after we strike."

After Lavena and Stena had found one more Roman cloak and jacket and were ready, Lavena said, "Tultas, we have no Roman saddle for you. Keep your head bowed and be a good servant, or a good prisoner. Those stinking riders need to see Stena and me first and think nothing of us, and that you serve us…but ready your bow. Stena, you and I will take our tethering sticks."

Lavena waited until no more riders came out to watch the grazing animals, and she could tell the drift of the four bullocks. The soft light of the moon allowed that.

As she mounted, the long sword from Stena's main hut hung from her left side and her falcata from her right. "We will be good Romans riding back in—until you see me move on them. We must not say a word, must not shout. If any of us makes one sound, we are no longer Romans. Tultas, if you must loose your arrows at any shadows, I pray they do not cry out before Stena and I are done. We go."

The four bullocks moved about of their own will for the first time that Lavena had seen. They tromped in the fresh uncut grass, heads low, the chains on their front feet clinking out their locations. Every now and then, they raised up their massive heads to breathe and chew and swallow. They took no notice of any riders on Roman horses, stayed in one place for a time, then moved on, one short step and then the next.

From somewhere Lavena remembered that cows always searched out the softest new growth. When in fields of young grass, no animal had greater persistence than a hungry cow.

The mules foraged far from the oxen. Lavena thought the mules must have learned to keep their distance from the big animals with sharp horns.

Lavena led Stena and Tultas on a line to the army's riders in tents and to their horses tied to wooden posts in the long line of the camp. As she passed the shadow of the nearest Roman rider keeping the grazing animals close, Lavena thought he might have waved but could not be sure in the nearly black night. She returned the wave.

Sentries stood side-by-side away from the camp, though Lavena had not seen them from her group's look-out place now far behind her. She kept riding as if coming into the camp, calmly, letting their horses find sure footing for every step. Closer, the sentries' heads seemed to sweep everything out there in front of them but did not linger on Lavena and the two with her.

Lavena veered to their right but did not change the pace, as she eased toward the oxen.

A night breeze washed down the hill from the forest, over the women and into the camp. No dog sounded an alarm. She thanked the god of night and moon for the smell of these horses and her garments. Even the oxen, much closer now, had not yet noticed.

She heard their every breath, the ripping of little clumps of grass, the chewing of each bite. One of the two pairs faced her. The other pair faced away. And she remembered that too, the natural arrangement of grazing animals to protect each other from opposite sides.

Their hulking shoulders, heavy heads and the tails slapping around their back sides were now not five paces ahead. She headed her horse at the hind quarters of the nearer pair, away from the big heads and horns.

Her horse obeyed and snorted not an arm's length from the rear of the closest bullock, as if to nudge him to turn and move closer to the other two. It worked. The first pair moved closer to the other oxen.

Stena closed on the other pair, also from behind.

Lavena jumped off her horse and stuck the tethering sticks into the soft ground. Stena did the same.

Lavena took a quick look up and around. The two tethered horses now joined the oxen in searching out the freshest shoots that the bigger beasts had missed—four oxen and two horses foraging peacefully by dappled moonlight with one rider watching over them. Dismounted, the tall grass in darkness provided some cover from the scrutiny of any Roman riders not far out beyond them.

This close, these beasts were larger and more brutish than any she had ever seen, their shoulders and rumps, darker against the dark sky, as tall as she and Stena. Waiting for her eyes to lock on, for that deeper quiet to come on her, she understood these beasts had become accustomed to walking side-by-side with Roman soldiers, with men and women from the supply train, and took no particular notice of them. They had marched in tight formation with many more soldiers far noisier and more menacing. They might allow her and Stena to finish this.

Lavena reached out and found Stena's arm, tugged on it, pointed at herself and the nearer pair of oxen, then at Stena and the other pair. Stena eased away to them.

Lavena slid closer to the nearest bullock, at its high dark rump and flicking tail, closer and closer. This one ignored her still, kept its head down and its mouth working. She thought she heard a heavy thumping sound behind her and to the left—perhaps a mule flopping down to rest, or Tultas dismounting. It didn't matter, no time to look over, no time to wait.

The women closed the last distance in two bounds, and struck at the same time. They swung their long swords around in a cutting slicing swipe aimed at the lower hind legs. Both swords hit hard and true, laying open the hide deep into muscle and tendons down to bone. With a return swipe the women cut down at the other hind leg of their targeted bull.

Before the bulls could spin or swing their heads and horns at whatever had done this, the hind half of their heavy bodies collapsed, grotesquely, as if a great weight made them sit, only their chained front legs able to move, able to hold up the their chests and shoulders.

Lavena looked at Stena, tried to see what her face might say, whether to lunge at the second of her pair or run to their horses and try to vanish.

The reactions of the second bullock of each pair showed them what to do next. Without needing to stop to think, Lavena understood that perhaps it was the night, or fatigue, or the chains on their front legs, or the feeling that they had no enemies, that no one could hurt them.

The unharmed bulls did not soon enough take notice of the calamity so close to them. They looked over at their mates, hind legs crumpled, and stood for an instant as if trying to figure out what to do, what had happened, how to react to the fallen bullock. They had not been trained for this, had lost all fear of Romans—their instinct and fear of two-footed animals trained out of them.

The women struck again.

A deep bellow rose from the first fallen pair, not the bleat of a lost calf, not even a cry of pain, but a low roar of anger and terror. The four fallen oxen made enough noise to fill the night, cover all other sounds, and draw the attention of anyone within a thousand paces.

By the first or second loud noise from the first fallen beast, Lavena and Stena found their horses, jumped on them, yanked up the tethering sticks and rode toward the tree line.

Riders near them yelled, and the yells came closer, dogs from the camp barked, then many more. Men and some women from the camp shouted and cried out.

None of the riders in the meadow with the animals rode at Lavena, Stena and Tultas. The bellowing beasts drew all of them. None of the riders chased after other riders out there. None suspected their own kind had done this.

Lavena kept her lead horse at a steady walk, no sense that the sound of hoofs, the shadows of riders leaving fast should attract attention. The noises and lights from the army camp increased, but all focused on the place of the fallen beasts, still not on any Roman riders.

They made it to the tree line without noticing anyone riding after them.

Tultas said, "I had to slay one of them."

Lavena let out a sound of surprise and question, less than a word. "Ah, that sound was one of them on horse close to us?"

"You were intent on those beasts. He saw you and came up behind you slowly, quietly. He had no concern about me, or maybe did not know what to make of me, just sitting there watching over your horses. The moon showed me the line to his head and neck. My arrow struck him flush on the cheek or upper neck. I could not be sure."

Lavena breathed deeply. The many ways of how this night might have ended whirled through her. After a time, she said, "The spirits of Father and Mother protected us this night, and surely guided your arrow."

Tultas said, "I, not your mother or father, shot that arrow."

Lavena said, "Did you aim there knowing that was the one, perhaps the only place, he could not cry out when hit?"

After a long moment, Tultas said, "No, daughter of Sinorix, I had not thought about him crying out. I had not thought what to do if he did. If he had cried out..." He paused. "Perhaps your father did guide us all on this night."

They arrived at the tree line, but did not see Caciro.

Then a loud whisper, "Over here, over here. I never thought you three could bring such joy, just finding you, seeing you. Come, Habo is waiting at a place that will be safe until morning."

#

By the time they reached the hiding place deep in the forest, the clouds had left, and the moon cast enough light through the trees so all five could see each other easily.

Tultas laughed. "I have never been more afraid, not of dying, but of failing." He let out a deep breath. "You two make good Romans, you rode slowly like Romans, must have smelled like Romans."

Lavena said, "I pray there will come a time when we no longer have to stink like them."

After they had rolled out their pelts, eaten some of the remaining food, and made sure no sounds of horses or dogs came near, Lavena said, "That's the first and the last time the army will not be ready for a night-time raid, the last time it'll let its animals forage in darkness."

She waited for them to think, to say something. None did. They waited for her next thoughts, her commands. "Tultas, before the sun is up, send Habo or Caciro back to find Daleninar. Tell her about this night. Tell her what five of us have done. Tell her what five more, ten, twenty more can do to this stinking army of Gracchus. Tell her, tell her uncle, if they want to chase the stinking Romans off our land, to send more fighters to Stena and me."

After a brief silence, Stena said, "Tell Daleninar to send her fastest riders on the strongest horses to the south of the main army camp that it heads back now. That army will go south next. All the armies of Carthage and Rome always went from the farms and villages here to the south and the silver mines. This one will too after it thinks it has cleansed our region of us. Make all the village elders listen, make them hasten their women and children away into the high country—and make them send us their best warriors. Only five more from each village will be enough."

Stena walked to the big packs taken off the pack horse. She groped around in the dark until she found and pulled out a garment. "Take this cloak stained with the blood of the stinking scout and torn by our arrows. Show it to your leader."

Lavena finished, "You will find us as the smallest shadow of this army, wherever it goes or even if it just sits at the main camp. Every morning look for us on the side where the sun comes over the land, at the end of the day on the side the sun drops down. And when the army is on the move, look for us behind the hindmost soldier." She paused in thought. "Leave all your arrows and your bow with us—and bring more fighters by the time we have used the last arrow."

Caciro left before light, back to his village now burned out, and far past it to find Daleninar. Before he rode off, he held high the cloak from one of the scouts slain in the forest. "The gods of earth and sky and water go with you. Daleninar will believe you now, and will send what she can. May the gods and the spirit of our people who have left us keep you safe until we find you once again."

Chapter XXXV

Death-Dealing Ghosts

The dogs, the sentries on foot and horse protected the army with a new intensity. They swept far on both sides of the marching army during the day and in constant tight circles around the camp at night.

Lavena's group found no unprotected rider or foot soldier, not even a mule, without too many riders and foot soldiers too close. She and Stena could not take the chance that their Roman garb and saddles would deflect away all attention from newly alerted eyes.

Late on the first morning after the attack on the bullocks, Lavena said, "As the moon lets us, we'll ride far ahead and help make preparations for the army's triumphant return to its base. But first, we must find a forest of stout pine trees."

The rest of that day, her group cut straight poles out of tree branches, shaping the ends to sharp points.

That night and every night until exhausted or stopped by rain blocking the moonlight, her group dug holes with the shovel taken from Daleninar's village and planted the stakes, points upward, in the freshly dug hole. Then they covered the holes with long grass or other branches and dirt.

All the holes lay on the path the army had made—flattening the grass, tearing up the low bushes, and mashing down fallen leaves—on its way to The Village on The Hill. The quickest way back for it was the path it had already cleared on the way out.

In the daytime when the wind was right, Lavena and the three with her heard the far off screams and shouts as the spikes impaled another horse or soldier. Stena said, "Lavena, your holes and spikes are a small menace, but so sudden and unexpected their impact is far greater than the wounds they make."

Tultas said, "There are so many of them, and we can't dig enough holes ahead of them while the night shields us."

Lavena answered, "As long as they don't know, as long as they don't see us, we are as many as they think we are."

#

Marcus heard the early morning yells. They came from the higher ground up where the whole army camped when not attacking villages far off.

"They've come back..."

"It's here..."

"By the great god *Iuppiter*, it comes back victorious. Brings bounty, brings slaves,..."

"Enough for each of us."

Twenty days of idleness, dice games, pock-marked flirting women—the ones who stayed behind and did not have a man among the fighting men or laborers—would end on this day.

Most of the men in his area of the camp, who the army had not taken, ran up the hill. Marcus stayed in the low area near the oxen pens. The first bearers of news from a returning army seldom had it right. They were the lookouts from the high places far out from the permanent camp, the first ones to see the returning riders. Those lookouts, here or with other armies in the high mountains, always relayed back to the main camp better tidings than the truth.

Marcus hoped they were right this time. He hoped the army had found useful bounty, enough to please all the old men, enough for some of the bounty to trickle down to the common soldiers, perhaps a few more bronze coins than their meager wages, an extra ration of salt. Marcus knew he would be among the very last to receive anything.

The excited shouts did not last, did not spread with details of battles won, new prisoners, and spoils.

By mid afternoon, the noises and dust from many horses, mules, carts and men welled up. This noise was made mostly by wheels turning, by mules and horses, the tromping of many feet, and the tired groans from thousands.

Closer to evening, some made their way down to the oxen area below the main camp. They did not search out the men, like Marcus, left behind to greet them and share good news. They looked only ahead at their empty tents or at the place on the ground where they might dump their bed rolls and tools. Some left to fetch water, to clean themselves in one of the washing areas, or to be alone.

Near the last, Brutus, heavy pack slung over his shoulders, stomped to his and his sons' tent, dropped his pack and headed straight for the oxen pens and the four bullocks that had remained behind.

Marcus and some of the others looked up the path to the rest of the returning army, and wondered and mumbled why no pairs of yoked oxen followed. Only one of Brutus' two sons who had left with him now came in, quiet, behind his father, also carrying big loads.

Brutus climbed through the rails, and approached the two bullocks in that pen, both standing, their heads over the top rail, curious at the noises and new commotion. These two let him come up to them. He patted the neck of the nearest one, ran its ear through his hand, and rested his cheek against the far larger cheek of the animal.

A loud noise of pain and anguish, and another, burst from him. His shoulders shook, and he began to sob. Marcus had never seen a grown man cry, not like this, wail and gasp for air, his face taking on the wet gloss of tears mixed with sweat, unable to utter a coherent word.

Two of his sons and others now stood along the fence but did not go in. Many laborers, some of whom had just carried back sets of yokes, whips, reins and long sticks, came up to the fence. Mule drivers and dark-skinned waste-hole diggers, wives of common soldiers and women who belonged to no one, and after them foot soldiers from up on the hill gathered behind them—all looking at Brutus.

Through his sobs he started to speak, single words that at first meant nothing to Marcus. In time, he recognized the words—names Brutus had given the four oxen which had not come back, and the name of his first son, Biticus. Marcus had not seen him come back either.

Brutus stood up and draped his arm over the neck of the second bull, then climbed through to the next paddock over and caressed both bulls there. At last, he turned to the many gathered to stare at him in his spectacular grief.

He wiped his face with a dirty sleeve and came over so that only the fence rails separated him from the front of the curious throng. Marcus stood less than an arm's length from Brutus, who said, "Ghosts prowl this land. Took four of my beauties, and my oldest son too."

Those gathered released a collective, "Oh, no...."

Someone said, "All four. In the name of *Iuppiter*, how?"

Marcus noticed the silent ones were the ones who had left with the army and come back tired, with a beaten look. They knew how.

Brutus talked on. "Biticus, my oldest, my best at all things..." He gulped down a sob. "Slain by a single arrow." Brutus put a big fist up to the side of his face under his ear. "Here, the arrow struck him here, clean through. A strong arrow as made only by the best metal workers."

Talking helped him gain control.

"The *barbari* villages, all the villages within four days west, sat empty, gates open, nothing there for us, no women, no gold, the *barbari* and their animals all gone."

Marcus silently agreed. He knew about that.

"Our only losses other than mine—from spikes under the ground around the village and on the way back to here. Stupid our infantry leaders, old lessons they've never learned. The *barbari* dug those holes—then fled and are running still."

He raised both hands to the sky and let them flop down. "I am but a poor oxen driver, never laid a hand in anger on anyone. Why did the gods give me this bitter drink?"

Those near Marcus murmured, then shouted. "It's not right...."

"Where is justice?"

"How?"

"After we set fire to the last village four days to the west and our riders and fighters had cleared the whole region, every spot of land between here and there, of all the *barbari*, I let my beauties graze. They had not seen grass like that since spring came to the hills back home, maybe ever." He whined once more and wiped away more tears.

"They had chains as always, couldn't go far, the whole army camped right there, our sentries beyond. My son...watched them too, kept them close to the camp. Nothing could happen to them—or to him." He breathed in deeply and scrunched his eyes to stop from crying.

"I heard a bellow from one of my beauties and three more, wouldn't stop. They had fallen, each of their hind legs cut... through the muscle...cut to bone. They couldn't stand up, that muscle rolled up the back of their blood-covered leg into a stone."

Many yelled, "No...."

"The treachery."

"The vile treachery."

"Who did this cursed cruel thing?"

"All four at once, how?"

"Someone must have seen."

"Biticus, he must have seen. Who did this to him for no cause?"

Brutus looked up to the cloudless sky. "I don't know. None of us knows. Had to kill my beauties—burned them to *Iuppiter* and Mars."

He sobbed again. "The army's best surgeon cut out the arrow, but Biticus left us before the arrow was out of him. Had to burn my oldest son."

He waited. Many standing at the fence started to wail with him amid shouts of, "Unfair…"

"Biticus and your beauties never hurt anyone…"

"Who did this vile thing?"

After a time Brutus talked on. "We questioned our patrols that night, and questioned them again in the morning—and no one is better than Legate Apollonius at that."

In hushed tones, some agreed.

"They let me sit in. Our scouts saw nothing, heard nothing. Only our riders and infantry coming back to camp by moonlight. One, maybe two of ours gave chase after the ghosts that had done this. But too dark, too unknown the terrain to search far in the night."

Someone yelled out, "We'll find more big bullocks, and burn alive whoever did this."

Another yelled, "Your son rides with the gods now, and they will avenge."

Brutus shook his head. "In the morning, our best trackers looked for tracks made by strange horses, but found only our tracks where my beauties had fallen. We sent dogs out, but they ran in circles. No trace left by whoever had done this. Only the one arrow—shot by a ghost in the night."

Someone near the front said, "Don't be troubled. There are many cows, even oxen in Iberia. We'll take the best and give them to you. You'll have more sons, many more."

Brutus looked over in the direction of whoever had said this and shook his big head again. "Takes a bull's whole growing up to train a good one. And…I'm too old for more sons." He paused, wiped his face again. He turned back to one of his last trained bulls, stood next to it, draped his arm around it again and rested his head on its neck. Soon those gathered dispersed, all but the two sons and Marcus.

Many who walked off grumbled and shook their heads at what had happened, at the oxen man, who had lost half his brood, his oldest son, and likely his only chance at glory in Iberia. Many talked of ghosts in this strange land.

Before Marcus left, he said in the direction of Brutus, "I'll clean out these pens when you want, sir."

Brutus waved him off in a manner that told him to get out of his sight.

#

After a time of idleness, listening to the low grumbling of tired men with nothing to do, sullen and angry, Marcus heard running footsteps getting closer, and as he turned a runner came at him.

It was Jove, once a dog handler and now a scout. "Marcus, Marcus, Celer did it again. You should know. You and I are the only ones left who really know what's out there."

"Celer did what again? What do mean the only ones left?"

"Came into our camp with no rider late in the day, Celer and another horse. Nicator and the scout next in the line closest to him never came in….Gone, like Martis and his men."

"What are you saying? Speak more slowly."

Jove looked down. "In the morning, we saw vultures circle high over an oak forest behind us. Many vultures. When we got there, the vultures had a good start on the naked bodies—of Nicator and another scout."

"What…? Who was that other scout?"

"You didn't know him. I didn't either. One of the horsemen sent up to take the place of all the lost scouts. A heavy sword or ax got Nicator across the face, and the other one through the neck. They stripped them and dumped their bodies in a gully. You should know. You did the right things up there on the mountain, Marcus. You were right to be careful and track back for anyone behind us, even if on a false trail. Nicator should have taken greater care, should have learned from you and not betrayed you. The gods be with you, Marcus."

"Thank you, Jove."

And Jove left.

Marcus said aloud but only to himself, "If Celer could talk, he'd talk of the ghosts he has seen, ghosts that see us but don't let us see them, ghosts that kill us with arrows and heavy swords and dig death-dealing holes in darkness." He thought but then dared not think the young one, whose name might be Lavena, had done these things.

Chapter XXXVI

Running After a Butterfly

The next morning, Marcus rose with the roosters. He crawled to the tent flap without waking the other men and slid out into the dawn. The scout in him woke him, made him want to see what was out there, what the day might bring.

As light crept up over the flat land to the south and east, he made his way to the far end of the awakening camp, past the big tents to the watch tower on the highest knoll. The tower sentries knew him. In former days when he was still a scout, they had welcomed him up to the top—his eyes were the best of any.

At day break, they always wanted to know what he saw, or that he saw nothing to alarm him. Later in the day, riders covered the land away from this main camp, and the men in the watch towers stood easy.

But every night those riders came back to this camp, not daring to remain out there in darkness. The early morning was the most vulnerable time for this camp and any who ventured out from it.

"Hey, Marcus. How's the cow shit?" The tower watchman laughed as he reached out a hand to pull him up to the top of the ladder.

Marcus responded, "All last night the whole night through, your mother said I smelled so good."

The other pretended to push Marcus off the ladder and laughed.

They settled to stare far out over the land reclaiming its shapes and colors from the night.

Far to the southeast the brightening light of morning on a gentle rise in the rolling grass cast stripes of green and black against another darker line of trees or rocks. There, against the sun, Marcus' gaze locked onto two faint specks, then two more.

They did not belong where he saw them, too thin, too straight for lone trees, bushes or boulders. Their color, what he could make out through the brighter light around them, was wrong. At first he was not sure. They were no larger than fleas—or spots in his eyes from looking into the day's first sunlight too long.

One of the specks moved. Then the speck next to it moved also, followed by the other two. They were too far out to have come from this camp, and too tall and thin to be wolves or bears or big animals lost. He slowed his breath and held his head still so his eyes would not lose them in the ever whiter light.

The four specks seemed to increase in size, merge into two, then one, and then stop.

Now he was sure.

Four riders looked at this camp, at this watchtower and, if their eyes were keen, at him. Did any of the four see him and the other watchmen as two specks? Likely they did with the sun behind them now shining on him brightly.

From the bits of color of their garb under the sun's streaks of light on the green grass, from how they sat in their saddles, they might have been Roman riders on Roman horses.

Then they turned, moved across his line of sight away from the direct light of the sun until they faded into the ground.

As the distant riders turned and presented to him the sides of their horses and themselves, it hit him, jolted hard, his insides a jumble of recollections, competing thoughts, then conclusions that had to be all wrong, but conclusions that in the end he knew were right.

Two of those riders, the height of one compared to the other, how they leaned and other things he could not see but felt through senses behind his eyes brought back to him the two floating above the trees on the mountain trail. One of them might have been—was—the fair girl and the other one that woman or older man with her on the day they brought Celer back to him.

Undeniable thoughts told him more. Those two might have, could have, perhaps did, wear Roman garb and sat high in Roman saddles on horses taken from Martis' scouts. Those two—could have—did get close to Nicator in the forest, the scout who rode with him, and close to the bullocks in the dark night and high grass, and were not noticed by anyone in this army.

Those two and the others who rode with them could have warned all the *barbari* to flee from the little village in the mountain valley and the larger village on the hill to the west, and from all the other villages the army chased down but found empty.

Marcus slid a glance at the lookout right next to him, also leaning over the railing and peering in the same direction. His face and shoulders, relaxed, bored, nearly yawning. He must have felt Marcus looking at him and said too loudly, "Nothing out there?"

At this moment, Marcus understood that what he did or said next would set the path of all his remaining days. "No, nothing, another quiet day out there."

Deep in thought, he walked back to the low part of the camp to help with the oxen however needed, though only four were left.

#

Every evening Marcus, carrying his two heavy buckets and tools for digging, trudged farther away from the permanent Roman camp. The easy places of soft soil close by foot paths had long ago been found and used by those who had done this task before him. It would take more than one cycle of rain and sun, of grass and fast-growing bushes to cleanse the ground in those spots so they could be used for this purpose once again.

On this the fifth day after the return of the army, for the fifth time Marcus broke the one rule of all scouts. And he knew it.

He lugged his burden beyond sight or hearing of anyone in the army camp before stopping to flex his hands and fingers. Then he continued farther down a gully into unfamiliar thickets fed by a spring or stream. He carried no horn and no weapon other than his short dagger for cutting meat and small items.

He might have asked one of the armed men to come with him, and they would have. There were many, all bored. But, he thought, there was nothing out here to alarm him. All large animals and locals had been chased off by the army of Gracchus and its many riders, and the fighting men of Piso before that. And he wanted to do this alone.

Marcus shook his head at his self-deception. He, and perhaps only he, knew that clever locals stalked this area. After what they had done to the four oxen, to the oldest son of Brutus, to Nicator and the scout who rode with him, and after all the spiked holes they dug, he should have not disobeyed the scout rule on this or any late afternoon.

He knew too that he had given in to a quieter, stronger yearning, the yearning of a child running after a butterfly, the yearning of boy racing by the side of a colt galloping in a mountain meadow, the yearning of a young man for his life's mate.

Other, more adult thoughts, piled in. Was all this just an idle wish? Did he wish that the riders he had seen from the top of the tower were the same as on the mountain? Did he wish that a fair maiden looked at him and felt as he felt? Did he wish that the one who Aunia said she knew was that one—the one who might have the worth of a thousand captured locals? And, most of all, did he wish that she now might seek out the same secluded place close to that army?

Marcus smiled to himself, smiled at his youth, at his foolishness. These thoughts, he knew, flew on the edge of madness.

If he found them—her—what was he to do? If they—she—found him, they would surely try to kill him again.

He was more sure of one thing. His still sore tongue and scarred mouth, and what happened to Martis, reminded him every waking moment how a Roman could become a traitor to the Great Empire, and that he was Roman did not stop him now.

If the women found him, he did have one thing that might save him from them, that might give him time, but only if he had guessed right about them this time.

#

They took turns watering their horses in a stream at the bottom of a gully far enough away from the army for the water to be untainted and the terrain safe. As each one rode down into the thicket of tall grass, bushes, and trees, the other three hung back on the flatter open land above, searching for any strangers, listening for noises that should not be near. On this late afternoon, Lavena was the last to lead her horse to water.

The night would be clear, with a large moon helping them to dig more holes far south of the main camp. Holes, digging them, was all they had done for the last ten nights. After the attack on the bullocks, the army's riders, its dogs and sentries on foot cast a wide protecting circle. Far too many alert eyes watched everyone else for Stena and Lavena to ride close, to let any of the army see them.

Now her belly growled, her arms ached, and her legs trembled as she dismounted and landed on the edge of the stream. Raw fish kept her moving and her head clear, barely. No rabbits were left in this area near the Roman camp. Stena had found wild beets and mushrooms, but not enough to keep away the hunger. Over the last days and nights, Lavena had come to understand that not enough sleep, not enough to eat, would in the end protect the Romans from her little band as much as all its soldiers.

While her horse drank, Lavena took off her Roman coat and cap, slapped them across her knees to shake out the dust. She trailed the cap through the flowing water, hung it on a tuft of grass, and scooped water up into her face, over her arms and shoulders.

The water was warm, warmer than the air, and it washed away the grime and sweat. She wished this stream were wider, deeper, big enough to swim in, and thought about shedding her clothes to roll in the warm water and soft mud or sand in the deepest part.

She looked up and around to see if Habo or Tultas watched her, but did not see them or their horses.

She started to untie the cord holding up her trousers but stopped at the new sound of silence, a sudden deeper quiet. The birds settling for the night had stilled. Her horse lifted up its head from drinking, and she followed its ears to where they pointed.

A man stood downstream, not far. He watched her from behind the darkest shadow cast by a clump of trees and bushes. She would not have noticed him if her horse had not. He held a bucket in each hand, but held them easily as if they were empty.

She thought he smiled. She looked for a sword on him, any weapon, looked past him for others. She reached across to the hilt of her falcata hanging from her left side, but her move for a weapon felt wrong, unneeded.

He took one slow step forward out of the shadows, set the buckets on the ground and stood there relaxed, as if he knew her.

In the day's last sunlight, she saw him well. He was older than she, but not much, taller than she, but not much. His hair was lighter than hers and his skin smooth. His eyes smiled and his mouth held no meanness. He looked as fine as Turibas, better than most other men of age in her village, lean though his arms and shoulders were strong. But his coat, trousers and sandals were not those of locals—and she got it. He was the one on the mountain.

For a long moment, she thought about how that could be, the same one with buckets of a laborer this time, no fine horse, nothing to alarm her. Yet, if she let him live and he told others what he had seen, her little band would have to leave on this night, would have to follow Caciro and not come back to the army until a thousand men rode with her.

Was this a dream? Was this one the spirit of that foul man she had knifed to an ugly death stalking her again? They should have kept his head after all.

Should she whistle for the three others? If she did, and this one carried a horn or shouted out, the whole army would descend on this little stream. If she whistled, and the others did not see him, they would think she was mad.

Should she kill him now, quietly? If he ran, she might not catch him. But she could pull him in—and take her first strike, again—bastard sons of Rome, each and every one of them.

She eased out of her top, and tossed it over onto dry ground.

But unlike those others by the oak forest, he did not move, his expression did not change, his gaze remained on her face.

This time, Lavena did not want to step out of her trousers. Standing in the stream, she wanted to keep her garments dry, and felt a discomfort in nakedness before this one.

But night descended fast and she had to do something. She tugged on the reins and began to walk her horse onto dry land—closer to him. A few more steps and if he then ran down the stream bed, she could ride him down, kill him quickly.

If he scrambled up away through the dense growth, the other three would be on him fast—as long as he kept quiet for moments more. If he was but a spirit and vanished, she would laugh but not tell anyone.

He did not move, just kept staring at her, at her horse, in a way that showed no fear, and as if he saw but did not see, as if in a trance.

Now close enough to see, to hear, that he breathed and his chest moved with each breath. He was real, and that made her decide.

She eased around to the other side of her horse in a manner to not alarm him. Let him stand there stupefied at a half naked woman, let him stand there long enough for her to pull the long sword out of its leather covering hanging on the Roman saddle, long enough for her to walk her horse closer, her sword shielded from his view.

He reached out and touched her horse's searching nose, patted its cheek, and the horse nuzzled him. They would do that, both of them smelling the Roman in the other, she thought.

He looked at her across the horse's head and chest, even while she slid her long sword out of its scabbard at an angle he could not see. His face was still open, almost happy, and unprepared for what was to come. But she had no choice.

The instant before she took the closing step, the instant before she brought her sword around, before she thrust it into him, the names made her stop. At first, she did not comprehend the Latin words, but the names were clear. She could not ignore the names. The names made every part of her stop as if the gods had turned her to stone.

The message out of him was dream-like, not of this earth, this life. He said the words once and then again, smiling, pleading, and she understood fully.

"Daughter of Sinorix? Yes? That is you? Daughter of Sinorix. It must be you. Yes? Aunia," he touched his lips at the same place of Aunia's opening, "spoke of you."

Marcus' words made her stop and push her horse around so she faced him. He now saw the long sword in its scabbard hanging from the saddle, her left hand resting on its hilt. But that did not break the spell she had on him, did not make him afraid. He said, "I first saw you on the mountain, and then at the edge of the meadow."

They stood within touching distance, if he reached out and she did not move away.

She shook her head, stepped over to her shirt lying on the ground, turned her back to him and slipped it over her head, while she tried to keep looking at him over her shoulder.

She retrieved her jacket and cap from the tufts of grass and placed them behind the saddle. She put her finger up to her lips, telling him to talk softly. She spoke in Latin, clearly slowly, surprising him so that he had to listen twice, the first time to hear her soft voice, her words in his language, and then try again to remember what she had said.

"Whatever you think you saw, whoever you think I am, leave now." She tipped her head up to her right. "If those with me see you, they will kill you—and kill me for letting you live."

Then she smiled, a beautiful smile of good teeth. He wanted to reach for her face—tired, but the fairest he had ever seen—a straight delicate nose, alert eyes, her hair the color of ripe berries. He had seen but forced himself to not think of her other parts.

Questions about Martis, about Celer, tumbled in, but he knew that asking about them might be his last questions, might end this encounter wherever it led. He said, "That was you on the mountain? That was you with another looking at the encampment out of the morning sun, yes?"

An older woman's voice in a loud whisper rolled down to them. "Lavena..." He did not understand the rest of it.

The fair one in front of him smiled again and yelled something back, then to him in a whisper. "I must go, and you must too."

As she mounted up, she said, "Is Aunia your friend? Is she well?"

He nodded furiously in response and to try to think of a way to make her stay longer. "*Noli discere*, don't go." She pulled on her horse's reins and looked down at him. "If you must leave now, come back here as the day goes to its resting place. I will look for you and will have more messages from Aunia."

He reached up to her—and noticed the short sword in its scabbard on her left thigh. It made his hand stop before they touched. She could have killed him easily this time. She and whoever rode with her could have done everything they said ghosts had done to the army, to Brutus and all the others. He managed, "Every evening I come here, or not far from here."

She looked down into his eyes with a look that said she understood, understood his bullock chores, understood his desires, his dreams. She said, "When next you talk to Aunia, ask her about a young man called Turibas."

She wheeled her horse away and did not look at him again as the back of her horse moved through tall grass and dense growth until out of sight.

Marcus found his clean buckets and headed back to camp, knowing what he must do next.

Chapter XXXVII

Trouble in the Army

Gracchus put on a calm and strong face. The great feast he ordered up and the good wine lugged all the way from Rome had shifted the mood but not enough. Plutarch had just given his report, and the old men grumbled and talked in low tones to those next to them. Gracchus had to make them listen before they cycled to anger and turned on him, blamed him for all the troubles of this army.

Quaestor Plutarchus kept the army's records on debts, payments, the collected bounties of gold, silver, and slaves. Just now he had told them where all that stood. Since its landing seven months back, the army had not found one uncial of gold, one *libra* of silver in this region of northern Hispania.

It had captured no more than eighty healthy male slaves, fewer than fifty women. More than half of the captured killed themselves by their own hands, of self-starvation or a broken spirit. The living sat in cages waiting for the auction merchants.

Gracchus had to ask, before any of the old men thought to. "Quaestor Plutarchus, how much will the captured fetch at auction?"

Plutarchus said, "If the slave merchant must come to us and take them back, perhaps the worth of one good horse for three good slaves. If we take them to Rome and deliver them healthy and strong, three times more, one horse for one slave."

Silence in the tent. They all could make the simple calculation. Years and a fortune spent gathering, equipping, transporting and feeding this army had yielded the worth of less than thirty horses. Every year one mid-sized stable on the outskirts of Rome produces that much and a good profit, and does it with a hand-full of laborers, five horse men and no borrowings from anyone.

Then there was that other thing. At first laughing talk, then rumors, then belief swept through his men. Killer ghosts hid in the mountains and forests of this land. All the villages west and north of the main army camp sat empty—no *barbari*, no animals, nothing—as if ghosts had announced his orders to the *barbari* before he gave them out. His men had begun to fight each other, and fifty-seven had died that way. A like number lay wounded, and some of those would die soon.

He had to take control. Else they would sit here and rot through the coming winter. In the spring, one of the Senate scribes with him would present a full report to the Senate. It would recall and sack him of all possessions—as it had Piso before him—and if the gods were not on his side, would drown or crucify him. But if he succeeded, a triumph in the Colosseum might still be his. His last path to glory lay far to the south and the silver mines.

He stood up and, one by one, locked onto the eyes of those still sober enough to know and feel his power, whatever was left of it. "Generous benefactors," he turned to the Legate Apollonius, "and wise leader of our fighting men, there is nothing more here for us. We have rid this region of all *barbari* and scraped them off the land up to the mountains. With your wise counsel, I will give the order that we winter in the south with our brother army and together harvest the silver mines of Tartessos. You will remember that when finished here, we were to rejoin them down there."

Apollonius responded first. "I have said that from the beginning. Follow the silver, I have always counseled. Follow the silver."

Gracchus said. "I will issue the order now, and our council will meet tomorrow morning to plan the best way."

Apollonius said, "Then it is done, but…one more thing. What of this Marcus Flavius? Everything he touches dies or vanishes. Our priest has it right. He and his brother know more, hide more, than he tells us. Watch that one."

Gracchus had not thought of his former scout since their last meeting, but the dog-faced legate saw Marcus in everything bad on this campaign. True or not, Marcus did seem connected to all of it. True or not, the legate had command over all tactics of war, and Gracchus must not interfere with mere tactics.

#

Brutus, his two surviving sons, two wagon drivers, and three laborers sat in a half circle. They ate the day's last meal of bread slathered with honey and hunks of beef cooked over their fire pit. After the sun fell below the land, a cold wind came down from the mountains to the north, and they sat close to the heat and pot hanging over it.

Brutus said, "Marcus, you take longer to clean out the shit from four bulls than you did for all eight. If you want to eat, hurry and then listen."

"Sorry, sir, have to go ever farther away to find a place not fouled."

Brutus held a piece of meat skyward at the end of a rusty fork, his signal that he wanted them to listen. "Tomorrow, we prepare to leave this camp. The orders have been issued, every group's place on the march assigned."

Several made questioning sounds. He said, "Can't stay here. No gold, no more women, no strong young men, no boys even." That brought a scoff. "The auction merchants will laugh when they see our slaves. Deer hunters come back with nothing most days, and the old men who pay us grumble."

One of the listeners said, "The old men who *don't* pay us."

Those on either side of Marcus grunted agreement. He earned only food and a place in a crowded tent to sleep. He had not spent the few coins paid him as a scout leader. Unless this army found bounty, in great amounts, he would return to his father's small farm with no more than when he left.

Brutus talked on, "The priest says bad ghosts walk this ground, says in the summer they live high in the mountain but come down now. Says that's who killed my son...and lamed my beauties...." He jabbed his fork in Marcus' direction. "And ghosts took your brother and all his men."

Marcus nodded slightly.

Brutus talked on. "The old men say that perhaps next summer we'll return to this camp. Have to keep the *barbari*, the few that might be left, from coming back to their old ground."

The thoughts, the questions piled into him as they never had in his eighteen years, and his yearnings of the last days, of what might be, confounded every sensible thought.

This camp, Marcus had to think about this camp as he never had before, not with the focus of this moment. From the gray wood of the storage huts, the well-trodden stones on the pathways, and the way the water had drained off in culverts during big rains, this camp had been here a long time. Its earthen walls topped by big posts, their sharp tips pointed up, the lookout towers on each corner, dogs and sentries posted on the perimeter protected all those inside well.

But strung out in open country and moving no faster than the slowest laborers, this army would make a fine target—for her and those who rode with her.

Giant tents had to be unstitched, folded, and loaded carefully so the cloth would not tear on the long trek. The old men had to be made comfortable in their chariots and carts or on litters carried by four servants. The engineers and carpenters needed to dismantle the many structures not built of stone. He might meet her again late in the coming days, if no one followed him, if the army stayed a while longer to dismantle the camp, if she returned alone.

Late at night before turning into his crowded tent, he whispered to himself, "*Haec est insania*," and again, "This is madness, but I must."

#

Getting close to Aunia, talking to her, was harder now. The army swarmed through the camp, breaking it up, breaking it down, readying all the carts and everything worth taking. The times of quiet, of waiting for nothing in particular, had ended. The guards of the women captives were more alert and changed from one day to the next.

Marcus had to help. The bullock fence posts had to be dug up. Once dug up, the bullocks had to be tethered and watched every moment, nudged or whipped back when they wandered where not wanted. They might have been tied up with heavy chains, but there was nothing in the camp to attach the chains that they could not pull out or pull over, such was their brute power.

And he still had to lug away their droppings. Every evening, he hauled them down to the same place, but she did not come there again.

In the middle of the fourth day after his encounter with the one named Lavena, the area around the women's cage quieted. Guards at the corners of the cage dozed in the warmth of the sun. She again sat at the edge of the raised platform, her legs hanging outside the cage.

This time he did not wait, did not ask permission from any of the guards for fear of what they would say. He did not idle pretending to be doing nothing in particular—the pressure of time passing, of the army leaving, of the slave merchant coming to take Aunia and the others away all too great.

The instant she spotted him, Aunia looked at him and got up as if to leave, to hide in the middle of the others.

He said loudly, almost yelling, "She asked me to ask you about a young man whose name is Turibas." The crooked mouth opened wider, and Aunia sat back down. The other women in the cage came round her. "I saw her three days back. She asked if you are well—and if you know what came of this one she called Turibas."

"What did you say?"

"I saw her, the one who answers to Lavena, the one whose hair is the color of ripe berries. She is a fighter now. She asked what you know of someone called Turibas."

Aunia dropped to her knees, buried her face in her hands. Others started to come closer to the cage, but Marcus tried to ignore them. The snoozing guards snapped their heads, stood up, and looked at Aunia, at Marcus. He crept closer to the cage, closer than all the others, keeping his gaze hard on Aunia.

She, still kneeling, looked at him as if they were alone in a small room. "Mother of all that is good, she is alive, Lavena is alive and a she-warrior still?"

He nodded and whispered, "Carries two swords, and handles a big horse as if born to ride." He felt the many eyes on him, felt others coming nearer to him. He dared whisper only, "What can you tell me of this Turibas?"

Aunia looked up and past Marcus. "Nothing...nothing. Get away from me, young Marcus. Trouble is all around you, around me, around us." And she got up and hid in the circle of the other captured women.

As Marcus turned, two of the armed guards closed on him.

They held him in his own cage, empty of others, until darkness.

Again Gracchus was not alone. But the only ones Marcus recognized were the Legate Apollonius, sitting in the big chair as he had on the day of the tongue burning test, and Brutus off to the side, larger than all the others, but standing defensively, not happy, without any hint of power. Marcus understood the oxen man was no longer needed, his bulls no longer prized. Brutus had lost all influence.

"Well, Marcus, you with the eyes of an eagle, tell us about your interest in the *venefica*?" As he talked, Gracchus smiled a smile of friendship and curiosity, not meanness, the same as at their first meeting.

Marcus was not cowed this time. "I had to ask about ghosts in the mountain, ghosts maiming the oxen of my new master."

He leaned in the direction of his new master and shrugged, to indicate how routine his curiosity. He could not point, his hands bound behind him. "Our whole camp knows she might know, but only she."

The dog-faced legate, said, "Well, what did she say?"

"She said ghosts are in children's stories, to make them behave." Some of the old men laughed, but not the dog-faced one. "She said the spirits of her people are in this land and have powers greater than any living." Marcus spoke without fear—he believed what he had just said, that much of it anyway.

Apollonius leaned in some and further until he seemed to nearly spill out of his chair, and cupped his right ear forward. His mouth opened in apparent disbelief at what he might have heard. "Tell us again why you have interfered with our most precious slave?"

"I was not sure what my eyes had seen—or not seen at all—honorable Legate. Those ghosts, or whatever they are, have done your army great harm, and greater harm to Brutus. I had to know."

The old legate came out of his chair and straight at Marcus, almost as tall as Marcus. His breath smelled of garlic and his hair of flowers. "Who, what gives you permission to meddle with our slaves, to drive them to more starvation, or to kill themselves? Our most precious slave, but the one who is the most dangerous to us all? You, you and she are curses on this army."

At this moment, the growling, spitting tone of the legate made Marcus understand he had risked more chasing butterflies than he had understood. The greater danger came from inside this tent, not from the one named Lavena.

Then the Legate said, "Why do you lie still?" The voice pitched higher, raspier. The face turned red and the old head began to shake up and down, as it had once before. "We have talked to Aunia, asked her, and you, Marcus Flavius, are a lying traitor of Rome."

Apollonius stood up, waved the back of his hand at Marcus and at the rear entrance flap of the tent. "Be gone, Marcus

Flavius. You and your brother have brought far too much dishonor and confusion on this army. You and that *venefica*, whatever you say is her name, are foul curses on glorious Rome. You interfere far too much in the lasting peace and honor glorious Rome spreads through all lands and to all people."

The second to last things Marcus remembered was Gracchus and Brutus both, heads down, shoulders slumped, standing off to the side, not once looking up at him, when four men dragged him out the back of the great tent.

The last things he remembered was the noise—grunt, whistle, slap—repeated again and again, each slap pounding into his ribs, exploding the air out of him, again and again past any ability to feel pain, then a whimper not far from him—and the faint smell of old worn leather.

Chapter XXXVIII

Strangers and Friends

Lavena and her group watched the monstrous snake slither along in the warming sun. Stena had been right. Over the past days, the Romans had leveled the wooden watch towers, fences, and huts. The whole army formed up in one long line pointing south out of the permanent encampment.

Tultas said, "I think this night or the next the gods may give us another chance to do more than dig holes."

They waited from far off for the last riders and stragglers to pass out of sight and then circled to get behind it. They waited the rest of that day until late, to see if anyone might start a cooking fire in the empty encampment, but no one did.

They crept up to and searched for what might have been left behind. No living creature other than crows and rats, no useful implements, remained. The only structures still standing were kilns, latrines, and baths of cement and stone on the higher ground.

The lower ground stank of animal and human waste more powerfully than Lavena had ever encountered. She held her hand over her mouth and nose and said to the others, "If we let them, the stinking Romans will foul all of Iberia."

Stena said, "The stench left by armies ten times greater than this one, the stench of the dead among them never leaves me."

Lavena said, "While we can still see on this day, let us get far away to a brook deep in the forest. This army will be easy to catch."

They rode away from the fouled earth, to a forest south and east, rode in deep until they found a gurgling brook that ran clear. A wind from the north had strengthened, and they quickly started to build lean-tos but dared not build a fire.

As the day held onto the last of its light, Lavena heard a sound that did not belong. No wind pressing through pine trees or running down a gorge made this noise, more the sound of an animal—but not an animal wounded or mourning over its dead young. Whatever made this sound no longer cared that the wail might attract predators.

She looked at the others in her group, all cutting and arranging pine branches, not hearing what she heard.

In a low urgent voice she said, "Stena, bring your long sword. You others stay here, and keep building but listen for us."

One hundred paces or so into the trees, Lavena knew no animal wailed like this—a sing-song cry of words that she thought she might understand, but dared not try to make out, not yet, the voice too disturbing, the shape of the words, if they were words, too familiar.

She ran to the sounds, catching her clothes on low thorny bushes, yanking at the cloth and scratching her legs.

In the dark gray light against the darker forest floor, a round white form hunched curled over on its haunches, its dark head turned away, its arms and hands bound behind its back in a truss impossible to slither out of. The figure, a woman, stood up and turned to face whoever came at her. She then hunched over to present a smaller target, kept her head low and forward, and snapped her jaw clattering her teeth—her only weapon—as if readying to bite.

Lavena did not hesitate, did not slow. She clasped the face of the dark-haired woman, pulled her up so she was forced to stand straight and look at her. Then she said, "Aunia, Aunia."

Aunia, her skin cold as the air, shivered, and her damp hair and face leaned into Lavena's face.

Lavena cut the leather strips that bound the hands and arms. She touched the raw skin of the wrists. She took Aunia's hands, lifted them up over her, Lavena's, shoulders, and pulled Aunia close. She held her for a long time then lightly stroked one cold cheek with back of a finger and then the other cheek. "Aunia, where ever you have been, whatever they have done to you, you are safe this night."

As she talked, Lavena became aware of another form, this one lying motionless behind Aunia, as if Aunia, when crouched over, had wailed not for herself but for this other. As she pressed Aunia close, tried to pour her warmth into her best friend, Lavena glanced at this other one, tried to learn about him without asking. There would be time enough for questions.

He was a grown man, dressed in a plain robe and sandals, from the side of his face a young man. His shoulders and back were covered by deep, dark bloody gashes, some edged by open skin exposing the red muscles below. The rough slashes extended down to his legs. His hands were tied behind his back too.

He breathed a rasping breath, coughed once, but his eyes did not open. Lavena had seen men whipped for stealing or trying to take another's wife, but never whipped this badly, had never seen them this close.

Lavena felt Stena standing beside her. "Stena, this night before rain comes, we need to build a fire. In this light no one will see it, and we'll put it out before we sleep."

Stena left quickly, Tultas and Habo taking her place next to Lavena.

Aunia wore only one thin garment that covered her whole length. Lavena half carried, half pushed Aunia to the others. There she quickly found another cloak on the pack horse and wrapped a pelt around Aunia too, then made her sit near where Stena had already sparked a small ball of straw.

The two men lifted the stranger by his hands and feet, set him on a pelt, face down, and built a lean-to over him. He still breathed fast but did not open his eyes or utter a sound.

Stena heated water in their one small pot and stirred in the fattiest remaining chunks of salted meat, then crumpled pieces of dried bread. She squinted as she worked, the wood too cold and damp to make a clean fire. When the stew boiled, she made Aunia eat and held some under the nose of the man.

He licked his lips, licked at the spoon Stena held closer, moved his face to the side, and began to eat.

Lavena said, "God of the forest. I know this one..." They all stopped what they had been doing and stared at her. "Not now. Will tell you later."

She brought water from the stream in a drinking gourd. He drank the cold water, drank more, the water splashing over his face and hair and shoulder. But he did not seem to mind or notice. His eyes did not seem to open, or if they did, he did not see.

After Aunia had eaten, after she, turning her face away from them, had finished chewing the last chunk of meat, she leaned into Lavena and whispered. "Every night"—it came out *every nigh*, but Lavena understood—"I scraped the ground and prayed to your spirit, prayed that after I crossed over I might soon find you or that you found me, prayed that your end came quickly."

She looked up directly at Lavena, "Have we crossed over? Have I dreamed all this?"

Lavena put her arm around Aunia's shoulder and pulled her ever tighter. "No, Aunia. The one with you has not crossed yet, and we are with him."

Aunia breathed deeply. "Yes, yes. That one lying there—his name is Marcus—told me he had seen you, but I did not believe him." This time Aunia reached out to touch Lavena on her arm, on her cheek. "But I believe him now. I have not slept in two days and nights. Wanted to watch over him—keep the vultures off him until he left. Then I would walk until I found deep water—if the wolves or bears did not find me first—and cross over in whatever water I found."

She leaned into Lavena with her whole body, and Lavena knew Aunia would sleep now, so soundly that nothing could keep her awake. Lavena eased Aunia under the lean-to where they had been sitting, checked that all but Aunia's face was under the heavy pelt and that another pelt covered the ground under every part of her.

The one called Marcus did not revive enough to keep his eyes open for long, to utter one word. Lavena watched him fall into unconsciousness of a deeper kind, shivering from the heat in him, sweating in the cold damp air, moaning, breathing fast, grinding his teeth, and sometimes crying out but with no words.

They had all seen this before, and knew only the gods could take the fever from him and heal his wounds.

#

Marcus felt the fur on his face, the fur familiar but a smell he did not know. He blinked twice. His eyes worked as they should, and, for a moment, that stilled the terror. It was the pelt of a bear, a hot pelt, hotter than he had ever known. He swallowed and licked his lips with a dry tongue and to a bitter taste.

He had the feeling in his hands, and his fingers felt the fur too. His hands, they were free again. He tried to push himself up, but managed to only raise his head and turn it to the side. The odor of blood and oozing skin close by came to him, with the odor of freshly-cut pine branches.

His head hurt, and hurt worse when he tried to lift it. His hands and arms were dry and hot, though the air was cold and the ground not far from his face wet from a fresh rain. He breathed fast and tried to breathe deeply but could not. His chest did not allow that.

He looked around as best he was able—and wanted to jump up, but the muscles of his back and legs ignored his commands. Had he been able to reach high, he could have touched her face. She stared at his back with a look of concern so intense she did not notice him gaze back and up at her. This time, he fixed on the lines of her neck and shoulders, on her strong arms.

But he let his eyes linger on her only for a long moment, the urge to breathe, the heat of his skin too strong, his head too painful to keep his eyes open.

Then he recovered for one moment more, the jolt of recognition too powerful to ignore through the hot ache of his whole body. The older woman standing next to her, both of them now wearing Roman cloaks, sandals and outer coats, they were the ones.

Accepting that he could not move much, that he was at their mercy, he tried to look awake, alert, and struggled to say, "Lavena, *ubi sum? Quis estis*?" He had no idea of where he was. He wanted to ask much more, but he was tired and started to cough.

"You are in a forest far from your camp. After your own kind whipped you and bound you and the girl with you, they dumped you out here."

He recovered a bit and tried to move his head to show he understood, tried to watch her face.

She said, "They laughed at you both, called her a *venefica* and you a lying traitor, told her to use her power to save you and herself. They were too cowardly to kill you themselves, afraid that whoever killed her would die a horrible death, and her freed spirit would kill many more."

As the Daughter of Sinorix talked, memories rushed in. He struggled to point over to the older woman. That was hard, his body too weak, too hot, breathing too hard. He said, "You and she brought Celer to me...." Both women stared as if they did not understand. "Brought the big beautiful stallion...clever, you did that."

Lavena touched his elbow. "We did. Do not say more. Save your strength, Marcus." She put her cool hand on his forehead.

At another time not long past, he would have placed his hand on hers and pulled her close, but none of that was in him now, only, "Tell me of the one who rode that horse—before you found it."

After what seemed like a long time, Lavena answered softly. "He and his scouts died in a valley in the mountains—after they did terrible things to the men of that valley."

All Marcus could to say, to squeeze out was, "*Martis frater meus fuit.* Martis was my brother...."

Then the light and smells and sounds of the earth and those standing close to him faded to hard dreams of places far away and people he did not know.

#

Lavena did not ask Aunia how she had survived the battle for their village, whether the army held others who they might know. There would be time for that when Aunia might be ready.

The five did not move from their little camp, stayed with Marcus through the day and into night.

Lavena remembered well—dreamed of it—the shouting out for help by the two at the door of the burning hut in Stena's valley, the shouting out of Martis' name, brother of this one nearly whipped to death by his own army. She knew that she would remember the two brothers for as long as she had memory, and some day might think more about what impelled one to brutality and the other to what might have been. But she could not dwell on that now, too much to do, far too much.

From time to time, she checked on Marcus, how he breathed, touched his face or head to measure his fever, listened for his cough, and witnessed his slow dying.

At first light, he lay still and cold. They lifted him as high as they could into the branches of the biggest nearby pine tree, and set his body so that he would not fall. They said a prayer that the big meat-eating birds would carry his spirit to all warriors wherever warriors waited until they came to ground in lightning.

Then they left to chase his army.

Aunia rode their pack horse, the packs now smaller and easily distributed among the other horses. Aunia rode well but silently, her eyes always on Lavena.

That night, Aunia told Lavena how she had pretended to be a witch, how she pretended she could talk to the dead spirits waiting deep in the ground, how the soldiers who found her saw her scrapings in the dirt, and did not touch her.

Lavena said, "Dear Aunia, I do not know how that is, but I am glad."

"The stupid Romans believe witches make their little ones take small amounts of bad potions from before they can talk. That makes them not die of any poisons later when they are grown, but they can kill by merely touching another, by breathing on them. That comes from their bodies being so poisoned. I knew that, and they dared not touch me, let me live."

For two days Lavena's group followed the wide scar in the land left by the army of Gracchus. On the evening of the second day, they found the back of their target.

Chapter XXXIX

Targets Too Easy

On a late evening Lavena and Stena eased close to the back of the army. The last riders behind the last of the supply train rode with heads down as if dozing in their saddles. They jerked up and looked over, but otherwise did not react to a couple more of their own coming into camp.

Some of these soldiers at the rear seemed young and untrained, others old with bad hearing and worse sight. They rode behind tired men and women on foot carrying heavy loads. Lavena wondered if these hindmost riders, about twenty in all, knew they were the most vulnerable, if their commanders knew or cared.

Lavena's group did not strike that first night. No rocks or trees provided cover. The evening light from the south shone on them too brightly, and too many Roman horsemen rode too close to each other, even if half asleep or half blind.

The next day, the army coursed through a valley with a stream at the bottom running south. Lavena thought this stream might in time run to her river.

By evening, the slopes covered by scrub bushes and trees on both sides were too steep for easy walking or riding. The rear guard had to string out, one rider behind the other. The last rider rode alone.

When darkness took most light out of this hollow, Lavena's group closed on that solitary rider.

He glanced back at them, nodded and Lavena thought he smiled, smiled that he was not the last in line after all, that he had protection from behind. She did not feel for him, felt nothing about him. It was routine now, and part of her knew she had become a killer. Only the clean kill and clean escape mattered.

Tultas needed to use only one arrow. It struck squarely in the back between his shoulders at the base of the neck. His horse snorted and trotted forward, bouncing him until he fell off sideways falling softly in the sandy bottom of the hollow. His horse stopped, lowered its head to check its fallen master, stood still for a moment and then cantered up ahead around a bend.

Lavena looked back from where they had come. Nothing, no one followed them from the trail back to Aunia and Habo. She whispered, "Over here, into the darkest corners, off our horses, ready our bows—and wait. Tultas, you take that side, Stena and I will take this. Next time, we can't let the horse run off. Remember what we must do if they challenge us."

They did not have long to wait. Two riders came down the gully and stopped at the fallen one lying face down on the trail, jumped off their horses and to him—like two herders reacting to a fallen calf, not hardened fighters suspecting an ambush.

They knelt down, turned his head, touched the arrow in him but did not try to remove it. Then they stood up, drew their short swords and peered into the trees and rocks on either side, but too late. They dropped to their knees and fell over near the first one, their falls barely making a sound.

Lavena, Stena and Tultas ran out to the horses and wrapped their reins around tree branches, but loosely to slip easily, so that the riderless horses might find the safety of the army but not too soon. Tultas made sure the three were dead, started to pull out the arrows but left them. They were embedded too well and would be useless if ripped out breaking any part of them. They had no time to cut the arrows free.

Lavena said, "Each time, I think this will be our last easy strike. This whole army must be made of farmers and herdsmen. Must get back fast to Aunia and Habo. No moon this night."

The pattern repeated for the better part of a month. Some evenings the terrain was too flat, the rear riders too many for a safe attack, and Lavena and Stena rode off ahead of the army. Where the ground was soft, they dug the spiked holes in the night.

More often, a lone sleeping sentry, a last straggler into camp, the last rider behind the last mule cart or behind the last laborer on foot, allowed them to come too close. Sometimes he said something. Sometimes Stena answered in her deepest voice. Whatever Stena said did not alarm them.

Tultas always took the first shot but not unless he was close, sure that he had clear line to the killing spot. He never shot unless the victim was separated from all others.

Late one night, Stena said, "I see a place. Lavena, walk down there with me in your best Roman walk."

Lavena and Stena walked unchallenged to the nearest waste hole. This hole was the farthest from the sleeping camp, and not used much at this time of night. Soon, two Roman men staggered out to them. When they saw Stena and Lavena, they grumbled, said something Lavena did not understand, but stopped to wait their turn, shifting from foot to foot, yawning, sleepy, not aware.

Stena and Lavena left the two severed heads where they landed next to their bodies sprawled over the waste holes.

On nights after Stena caught rabbits or fish, Lavena's group stayed far away from the army and dared to build a fire. They gulped down the fresh meat and warmed themselves as best they could. But they still doused or smothered the fires and rode far off to sleep. Every night, one of them stayed awake and watched over them from a tree or high point. Aunia took her turn too.

Over the days and weeks after the attack on the bullocks, Lavena began to understand this army. These Romans had not yet figured out who did this killing, where the killers came from, how to stop them. Or perhaps there were so many men, their leaders did not care about losing a few poor fighters from among thousands on the way south. No matter the cause of the easy targets, each arrow shot could not be used again.

#

Gracchus held the arrows high, so many arrows that he could not grasp them all. More arrows lay at his feet. Many of the shafts were broken. On others the points had bent into ugly shapes by the impact against metal or bone. Some arrows tips still held bits of flesh and dark spots of dried blood.

One by one, he again faced all the old men sitting or lying around him, his war council, starting with the Legate Apollonius. This time he had summoned them to his tent before feeding them or letting their heads cloud up with wine. This time and from now on, he would take control, make all the decisions, allow not one more mistake—and live or die with the consequences.

He stopped his circling at Apollonius, and shook one fist filled with arrows in the old man's face. He yelled, "You, you stupid old man who listens to the bones of birds and sees treachery in good soldiers."

The old dog-faced man returned the stare and leaned forward. "Gracchus, you know nothing of fighting men on foot or horse. The Senate will hear about your ignorant insults." Then he let out a rasping shout, "Scribe, Scribe, do you have that?"

The time for charm, for fawning, for trying to placate them with feasts had ended. Gracchus kept yelling. "More than thirty arrows here in my hands and at my feet, the first one cut out of the oldest son of Bovis. Look at these arrows. Each one took one of my riders or sentries. And not one man next to or near the fallen saw anyone who did this. My men piss in the night, and someone takes their heads."

Apollonius shook his head showing impatience, anger. "I know. I know. Ghosts in the land—or that brother of Marcus and his men trying to chase us away and off our gold, or other traitors in your army."

"Yes, my army. Your stupidity destroys my army. You, you who ordered the tongue burning and then whipping of my last best scout, you who banished my best prisoner because your priest said she was a *venefica*, you know nothing. What say you to thirty and more arrows buried deep into the flesh of our men? Another twenty horses and ten men lost to pikes in the ground. No ghost or Martis or preditor, no traitor could do that without us knowing it, without someone seeing it, again and again."

The eyes of the Legate darted to the sides and behind his accuser and out around the tent walls looking for, measuring the support from the others. This tent was smaller than the permanent tent at the old camp and could not contain the voice of the accuser.

Gracchus saw others outside, their shadows on the tent walls, close, listening. He was glad of that. Time they too knew who held the supreme power in this army and who was the fool.

The old one rasped out, "The vile ambushers have nothing to do with the *venefica* or with your traitorous scout—even if they are men and not ghosts."

That last took Gracchus to a place he had not been since his mother died for no good reason—the place of unchecked rage. But he would channel it, use it, not let it use him. "Your whipping of my last best scout and banishing of the *venefica* with the boar's snout killed fifty men and more as if by your own hand. They died far, far too easily. We have not caught or killed a single one who did this. But your evil is far greater than that. You have allowed my whole army to be spooked by ghosts that do not exist."

Gracchus screamed as he had never screamed. "By a handful of riders wearing our garments, riding our horses. That's who has done this. Those garments, those horses came from Martis and his scouts and are worn by locals, not by ghosts. By all the powers of *Iuppiter* and Mars, that makes you the fool, for not seeing that, for not listening to Marcus."

Apollonius raised a gnarled hand and balled it into a fist as if he wanted to strike away the words and Gracchus. He rasped out, "No *barbari* could ever do this to a Roman army, and army that I still lead."

Gracchus chortled and said, "This army of young farmers with no land to farm, of tradesmen with no place to ply their trade, is so easily spooked by talk of ghosts and your bird bones. They fear standing watch at night, fear relieving themselves without guards surrounding them. Not one wants to ride behind my supply train. Not one wants to ride at the head for fear of holes in the ground. Marcus Flavius."

He slowed down, made every word sit by itself, "Had it right. *Barbari* dressed in our garb stripped from our men, using our weapons, riding our horses, are doing this. Both Marcus and the witch told us of *barbari* fighters, of their cleverness. But you listened to lies in dead bird bones."

Gracchus waited, waited for the dog-faced Legate to answer. After a long time, Apollonius shrugged and lifted his hands palms up, as if to say he had nothing more.

Gracchus looked at the armed men standing at the tent flap. They seemed to nod gently. They too had been spooked by unseen ghosts cutting down soldiers, but now understood. Gracchus snapped his fingers at them and curled his index finger for them to come to him. They obeyed.

"Take our Legate Apollonius to his tent and keep him there. Allow only one of his servants to tend his needs. One of you must go with his servant where ever he goes. Legate Apollonius will give no more orders. If he tries to send one order to my army, you have my command to make it his last. Understand?"

Both guards said, "Yes, sir."

Gracchus said, "Take him to his tent, now. His servant will bring him the evening meal."

One of the guards reached to take the old man's arm, but Apollonius stood up and hurried out on his old legs. As he passed in front of Gracchus, he said, "The Senate will hear about this and have you on the cross."

Gracchus said, "Yes it will hear about this, if you insist. And then everyone will know why it selected you for this easy little campaign to subdue the *barbari* in Iberia."

Gracchus turned back to those remaining. "Out, all of you. Lucius, you who leads my horsemen, stay."

When all but one of them had left, Gracchus said, "Lucius, the *barbari* must be watching us, but we do not see them."

Lucius said, "They come at us from the rising sun in the morning and the setting sun at night."

"Yes," said Gracchus. "Every night they must camp to the east of us, but far enough away we do not see their fire. Time to set a trap for these locals more clever and courageous than my men. But the trap will not succeed if my army knows of it before it is set. Listen to me now, but do not tell your riders the plan. I will do that after you gather them ready to ride and fight before the sun is up again. I will tell them where to go and what to do. If any locals are among us, they must not know."

Chapter XL

Fine Day for a Noble Death

Ten arrows left. On this night, Lavena said, "Thousands more must fall—to our ten arrows."

Tultas said, "They are leaving our region."

Stena said, "But not leaving our land. When they've taken all the silver out of the ground, they will return, build their own houses, their own walls and watch towers, swarm over here from *Italoi*, and—choke us out, push us north into the Endless Sea, or kill and enslave us all."

Tultas said, "We cannot know if Caciro found Daleninar, if he is alive, if anyone brings us more arrows."

#

The next morning, Lavena opened her eyes and took three deep breaths, threw off her pelts, stood up and looked around their camp. It sat in sheltering pine trees on both sides of a stream. She scrambled up above the little gully. White tops of an unfamiliar mountain range greeted the sun. The shining distant snow promised a clear cold day.

The army of Gracchus sat a half morning's ride toward those mountains. It too would be breaking camp and forming up to trudge south.

Their five horses stood close by, and now Stena, Tultas and Aunia stirred.

All at once Lavena felt an unease deeper than on any other morning spent chasing the army. It came not from Habo, last night's watchman, bundled up and snoring at the base of the biggest tree on the flat above the little camp. It came not from being one day farther away from the place she had once called home, not from only ten arrows left, not from never enough to eat.

The unease came from out there. Out there in the cold dead high grass, the songs and chirping of the morning birds should have sounded different, louder. The cold air should have smelled cleaner.

Most of all, the horses should not have stood this quietly, held their heads this high facing the sunrise, only their ears moving and pointed forward. They should not have been this alert listening for, perhaps smelling, the same thing.

She whispered, "Father, guide us through this day," and nudged Habo awake, pointing for him to fetch his horse and prepare to leave fast.

All of them up, she said softly but loudly enough for them all to hear, "Something or someone is out there."

In the time it took the two men and three women to put on their day cloaks, fasten their weapon belts and personal pouches, fetch and pack up the horses, they knew. Habo had climbed up one of the trees and yelled, "Look, get up here. Fast."

Out of the sun breaking above the land, riders, many riders, headed for this stream, this line of trees.

Though they were far off, Lavena saw enough. She said, "No one hunts for deer carrying shields. This hunting party can only be hunting us."

She quickly loosened the Roman saddle on her horse, pulled it off, and said, "Today we ride as we ride best—no saddles, no stinking Roman cloaks—lighter, faster."

She tossed away her sleeping pelts. The others did too, and left behind all the Roman clothes. Done, she waited for any response or question before mounting up, though time was running out.

Tultas and Habo both moved fast and without hesitation, as if they had known it would come to this and were not troubled. They carried the bows and five arrows each.

Stena nodded a nod of power and acceptance.

Aunia pulled back her long black hair and quickly tied it into a knot, then raised her face and let the morning light shine on all of it. This was no time to remain downcast about how she might appear to strangers. She slapped the hilt of the falcata tied to her left thigh. Until this morning, it had been Lavena's.

Lavena carried her long sword and a pike across her back. As she wheeled her horse to the right of the mountains and north, she said, "Habo and Aunia, lead us and stay together until the end, or until we find you. Head north where we came from on a pace your horse can hold. If we lose you, find Daleninar and stay with her until we come to you. Tultas, ride with Stena and me...."

Then, "If they catch us, let us make them remember two she-warriors and the best men with a bow and arrow Daleninar's tribe has ever known. And, Aunia, if they catch you, be a good witch once more."

Already cantering out behind Habo, Aunia laughed for the first time since they had found her. One by one, the others laughed too.

Lavena's horse reacted instantly to signals from Lavena's body and legs. At times it wanted to surge past Aunia and Habo, but responded to Lavena's slight squeeze of her thighs or gentle tug on the reins and stayed in line.

The air cooled her face and lifted her hair off her shoulders. She touched the wrist torcs and the great neck torc under her cloak, wearing them for the first time since the meeting with Daleninar's nobles. The torcs calmed her. The air, the distant mountains seeming to rise higher with the sun's light, the power of her horse, and thoughts of whatever was to come poured into her, poured into her all the songs of life.

This was a fine day for a noble death.

From time to time, she heard a ram's horn sound three times and a fainter response from farther away and a different direction, though she saw nothing ahead to alarm her—rolling grass land, broken by hills, rocks, pockets of trees bare of leaves running away up to hills in the distance.

When she glanced back, the line of chasers appeared and then vanished. When she did see it, she only saw one or two. The pursuing riders had strung out, those on the better horses leaving the others behind. That was good. When the fighting began, best to be able to fight one at a time.

After a long steady ride, the horns sounded closer, and she began to hear faint cries, "*Veni, veni, eos*, over here, I see them," and other words she did not understand, along with yips and shouts.

The cries died down again, and some of the horn sounds grew slightly fainter. The scout horses Lavena's group rode and those of Tultas and Habo must have been as strong and sure-footed as any left in the Roman army.

Without warning or any cause that she could see, Habo raised his hand for them to slow. Perhaps his horse had to walk for a while, find water.

But that was not it.

A line of Roman horsemen broke the top of a low rise in the rolling land ahead, close enough that Lavena could see their open mouths of broken and missing teeth, see their eyes that said this would be an easy fight, a tasty prize.

She and her group had been flushed like rabbits, and like rabbits followed or chased to their old homes where this line of ready fighters waited. The five of Lavena's group circled up trying to control their heated, restless horses. The others looked at her.

She did not have to think, the only choice clear. "Tultas and Habo ready your bows, and come up to both sides of me. Don't shoot until you know your shots will kill. Stena, Aunia follow close behind—and whatever you do, stay on your horses. On ground we die too easily."

Lavena kicked her horse and slapped the reins on both sides of its neck, leaned low behind her horse's head and charged the nearest Roman rider.

He, sitting high in a Roman saddle and cloaked with a vest of interlocking chains, held a short sword and pointed it at Lavena with his free hand. The instant she charged, she saw he lost the smirk and tried to back his horse. Another untrained farmer reacting too slowly and too late.

Lavena heard the arrow from close behind her and saw it hit him flush in the face. He toppled backwards, as did the rider to his left, and two more riders on either side of them.

Stupid stinking Romans. She screamed a scream of killing rage and vengeance. Her scream made the other horsemen back up awkwardly, not trained to handle weapons and spooked horses both. But rage did not make her lose her next target, the nearest rider still on horse to her right.

That rider did not think to duck, did not think to ride away. He rose up high in his confining saddle and pointed his pike at Lavena, as if by holding it there she would impale herself for him. Instantly, she knew this would be easy. She slid her long sword under the pike and rotated her arm in an outside circle.

The pike deflected away, she closed inside his reach, so close she saw the fright, the confusion, the shock, as she thrust deep into his chest, his leather cloak no protection against sharp steel. She pulled it out feeling it rip his insides as he fell toward her then off his horse to the ground. He tried to get to his feet, but fell again gripping his stomach and yelling, "*Sanguis et viscera…non possim continere.*"

Lavena understood his last words and thought it was right that he could not hold in his blood, his guts.

The line of Romans parted, chaotically, with shouts of men trying to hang onto frightened horses backing up, rearing. One by one or in pairs the four Roman riders hit by arrows fell to the side or over backwards. On the ground they staggered and fell or never got to their feet.

The Roman riders on either side managed to turn their horses away and flee to Lavena's right and left. Lavena guessed twenty or so had awaited them, five now dead or dying in the grass, their riderless horses off with the others.

To her left Tultas and Habo each loaded another arrow and took aim, but their targets were already too far for a certain kill. Stena and Aunia had closed up tight from behind, and Lavena led them through the wide opening in the Roman line.

But this first encounter had been too easy. Down the gentle slope on the far side of the low ridge, two more lines of riders waited, behind them shallow water of a wide stream. They had seen the sudden carnage above them, and their group leaders must have seen battles on horse before.

As Lavena sent her horse at the lead rider of the first line, all horsemen with him quickly formed a loose half circle. An attack by her on any rider in that circle would naturally cause her and any of her group with her to be swallowed, outnumbered, four or five to one, by slashing, jabbing soldiers to a certain and quick death.

Lavena pulled up twenty paces from these better prepared Roman horsemen. Shouts of glee and victory from behind grew louder, closer. Soon very soon, her little group would be surrounded and, if the gods were kind, slaughtered, and, if not, disarmed and dragged off.

She said, "Tultas and Habo, stay close again. When I throw the first one and you have a good target let your arrows fly."

The men looked at her in puzzlement. Lavena, Tultas and Habo on either side, walked her horse into the Roman half circle. All the Romans in the half circle quieted, puzzled at what was to come, braced for a charge on one of them with the others in position to crush in.

When so close that even the half blind among them could see, Lavena pulled the torc off her left wrist, straightened it, held it high, let the morning light play on all shades of yellow gold.

A murmur rose from the Romans and all stared at the thick snake in her hand high above her hair, then, "*Argentum…argentum.*"

She leaned back and hurled the torc with all her strength over them to the right. All of them followed its tumbling flight against the bright blue sky. As they watched, Lavena whispered, "Habo, Tultas, wait."

A rider broke into the stream where the torc had splashed and disappeared, jumped off his horse, and dove into the water—followed by three more and more after him. When not one of them found it quickly, or having found it could not keep the others from knocking him down, short swords came out and slashed at the others.

Lavena shifted to the center of the remaining Romans still on horse and flung the other wrist torc to her left. This time they all charged after the most precious bounty.

The Roman horsemen who had waited and fought briefly on the ridge behind Lavena's group again formed up, now joined by those who had chased Lavena's group out of their camp, thirty or more all together. She said, "Wait here. Protect me from behind. I will come back to you."

She turned her horse at the group behind and walked it back to them, but not close before she stopped, reached under the neck line on her cloak with both hands and pulled off the last and most glorious solid gold torc.

Its heft and balance allowed her to throw it the farthest, made it hang in the sky the longest, the light playing with the gold and the green eyes. This time a low roar rose from the riders and they, each one, charged to the place where her father's great torc disappeared in the high grass.

Their horses collided hard and noisily. The riders jumped off, short swords drawn, slashing at the grass, at searching hands and arms, and horse's feet that they thought were in the way or tromped the torc into the grass.

Heavy pikes jammed into low heads looking for it. The roars and shouts, screams of pain, anger and revenge, now came from three places. Deadly wounds did not dampen the fight for gold.

Lavena rejoined the others of her group. "Let us leave this place. When they finish fighting over three torcs, they will have only us for bounty."

It did not take long enough for the Romans to finish fighting or for those with no bounty to think Lavena's little group must be carrying more. She had not led them a thousand paces farther north, when new yells and shouts reached them.

Again, her group urged the horses to run, but they struggled. The hard ride since morning, the many maneuvers at the fight on the ridge and at the stream, the days of chasing the army with not one day to rest and forage had worn them down. And the Romans who had waited for the trap to close rode fresh horses.

Lavena understood that any further running was useless, could cause one of their mounts to stumble, its heart to explode. She stopped. The others stopped with her. "Stena, come up next to me, your long sword out. Habo and Tultas, ready your last arrows. Aunia, stay behind us."

Aunia said, "Lavena, I love you like I never knew I could love another. But I will not let you shield me any longer. I will come up with you and face them with you." She moved up to the line with the other four.

Fifty or more armed riders closed on them, but as they got closer, they slowed. Already, they had lost four to arrows, one to Lavena's sword and uncounted others to the fight for torcs of solid gold. This time, the Romans were not so foolish.

They again formed up in a large half circle. Some hoisted light spears made for throwing. Any one of Lavena's group or their horses, standing, waiting, made an easy target for a well thrown spear. But they stopped before they got into a good throwing range, seeming to understand that arrows flew just as far.

But the half circle crept up behind the waiting five, who could no longer remain in a straight line. Soon the Romans surrounded Lavena's group completely. They must have been leaderless now, or their leader did not care to yell out or charge. The circle closed tighter, all of them on both sides knowing after one more shot from Tultas and Habo, the circle could collapse on the center, the spears could be flung, and the battle would end with no more resistance to frighten even a farmer pressed to serve as a soldier.

Through the low din of horses snorting, their heavy foot falls and swishing tales, the breathing and groaning men, Lavena whispered loudly enough for her group to hear, "Save your last strike to take you to the next life. It is better than whatever the stinking Romans will do to us. Habo, Tultas, no sense leaving our good arrows for the Romans unused."

Two arrows whistled out and this time found the broad chests of the closest two horses, causing chaos for their riders and those near them. Two more arrows hit the chests of the closest two spearmen readying to throw, but not getting their spears into the air.

Habo and Tultas loaded the last arrows and pointed at the next closest in the closing circle.

Lavena placed her long sword across the back of her horse. She grabbed the handle with both hands backwards, turning its point inward and up under her chin. However she fell, as long as she fell forward, that would be the sword's last thrust. Her insides quieted.

She didn't hear the Romans any longer, didn't hear anything except as if from far away the calming notes of carnyxes, trumpets of war used by her tribe she had last heard on that first morning of the first battle—good sounds to send her to Father and Mother and all the other spirits of the dead.

Stena did the same. Aunia on her right set her falcata blade on her left shoulder readying to pull it across her throat.

The approaching riders grumbled in surprise and disbelief, but none said anything. They too grew quiet—the kind of quiet before a great storm, before the earth shakes, before the big cat leaps at the youngest deer.

Through the quiet, the sounds of the carnyxes grew louder. And that was good. She could fall forward off her good Roman horse now, listening to those deep beautiful sounds as her last on this side of the living. She leaned forward and to the side to fall off her horse and onto the sharp point.

She glanced up for the last time and caught one last Roman moving—but in a way that did not fit. That rider, directly in front of her, turned his head to the side, then behind, started talking to the rider next to him in a voice of surprise and fear.

She dropped the point and turned the sword at them, looked at them, all turned now, and listened. The sounds she had heard came from real trumpets.

The riders in front of her parted, and she spotted the brightly-striped cloaks streaming behind riders cresting over the same ridge in the distance. The cloaks streamed behind riders who screamed so loudly now that they drowned out their own trumpets of war.

The Roman riders backed away, turned and rode in all directions fast.

Tultas waved and yelled out first, "Here, over here." Then more quietly, "Those are the colors of my village, the same as my cloak...you made me take off." And then he laughed.

They all laughed, and cried, and shouted.

Caciro reached them first. After raucous greetings and more laughter, he said, "We followed their scout horns. It could be only you they chased."

Chapter XLI

Harvest Festival

178 B.C.

Daleninar, her uncle, and their nobles broadcast the news to everyone within two days ride of the Village on The Hill. They had much to celebrate. Gracchus and his army had left Iberia with a promise to never return.

Pestered day and night by the riders who had saved Lavena's group, the Roman army never sought out or attacked another village, menaced another farmer, or took what did not belong to it. Under a treaty hastily negotiated, Gracchus was allowed to leave rather than both sides fight to the last death.

The harvest of that summer and autumn had been bountiful, most of the burned-out houses and huts rebuilt. The Romans had not flattened the stout stone walls of the structures, and the roofs of straw did not take long to replace.

On the second night of the festival Tultas and Aunia, along with many other couples of the region, would become husband and wife. Word spread down the valley of the Eberus and up into the Burnt Rocks. Stena came with some of her clan as did many other out villagers.

All who came wanted to be part of the largest festival of the region since the summer of two years before, and they came to see the great she-warrior, *Daughter of Sinorix*. After the mass wedding, Daleninar clapped for attention. Those near her quieted and gathered, and that caused the ones farther out to come closer and listen. They gathered at the main gate, up on and along the walls, and out to the nearby houses and stables, many more than only the local villagers.

Daleninar climbed to the top of the wall and from there shouted out in a loud voice for a small woman, the voice of a leader. "Daughter of Sinorix, Lavena, where are you?"

The name passed through the throng until they found her with Stena's clan far down the wall. The throng parted for Lavena to join Daleninar up on the wall above the main gate.

The cheering started near her, grew as she made her way along the wall, through the gate, and up next to Daleninar. Lavena had wanted to ask Stena to come with her, but only her own name came to her again and again, and soon she could not think at all, just let herself be swept along by the joyous noise, the smiles, the hands held high in gratitude.

When Lavena neared Daleninar, the village ruler raised her hands high for quiet. It took a long time, the cheers and shouts of her name dying but bursting out again from another direction. In time it was quiet enough for Daleninar to speak, to shout out. "Never has our land had such a warrior."

Another wave of cheers and shouts of Lavena, Daughter of Sinorix, circled the village.

"We honor you, we love you. We have these for you to wear all your days, and never give to anyone. My men found them on the Roman riders they chased down on the day my men reached you."

Before the cheers started up again, Daleninar raised her hands again for quiet. She hugged Lavena and, as she released, pulled Lavena's arms forward, making Lavena hold out her wrists.

Daleninar reached into a deep pocket of her full white cloak and, one by one, pulled out Sinorix's torcs, placed the two small ones around each wrist and the large one around Lavena's neck. At the first glimpse of yellow, the cheering started up again and could not be quelled.

Though only she and Daleninar could hear, Lavena said, "All our gods have smiled on me from the day Little Bear found me, from the day Stena took me in, from the day you sent us Tultas, Habo and Caciro."

She touched each torc in turn, and whispered, "When I can no longer wear these, I shall return them to the waters that flow around Sagunto. Until then, I am honored and I thank you."

It was a clear night of a full moon. Lavena rode the same horse as in her last battle. The bed roll behind her held clothes and enough food for days. With fish netting and rabbit snares, she did not need to come in until winter. She had no clear plan, no route she wanted to take. Without thinking, she headed east and south, back to her river, her village, and her memories from before the gruesome time.

On this night, Turibas came into her thoughts more powerfully than ever since that early morning when she had last touched him on the village wall. That memory of their last meeting made her smile. She had more than once asked Aunia if he had been taken prisoner, if Aunia had seen his body, if any of the prisoners in the cage had mentioned him. None had.

She whispered, "Mother, if he is alive, show me the way to him. If he is with you, ask that he waits for me."

#

In later decades, Roman historians wrote of Iberian-Celtic she-warriors fighting naked side-by-side with their men. School-aged children of the upper class read those histories but did not believe what they read. Women did not, were not supposed to, do those things.

The Iberian Celts never developed a written language of their own. They passed their lessons down by telling them.

For hundreds of years, mothers told their youngsters true stories of the greatest she-warrior of all, the last survivor of the Roman army's destruction of the Village on The Cliff and who, though not much older than a girl, by herself brought a whole Roman army to its knees. And that, they said, was just the beginning of her life lived with great glory.

THE END

Author's Notes

I give these notes to any reader who wonders, did this happen, in this way, really? Although Lavena, Sinorix, Edereta, The Village On the Cliff are fictional, most of the main events did take place. The main background characters lived as they do in this novel.

Throughout this story, I have tried to remain true to the events historians of the time have passed down to those who came after, and to what coins and other traces from back then tell us. I have walked in a number of the places Lavena and Sinorix rode or walked. Where I am unsure, I have portrayed what seems reasonable based on all accounts available to me.

Perhaps the biggest unknown is how Lavena and those close to her spoke. Roman historians, writing decades afterwards, have given us their recreations of some of Hannibal's speeches, but not more. Common people from ancient Greece, Carthage, Assyria, Italy and the many Celtic tribal regions intermingled as friends, traders or adversaries, but their dialogue is not preserved in any record I have found.

Below I sketch some of the history before and after the brief span of my novel.

The people usually referred to as Celts or Keltoi, with their common language, jewelry, every-day implements, methods of farming, styles of houses, villages and walls, swept out of the British Isles, across the whole of what is Europe today all the way to Asia minor. They settled in most of Iberia intermingling with early locals as well as with Greeks. The history of the Iberian Celts, sometimes called Celtiberians, ties closely to the empires of Carthage, of Rome, and the three great wars Rome and Carthage fought.

Carthage and The Punic Wars. Historians closest in time to the strife between Rome and Carthage wrote not only from the point of view of Rome but wrote decades or centuries afterwards. Hence, it is not known how much they exaggerated or unfairly demeaned Rome's greatest adversary, and looked down their Roman noses at the Celts wherever Rome engaged them.

Carthage began as a one-town colony in about 600 B.C. on the present site of Tunis in North Africa. It had the best seafarers and ship builders and became the strongest seafaring empire of the Mediterranean. At its height, it controlled all of North Africa west of Egypt, all of Iberia, and islands in the Mediterranean, including Sicily (called Trinacria by the ancients).

It built a second city center, New Carthage, on the present site of Cartagena, Spain. There Hannibal collected his army and from there launched his astounding invasion over the Alps and down the backside of Rome. Today some of the walls erected by Carthage still look down from the five hills of Cartagena.

Rome and Carthage fought three wars. Hannibal Barca (sometimes Barka) led Carthage in the second of the three.

At the beginning of his march, the Iberian Celts were happy to join him. They had helped his siege of Saguntum the year before. But soon, some seven thousand left Hannibal and returned to their homes and farms. I have not found the name of their tribal leader and have given him the name Sinorix.

Many of the Celtic tribes from Iberia and elsewhere fought wearing only shields, a helmet, and weapons. They wanted freedom of movement in a fight and to run fast. They believed dirty leather or cloth thrust deep into a wound would more likely lead to a slow death than a clean wound.

After Hannibal took his army out of Iberia, a small Roman force attacked the city of New Carthage. The city surrendered in a few days. The soldiers Hannibal had left to guard Iberia lingered in the interior never expecting a direct attack on the well-fortified city.

Hannibal was captured by the Romans and lived into his seventh decade exiled in Tyre, close by the site of the Phoenician city that had sent its young queen to found the original colony of Carthage.

After decades of an uneasy peace and unbearable tribute paid by Carthage, Rome started the Third Punic War. Historians are divided on whether Rome was provoked by some dishonorable act of Carthage, or decided to eradicate its rival while still weak.

Rome prevailed once more. This time it knocked down every building, confiscated every item of value and burned to ash all else in the city of Carthage. It tilled salt into the soil so that no living thing could again grow out of that ground.

The empire of Carthage lasted more than 400 years. But its people showed no urge to record their own exploits and wrote sparingly on other subjects.

"Punic" is derived from the Latin word for a person of Carthage.

Rome In Iberia After Carthage Collapsed. As with the Punic wars, most of what we know today comes down the ages from Roman historians--principally Livy, Polybius, and Appian--and archeological sites. But the accounts are sketchy, usually written long after the main events, and are Rome centric. Some common themes emerge and are likely true.

For many decades Rome had coveted the strong bodies of the Iberians as well as the tin and silver from its mines in the south. Starting around 195 B.C. a series of Roman aristocrats spent small fortunes on armies and weapons to roam around Iberia and collect up slaves and precious metals.

But the proud, strong and intelligent locals were not easily subdued. For many years the Iberian peninsula saw cycles of war, truce, peace and then another ambitious Roman entering the land to set down the revolt, revoke the peace, and loot more bounty.

Two such Romans were Piso and Gracchus. After early successes in battle, Piso found the going rough and made treaties with some of the local tribes. The Roman Senate recalled Piso, literally tore up the treaties, and sent Gracchus in his place. The campaign of Gracchus was short and brutal. Historians proclaim that in a matter of months he destroyed either 100 or 300 villages. He returned to Rome only two years later.

Anecdotal accounts by Romans suggest Celtic women were far more the equals of men than Roman women. Some Romans wrote that select Celtic women fought side-by-side with their men, chose their mates, shared their own and their husband's property.

Enlightening and helpful sources for this novel include my travels to modern day Cartagena, to Sagunt, the Ebro River and the beautiful countryside of Spain. Not far from the town of Soria in north central Spain sits Numancia. There, some fifty years after the events of this story, the Iberian Celts fought their greatest and last battle against the Roman oppressor. Today Spain is rebuilding that town to what it might have appeared then.

I am indebted for the information imparted by more contemporary writers. J. S. Richardson, Professor of Classics at the University of Edinburgh (retired), has given us a translation of Appian's *Wars of the Romans in Iberia* (Aris & Phillips, Ltd, 2000). J. S. Richardson has also given us his treatise, *The Romans in Spain* (Blackwell Publishers, 1996). Each is wonderful and indispensable to me.

Sir Barrington Windsor Cunliffe (writing under Barry Cunliffe), Emeritus Professor of European Archaeology at the University of Oxford, has written the beautifully illustrated, *The Ancient Celts* (Penguin Books, 1997).

Dr. Simon James, Professor at the University of Leicester, has compiled the also beautifully illustrated *Exploring the World of the Celts* (Thames & Hudson, 1993).

Stephen Allen has written and Wayne Reynolds has illustrated the compendium of Celtic weapons and armor in their *Celtic Warrior, 300 BC - AD 100* (Osprey Publishing 2001).

Juan Soler Canto has written the interesting *The History of Cartagena* (Rodriguez & Carlson, 2004). From each of these I gleaned valuable information.

A special thanks to Nicole B. Morgan, archaeologist and classics scholar, for help in all things related to old Latin and all the Latin phrases and words in this book.

www.ingramcontent.com/pod-product-compliance
Lightning Source LLC
Chambersburg PA
CBHW030812310726
48980CB00006B/467/J